The Drums Of Jeopardy

Harold MacGrath

Contents

THE DRUMS OF JEOPARDY

BY

Harold MacGrath

CHAPTER I

A fast train drew into Albany, on the New York Central, from the West. It was three-thirty of a chill March morning in the first year of peace. A pall of fog lay over the world so heavy that it beaded the face and hands and deposited a fairy diamond dust upon wool. The station lights had the visibility of stars, and like the stars were without refulgence--a pale golden aureola, perhaps three feet in diameter, and beyond, nothing. The few passengers who alighted and the train itself had the same nebulosity of drab fish in a dim aquarium.

Among the passengers to detrain was a man in a long black coat. The high collar was up. The man wore a derby hat, well down upon his head, after the English mode. An English kitbag, battered and scarred, swung heavily from his hand. He immediately strode for the station wall and stood with his back to it. He was almost invisible. He remained motionless until the other detrained passengers swam past, until the red tail lights of the last coach vanished into the deeps; then he rushed for the exit to the street.

Away toward the far end of the platform there appeared a shadowy patch in the fog. It grew and presently took upon itself the shape of a man. For one so short and squat and thick his legs possessed remarkable agility, for he reached the street just as the other man stopped at the side of a taxicab.

The fool! As if such a movement had not been anticipated. Sixteen thousand miles, always eastward, on horses, camels, donkeys, trains, and ships; down China to the sea, over that to San Francisco, thence across this bewildering stretch of cities and plains called the United States, always and ever toward New York--and the fool thought he could escape! Thought he was flying, when in truth he was being driven toward a wall in which there would be no breach! Behind and in front the net was closing. Up to this hour he had been extremely clever in avoiding contact. This was his first stupid act--thought the fog would serve as an impenetrable cloak.

Meantime, the other man reached into the taxicab and awoke the sleeping chauffeur.

"A hotel," he said.

"Which one?"

"Any one will do."

"Yes, sir. Two dollars."

"When we arrive. No; I'll take the bag inside with me." Inside the cab the fare chuckled. For those who fished there would be no fish in the net. This fog--like a kindly hand reaching down from heaven!

Five minutes later the taxicab drew up in front of a hotel. The unknown stepped out, took a leather purse from his pocket and carefully counted out in silver two dollars and twenty cents, which he poured into the chauffeur's palm.

"Thank you, sir."

"You are an American?"

"Sure! I was born in this burg."

"Like the idea?"

"Huh?"

"The idea of being an American?"

"I should say yes! This is one grand little gob o' mud, believe me! It's going to be dry in a little while, and then it will be some grand little old brick. Say, let me give you a tip! The gas in this joint is extra if you blow it out!"

Grinning, the chauffeur threw on the power and wheeled away into the fog.

His late fare followed the vehicle with his gaze until it reached the vanishing point, then he laughed. An American cockney! He turned and entered the hotel. He marched resolutely up to the desk and roused the sleeping clerk, who swung round the register. The unknown without hesitance inscribed his name, which was John Hawksley. But he hesitated the fraction of a second before adding his place of residence--London.

"A room with a bath, if you please; second flight. Have the man call me at seven."

"Yes, sir. Here, boy!"

Sleepily the bellboy lifted the battered kitbag and led the way to the elevator.

"Bawth!" said the night clerk, as the elevator door slithered to the latch. "Bawth! The old dear!"

He returned to his chair, hoping that he would not be disturbed again until he was relieved.

What do we care, so long as we don't know? What's the stranger to us but a fleeting shadow? The Odysseys that pass us every day, and we none the wiser!

The clerk had not properly floated away into dreams when he was again roused. Resentfully he opened his eyes. A huge fist covered with a fell of black hair rose and fell. Attached to this fist was an arm, and joined to that were enormous shoulders. The clerk's trailing, sleep-befogged glance paused when it reached the newcomer's face. The jaws and cheeks and upper lip were blue-black with a beard that required extra-tempered razors once a day. Black eyes that burned like opals, a bullet-shaped head well cropped, and a pudgy nose broad in the nostrils. Because this second arrival wore his hat well forward the clerk was not able to discern the pinched forehead of the fanatic. Not wholly unpleasant, not particularly agreeable; the sort of individual one preferred to walk round rather than bump into. The clerk offered the register, and the squat man scratched his name impatiently, grabbed the extended key, and trotted to the elevator.

"Ah," mused the clerk, "we have with us Mr. Poppy--Popo--" He stared at the signature close up. "Hanged if I can make it out! It looks like some new brand of soft drink we'll be having after July first. Greek or Bulgarian. Anyhow, he didn't awsk for a bawth. Looks as if he needed one, too. Here, boy!"

"Ye-ah!"

"Take a peek at this John Hancock."

"Gee! That must be the guy who makes that drugstore drink--Boolzac."

The clerk swung out, but missed the boy's head by a hair. The boy stood off, grinning.

"Well, you ast me!"

"All right. If anybody else comes in tell 'em we're full up. I'll be a wreck to-morrow without my usual beauty sleep." The clerk dropped into his chair again and elevated his feet to the radiator.

"Want me t' git a pillow for yuh?"

"No back talk!"--drowsily.

"Oh! boy, but I got one on you!"

"What?"

"This Boolzac guy didn't have no baggage, and yuh give 'im the key without little ol' three-per in advance."

"No grip?"

"Nix. Not a toot'brush in sight."

"Well, the damage is done. I might as well go to sleep."

It was not premeditated on the part of the clerk to give the squat man the room adjoining that of Hawksley's. The key had been nearest his hand. But the squat man trembled with excitement when he noted that it was stamped 214. He had taken particular pains to search the register for Hawksley's number before rousing the clerk. He hadn't counted on any such luck as this. His idea had been merely to watch the door of Room 212.

He had the feline foot, as they say. He moved about lightly and without sound in the dark. Almost at once he approached one of the two doors and put his ear to the panel. Running water. The fool had time to take a bath!

A plan flashed into his head. Why not end the affair here and now, and reap the glory for himself? What mattered the net if the fish swam into your hand? Wasn't this particularly his affair? It was the end, not the means. A close touch in Hong-Kong, but the fool had slipped away. But there, in the next room, assured that he had escaped--it would be easy. The squat man tiptoed to the window. Luck of luck, there was a fire-escape platform! He would let half an hour pass, then he would act. The ape, with his British mannerisms! Death to the breed, root and branch! He sat down to wait.

On the other side of the wall the bather finished his ablutions. His body was graceful, vigorous, and youthful, tinted a golden bronze. His nose was hawky; his eyes a Latin brown, alert and roving, though there was a hint of weariness in them, the pressure of long, racking hours of ceaseless vigilance. His top hair was a glossy black inclined to curl; but the four days' growth of beard was as blond as a ripe chestnut burr. In spite of this mark of vagabondage there were elements of beauty in the face. The expanse of the brow and the shape of the head were intellectual. The mouth was pleasure-loving, but the nose and the jaw neutralized this.

After he had towelled himself he reached down for a brown leather pouch which lay on the three-legged bathroom stool. It was patently a tobacco pouch, but there was evidently something inside more precious than Saloniki. He held the pouch on his palm and stared at it as if it contained some jinn clamouring to be let out. Presently he broke away from this fascination and rocked his body, eyes closed--like a man suffering unremitting pain.

"God's curse on them!" he whispered, opening his eyes. He raised the pouch swiftly, as though he intended dashing it to the tiled floor; but his arm sank gently. After all, he would be a fool to destroy them. They were future bread and butter.

He would soon have their equivalent in money--money that would bring back no terrible recollections.

Strange that every so often, despite the horror, he had to take them out and gaze at them. He sat down upon the stool, spread a towel across his knees, and opened the pouch. He drew out a roll of cotton wool, which he unrolled across the towel. Flames! Blue flames, red, yellow, violet, and green--precious stones, many of them with histories that reached back into the dim centuries, histories of murder and loot and envy. The young man had imagination--perhaps too much of it. He saw the stones palpitating upon lovely white and brown bosoms; he saw bloody and greedy hands, the red sack of towns; he heard the screams of women and the raucous laughter of drunken men. Murder and loot.

At the end of the cotton wool lay two emeralds about the size of half dollars and half an inch in thickness, polished, and as vividly green as a dragonfly in the sun, fit for the turban of Schariar, spouse of Scheherazade.

Rodin would have seized upon the young man's attitude--the limp body, the haggard face--hewn it out of marble and called it Conscience. The possessor of the stones held this attitude for three or four minutes. Then he rolled up the cotton wool, jammed it into the pouch, which he hung to his neck by a thong, and sprang to his feet. No more of this brooding; it was sapping his vitality; and he was not yet at his journey's end.

He proceeded to the bedroom, emptied the battered kitbag, and began to dress. He put on heavy tan walking shoes, gray woollen stockings, gray knickerbockers, gray flannel shirt, and a Norfolk jacket minus the third button.

Ah, that button! He fingered the loose threads which had aforetime snugged the button to the wool. The carelessness of a tailor had saved his life. Had that button held, his bones at this moment would be reposing on the hillside in far-away Hong-Kong. Evidently Fate had some definite plans regarding his future, else he would not be in this room, alive. But what plans? Why should Fate bother about him further? She had strained the orange to the last drop. Why protect the pulp? Perhaps she was only making sport of him, lulling him into the belief that eventually he might win through. One thing, she would never be able to twist his heart again. You cannot fill a cup with water beyond the brim. And God knew that his cup had been full and bitter and red.

His hand swept across his eyes as if to brush away the pictures suddenly conjured up. He must keep his thoughts off those things. There was a taint of madness in his blood, and several times he had sensed the brink at his feet. But God had been kind to him in one respect: The blood of his glorious mother predominated.

How many were after him, and who? He had not been able to recognize the man that night in Hong-Kong. That was the fate of the pursued: one never dared pause to look back, while the pursuers had their man before them always. If only he could have broken through into Greece, England would have been easy. The only door open had been in the East. It seemed incredible that he should be standing in this room, but three hours from his goal.

America! The land of the free and the brave! And the irony of it was that he must seek in America the only friends he had in the world. All the Englishmen he had known and loved were dead. He had never made friends with the French, though he loved France. In this country alone he might successfully lose himself and begin life anew. The British were British and the French were French; but in this magnificent America they possessed the tenacity of the one and the gayety of the other--these joyous, unconquered, speed-loving Americans.

He took up the overcoat. Under the light it was no longer black but a very deep green. On both sleeves there were narrow bands of a still deeper green, indicating that gold or silver braid had once befrogged the cuffs. Inside, soft silky Persian lamb; and he ran his fingers over the fur thoughtfully. The coat was still impregnated with the strong odour of horse. He cast it aside, never to touch it again. From the discarded small coat he extracted a black wallet and opened it. That passport! He wondered if there existed another more cleverly forged. It would not have served an hour west of the Hindenburg Line; but in the East and here in America no one had questioned it. In San Francisco they had scarcely glanced at it, peace having come. Besides this passport the wallet contained a will, ten bonds, a custom appraiser's receipt and a sheaf of gold bills. The will, however, was perhaps one of the most astonishing documents conceivable. It left unreservedly to Capt. John Hawksley the contents of the wallet!

Within three hours of his ultimate destination! He knew all about great cities. An hour after he left the train, if he so willed, he could lose himself for all time.

From the bottom of the kitbag he dug up a blue velours case, which after a moment's hesitation he opened. Medals incrusted with precious stones; but on the top was the photograph of a charming girl, blonde as ripe wheat, and arrayed for the tennis court. It was this photograph he wanted. Indifferently he tossed the case upon the centre table, and it upset, sending the medals about with a ring and a tinkle.

The man in the next room heard this sound, and his eye roved desperately. Some way to peer into yonder room! But there was no transom, and he would not yet dare risk the fire escape. The young man raised the photograph to his lips and kissed it passionately.

Then he hid it in the lining of his coat, there being a convenient rent in the inside pocket.

"I must not think!" he murmured. "I must not!"

He became the hunted man again. He turned a chair upend and placed it under the window. He tipped another in front of the door. On the threshold of the bathroom door he deposited the water carafe and the glasses. His bed was against the connecting door. No man would be able to enter unannounced. He had no intention of letting himself fall asleep. He would stretch out and rest. So he lit his pipe, banked the two pillows, switched out the light, and lay down. Only the intermittent glow of his pipe coal could be seen. Near the journey's end; and no more tight-rope walking, with death at both ends, and death staring up from below. Queer how the human being clung to life. What had he to live for? Nothing. So far as he was concerned, the world had come to an end. Sporting instinct; probably that was it; couldn't make up his mind to shuffle off this mortal coil until he had beaten his enemies. English university education had dulled the bite of his natural fatalism. To carry on for the sport of it; not to accept fate but to fight it.

By chance his hand touched his spiky chin. Nevertheless, he would have to enter New York just as he was. He had left his razor in a Pullman washroom hurriedly one morning. He dared not risk a barber's chair, especially these American chairs, that stretched one out in a most helpless manner.

Slowly his pipe sank toward his breast. The weary body was overcoming the will. A sound broke the pleasant spell. He sat up, tense. Someone had entered through the window and stumbled over the chair! Hawksley threw on the light.

CHAPTER II

When the day clerk arrived the night clerk sleepily informed him that the guest in Room 214 was without baggage and had not paid in advance.

"Lave a call?"

"No. I thought I'd put you wise. I didn't notice that the man had no grip until he was in the elevator."

"All right. I'll send the bell-hop captain up with a fake call to see if the man's still there."

When the captain--late of the A.E.F. in France--returned to the office he was mildly excited.

"Gee, there's been a whale of a scrap in Room 212. The chambermaid let me in."

"Murder?" whispered the clerks in unison.

"Murder your granny! Naw! Just a fight between 212 and 214, because both of 'em have flown the roost. But take a peek at what I found on the table."

It was a case of blue velours. The boy threw back the lid dramatically.

"War medals?"

"If they are I never piped 'em before. They ain't French or British." The captain of the bell-boys scratched his head ruminatively. "Gee, I got it! Orders, that's what they all 'em. Kings pay 'em out Saturdays when the pay roll is nix. Will you pipe the diamonds and rubies? There's your room rents, monseer."

The day clerk, who considered himself a judge, was of the opinion that there were two or three thousand dollars tied up in the stones. It was a police affair. Some ambassador had been robbed, and the Britisher and the Greek or Bulgarian were mixed up in it. Loot.

"I thought the war was over," said the night clerk.

"The shootin' is over, that's all," said the captain of the bellboys, sagely.

What had happened in Room 212? A duel of wits rather than of physical contact. Hawksley realized instantly that here was the crucial moment. Caught and overpowered, he was lost. If he shouted for help and it came, he was lost. Once the police took a hand in the affair, the newspaper publicity that would follow would result in the total ruin of all his hopes. There was only one chance--to finish this affair outside the hotel, in some fog-dimmed street. There leaped into his mind, obliquely and queerly, a picture in one of Victor Hugo's tales--Quasimodo. And there he stood, in every particular save the crooked back. And on the top of this came the recollection that he had seen the man before.... The torches! The red torches and the hobnailed boots!

There began an odd game, a dancing match, which the young man led adroitly, always with his thought upon the open window. There would be no shooting; Quasimodo would not want the police either. Half a dozen times his fingers touched futilely the dancing master's coat. Bank and forth across the room, over the bed, round the stand and chairs. Persistently, as if he understood the young man's manoeuvres, the squat individual kept to the window side of the room.

An inspiration brought the affair to an end. Hawksley snatched up the bedclothes and threw them as the ancient retiarius threw his net. He managed to win to the lower platform of the fire escape before Quasimodo emerged.

There was a fourteen-foot drop to the street, and the man with the golden stubble on his chin and cheeks swung for a moment to gauge his landing. Quasimodo came after with the agility of an ape. The race down the street began with about a hundred yards in between.

Down the hill they went, like phantoms. The distance did not widen. Bears will run amazingly fast and for a long while. The quarry cut into Pearl Street for a block, turned a corner, and soon vaguely espied the Hudson River. He made for this.

To the mind of Quasimodo this flight had but one significance--he was dealing with an arrant coward; and he based his subsequent acts upon this premise, forgetting that brave men run when need says must. It would have surprised him exceedingly to learn that he was not driving, that he was being led. Hawksley wanted his enemy alone, where no one would see to interfere. Red torches and hobnailed boots! For once the two bloods, always more or less at war, merged in a common purpose--to kill this beast, to grind the face of him into pulp! Red torches and hobnailed boots!

Presently one of the huge passenger boats, moored for the winter, loomed up through the fog; and toward this Hawksley directed his steps. He made a flying leap aboard and vanished round the deckhouse to the river side.

Quasimodo laughed as he followed. It was as if the tobacco pouch and the appraiser's receipt were in his own pocket; and broad rivers made capital graveyards. They two alone in the fog! He whirled round the deckhouse--and backed on his heels to get his balance. Directly in front, in a very understandable pose, was the intended victim, his jaw jutting, his eyelids narrowed.

Quasimodo tried desperately to reach for his pistol; but a bolt of lightning stopped the action. There is something peculiar about a blow on the nose, a good blow. The Anglo-Saxon peoples alone possess the counterattack--a rush. To other peoples concentration of thought is impossible after the impact. Instinctively Quasimodo's hands flew to his face. He heard a laugh, mirthless and terrible. Before he could drop his hands from his face-blows, short and boring, from this side and from that, over and under. The squat man was brave enough; simply he did not know how to fight in this manner. He was accustomed to the use of steel and the hobnails on his boots. He struck wildly, swinging his arms like a Flemish mill in a brisk wind.

Some of his blows got home, but these provoked only sardonic laughter.

Wild with rage and pain he bored in. He had but one chance--to get this shadow in his gorilla-like arms. He lacked mental flexibility. An idea, getting into his head, stuck; it was not adjustable. Like an arrow sped from the bowstring, it had to fulfill its destiny. It never occurred to him to take to his heels, to get space between himself and this enemy he had so woefully underestimated. Ten feet, and he might have been able to whirl, draw his pistol, and end the affair.

The coup de grace came suddenly: a blow that caught Quasimodo full on the point of the jaw. He sagged and went sprawling upon his face. The victor turned him over and raised a heel.... No! He was neither Prussian nor Sudanese black. He was white; and white men did not stamp in the faces of fallen enemies.

But there was one thing a white man might do in such a case without disturbing the ethical, and he proceeded about it forthwith: Draw the devil's fangs; render him impotent for a few hours. He deliberately knelt on one of the outspread arms and calmly emptied the insensible man's pockets. He took everything--watch, money, passport, letters, pistol, keys--rose and dropped them into the river. He overlooked Quasimodo's belt, however. The Anglo-Saxon idea was top hole. His fists had saved his life.

CHAPTER III

Hawksley heard the panting of an engine and turned his head. Dimly he saw a giant bridge and a long drab train moving across it. He picked up the fallen man's cap and tried it on. Not a particularly good fit, but it would serve. He then trotted round the deckhouse to the street side, jumped to the wharf, and sucking the cracked knuckles of his right hand fell into a steady dogtrot which carried him to the station he had left so hopefully an hour and a half gone.

An accommodation train eventually deposited him in Poughkeepsie, where he purchased a cap and a sturdy walking stick. The stubble on his chin and cheeks began to irritate him intensely, but he could not rid himself of the idea that a barber's chair would be inviting danger. He was now tolerably certain that from one end of the continent to the other his presence was known. His life and his property, they would be after both. Even now there might be men in this strange town seeking him. The closer he got to New York, the more active and wide-awake they would become.

He walked the streets, his glance constantly roving. But apparently no one paid the least attention to him. Finally he returned to the railway station; and at six o'clock that evening he left the platform of the 125th Street Station, and appraised covertly the men who accompanied him to the street. He felt assured that they were all Americans. Probably they were; but there are still some stray fools of American birth who cannot accept the great American doctrine as the only Ararat visible in this present flood. Perhaps one of these accompanied Hawksley to the street. Whatever he was, one had upon order met every south-going train since seven o'clock that morning, when Quasimodo, paying from the gold hidden in his belt, had sent forth the telegraphic alarm. The man hurried across the street and followed Hawksley by matching his steps. His business was merely to learn the other's destination and then to report.

Across the earth a tempest had been loosed; but Ariel did not ride it, Caliban did. The scythe of terror was harvesting a type; and the innocent were bending with the guilty.

Suddenly Hawksley felt young, revivified, free. He had arrived. Surmounting indescribable hazards and hardships he walked the pavement of New York. In an hour the mutable quicksands of a great city would swallow him forever. Free! He wanted to stroll about, peer into shop windows, watch the amazing electric signs, dally; but he still had much to accomplish.

He searched for a telephone sign. It was necessary that he find one immediately. He had once spent six weeks in and about this marvellous city, and he had a vague recollection of the blue-and-white enamel signs. Shortly he found one. It was a pay station in the rear of a news and tobacco shop.

He entered a booth, but discovered that he had no five-cent pieces in his purse. He hurried out to the girl behind the cigar stand. She was exhibiting a box of cigars to a customer, who selected three, paid for them, and walked away. Hawksley, boiling with haste to have his affair done, flung a silver coin toward the girl.

"Five-cent pieces!"

"Will you take them with you or shall I send them?" asked the girl, earnestly.

"I beg pardon!"

"Any particular kind of ribbon you want the box tied with?"

"I beg your pardon!" repeated Hawksley, harried and bewildered. "But I'm in a hurry--"

"Too much of a hurry to leave out the bark when you ask a favour? I make change out of courtesy. And you all bark at me Nickel! Nickel! as if that was my job."

"A thousand apologies!"--contritely.

"And don't make it any worse by suggesting a movie after supper. My mother never lets me go out after dark."

"I rather fancy she's quite sensible. Still, you seem able to take care of yourself. I might suggest--"

"With that black eye? Nay, nay! I'll bet somebody's brother gave it to you."

"Venus was not on that occasion in ascendancy. Thank you for the change." Hawksley swung on his heel and reentered the booth.

A great weariness oppressed him. A longing, almost irresistible, came to him to go out and cry aloud: "Here I am! Kill me! I am tired and done!" For he had recognized the purchaser of the cigars as one of the men who had left the 125th Street Station at the same time as he. He remembered distinctly that this man had been in a hurry. Perhaps the whole dizzy affair was reacting upon his imagination psychologically and turning harmless individuals into enemies.

"Hello!" said a man's voice over the wire.

"Is Mr. Rathbone there?"

"Captain Rathbone is with his regiment at Coblenz, sir."

"Coblenz?"

"Yes, sir. I do not expect his return until near midsummer, sir. Who is this talking?"

"Have you opened a cable from Yokohama?"

"This is Mr. Hawksley!" The voice became excited.

"Oh, sir! You will come right away. I alone understand, sir. You will remember me when you see me. I'm the captain's butler, sir--Jenkins. He cabled back to give you the entire run of the house as long as you desired it. He advised me to notify you that he had also prepared his banker against your arrival. Have your luggage sent here at once, sir. Dinner will be at your convenience."

Hawksley's body relaxed. A lump came into his throat. Here was a friend, anyhow, ready to serve him though he was thousands of miles away.

When he could trust himself to speak he said: "Sorry. It will be impossible to accept the hospitality at present. I shall call in a few days, however, to establish my identity. Thank you. Good evening."

"Just a moment, sir. I may have an important cable to transmit to you. It would be wise to leave me your address, sir."

Hawksley hesitated a moment. After all, he could trust this perfect old servant, whom he remembered. He gave the address.

As he came out of the booth the girl stretched forth an arm to detain him. He stopped.

"I'm sorry I spoke like that," she said. "But I'm so tired! I've been on my feet all day, and everybody's been barking and growling; and if I'd taken in as many nickels as I've passed out in change the boss would be rich."

"Give me a dozen of those roses there." She sold flowers also. "The pink ones. How much?" he asked.

"Two-fifty."

He laid down the money. "Never mind the box. They are for you. Good evening."

The girl stared at the flowers as Ali Baba must have stared at the cask with rubies.

"For me!" she whispered. "For nothing!"

Her eyes blurred. She never saw Hawksley again; but that was of no importance. She had a gentle deed to put away in the lavender of recollection.

Outside Hawksley could see nothing of the man who had bought the cigars. At any rate, further dodging would be useless. He would go directly to his destination. Old Gregor had sent him a duplicate key to the apartment. He could hide there for a day or two; then visit Rathbone's banker at his residence in the night to establish his identity. Gregor could be trusted to carry the wallet and the pouch to the bank. Once these were walled in steel half the battle would be over. He would have nothing to guard thereafter but his life. He laughed brokenly. Nothing but the clothes he stood in. He never could claim the belongings he had been forced to leave in that hotel back yonder. But there was loyal old Gregor. Somebody would be honestly glad to see him. The poor old chap! Astonishing, but of late he was always thinking in English.

He hailed the first free taxicab he saw, climbed in, and was driven downtown. He looked back constantly. Was he followed? There was no way of telling. The street was alive with vehicles tearing north and south, with frequent stoppage for the passage of those racing east and west. The destination of Hawksley's cab was an old-fashioned apartment house in Eightieth Street.

Gregor would have a meal ready; and it struck Hawksley forcibly that he was hungry, that he had not touched food since the night before. Gregor, valeting in a hotel, pressing coats and trousers and sewing on buttons! Groggy old world, wasn't it? Gregor, pressing the trousers of the hoi polloi! Gregor, who could have sent New York mad with that old Stradivarius of his! But Gregor was wise. Safety for him lay in obscurity; and what was more obscure than a hotel valet?

He did not seek the elevator but mounted the first flight of stairs. He saw two doors, one on each side of the landing. He sought one, stooped and peered at the card over the bell. Conover. Gregor's was opposite. Having a key he did not knock but unlocked the door and stepped into the dark hall.

"Stefani Gregor?" he called, joyously. "Stefani, my old friend, it is I!"

Silence. But that was understandable. Either Gregor had not returned from his labours or he was out gathering the essentials for the evening meal. Judging from the variety of odours that swam the halls of this human warren many suppers were in the process of making, and the top flavour was garlic. He sniffed pleasurably. Not that the smell of garlic quickened his hunger. It merely sent his thought galloping backward a score of years. He saw Stefani Gregor and a small boy in mountain costume footing it sturdily along the dizzy goat paths of the rugged hills; saw the two sitting on some ruddy promontory and munching black bread rubbed with garlic. Ambrosia! His mother's horror, when she smelt his breath--as if garlic had not been one of her birthrights! His uncle, roaring out in his bull's voice that black bread and garlic were good for little boys' stomachs, and made the stuff of soldiers. Black bread and garlic and the Golden Age!

After he had flooded the hall with light he began a tour of inspection. The rooms were rather bare but clean and orderly. Here and there were items that kept the homeland green in the recollection. He came to the bedroom last. He hesitated for a moment before opening the door. The lights told him why Gregor had not greeted his entering hail.

The overturned reading lamp, the broken chair, the letters and papers strewn about the floor, the rifled bureau drawers--these things spoke plainly enough. Gregor was a prisoner somewhere in this vast city; or he was dead.

Hawksley stood motionless for a space. And he must remain here at least for a night and a day! He would not dare risk another hotel. He could, of course, go to the splendid Rathbone place; but it would not be fair to invite tragedy across that threshold.

A ball of crushed paper at his feet attracted his attention. He kicked it absently, followed and picked it up, his thought on other things. He was aimlessly smoothing it out when an English word caught his eye. English! He smoothed the crumpled sheet and read:

> If you find this it is the will of God. I have been watched
> for several days, and am now convinced that they have always
> known I was here but were leaving me alone for some unknown
> purpose. I roll this ball because anything folded and left
> in a conspicuous place would be useless should they come for
> me. I understand. It is you, poor boy. They are watching
> me in hopes of catching you, and I've no way to warn you not
> to come here. It was after I sent you the key that I learned
> the truth. God bless you and guard you!
> STEFANI.

Hawksley tore the note into scraps. Food and sleep. He walked toward the kitchen, musing. What an odd mixture he was! Superficially British, with the British outlook; and yet filled with the dancing blood of the Latin and the cold, phlegmatic blood of the Slav. He was like a schoolmaster with two students too big for him to handle. Always the Latin was dispossessing the Slav or the Slav was ousting the Latin. With fatalistic confidence that nevermore would he look upon the kindly face of Stefani Gregor, alive, he went in search of food.

Not a crust did he find. In the ice-chest there was a bottle of milk--soured. Hungry; and not a crumb! And he dared not go out in search of food. No one had observed his entrance to the apartment, but it was improbable that such luck would attend him a second time.

He returned to the bedroom. He did not turn on the light because a novel idea had blossomed unexpectedly--a Latin idea. There might be food on some window ledge. He would leave payment. He proceeded to the window, throwing up both it and the curtain, and looked out. Ripping! There was a fire escape.

As he slipped a leg over the sill a golden square sprang into existence across the way. Immediately he forgot his foraging instincts. In a moment he was all Latin, always susceptible to the enchantment of beauty.

The distance across the court was less than forty feet. He could see the girl quite plainly as she set about the preparation of her evening meal. He forgot his danger, his hunger, his code of ethics, which did not permit him to gaze at a young woman through a window.

Alone. He was alone and she was alone. A novel idea popped into his head. He chuckled; and the sound of that chuckle in his ears somehow brought back his resolve to carry on, to pass out, if so he must, fighting. He would knock on yonder window and ask the beautiful lady slavey for a bit of her supper!

CHAPTER IV

Kitty Conover had inherited brains and beauty, and nothing else but the furniture. Her father had been a famous reporter, the admiration of cubs from New York to San Francisco; handsome, happy-go-lucky, generous, rather improvident, and wholly lovable. Her mother had been a comedy actress noted for her beauty and wit and extravagance. Thus it will be seen that Kitty was in luck to inherit any furniture at all.

Kitty was twenty-four. A body is as old as it is, but a brain is as old as the facts it absorbs; and Kitty had absorbed enough facts to carry her brain well into the thirties.

Conover had been dead twenty years; and Kitty had scarcely any recollections of him. Improvident as the run of newspaper writers are, Conover had fulfilled one obligation to his family--he had kept up his endowment policies; and for eighteen years the insurance had taken care of Kitty and her mother, who because of a weak ankle had not been able to return to the scenes of her former triumphs. In 1915 this darling mother, whom Kitty loved to idolatry, had passed on.

There was enough for the funeral and the cleaning up of the bills; but that was all. The income ceased with Mrs. Conover's demise. Kitty saw that she must give up writing short stories which nobody wanted, and go to work. So she proceeded at once to the newspaper office where her father's name was still a tradition, and applied for a job. It was frankly a charity job, but Kitty was never to know that because she fell into the newspaper game naturally; and when they discovered her wide acquaintance among theatrical celebrities they switched her into the dramatic department, where she had astonishing success as a raconteur. She was now assistant dramatic editor of the Sunday issue, and her pay envelope had four crisp ten-dollar notes in it each Monday.

She still remained in the old apartment; sentiment as much as anything. She had been born in it and her happiest days had been spent there. She lived alone, without help, being one of that singular type of womanhood that is impervious to the rust of loneliness. Her daily activities sufficed the gregarious instincts, and it was often a relief to move about in silence.

Among other things Kitty had foresight. She had learned that a little money in the background was the most satisfying thing in existence. So many times she and her mother had just reached the insurance check, with grumbling bill collectors in the hall, that she was determined never to be poor. She had to fight constantly her love of finery inherited from her mother, and her love of good times inherited from her father. So she established a bank account, and to date had not drawn a check against it; which speaks well for her will power, an attribute cultivated, not inherited.

Kitty was as pleasing to the eye as a basket of fruit. Her beauty was animated. There was an expression in her eyes and on her lips that spoke of laughter always on tiptoe. An enviable inheritance, this, the desire to laugh, to be searching always for a vent to laughter; it is something money cannot buy, something not to be cultivated; a true gift of the gods. This desire to laugh is found invariably in the tender and valorous; and Kitty was both. Brown hair with running threads of gold that was always catching light; slate-blue eyes with heavy black fringe-Irish; colour that waxed and waned; and a healthy, shapely body. Topped by a sparkling intellect these gifts made Kitty desirable of men.

Kitty had no beau. After the adolescent days beaux ceased to interest her. This would indicate that she was inclined toward suffrage. Nothing of the kind. Intensely romantic, she determined to await the grand passion or go it alone. No experimental adventures for her. Be assured that she weighed every new man she met, and finding some flaw discarded him as a matrimonial possibility. Besides, her unusual facilities to view and judge men had shown her masculine phases the average woman would have discovered only after the fatal knot was tied. She did not suspect that she was romantical. She attributed her wariness to common sense.

If there is one place where a pretty young woman may labour without having to build a wall of liquid air about her to fend off amatory advances that place is the editorial room of a great metropolitan daily. One must have leisure to fall in love;

and only the office boys could assemble enough idle time to call it leisure.

Her desk faced Burlingame's; and Burlingame was the dramatic editor, a scholar and a gentleman. He liked to hear Kitty talk, and often he lured her into the open; and he gathered information about theatrical folks that was outside even his wide range of knowledge.

A drizzly fog had hung over New York since morning. Kitty was finishing up some Sunday special. Burlingame was reading proofs. All day theatrical folks had been in and out of this little ten-by-twelve cubby-hole; and now there would be quiet.

But no. The door opened and an iron-gray head intruded.

"Will I be in the way?"

"Lord, no!" cried Burlingame, throwing down his proofs. "Come along in, Cutty."

The great war correspondent came in and sat down, sighing gratefully.

Cutty was a nickname; he carried and smoked--everywhere they would permit him--the worst-looking and the worst-smelling pipe in Christendom. You may not realize it, but a nickname is a round-about Anglo-Saxon way of telling a fellow you love him. He was Cutty, but only among his dear intimates, mind you; to the world at large, to presidents, kings, ambassadors, generals, and capitalists he is known by another name. You will find it on the roster of the Royal Geographical; on the title page of several unique books on travel, jewels, and drums; in magazines and newspapers; on the membership roll of the Savage in London and the Lambs in New York. But you will not find it in this story; because it would not be fair to set his name against the unusual adventures that crossed his line of life with that of the young man who wore the tobacco pouch suspended from his neck.

Tall, bony, graceful enough except in a chair, where his angles became conspicuous; the ruddy, weather-bitten complexion of a deep-sea sailor, and a sailor man's blue eye; the brow of a thinker and the mouth of a humourist. Men often call another man handsome when a woman knows they mean manly. Among men Cutty was handsome.

Kitty considerately rose and gathered up her manuscript.

"No, no, Kitty! I'd rather talk to you than Burly, here. You're always reminding me of that father of yours. Best comrade I ever had. You laugh just like him. Did your mother ever tell you that old Cutty is your godfather?"

"Good gracious!"

"Fact. I told your dad I'd watch over you."

"And a fat lot of watching you've done to date," jeered Burlingame.

"Couldn't help that. But I can be on the job until I return to the Balkans."

Kitty laughed joyously and sat down, perhaps a little thrilled. She had always admired Cutty from afar, shyly. Once in a blue moon he had in the old days appeared for tea; and he and Mrs. Conover would spend the balance of the afternoon discussing the lovable qualities of Tommy Conover. Kitty had seen him but twice during the war.

"Every so often," began Cutty, "I have to find listeners. Fact. I used to hate crowds, listeners; but those ten days in an open boat, a thousand miles from anywhere, made me gregarious. I'm always wanting company and hating to go to bed, which is bad business for a man of fifty-two." Cutty's ship had been torpedoed.

To Kitty, with his tired eyes and weather-bitten face, his bony, gangling body, he had the appearance of a lazy man. Actually she knew him to be a man of tremendous vitality and endurance. Eagles when they roost are heavy-lidded and clumsy. She wondered if there was a corner on the globe he had not peered into.

For thirty years he had been following two gods--Rumour and War. For thirty years he had been the slave of cables and telegrams. Even now he was preparing to return to the Balkans, where the great fire had started and where there were still some threatening embers to watch.

Cutty was not well known in America; his reputation was European. He played the game because he loved it, being comfortably fortified with worldly goods. He was a linguist of rare attainments, specializing in the polyglot of southeastern Europe. He came and went like cloud shadow. His foresight was so keen he was seldom ordered to go here or there; he was generally on the spot when the orders arrived.

He was interested in socialism and its bewildering ramifications, but only as an analytical student. He could fit himself into any environment, interview a prime minister in the afternoon and take potluck that night with the anarchist who was planning to blow up the prime minister.

Burlingame, an intimate, often exposed for Kitty's delectation the amazing and colourful facets of Cutty's diamond-brilliant mind. Cutty wrote authoritatively on famous gems and collected drums. He had one of the finest collections of chrysoprase in the world. He loved these semi-precious stones because of their unmatchable, translucent green--like the pulp of a grape. From Burlingame Kitty had learned that Cutty, rather indifferent to women, carried about with him the photographs--large size--of famous professional beauties and a case filled with polished chrysoprase. He would lay a photograph on a table and adorn the lovely throat with astonishing necklaces and the head with wonderful tiaras, all the while his brain at work with some intricate political puzzle.

And he collected drums. The walls of his apartment--part of the loft of a mid-town office building--were covered with a most startling assortment of drums: drums of war, of the dance, of the temples of the feast, ancient and modern, some of them dreadful looking objects, as Kitty had cause to remember.

Though Cutty had known her father and mother intimately, Kitty was a comparative stranger. He recollected seeing her perhaps a dozen times. She had been a shy child, not given to climbing over visitors' knees; not the precocious offspring of the average theatrical mother. So in the past he had somewhat overlooked her. Then one day recently he had dropped in to see Burlingame and had seen Kitty instead; which accounts for his presence here this day. Neither Kitty nor Burlingame suspected the true attraction. The dramatic editor accepted the advent as a peculiar compliment to himself. And it is to be doubted if Cutty himself realized that there was a true magnetic pole in this cubbyhole of a room.

Kitty, however, had vivid recollections. Actually the first strange man she had ever met. But not having been visible on her horizon, except in flashes, she knew of the man only what she had read and what Burlingame had casually offered during discussions.

"Well, anyhow," said Burlingame, complacently, "the war is over."

Cutty smiled indulgently. "That's the trouble with us chaps who tramp round the world for news. We can't bamboozle ourselves like you folks who stay at home. The war was only the first phase. There's a mess over there; wanting something and not knowing exactly what, those millions; milling cattle, with neither shed nor pasture. The Lord only knows how long it will take to clarify. Would you mind if I smoked?"

"Wow!" cried Burlingame.

"Not at all," answered Kitty. "I don't see how any pipe could be worse than Mr. Burlingame's."

"I apologize," said the dramatic editor, humbly.

"You needn't," replied the girl. She turned to the war correspondent. "Any new drums?"

"I remember that day. You were scared half to death at my walls."

"Small wonder! I was only twelve; and I dreamed of cannibals for weeks."

"Drums! I wonder if any living man has heard a greater variety than I? What a lot of them! I have heard them calling a jehad in the Sudan. Tumpi-tum-tump! tumpitum-tump! Makes a white man's hair stand up when he hears it in the night. I don't know what it is, but the sound drives the Oriental mad. And that reminds me--I've had them in mind all day--the drums of jeopardy!"

"What an odd phrase! And what are the drums of jeopardy?" asked Kitty, leaning on her arms. Odd, but suddenly she felt a longing to go somewhere, thousands and thousands of miles away. She had never been west of Chicago or east of Boston. Until this moment she had never felt the call of the blood--her father's. Cocoanut palms and birds of paradise! And drums in the night going tumpi-tum-tump! tumpi-tum-tump!

"I've always been mad over green things," began Cutty. "A wheat field in the spring, leafing maples. It's Nature's choice and mine. My passion is emeralds; and I haven't any because those I want are beyond reach. They are owned by the great houses of Europe and Asia, and lie in royal caskets; or did. If I could go into a mine and find an emerald as big as my fist I should be only partly happy if it chanced to be of fine colour. In a little while I should lose interest in it. It wouldn't be alive, if you can get what I mean. Just as a man would rather have a homely woman to talk to than a beautiful window dummy to admire. A stone to interest me must have a story--a story of murder and loot, of beautiful women, palaces."

"Br-r-r!" cried Burlingame.

"Why, I've seen emeralds I would steal with half a chance. I couldn't help it. Fact," declared Cutty, earnestly. "Think of the loot in the Romanoff palaces! What's become of all those magnificent stones? In a little while they'll be turning up in Amsterdam to be cut--some of them. Or maybe Mister Bolsheviki's inamorata will be stringing them round her neck. Loot."

"But the drums of jeopardy!" said Kitty.

"Emeralds, green as an English lawn in May after a shower, Kitty. By the way, do you mind if I call you Kitty? I used to."

"And I've always thought of you as Cutty. Fifty-fifty."

"It's a bargain. Well, the drums to my thinking are the finest two examples of the green beryl in the world. Polished, of course, as emeralds always should be. I should say that they were about the size of those peppermint chocolate drops there."

"Have one?" said Kitty.

"No. Spoil the taste of the pipe."

"You ought to spoil that taste once in a while," was Burlingame's observation. "But go on."

"I suppose originally there was a single stone, later cut into halves, because they are perfect matches. The drums proper are exquisitely carved ivory statuettes, of Hindu or Mohammedan drummers, squatting, the golden base of the drums between the knees, and the drumheads the emeralds. Lord, how they got to me! I wanted to run off with them. The history of murder and loot they could tell! Some Delhi mogul owned them first. Then Nadir Shah carried them off to Persia, along with the famous peacock throne. I saw them in a palace on the Caspian in 1912. Russia was very strong in Persia at one time. Perhaps they were gifts; perhaps they were stolen--these emeralds. Anyhow, I'd never heard of them until that year. And I travelled all the way up from Constantinople to get a glimpse of them if it were possible. I had to do some mighty fine wire-pulling. For one of those stones I would give half of all I own. To see them in the possession of another man would be a supreme test to my honesty."

"You old pirate!" said Burlingame.

"But why the word jeopardy?" persisted Kitty, who was intrigued by the phrase.

"Probably some Hindu trick. It is a language of flowery metaphors. It means, I suppose, that when you touch the drums they bite. In journeying from one spot to another they always leave misfortune behind, as I understand it. Just coincidence; but you couldn't drive that into an Oriental skull. This is what makes the study of precious stones so interesting. There is always some enchantment, some evil spell.

To handle the drums is to invite a minor accident. Call it twaddle; probably is; and yet I have reason to believe that there's something to the superstition."

Burlingame sniffed.

"I can prove it," Cutty declared. "I held those drums in my hands one day. I carried them to a window the better to observe them. On my return to the hotel I was knocked down by a horse and laid up in bed for a week. That same night someone tried to kill the man who showed me the emeralds. Coincidence? Perhaps. But these days I'm shying at thirteen, the wrong side of the street, ladders, and religious curses."

"An old hard-boiled egg like you?" Burlingame threw up his hands in mock despair.

"I laugh, too; but I duck, nevertheless. The chap who showed me the stones was what you'd call the honorary custodian; a privileged character because of his genius. Before approaching him I sent him a copy of my monograph on green stones. I found that he was quite as crazy over green as I. That brought us together; and while I drew him out I kept wondering where I had seen him before. Both his name and his face were vaguely familiar. It seems a superstition had come along with the stones, from India to Persia, from there to Russia. A maid fortunate enough to see the drums would marry and be happy. The old fellow confessed that occasionally he secretly admitted a peasant maid to gaze upon the stones. But he never let the male inmates of the palace find this out. He knew them a little too intimately. A bad lot."

"And this palace?" asked Kitty.

"Not one stone on another. The proletariat rose up and destroyed it. To mobs anything beautiful is offensive. Palaces looted, banks, museums, houses. The ignorant toying with hand grenades, thinking them sceptres. All the scum in the world boiling to the top. After the Red Day comes the Red Night."

"Whatever will become of them--the little kings and princes and dukes?" After all, thought Kitty, they were human beings; they would not suffer any the less because they had been born to the purple.

"Maybe they'll go to work," said Cutty, dryly. "Sooner or later, all parasites will have to work if they want bread. And yet I've met some men among them, big in the heart and the mind, who would have made bully farmers and professors.

The beautiful thing about the Anglo-Saxon education is that the whole structure is based upon fair play. In eastern and southeastern Europe few of them can play solitaire without cheating. But I would give a good deal to know what has happened to those emeralds--the drums of jeopardy. They'll probably be broken up and sold in carat weights. The whole family was wiped out in a night.... I say, will you take lunch with me to-morrow?"

"Gladly."

"All right. I'll drop in here at half after twelve. Here's my telephone number, should anything alter your plans. If I'm going to be godfather I might as well start right in."

"The drums of jeopardy; what a haunting phrase!"

"Haunting stones, too, Kitty. For picking them up in my hands I went to bed with a banged-up leg. I can't forget that. We Occidentals laugh at Orientals and their superstitions. We don't believe in the curse. And yet, by George, those emeralds were accursed!"

"Piffle!" snorted Burlingame. "Mush! It's greed, pure and simple, that gives precious stones their sinister histories. You'd have been hit by that horse if you had picked up nothing more valuable than a rhinestone buckle. Take away the gold lure, and precious stones wouldn't sell at the price of window glass."

"Is that so? How about me? It isn't because a stone is worth so much that makes me want it. I want it for the sheer beauty; I want it for the tremendous panorama the sight of it unfolds in my mind. I imagine what happened from the hour the stone was mined to the hour it came into my possession. To me--to all genuine collectors--the intrinsic value is nil. Can't you see? It is for me what Balzac's La Peau de Chagrin would be to you if you had fallen on it for the first time--money, love, tragedy, death."

An interruption came in the form of one of the office boys. The chief was on the wire and wanted Cutty at once.

"At half after twelve, Kitty. And by the way," added Cutty as he rose, "they say about the drums that a beautiful woman is immune to their danger."

"There's your chance, Kitty," said Burlingame.

"Am I beautiful?" asked Kitty, demurely.

"Lord love the minx!" shouted Cutty. "A corner in Mouquin's."

"Rain or shine." After Cutty had departed Kitty said: "He's the most fascinating man I know. What fun it would be to jog round the world with a man like that, who knew everybody and everything. As a little girl I was violently in love with him; but don't you ever dare give me away."

"You'll probably have nightmare to-night. And honestly you ought not to live in that den alone. But Cutty has seen things," Burlingame admitted; "things no white man ought to see. He's been shot up, mauled by animals, marooned, torpedoed at sea, made prisoner by old Fuzzy-Wuzzy. An ordinary man would have died of fatigue. Cutty is as tough and strong as a gorilla and as active as a cat. But this jewel superstition is all rot. Odd, though; he'll travel halfway round the world to see a ruby or an emerald. He says no true collector cares a cent for a diamond. Says they are vulgar."

"Except on the third finger of a lady's left hand; and then they are just perfectly splendid!"

"Oho! Well, when you get yours I hope it's as big as the Koh-i-noor."

"Thank you! You might just as well wish a brick on me!"

Kitty left the office at a quarter of six. The phrase kept running through her head--the drums of jeopardy. A little shiver ran up her spine. Money, love, tragedy, death! This terrible and wonderful old world, of which she had seen little else than city streets, suddenly exhibited wide vistas. She knew now why she had begun to save--travel. Just as soon as she had a thousand she would go somewhere. A great longing to hear native drums in the night.

Even as the wish entered her mind a new sound entered her ears. The Subway car wheels began to beat--tumpitum-tump! tumpitum tump! Fudge! She opened her evening paper and scanned the fashions, the dramatic news, and the comics. Being a woman she read the world news last. On the front page she saw a queer story, dated at Albany: Mysterious guests at a hotel; how they had fought and fled in the early morning. There had been left behind a case with foreign orders incrusted with several thousand dollars' worth of gems. Bolsheviki, said the police; just as they said auto bandits a few years ago when confronted with something they could not understand. The orders had been turned over to the Federal authorities from whom it was learned that they were all royal and demi-royal. Neither of the two guests had returned up to noon, and one had fled, leaving even his hat and coat. But there was nothing to indicate his identity.

"Loot!" murmured Kitty. "All the scum in the world rising to the top"--quoting Cutty. "Poor things!" as she thought of the gentle ladies who had died horribly in bedrooms and cellars.

Kitty was beginning to cast about for more congenial quarters. There were too many foreigners in the apartments, and none of them especially good housekeepers. Always, nowadays, somebody had a washing out on the line, the odour of garlic was continuously in the air, and there were noisy children under foot in the halls. The families she and her mother had known were all gone; and Kitty was perhaps the oldest inhabitant in the block.

The living-room windows faced Eightieth Street; bedrooms, dining room, and kitchen looked out upon the court. From the latter windows one could step out upon the fire-escape platform, which ran round the three sides of the court.

Among the present tenants she knew but one, an old man by the name of Gregory, who lived opposite. The acquaintance had never ripened into friendship; but sometimes Kitty would borrow an egg and he would borrow some sugar. In the summertime, when the windows were open at night, she had frequently heard the music of a violin swimming across the court. Polish, Russian, and Hungarian music, always speaking with a tragic note; nothing she had ever heard in concerts. Once, however, she had heard him begin something from Thais, and stop in the middle of it; and that convinced her that he was a master. She was fond of good music. One day she asked Gregory why he did not teach music instead of valeting at a hotel. His answer had been illuminative. It was only his body that pressed clothes; but it would have torn his soul to listen daily to the agonized bow of the novice. Kitty was lonely through pride as much as anything. As for friends, she had a regiment of them. But she rarely accepted their hospitality, realizing that she could not return it. No young men called because she never invited them. All this, however, was going to change when she moved.

As she turned on the hail light she saw an envelope on the floor. Evidently it had been shoved under the door. It was unstamped. She opened it, and stepped out of the humdrum into the whirligig.

DEAR MISS CONOVER:

If anything should happen to me all the things in my apartment
I give to you without reservation.

STEPHEN GREGORY.

She read the letter a dozen times to make sure that it meant exactly what it said. He might be ill. After she had cooked her supper she would run round and inquire. The poor lonely old man!

She went into the kitchen and took inventory. There was nothing but bacon and eggs and coffee. She had forgotten to order that morning. She lit the gas range and began to prepare the meal. As she broke an egg against the rim of the pan the nearby Elevated train rushed by, drumming tumpitum-tump! tumpitum-tump! She laughed, but it wasn't honest laughter. She laughed because she was conscious that she was afraid of something. Impulse drove her to the window. Contact with men--her unusual experiences as a reporter--had developed her natural fearlessness to a point where it was aggressive. As she pressed the tip of her nose against the pane, however, she found herself gazing squarely into a pair of exceedingly brilliant dark eyes; and all the blood in her body seemed to rush violently into her throat.

Tableau!

CHAPTER V

Kitty gasped, but she did not cry out. The five days' growth of blondish stubble, the discoloured eye--for all the orb itself was brilliant--and the hawky nose combined to send through her the first great thrill of danger she had ever known. Slowly she backed away from the window. The man outside immediately extended his hands with a gesture that a child would have understood. Supplication. Kitty paused, naturally. But did the man mean it? Might it not be some trick to lure her into opening the window? And what was he doing outside there anyhow? Her mind, freed from the initial hypnosis of the encounter, began to work quickly. If she ran from the kitchen to call for help he might be gone when she returned, only to come back when she was again alone.

Once more the man executed that gesture, his palms upward. It was Latin; she was aware of that, for she was always encountering it in the halls. Another gesture. She understood this also. The tips of the fingers bunched and dabbed at the lips. She had seen Italian children make the gesture and cry: "Ho fame!" Hungry. But she could not let him into the kitchen. Still, if he were honestly hungry--She had it!

In the kitchen-table drawer was an imitation revolver--press the trigger, and a fluted fan was revealed--a dance favour she had received during the winter.

She plucked it out of the drawer and walked bravely to the window, which she threw up.

"What do you want? What are you doing out there on the fire escape?" she instantly demanded to know.

"My word, I am hungry! I was looking out of the window across the way and saw you preparing your dinner. A bit of bread and a glass of milk. Would you mind, I wonder?"

"Why didn't you come to the door then? What window?" Kitty was resolute;

once she embarked upon an enterprise.

"That one."

"Where is Mr. Gregory?" Kitty recalled that odd letter.

"Gregory? I should very much like to know. I have come many miles to see him. He sent me a duplicate key. There was not even a crust in the cupboard."

Gregory away? That letter! Something had happened to that poor, kindly old man. "Why did you not seek some restaurant? Or have you no money?"

"I have plenty. I was afraid that I might not be able conveniently to return. I am a stranger. My actions might be viewed with suspicion."

"Indeed! Describe Mr. Gregory."

Not of the clinging kind, evidently, he thought. A raving beauty--Diana domesticated!

"It is four years since I saw him. He was then gray, dapper, and erect. A mole on his chin, which he rubs when he talks. He is a valet in one of the fashionable hotels. He is--or was--the only true friend I have in New York."

"Was? What do you mean?"

"I'm afraid something has happened to him. I found his bedroom things tossed about."

"What could possibly happen to a harmless old man like Mr. Gregory?"

"Pardon me, but your egg is burning!"

Kitty wheeled and lifted off the pan, choking in the smother of smoke. She came right-about face swiftly enough. The man had not moved; and that decided her.

"Come in. I will give you something to eat. Sit in that chair by the window, and be careful not to stir from it. I'm a good shot," lied Kitty, truculently. "Frankly, I do not like the looks of this."

"I do look like a burglar, what?" He sat down in the chair meekly. Food and a human being to talk to! A lovely, self-reliant American girl, able to take care of herself. Magnificent eyes--slate blue, with thick, velvety black lashes. Irish.

In a moment Kitty had three eggs and half a dozen strips of bacon frying in a fresh pan. She kept one eye upon the pan and the other upon the intruder, risking strabismus. At length she transferred the contents of the pan to a plate, backed to the ice chest, and reached for a bottle of milk. She placed the food at the far end of the table and retreated a few steps, her arms crossed in such a way as to keep the revolver in view.

"Please do not be afraid of me.

"What makes you think I am?"

"Any woman would be."

Kitty saw that he was actually hungry, and her suspicions began to ebb. He hadn't lied about that. And he ate like a gentleman. Young, not more than thirty; possibly less. But that dreadful stubble and that black eye! The clothes would have passed muster on any fashionable golf links. A fugitive? From what?

"Thank you," he said, setting down the empty milk bottle.

"Your accent is English."

"Which is to say?"

"That your gestures are Italian."

"My mother was Italian. But what makes you believe I am not English?"

"An Englishman--or an American, for that matter--with money in his pocket would have gone into the street in search of a restaurant."

"You are right. The fundamentals of the blood will always crop out. You can educate the brain but not the blood. I am not an Englishman; I merely received my education at Oxford."

"A fugitive, however, of any blood might have come to my window."

"Yes; I am a fugitive, pursued by the god of Irony. And Irony is never particular; the chase is the thing. What matters it whether the quarry be wolf or sheep?"

Kitty was impressed by the bitterness of the tone. "What is your name?"

"John Hawksley."

"But that is English!"

"I should not care to call myself Two-Hawks, literally. It would be embarrassing. So I call myself Hawksley."

A pause. Kitty wondered what new impetus she might give to the conversation, which was interesting her despite her distrust.

"How did you come by that black eye?" she asked with embarrassing directness.

Hawksley smiled, revealing beautifully white teeth. "I say, it is a bit off, isn't it! I received it"--a twinkle coming into his eyes--"in a situation that had moribund perspectives."

"Moribund perspectives," repeated Kitty, casting the phrase about in her mind in search of an equivalent less academic.

"I am young and healthy, and I wanted to live," he said, gravely. "I am curious to know what is going to happen to-morrow and other to-morrows."

Somewhere near by a door was slammed violently. Kitty, every muscle in her body tense, jumped convulsively, with the result that her finger pressed automatically the trigger of her pistol. The fan popped out gayly.

Hawksley stared at the fan, quite as astonished as Kitty. Then he broke into low, rollicking laughter, which Kitty, because her basic corpuscle was Irish, perforce had to join. For all her laughter she retreated, furious and alarmed.

"Fancy! I say, now, you're jolly plucky to face a scoundrel like me with that."

"I don't just know what to make of you," said Kitty, irresolutely, flinging the fan into a corner.

"You have revivified a celestial spark--my faith in human beings. I beg of you not to be afraid of me. I am quite harmless. I am very grateful for the meal. Yours is the one act of kindness I have known in weeks. I will return to Gregor's apartment at once. But before I go please accept this. I rather suspect, you know, that you live alone, and that fan is amusing and not particularly suitable." He rose and unsmilingly laid upon the table one of those heavy blue-black bull-dogs of war, a regulation revolver. Kitty understood what this courteous act signified; he was disarming himself to reassure her.

"Sit down," she ordered. Either he was harmless or he wasn't. If he wasn't she was utterly at his mercy. She might be able to lift that terrible-looking engine of murder, battle, and sudden death with the aid of both hands, but to aim and fire it--never in this world! "As I came in to-night I found a note in the hall from Mr. Gregory. I will fetch it. But you call him Gregor?"

"His name is Stefani Gregor; and years and years ago he dandled me on his knees. I promise not to move until you return."

Subdued by she knew not what, no longer afraid, Kitty moved out of the kitchen. She had offered Gregory's letter as an excuse to reach the telephone. Once there, however, she did not take the receiver off the hook. Instead she whistled down the tube for the janitor.

"This is Miss Conover. Come up to my apartment in ten minutes.... No; it's not the water pipes.... In ten minutes."

Nothing very serious could happen inside of ten minutes; and the janitor was reliable and not the sort one reads about in the comic weeklies. Her confidence reenforced by the knowledge that a friend was near, she took the letter into the kitchen. Apparently her unwelcome guest had not stirred. The revolver was where he had laid it.

"Read this," she said.

The visitor glanced through it. "It is Gregor's hand. Poor old chap! I shall never forgive my self."

"For what?"

"For dragging him into this. They must have intercepted one of my telegrams." He stared dejectedly at the strip of oilcloth in front of the range. "You are an Ameri-can?"

"Yes."

"God has been exceedingly kind to your country. I doubt if you will ever know how kind. I'll take myself off. No sense in compromising you." He laid a folded handkerchief inside his cap which he put on. "Know anything about this?"--indicating the revolver.

"Nothing whatever."

"Permit me to show you. It is loaded; there are five bullets in the clip. See this little latch? So, it is harmless. So, and you kill with it."

"It is horrible!" cried Kitty. "Take it with you please. I could not keep my eyes open to shoot it."

"These are troublous times. All women should know something about small arms. Again I thank you. For your own sake I trust that we may never meet again. Good-bye." He stepped out of the window and vanished.

Kitty, at a mental impasse, could only stare into the night beyond the window. This mesmeric state endured for a minute; then a gentle and continuous sound dissipated the spell. It was raining. Obliquely she saw the burnt egg in the pan. The thing had happened; she had not been dreaming. Her brain awoke. Thought crowded thought; before one matured another displaced it; and all as futile as the sparks from the anvil. An avalanche of conjecture; and out of it all eventually emerged one concrete fact. The man Was honest. His hunger had been honest; his laughter. Who was he, what was he? For all his speech, not English; for all his gestures, not Italian. Moribund perspectives. Somewhere that day he had fought for his life. John Two-Hawks. And there was the mysterious evanishment of old Gregory, whose name was Stefani Gregor. In a humdrum, prosaic old apartment like this!

Kitty had ideas about adventure--an inheritance, though she was not aware of that. There had to be certain ingredients, principally mystery. Anything sordid must not be permitted to edge in. She had often gone forth upon semi-perilous enterprises as a reporter, entered sinister houses where crimes had been committed, but always calculating how much copy at eight dollars a column could be squeezed out of the affair. But this promised to be something like those tales which were always clear and wonderful in her head but more or less opaque when she attempted to transfer them to paper. A secret society? Vengeance? An echo of the war?

"Johnny Two-Hawks," she murmured aloud. "And he hopes we'll never meet again!"

There was a mirror over the sink, and she threw a glance into it. Very well; if he thought like that about it.

Here the doorbell tinkled. That would be the faithful janitor. She ran to the door.

"Whadjuh wanta see me about, Miz Conover?"

"What has happened to old Mr. Gregory?"

"Him? Why, some amb'lance fellers carted him off this afternoon. Didn't know nawthin' was the matter with 'im until I runs into them in the hall."

"He'd been hurt?"

"Couldn't say, miz. He was on a stretcher when I seen 'im. Under a sheet."

"But he might have been dead!"

"Nope. I ast 'em, an' they said a shock of some sort."

"What hospital?"

"Gee, I forgot t'ast that!"

"I'll find out. Good-night."

But Kitty did not find out. She called up all the known private and public hospitals, but no Gregor or Gregory had been received that afternoon, nor anybody answering his description. The fog had swallowed up Stefani Gregor.

CHAPTER VI

The reportorial instinct in Kitty Conover, combined with her natural feminine curiosity, impelled her to seek to the bottom of affair. Her newspaper was as far from her as the poles; simply a paramount desire to translate the incomprehensible into sequence and consequence. Harmless old Gregor's disappearance and the advent of John Two-Hawks--the absurdity of that name!--with his impeccable English accent, his Latin gestures, and his black eye, convinced her that it was political; an electrical cross current out of that broken world over there. Moribund perspectives. What did that signify save that Johnny Two-Hawks had fought somewhere that day for his life? Had Gregor been spirited away so as to leave Two-Hawks without support, to confuse and discourage him and break down his powers of resistance? Or had there been something of great value in the Gregor apartment, and Johnny Two-Hawks had come too late to save his friend?

A word slipped into her mind like a whiff of miasma off an evil swamp. As she recognized the word she felt the same horror and repugnance one senses upon being unexpectedly confronted by a cobra. Internationalism. The scum of the world boiling to the top. A half-blind viper striking venomously at everything--even itself! A destroyer who tore down but who knew not how or what to build. Kitty knew that lower New York was seething with this species of terrorism--thousands of noisome European rats trying to burrow into the granary of democracy. But she had no particular fear of the result. The reacting chemicals of American humour and common sense would neutralize that virus. Supposing a ripple from this indecent eddy had touched her feet? The torch of liberty in the hands of Anarch!

Johnny Two-Hawks. Somehow--even if she never saw him again--she knew she would always remember him by that name. Phases of the encounter began to return. Fine hands; perhaps he painted or played. The oblong head of well-balanced mentality. A pleasant voice. Breeding. To be sure, he had laughed at that fan popping out. Anybody would have laughed. Never had she felt so idiotic. He had gravely expressed the hope that they might never meet again because his life was in danger. What danger? Conceivably the enmity of a society--internationalism. The word having found lodgment in her thoughts took root. Internationalism--Utopia while you wait! Anarchism and Bolshevism offering nostrums for humanity's ills! And there were sane men who defended the cult on the basis that the intention was honest. Who can say that the rattlesnake does not consider his intentions honourable?

The attribute lacking in the ape to make him human is continuity of thought and action in all things save one. He often starts out well but he never arrives. His interest is never sustained. He drops one thing and turns to another. The exception is his enmity, savage and cunning, relentless and enduring.

Kitty was awake to one fact. She could not venture to dig into this affair alone. On the other hand, she did not want one of the men from the city room--a reporter who would see nothing but news. If Gregor was only a prisoner publicity might be the cause of his death; and publicity would certainly react hardily against Johnny Two-Hawks. To whom might she turn?

Cutty!--with his great physical strength, his shrewd and alert mentality, and his wide knowledge of peoples and tongues. There was the man for her--Kitty Conover's godfather. She dumped the contents of her handbag upon the stand in the hallway in her impatience to find Cutty's card with his telephone number. It was not in the directory. She might catch him before he went out for the evening.

A Japanese voice answered her call.

"'Souse, but he iss out."

"Where?"

"No tell me."

"How long has he been gone?"

"'Scuse!"

Kitty heard the click of the receiver as it went down upon the hook. But she wasn't the daughter of Conover for nothing. She called up the University Club. No. The Harvard Club. No. The Players, the Lambs; and in the latter club she found him.

"Who is it?" Cutty spoke impatiently.

"Kitty Conover."

"Oh! What's the matter? Can't you have lunch with me?"

"Something very strange is happening in this old apartment house, Cutty. I'm afraid it is a matter of life and death. Otherwise I shouldn't have bothered you. Can you come up right away?"

"As soon as a taxi can take me!"

"Thanks."

Kitty then went through the apartment and turned out all the lights. Next she drew up a chair to the kitchen window and sat down to watch. All was dark across the way. But there was nothing singular in this fact. Johnny Two-Hawks would have sense enough to realize that it would be safer to move about in the dark. It was even probable that he was lying down.

Tumpitum-tump! Tumpitum-tump! went the racing Elevated; and Kitty's heart raced along with it. Queer how the echo of Cutty's description of the drums calling a jehad--a holy war--should adapt itself to that Elevated. Drums! Perhaps the echo clung because she had been interested beyond measure in his tale of those two emeralds, the drums of jeopardy. Mobs sacking palaces and museums and banks and homes; all the scum of the world boiling to the top; the Red Night that wasn't over.

She uttered a shaky little laugh. She would tell Cutty. The real drums of jeopardy weren't emeralds but the roll of warning that prescience taps upon the spine, the occult sense of impending danger. That was why the Elevated went tumpitum-tump! tumpitum-tump! She would tell Cutty. The drums of fear.

He over there and she here, in darkness; both of them waiting for something to happen; and the invisible drumsticks beating the tattoo of fear. If he were in her thoughts might not she be a little in his? She stood up. She would do it. Convention in a moment like this was nonsense. Hadn't he kept his side of the line scrupulously?

Nonchalance. It occurred to her for the first time that there must be good material in a man who could come through in a contest with death, nonchalant. She would fetch him and have him here to meet Cutty, this rather forlorn Johnny Two-Hawks, with his unshaven face, his black eye, and his nonchalance. She would fetch him at once. It would save a good deal of time.

There were but ten apartments in the building, two on a floor. The living room formed an L. Kitty's buttressed Gregor's. The elevator shaft was inside, facing the court; and the stair head was on the Gregor side of the elevator. The two entrances faced each other across the landing.

As Kitty opened her door to step outside she was nonplussed to see two men issue cautiously from the Gregor door. The moment they espied her, however, there was a mad rush for the stair head. She could hear the thud of their feet all the way down to the ground floor; and every footfall seemed to touch her heart. One of them carried a bundle.

She breathed quickly, and she knew that she was afraid. Neither man was Johnny Two-Hawks. Something dreadful had happened; she was sure of it. Reenforcing her sinking courage with nerve energy she ran across to the Gregor door and knocked. No answer. She knocked again; then she tried the door. Locked. The flutter in her breast died away; she became quite calm. She was going to enter this apartment by the way of the fire escape. The window he had come out of was still up. She had made note of this from the kitchen. In returning he had stepped on to the springe of a snare.

She hurried back to her kitchen for the automatic. She hadn't the least idea how to manipulate it; but she was no longer afraid of it. Bravely she stepped out on to the fire escape. To reach her objective she had to walk under the ladder. Danger often puts odd irrelevancies into the human brain. As she moved forward she wondered if there was anything in the superstition regarding ladders.

When she reached the window she leaned against the brick wall and listened. Silence; an ominous silence. The window was open, the curtain up. Within, what? For as long as five minutes she waited, then she climbed in.

Now as this bedroom was a counterpart of her own she knew where the light button would be. She might stumble over a chair or two, but in the end she would find the light. The fingers of one hand spread out before her and the other clutching the impossible automatic, she succeeded in navigating the uncharted reefs of an unfamiliar room. She blinked for a moment after throwing on the light, and stood with her back to the wall, the automatic wabbling at nothing in particular. The room was empty so far as she could see. There was evidence of a physical encounter, but she could not tell whether it was due to the former or to the latter invasion.

Where was he? From where she stood she could not see the floor on the far side of the bed. Timidly she walked past the foot of the bed--and the transient paralysis of horror laid hold of her. She became bereft of the power to grasp and hold, and the automatic slipped from her fingers and thudded on the carpet.

On the floor lay poor Johnny Two-Hawks, crumpled grotesquely, a streak of blood zigzagging across his forehead; to all appearances, dead!

CHAPTER VII

Twice before in her life Kitty had looked upon death by violence; and it required only this present picture to convince her that she would never be able to gaze upon it callously, without pity and terror. Newspaper life--at least the reportorial side of it--has an odd effect upon men and women; it sharpens their tragical instincts and perceptions and dulls eternally the edge of tenderness and sentimentality. It was natural for Kitty to possess the keenest perceptions of tragedy; but she had been taken out of the reportorial field in time to preserve all her tenderness and romanticism. Otherwise she would have seen in that crumpled object with the sinister daub of blood on the forehead merely a story, and would have approached it from that angle. But was he dead? She literally forced her steps toward the body and stared. She dropped to her knees because they were threatening to buckle in one of those flashes of physical incoordination to which the strongest will must bow occasionally. She was no longer afraid of the tragedy, but she feared the great surging pity that was striving to express itself in sobs; and she knew that if she surrendered she would forthwith become hysterical for the rest of the evening and incompetent to carry out the plan in her head.

A strong, healthy young man done to death in this fashion only a few minutes after he had left her kitchen! Somehow she could not look upon him as a stranger. She had given him food; she had talked to him; she had even laughed with him. He was not like those dead she had seen in her reportorial days. Her orbit and Johnny Two-Hawks' had indeterminately touched; she had known old Gregory, or Gregor, who had been this unfortunate young man's friend. And he had hoped they might never meet again!

The murderous scoundrels had been watching. They must have entered the apartment shortly after he had entered hers. Conceivably they would have Gregor's key. And they had watched and waited, striking him down it may have been at the very moment he had crossed the sill of the window.

Her hand shook so idiotically that it was impossible for a time to tell if the man's heart was beating. All at once a wave of hot fury rushed over her--fury at the cowardliness of the assault--and the vertigo passed. She laid her palm firmly over Johnny Two-Hawks' heart. Alive! He was alive! She straightened his body and put a pillow under his head. Then she sought water and towels.

There was no cut on his forehead, only blood; but the top of his head had been cruelly beaten. He was alive, but without immediate aid he might die. The poor young man!

There were two physicians in the block; one or the other would be in. She ran to the door, to find it locked. She had forgotten. Next she found the telephone wire cut and the speaking tube battered and inutile. She would have to return to her own apartment to summon help. She dared not leave the light on. The scoundrels might possibly return, and the light would warn them that their victim had been discovered; and naturally they would wish to ascertain whether or not they had succeeded in their murderous assault.

As she was passing the first-landing windows she saw Cutty emerging from the elevator. She flew across the fire-escape platform with the resilient step of one crossing thin ice.

Probably the most astonished man in New York was the war correspondent when the door opened and a pair of arms were flung about him, and a voice smothered in the lapel of his coat cried: "Oh, Cutty, I never was so glad to see any one!"

"What in the name of--"

"Come! We'll handle this ourselves. Hurry!" She dragged him along by the sleeve.

"But--"

"It is life and death! No talk now!"

Cutty, immaculate in his evening clothes, very much perturbed, went along after her. As she passed through the kitchen window and beckoned him to follow he demurred.

"Kitty, what the deuce is going on here?"

"I'll answer your questions when we get him into my apartment. They tried to murder him; left him there to die!"

Cutty possessed a great art, an art highly developed only in explorers and newspaper reporters of the first order--adaptability; of being able to cast aside instantly the conventions of civilization and let down the bars to the primordial, the instinctive, and the natural. Thus the Cutty who stepped out beside Kitty into the drizzle was not the Cutty she had admitted into the apartment. She did not recognize this remarkable transition until later; and then she discovered that Cutty, the suave and lackadaisical in idleness, was a tremendous animal hibernating behind a crackle shell.

Ordinarily Cutty would have declined to come through this shell, thin as it was; he liked these catnaps between great activities. But this lovely creature was Conover's daughter, and she would have the seventh sense-divination of the born reporter. Something big was in the air.

"Go on!" he said, briskly. "I'm at your heels. And stoop as you pass those hall windows. No use throwing a silhouette for somebody in those rear houses to see.... Old Tommy Conover's daughter, sure pop!... There you go, under the ladder! You've dished the whole affair, whatever it is.... No, no! Just spoofing, Kitty. A long face is no good anywhere, even at a funeral.... This window? All right. Know where the lights are? Very good."

When Cutty saw the man on the floor he knelt quickly. "Nasty bang on the head, but he's alive. What's this? His cap. Poughkeepsie. By George, padded with his handkerchief! Must have known something was going to fall on him. Now, what's it all about?"

"When we get him to my apartment."

"Yours? Good Lord, what's the matter with this?"

"They tried to kill him here. They might return to see if they had succeeded. They mustn't find where he has gone. I'm strong. I can take hold of his knees."

"Tut! Neither of us could walk backward over that fire escape. He looks husky, but I'll try it. Now obey me without question or comment. You'll have to help me get him outside the window and in through yours. Between the two windows I can handle him alone. I only hope we shan't be noticed, for that might prove awkward. Now take hold. That's it. When I'm through the window just push his legs outside." Panting, Kitty obeyed. "All right," said Cutty. "I like your pluck. You run along ahead and be ready to help me in with him. A healthy beggar! Here goes."

With a heave and a hunch and another heave Cutty stood up, the limp body disposed scientifically across his shoulders. Kitty was quite impressed by this exhibition of strength in a man whom she considered as elderly--old. There was an underthought that such feats of bodily prowess were reserved for young men. With the naive conceit of twenty-four she ignored the actual mathematics of fifty years of clean living and thinking, missed the physiological fact that often men at fifty are stronger and tougher than men in the twenties. They never waste energy; their precision of movement and deliberation of thought conserve the residue against the supreme moment.

As a parenthesis: To a young woman what is a hero? Generally something conjured out of a book she has read; the unknown, handsome young man across the street; the leading actor in a society drama; the idol of the movie. A hero must of necessity be handsome; that is the first essential. If he happens to be brave and debonair, rich and aristocratic, so much the better. Somehow, to be brave and to be heroic are not actually accepted synonyms in certain youthful feminine minds. For instance, every maid will agree that her father is brave; but tell her he is a hero because he pays his bills regularly and she will accept the statement with a smile of tolerant indulgence.

Thus Kitty viewed Cutty's activities with a thrill of amazed wonder. Had the young man hoisted Cutty to his shoulders her feeling would have been one of exultant admiration. Let age crown its garnered wisdom; youth has no objections to that; but feats of physical strength--that is poaching upon youth's preserves. Kitty was not conscious of the instinctive resentment. At that moment Cutty was to her the most extraordinary old man in the world.

"Forward!" he whispered. "I want to know why I am doing this movie stunt." The journey began with Kitty in the lead. She prayed that no one would see them as they passed the two landing windows. Below and above were vivid squares of golden light. She regretted the drizzle; no clothes-laden lines intervened to obscure their progress. Someone in the rear of the houses in Seventy-ninth Street might observe the silhouettes. The whole affair must be carried off secretly or their efforts would come to nothing.

Once inside the kitchen Cutty shifted his burden into his arms, the way one carries a child, and followed Kitty into the unused bedroom. He did not wait for the story, but asked for the telephone.

"I'm going to call for a surgeon at the Lambs. He's just back from France and knows a lot about broken heads. And we can trust him absolutely. I told him to wait there until I called."

"Cutty, you're a dear. I don't wonder father loved you."

Presently he turned away from the telephone. "He'll be here in a jiffy. Now, then, what the deuce is all this about?"

Briefly Kitty narrated the episodes.

"Samaritan stuff. I see. Any absorbent cotton? I can wash the wound after a fashion. Warm water and Castile soap. We can have him in shape for Harrison."

Alone, Cutty took note of several apparent facts. The victim's flannel shirt was torn at the collar and there were marks of finger nails on the throat and chest. Upon close inspection he observed a thin red line round the neck--the mark of a thong. Had they tried to strangle him or had he carried something of value? Silk underwear and a clean body; well born; foreign. After a conscientious hesitance Cutty went through the pockets. All he found were some crumbs of tobacco and a soggy match box. They had cleaned him out evidently. There were no tailors' labels in any of the pockets; but there were signs that these had once existed. The man on the bed had probably ripped them out himself; did not care to be identified.

A criminal in flight? Cutty studied the face on the pillow. Shorn of that beard it would be handsome; not the type criminal, certainly. A bit of natural cynicism edged into his thoughts: Kitty had seen through the beard, otherwise she would have turned the affair over to the police. Not at all like her mother, yet equally her mother's match in beauty and intelligence. Conover's girl, whose eyes had nearly popped out of her head at the first sight of those drum-lined walls of his.

Two-Hawks. What was it that was trying to stir in his recollection? Two-Hawks. He was sure he had heard that name before. Hawksley meant nothing at all; but Two-Hawks possessed a strange attraction. He stared off into space. He might have heard the name in a tongue other than English.

A sound. It came from the lips of the young man. Cutty frowned. The poor chap wasn't breathing in a promising way; he groaned after each inhalation. And what had become of the old fellow Kitty called Gregory? A queer business.

Kitty came in with a basin and a roll of absorbent cotton.

"He is groaning!" she whispered.

"Pretty rocky condition, I should say. That handkerchief in his cap doubtless saved him. Now, little lady, I frankly don't like the idea of his being here. Suppose he dies? In that event there'll be the very devil to pay. You're all alone here, without even a maid."

"Am I all alone?"--softly.

"Well, no; come to think of it, I'm no longer your godfather in theory. Give me the cotton and hold the basin."

He was very tender. The wound bled a little; but it was not the kind that bled profusely. It was less a cut than a smashing bruise.

"Well, that's all I can do. Who was this tenant Gregory?"

"A dear old man. A valet at a Broadway hotel. Oh, I forgot! Johnny Two-Hawks called him Stefani Gregor."

"Stefani Gregor?"

"Yes. What is it? Why do you say it like that?"

"Say it like what?"--sparring for time.

"As if you had heard the name before?"

"Just as I thought!" cried Cutty, his nimble mind pouncing upon a happy invention. "You're romantic, Kitty. You're imagining all sorts of nonsense about this chap, and you must not let the situation intrigue you. If I spoke the name oddly-- this Stefani Gregor--it was because I sensed in a moment that this was a bit of the overflow. Southeastern Europe, where the good Samaritan gets kicked instead of thanked. Now, here's a good idea. Of course we can't turn this poor chap loose upon the public, now that we know his life is in danger. That's always the trouble with this Samaritan business. When you commit a fine action you assume an obligation. You hoist the Old Man of the Sea on your shoulders, as it were. The chap cannot be allowed to remain here. So, if Harrison agrees, we'll take him up to my diggings, where no Bolshevik will ever lay eyes upon him."

"Bolshevik?"

"For the sake of a handle. They might be Chinamen, for all I know. I can take care of him until he is on his feet. And you will be saved all this annoyance.

"But I don't believe it's going to be an annoyance. I'm terribly interested, and want to see it through."

"If he can be moved, out he goes. No arguments. He can't stay in this apartment. That's final."

"Exactly why not?" Kitty demanded, rebelliously.

"Because I say so, Kitty."

"Is Stefani Gregor an undesirable?"

"You knew him. What do you say?" countered her godfather, evading the trap. The innocent child! He smiled inwardly.

Kitty was keen. She sensed an undercurrent, and her first attempt to touch it had failed. The mere name of Stefani Gregor had not roused Cutty's astonishment. She was quite positive that the name was not wholly unfamiliar to her father's friend.

Still, something warned her not to press in this direction. He would be on the alert. She must wait until he had forgotten the incident. So she drew up a chair beside the bed and sat down.

Cutty leaned against the footrail, his expression neutral. He sighed inaudibly. His delightful catnap was over. Stefani Gregor, Kitty's neighbour, a valet in a fashionable hotel! Stefani Gregor, who, upon a certain day, had placed the drums of jeopardy in the palms of a war correspondent known to his familiars as Cutty. And who was this young man on the bed?

"There goes the bell!" cried Kitty, jumping up.

"Wait!"

The ring was repeated vigorously and impatiently.

"Kitty, I don't quite like the sound of that bell. Harrison would have no occasion to be impatient. Somebody in a hurry. Now, attend to me. I'm going to steal out to the kitchen. Don't be afraid. Call if I'm needed. Open the door just a crack, with your foot against it. If it's Harrison he'll be in uniform. Call out his name. Slam the door if it is someone you don't know."

Kitty opened the door as instructed, but she swung it wide because one of the men outside was a policeman. The man behind him was a thickset, squat individual, with puffed, discoloured eyes and a nose that reminded Kitty of an alligator pear.

"What's going on here?" the policeman demanded to know.

CHAPTER VIII

A phrase, apparently quite irrelevant to the situation, shot into Kitty's head. Moribund perspectives. Instantly she knew, with that foretasting mind of hers, that the man peering over the policeman's shoulder and Johnny Two-Hawks had met somewhere that day. She was now able to compare the results, and she placed the victory on Two-Hawks' brow. Yonder individual somehow justified the instinct that had prompted her to play the good Samaritan. Whence had this gorilla come? He was not one of the men who had issued in such dramatic haste from the Gregor apartment.

"This man here saw you and another carrying someone across the fire escape. What's the rumpus?" The policeman was not exactly belligerent, but he was dutifully determined. And though he was ready to grant that this girl with the Irish eyes was beautiful, a man never could tell.

"There's been a tragedy of some kind," began Kitty. "This man certainly did see us carrying a man across the fire escape. He had been set upon and robbed in the apartment across the way."

"Why didn't you call in the police?"

"Because he might have died before you got here."

"Where's the man who helped you?"

"Gone. He was an outsider. He was afraid of getting mixed up in a police affair and ran away." Behind the kitchen door Cutty smiled. She would do, this girl.

"Sounds all right," said the policeman. "I'll take a look at the man."

"This way, if you please," said Kitty, readily. "You come, too, sir," she added as the squat man hesitated. Kitty wanted to watch his expression when he saw Johnny Two-Hawks.

Seed on rocky soil; nothing came of the little artifice. No Buddha's graven face was less indicative than the squat man's. Perhaps his face was too sore to permit mobility of expression. The drollery of this thought caused a quirk in one corner of Kitty's mouth. The squat man stopped at the foot of the bed with the air of a mere passer-by and seemed more interested in the investigations of the policeman than in the man on the bed. But Kitty knew.

"A fine bang on the coco," was the policeman's observation. "Take anything out of his pockets?"

"They were quite empty. I've sent for a military surgeon. He may arrive at any moment."

"This fellow live across the way?"

"That's the odd part of it. No, he doesn't."

"Then what was he doing there?"

"Probably awaiting the return of the real tenant who hasn't returned up to this hour"--with an oblique glance at the squat man.

"Kind o' queer. Say, you stay here and watch the lady while I scout round."

The squat man nodded and leaned over the foot of the bed. The policeman stalked out.

"I was in the kitchen," said Kitty, confidingly. "I saw shadows on the window curtain. It did not look right. So I started to inquire and almost bumped into two men leaving the apartment. They took to their heels when they saw me."

Again the squat man nodded. He appeared to be a good listener.

"Where were you when we crossed the fire escape?"

"In the yard on the other side of the fence." There was reluctance in the guttural voice.

"Oh, I see. You live there."

As this was a supposition and not a direct query, the squat man wagged his head affirmatively.

Kitty, her ears strained for disquieting sounds in the kitchen, laid her palm on the patient's cheek. It was very hot. She dipped a bit of cotton into the water, which had grown cold, and dampened the wounded man's cheeks and throat. Not that she expected to accomplish anything by this act; it relieved the nerve tension. This man was no fool. If her surmises were correct he was a strong man both in body and in mind. In a rage he would be terrible. However, had Johnny Two-Hawks done it--

beaten the man and escaped? No doubt he had been watching all the time and had at length stepped in to learn if his subordinates had followed his instructions and to what extent they had succeeded.

"If he dies it will be murder."

"It is a big city."

"And so many terrible things happen like this every day. But sooner or later those who commit them are found out. Nemesis always follows on the heels of vengeance."

For the first time there was a flash of interest in the battered eyes of the intruder. Perhaps he saw that this was not only a pretty woman but a keen one, and sensed the veiled threat. Moreover, he knew that she had lied at one point. There had been no light in the room across the court.

But what in the world was happening out there in the kitchen? Kitty wondered. So far, not a sound. Had Cutty really taken flight? And why shouldn't he have faced it out at her side? Very odd on Cutty's part. Shortly she heard the heavy shoes of the policeman returning.

"Guess it's all right, miss. I'll report the affair at the precinct and have an ambulance sent over. You'll have to come along with me, sir."

"Is that legally necessary?" asked the squat man, rather perturbed.

"Sure. You saw the thing and I verified it," declared the policeman. "It won't take ten minutes. Your name and address, in case this man dies."

"I see. Very well."

Kitty wasn't sure, but the policeman seemed embarrassed about something. The directness was gone from his eyes and his speech was no longer brisk.

"My name is Conover," said Kitty.

"I got that coming in," replied the policeman. "We'll be on our way."

Not once again did the squat man glance at the man on the bed. He followed the policeman into the hall, his air that of one who had accepted a certain obligation to community welfare and cancelled it.

Kitty shut the door--and leaned against it weakly. Where had Cutty gone? Even as she expressed the query she smelt burning tobacco. She ran out into the kitchen, to behold Cutty seated in a chair calmly smoking his infamous pipe!

"And I thought you were gone! What did you say to that policeman?"

"I hypnotized him, Kitty."

"The newspaper?"

"No. Just looked into his eye and made a few passes with my hands."

"Of course, if you believe you ought not to tell me--" said Kitty, which is the way all women start their wheedling.

Cutty looked into the bowl of his pipe.

"Kitty, when you throw a cobble into a pond, what happens? A splash. But did you ever notice the way the ripples have of running on and on, until they touch the farthest shore?"

"Yes. And this is a ripple from some big stone cast into the pond of southeastern Europe. I understand."

"That's just the difficulty. If you understood nothing it would be much easier for me. But you know just enough to want to follow up on your own hook. I know nothing definitely; I have only suspicions. I calmed that policeman by showing him a blanket police power issued by the commissioner. I want you to pack up and move out of this neighbourhood. It's not congenial to you."

"I'm afraid I can't afford to move until May."

"I'll take care of that gladly, to get you out of this garlicky ruin."

"No, Cutty; I'm going to stay here until the lease is up."

"Gee-whiz! The Irish are all alike," cried the war correspondent, hopelessly. "Petticoat or pantaloon, always looking for trouble."

"No, Cutty; simply we don't run away from it. And there's just as much Irish in you as there is in me."

"Sure! And for thirty years I've gone hunting for trouble, and never failed to find it. I don't like this affair, Kitty; and because I don't I'm going to risk my Samson locks in your lily-white hands. I am going to tell you two things: I am a secret foreign agent of the United States Government. Now don't light up that way. Dark alleys and secret papers and beautiful adventuresses and bang-bang have nothing at all to do with my job. There isn't a grain of romance in it. Ostensibly I am a war correspondent. I have handled all the big events in Serbia and Bulgaria and Greece and southwestern Russia. Boiled down, I am a census taker of undesirables. Socialist, anarchist and Bolshevik--I photograph them in my mental 'fillums' and transmit to Washington. Thus, when Feodor Slopeski lands at Ellis Island with the idea of blowing up New York, he is returned with thanks. I didn't ask for the job; it was thrust upon me because of my knowledge of the foreign tongues. I accepted it because I am a loyal American citizen."

"And you left me because you' didn't know who might be at the door!"

"Precisely. I am known in lower New York under another name. I'm a rabid internationalist. Down with everything! I don't go out much these days; keep under cover as much as I can. Once recognized, my value would be nil. In a flannel shirt I'm a dangerous codger."

"And Gregor and this poor young man are in some way mixed up with internationalism!"

"Victims, probably."

"What is the other thing you wish to tell me?"

"Because your eyes are slate blue like your mother's. I loved your mother, Kitty," said Cutty, blinking into his pipe. "And the singular fact is, your father knew but your mother never did. I was never able to tell your mother after your father died. Their bodies were separated, but not their spirits."

Kitty nodded. So that was it? Poor Cutty!

"I make this confession because I want you to understand my attitude toward you. I am going to elect myself as your special guardian so long as I'm in New York. From now on, when I ask you to do something, understand that I believe it best for you. If my suspicions are correct we are not dealing with fools but with madmen. The most dangerous human being, Kitty, is an honest man with a half-baked or crooked idea; and that's what this world pother, Bolshevism, is--honest men with crooked ideas, carrying the torch of anarchism and believing it enlightenment. What makes them tear down things? Every beautiful building is only a monument to their former wretchedness; and so they annihilate. None of them actually knows what he wants. A thousand will-o'-the-wisps in front of them, and all alike. A thousand years to throw off the shackles, and they expect Utopia in ten minutes! It makes you want to weep. Socialism--the brotherhood of man--is a beautiful thing theoretically; but it is like some plays--they read well but do not act. Lopping off heads, believing them to be ideas!"

"The poor things!"

"That's it. Though I betray them I pity them. Democracy; slowly and surely. As prickly with faults as a cactus pear; but every year there are less prickles. We don't stand still or retrogress; we keep going on and up. Take this town. Think of It to-day and compare it with the town your father knew. There's the bell. I imagine that will be Harrison. If we can move this chap will you go to a hotel for the night?"

"I'm going to stay here, Cutty. That's final."

Cutty sighed.

CHAPTER IX

At the precinct station the squat man gave a name and an address to the bored sergeant at the desk, passed out a cigar, lit one himself, expressed some innocuous opinions upon one or two topics of the day, and walked leisurely out of the precinct. He wanted to laugh. These pigheads had never thought to question his presence in the backyard of the house in Seventy-ninth Street. It was the way he had carried himself. Those years in New York, prior to the war, had not been wasted. The brass-buttoned fools!

Serenely unconscious that he was at liberty by explicit orders, because the Department of Justice did not care to trap a werewolf before ascertaining where the pack was and what the kill, he proceeded leisurely to the corner, turned, and broke into a run, which carried him to a drug store in Eightieth Street. Here he was joined by two men, apparently coal heavers by the look of their hands and faces.

"They will take him to a hospital. Find where, then notify me. Remember, this is your business, and woe to you if you fail. Where is it?" One of the men extended an object wrapped in ordinary grocer's paper.

"Ha! That's good. I shall enjoy myself presently. Remember: telephone me the moment you learn where they take him. He is still alive, bunglers! And you came away empty-handed."

"There was nothing on him. We searched."

"He has hidden them in one of those rooms. I'll attend to that later. Watch the hospital for an hour or so, then telephone for information regarding his condition. Is that motor for me? Very good. Remember!"

Inside the taxicab the squat man patted the object on his knees, and chuckled from time to time audibly. It would be worth all that journey, all he had gone through since dawn that morning. Stefani Gregor! After these seven long years--the man who had betrayed him! To reach into his breast and squeeze his heart as one might squeeze a bit of cheese! Many things to tell, many pictures to paint. He rode far downtown, wound in and out of the warehouse district for a while, then dismissed the taxi and proceeded on foot to his destination--a decayed brick mansion of the 40's sandwiched in between two deserted warehouses. In the hall of the first landing a man sat in a chair under the gas, reading a newspaper. At the approach of the squat man he sprang to his feet, but a phrase dissipated his apprehension and he nodded toward a door.

"Unlock it for me and see that I am not disturbed."

Presently the squat man stood inside the room, which was dark. He struck a match and peered about for the candle. The light discovered a room barren of all furniture excepting the table upon which stood the candle, and a single chair. In this chair was a man, bound. He was small and dapper, his gray hair swept back a la Liszt. His chin was on his breast, his body limp. Apparently the bonds alone held him in the chair.

The squat man laid his bundle on the table and approached the prisoner.

"Stefani Gregor, look up; it is I!" He drummed on his chest like a challenging gorilla. "I, Boris Karlov!"

Slowly the eyelids of the prisoner went up, revealing mild blue eyes. But almost instantly the mildness was replaced by an agate hardness, and the body became upright.

"Yes, it is Boris, whom you betrayed. But I escaped by a hair, Stefani; and we meet again."

What good to tell this poor madman that Stefani Gregor had not betrayed him, that he had only warned those marked for death? There was no longer reason inside that skull. To die, probably in a few moments. So be it. Had he not been ready for seven years? But that poor boy--to have come all these thousands of miles, only to walk into a trap! Had he found that note? Had they killed him? Doubtless they had or Boris Karlov would not be in this room.

"We killed him to-night, Stefani, in your rooms. We threw out the food so he would have to seek something to eat. The last of that breed, stem and branch! We are no longer the mud; we ourselves are the heels. We are conquering the world. Today Europe is ours; to-morrow, America!"

A wintry little smile stirred the lips of the man in the chair. America, with its keen perceptions of the ridiculous, its withering humour!

"No more the dissolute opera dancers will dance to your fiddling, Stefani, while we starve in the town. Fiddler, valet, tutor, the rivers and seas of Russia are red. We roll east and west, and our emblem is red. Stem and branch! We ground our heels in their faces as for centuries they ground theirs in ours. He escaped us there--but I was Nemesis. He died to-night."

The body in the chair relaxed a little. "He was clean and honest, Boris. I made him so. He would have done fine things if you had let him live."

"That breed?"

"Why, you yourself loved him when he was a boy!"

"Stem and branch! I loved my little sister Anna, too. But what did they do to her behind those marble walls? Did you fiddle for her? What was she when they let her go? My pretty little Anna! The fires of hell for those damned green stones of yours, Stefani! She heard of them and wanted to see them, and you promised."

"I? I never promised Anna! ... So that was it? Boris, I only saw her there. I never knew what brought her. But the boy was in England then."

"The breed, the breed!" roared the squat man. "Ha, but you should have seen! Those gay officers and their damned master--we left them with their faces in the mud, Stefani; in the mud! And the women begged. Fine music! Those proud hearts, begging Boris Karlov for their lives--their faces in the mud! You, born of us in those Astrakhan Hills, you denied us because you liked your fiddle and a full belly, and to play keeper of those emeralds. The winding paths of torture and misery and death by which they came into the possession of that house! And always the proletariat has had to pay in blood and daughters. You, of the people, to betray us!"

"I did not betray you. I only tried to save those who had been kind to me."

A cunning light shot into Karlov's eyes. "The emeralds!" He struck his pocket. "Here, Stefani; and they shall be broken up to buy bread for our people."

"That poor boy! So he brought them! What are you going to do with me?"

"Watch you grow thin, Stefani. You want death; you shall want food instead. Oh, a little; enough to keep you alive. You must learn what it is to be hungry."

The squat man picked up the bundle from the table and tore off the wrapping paper. A violin the colour of old Burgundy lay revealed.

"Boris!" The man in the chair writhed.

"Have I waked you, Stefani?"--tenderly. "The Stradivarius--the very grand duke of fiddles! And he and his damned officers, how they used to call out--'Get Stefani to fiddle for us!' And you fiddled, dragged your genius though the mud to keep your belly warm!"

"To save a soul, Boris--the boy's. When I fiddled his uncle forgot to drag him into an orgy. Ah, yes; I fiddled, fiddled because I had promised his mother!"

"The Italian singer! She was lucky to die when she did. She did not see the torch, the bayonet, and the mud. But the boy did--with his English accent! How he escaped I don't know; but he died to-night, and the emeralds are in my pocket. See!" Karlov held the instrument close to the other's face. "Look at it well, this grand duke of fiddles. Look, fiddler, look!"

The huge hands pressed suddenly. There was brittle crackling, and a rare violin became kindling. A sob broke from the prisoner's lips. What to Karlov was a fiddle to him was a soul. He saw the madman fling the wreckage to the floor and grind his heels into the fragments. Gregor shut his eyes, but he could not shut his ears; and he sensed in that cold, demoniacal fury of the crunching heel the rising of maddened peoples.

CHAPTER X

Meanwhile, Captain Harrison of the Medical Corps entered the Conover apartment briskly.

"You old vagabond, what have you been up to? I beg pardon!"--as he saw Kitty emerge from behind Cutty's bulk.

"This is Miss Conover, Harrison."

"Very pleased, I'm sure. Luckily my case was in the coat room at the club. I took the liberty of telephoning for Miss Frances, who returned on the same ship with me. I concluded that your friend would need a nurse. Let me have a look at him."

Callously but lightly and skillfully the surgeon examined the battered head. "Escaped concussion by a hair, you might say. Probably had his cap on. That black eye, though, is an older affair. Who is he?"

"I suspect he's some political refugee. We don't know a thing about him otherwise. How soon can he be moved?"

"He ought to be moved at once and given the best of care."

"I can give him that in my eagle's nest. Harrison, this chap's life is in danger; and if we get him into my lofty diggings they won't be able to trace him. Not far from here there's a private hospital I know. It goes through from one street to the next. I know the doctor. We'll have the ambulance carry the patient there, but at the rear I'll have one of the office newspaper trucks. And after a little wait we'll shoot the stretcher into the truck. The police will not bother us. I've seen to that. I rather believe it falls in with some of my work. The main idea, of course, is to rid Miss Conover of any trouble."

"Just as you say," agreed the surgeon. "That's all I can do for the present. I'll run down to the entrance and wait for The nurse."

"Will he live?" asked Kitty.

"Of course he will. He is in good physical condition. Imagine he has simply been knocked out. Serious only if unattended. Your finding him probably saved him. Twelve hours will tell the story. May be on his feet inside a week. Still, it would be advisable to keep him in bed as long as possible. Fagged out, I should say, from that beard. I'll go down and wait for Miss Frances."

"And ring three tunes when you return," advised Cutty.

"All right. Did they try to strangle him or did he have something round his neck?"

"Hanged if I know."

"All out of the room now. I want it dark. Just as soon as the nurse arrives I'll return. Three rings." Harrison left the apartment.

Cutty spent a few minutes at the telephone, then he joined Kitty in the living room.

"Kitty, what was the stranger like?"

"Like a gorilla. He spoke English as if he had a cold."

Cutty scowled into space. "Have a scar over an eyebrow?"

"Good gracious, I couldn't tell! Both his eyes were black and his nose banged dreadfully. Johnny Two-Hawks probably did it."

"Bully for Two-Hawks! Kitty, you're a marvel. Not a flivver from the start. And those slate-blue eyes of yours don't miss many things."

"Listen!" she interrupted, taking hold of his sleeve. "Hear it?"

"Only the Elevated."

"Tumpitum-tump! Tumpitum-tump! Cutty, you hypnotized me this afternoon with your horrid drums."

"The emeralds?" He managed to repress the start.

"I don't know what it is; drums, anyhow. Maybe it is the emeralds. Something has been happening ever since you told me about them--the misery and evil that follow their wake."

"But the story goes that women are immune, Kitty."

"Nonsense! No woman is immune where a wonderful gem is concerned. And yet I've common sense and humour."

"And a lot more besides, Kitty. You're a raving, howling little beauty; and how you've remained out of captivity this long is a puzzler to me. Haven't you got a beau somewhere?"

"No, Cutty. Perhaps I'm one of those who are quite willing to wait patiently. If the one I want doesn't come--why, I'll be a jolly, philosophical old maid. No seconds or culls for me, as the magazine editor says."

"Exactly what do you want?" Cutty was keenly curious, for some reason he could not define. He did not care for diamonds as stones; but he admired any personality that flashed differently from each new angle exposed.

"Oh, a man, among other things. I don't mean one of those godlike chromos in the frontispiece of popular novels. He hasn't got to be handsome. But he must be able to laugh when he's happy, when he's hurt. I must be his business in life. He must know a lot about things I know. I want a comrade who will come to me when he has a joke or an ache. A gay man and whimsical. The law can make any man a husband, but only God can make a good comrade."

"Kitty," said Cutty, his fine eyes sparkling, "I shan't have to watch over you so much as I thought. On the other hand, you have described me to a dot."

"Quite possibly. Vanity has its uses. It keeps us in contact with bathtubs and nice clothes. I imagine that you would make both husband and comrade; or you would have, twenty years ago"--without intentional cruelty. Wasn't Cutty fifty-two?

"Kitty, you've touched a vital point. It took those twenty years to make me companionable. Experience is something we must buy; it isn't left in somebody's will. Let us say that I possess all the necessary attributes save one."

"And what is that?"

"Youth, Kitty. And take the word of a senile old dotard, your young man, when you find him, will lack many of the attributes you require. On the other hand, there is always the possibility that these will develop as you jog along. The terrible pity of youth is that it has the habit of conferring these attributes rather than finding them. You put garlands on the heads of snow images, and the first glare of sunshine--pouf!"

"Cutty, I'm beginning to like you immensely"--smiling. "Perhaps women ought to have two husbands--one young and handsome and the other old and wise like yourself."

Cutty wished he were alone in order to analyze the stab. Old! When he knew that mentally and physically he could take and break a dozen Two-Hawks. Old! He had never thought himself that. Fifty-two years; they had piled up on him without his appreciation of the fullness of the score. And yet he was more than a match for any ordinary man of thirty in sinew and brain; and no man met the new morning with more zest than he himself met it. But to Kitty he was old! Lavender and oak leaves were being draped on his door knob. He laughed.

"Why do you laugh?"

"Oh, because--Hark!"

The two of them ran to the bedroom door.

"Olga! Olga!" And then a guttural level jumble of sounds.

Kitty's quick brain reached out for a similitude--water rushing over ragged boulders.

"Olga!" she whispered. "He is a Russian!"

"There are Serbian Olgas and Bulgarian Olgas and Rumanian Olgas. Probably his sweetheart."

"The poor thing!"

"Sounds like Russian," added Cutty, his conscience pricking him. But he welcomed that "Olga." It would naturally put a damper on Kitty's interest. "There's Harrison with the nurse."

Quarter of an hour later the patient was taken down to the ambulance and conveyed to the private hospital. Cutty had no way of ascertaining whether they were followed; but he hoped they would be. The knowledge that their victim was in a near-by hospital would naturally serve to relax the enemy vigilance temporarily; and this would permit safely and secretly the second leg of the journey--that to his own apartment.

He decided to let an hour go past; then Two-Hawks was taken through the building to the rear and transferred to the truck. Cutty sat with the driver while Captain Harrison and the nurse rode inside with the patient.

On the way Cutty was rather disturbed by the deep impression Kitty Conover had made upon his heart and mind. That afternoon he had looked upon her with fatherly condescension, as the pretty daughter of the two he had loved most. From the altitude of his fifty-two he had gazed down upon her twenty-four, weighing her as like all young women of twenty-four--pleasure-loving and beau-hunting and fashion-scorched; and in a flash she had revealed the formed mind of a woman of thirty. Altitude. He had forgotten that relative to altitudes there are always two angles of vision--that from the summit and that from the green valley below. Kitty saw him beyond the tree line, but just this side of the snows--and matched his condescension with pity! He chuckled. Doddering old ass, what did it matter how she looked at him?

Beautiful and young and full of common sense, yet dangerously romantical. To wait for the man she wanted, what did that signify but romance? And there was her Irish blood to consider. The association of pretty nurse and interesting patient always afforded excellent background for sentimental nonsense, the obligations of the one and the gratitude of the other. Well, he had nipped that in the bud.

And why hadn't he taken this Two-Hawks person--how easy it was to fall into Kitty's way of naming the chap!--why hadn't he taken him directly to the Roosevelt? Why all this pother and secrecy over a total stranger? Stefani Gregor, who lived opposite Kitty and who hadn't prospered particularly since the day he had exhibited the drums of jeopardy--he was the reason. These were volcanic days, and a friend of Stefani Gregor--who played the violin like Paganini--might well be worth the trouble of a little courtesy. Then, too, there was that mark of the thong--a charm, a military identification disk or something of value. Whatever it was, the rogues had got it. Murder and loot. And as soon as he returned to consciousness the young fellow would be making inquiries.

Perhaps Kitty's point of view regarding a certain duffer aged fifty-two was nearer the truth than the duffer himself realized. Second childhood! As if the drums of jeopardy would ever again see light, after that tempest of fire and death--that mud volcano!

One thing was certain--there would be no more cat-napping. The game was on again. He was assured of that side of it.

Green stones, the sunlight breaking against the flaws in a shower of golden sparks; green as the pulp of a Champagne grape; the drums of jeopardy! Murder and loot; he could understand.

Immediately after the patient was put to bed Cutty changed. A nondescript suit of the day-labourer type and a few deft touches of coal dust completed his make-up.

"I shan't be back until morning," he announced. "Work to do. Kuroki will be at your service through the night, Miss Frances. Strike that Burmese gong once, at any hour. Come along, Harrison."

"Want any company?" asked Harrison, with a belligerent twist to his moustache.

Cutty laughed. "No. You run along to your lambs. I'm running with the wolves to-night, old scout, and you might get that spick-and-span uniform considerably mussed up. Besides, it's raining."

"But what's to become of Miss Conover? She ought not to remain alone in that apartment."

"Well, well! I thought of that, too. But she can take care of herself."

"Those ruffians may call up the hospital and learn that we tricked them.

"And then?"

"Try to force the truth from Miss Conover."

"That's precisely the wherefore of this coal dust. On your way!"

Eleven o'clock. Kitty was in the kitchen, without light, her chair by the window, which she had thrown up. She had gone to bed, but sleep was impossible. So she decided to watch the Gregor windows. Sometimes the mind is like a movie camera set for a double exposure. The whole scene is visible, but the camera sees only half of it. Thus, while she saw the windows across the court there entered the other side of her mind a picture of the immaculate Cutty crossing the platform with Johnny Two-Hawks thrown over his shoulder. The mental picture obscured the actual.

She had called him old. Well, he was old. And no doubt he looked upon her as a child, wanting her to spend the night at a hotel! The affair was over. No one would bother Kitty Conover. Why should they? But it took strength to shoulder a man like that. What fun he and her father must have had together! And Cutty had loved her mother! That made Kitty exquisitely tender for a moment. All alone, at the age when new friendships were impossible. A lovable man like that going down through life alone!

Census taker of alien undesirables; a queer occupation for a man so famous as Cutty. Patriotism--to plunge into that seething revolutionary scum to sort the dangerous madmen from the harmless mad-men. Courage and strength and mental resource; yes, Cutty possessed these; and he would be the kind to laugh at a joke or a hurt.

One thing, however, was indelibly printed on her mind. Stefani Gregor--either Cutty had met and known the man or he had heard of him.

Suddenly she became conscious that she was blinking as one blinks from mirror-reflected sunlight. She cast about for the source of this phenomenon. Obliquely from between the interstices of the fire-escape platform came a point of moving white light. She craned her neck. A battery lamp! The round spot of light worked along the cement floor, vanished occasionally, reappeared, and then vanished altogether. Somebody was down there hunting for something. What?

Kitty remained with her head out of the window for some time, unmindful of the spatter of rain. But nothing happened. The man was gone. Of course the incident might not have the slightest bearing upon the previous adventures of this amazing night; still, it was suggestive. The young man had worn something round his neck. But if his enemies had it why should this man comb the court, unless he was a tenant and had knocked something off a window ledge?

She began to appreciate that she was very tired, and decided to go back to bed. This time she fell asleep. Her disordered thoughts rearranged themselves in a dazzling dream. She found herself wandering through a glorious translucent green cavern--a huge emerald. And in the distance she heard that unmistakable tumpitum-tump! tumpitum-tump! It drew her irresistibly. She fought and struggled against the fascinating sound, but it continued to draw her on. Suddenly from round a corner came the squat man, his hair a la Fuzzy-Wuzzy. He caught her savagely by the shoulder and dragged her toward a fire of blazing diamonds. On the other side of that fire was a blonde young woman with a tiara of rubies on her head. "Save me! I am Olga, Olga!" Kitty struggled fiercely and awoke.

The light was on. At the side of her bed were two men. One of them was holding her bare shoulder and digging his fingers into it cruelly. They looked like coal heavers.

"We do not wish to harm you, and won't if you're sensible. Where did they take the man you brought?"

CHAPTER XI

Kitty did not wrench herself loose at once. She wasn't quite sure that this was not a continuance of her nightmare. She knew that nightmares had a way of breaking off in the middle of things, of never arriving anywhere. The room looked natural enough and the pain in her shoulder seemed real enough, but one never could tell. She decided to wait for the next episode.

"Answer!" cried the spokesman of the two, twisting Kitty's shoulder. "Where did they take him?"

Awake! Kitty wrenched her shoulder away and swept the bedclothes up to her chin. She was thoroughly frightened, but her brain was clear. The spark of self-preservation flew hither and about in search of expediencies, temporizations. She must come through this somehow with the vantage on her side. She could not possibly betray that poor young man, for that would entail the betrayal of Cutty also. She saw but one avenue, the telephone; and these two men were on the wrong side of the bed, between her and the door.

"What do you want?" Her throat was so dry she wondered whether the words were projected far enough for them to hear.

"We want the address of the wounded man you brought into this apartment."

"They took him to a hospital."

"He was taken away from there."

"He was?"

"Yes, he was. You may not know where, but you will know the address of the man who tricked us; and that will be sufficient."

"The army surgeon? He was called in by chance. I don't know where he lives."

"The man in the dress suit."

"He was with the surgeon."

"He came first. Come; we have no time to waste. We don't want to hurt you, and we hope you will not force us.

"Will you step out of the room while I dress?"

"No. Tell us where the man lives, and you can have the whole apartment to yourself."

"You speak English very well."

"Enough! Do you want us to bundle you up in the bedclothes and carry you off? It will not be a pleasant experience for a pretty young woman like yourself. Something happened to the man you knew as Gregory. Will that make you understand?"

"You know what abduction means?"

"Your police will not catch us."

"But I might give you the wrong address."

"Try it and see what happens. Young lady, this is a bad affair for a woman to be mixed up in. Be sensible. We are in a hurry."

"Well, you seem to have acquired at least one American habit!" said a gruff voice from the bedroom doorway. "Raise your hands quickly, and don't turn," went on the gruff voice. "If I shoot it will be to kill. It is a rough game, as you say. That's it; and keep them up. Now, then, young lady, slip on your kimono. Get up and search these men. I'm in a hurry, too."

Kitty obeyed, very lovely in her dishevelment. Repugnant as the task was she disarmed the two men and flung their weapons on the bed.

"Now something to tie their hands; anything that will hold."

Kitty could see the speaker now. Another coal heaver, but evidently on her side.

"Tie their hands behind them... I warn you not to move, men. When I say I'll shoot I mean it. Don't be afraid of hurting them, miss. Very good. Now bandage their eyes. Handkerchiefs."

But Kitty's handkerchiefs did not run to the dimensions' required; so she ripped up a petticoat. Torn between her eagerness to complete a disagreeable task and her offended modesty, Kitty went through the performance with creditable alacrity. Then she jumped back into bed, doubled her knees, and once more drew up the bedclothes to her chin, content to be a spectator, her eyes as wide as ever they possibly could be.

Some secret-service man Cutty had sent to protect her. Dear old Cutty! Small wonder he had urged her to spend the night at a hotel. The admiration of her childhood returned, but without the shackles of shyness. She had always trusted him absolutely, and to this trust was now added understanding. To have him pop into her life again in this fashion, all the ordinary approaches to intimacy wiped out by these amazing episodes; the years bridged in an hour! If only he were younger!

"Watch them, miss. Don't be afraid to shoot. I'll return in a moment"--still gruffly. The secret-service man pushed his prisoners into chairs and left the bedroom.

Kitty did not care how gruff the voice was; it was decidedly pleasant in her ears. Gingerly she picked up one of the revolvers. Kitty Conover with shooting irons in her hands, like a movie actress! She heard a whistle. After this an interval of silence, save for the ticking of the alarm clock on the stand. She eyed the blindfolded men speculatively, swung out of bed, and put on her stockings and sandals; then she sat on the edge of the bed and waited for the sequence. Kitty Conover was going to have some queer recollections to tell her grandchildren, providing she had any. That morning she had risen to face a humdrum normal day. And here she was, at midnight, hobnobbing with quiescent murder and sudden death! To-morrow Burlingame would ask her to hustle up the Sunday stuff, and she would hustle. She wanted to laugh, but was a little afraid that this laughter might degenerate into incipient hysteria.

There was still in her mind a vivid recollection of her dream--the fire of diamonds and the blonde girl with the tiara of rubies. Olga, Olga! Russian; the whole affair was Russian. She shivered. Always that land and people had appeared to her in sinister aspect; no doubt an impression acquired from reading melodramas written by Englishmen who, once upon a time, had given Russia preeminence as a political menace. Russia, in all things--music, art, literature--the tragic note. Stefani Gregor and Johnny Two-Hawks had roused the enmity of some political society with this result. Nihilist or Bolshevist or socialist, there was little choice; and Cutty sensibly did not want her drawn into the whirlpool.

What a pleasant intimacy hers and Cutty's promised to be! And if he hadn't casually dropped into the office that afternoon she would have surrendered the affair to the police, and that would have been the end of it. Amazing thought--you might jog along all your life at the side of a person and never know him half so well as someone you met m a tense episode, like that of the immaculate Cutty crossing the fire escape with Two-Hawks on his shoulders!

She heard the friendly coal heaver going down the corridor to the door. When he returned to the bedroom two men accompanied him. Not a word was said. The two men marched off with the prisoners and left Kitty alone with her saviour.

"Thank you," she said, simply.

"You poor little chicken, did you believe I had deserted you?" The voice wasn't gruff now.

"Cutty?" Kitty ran to him, flinging her arms round his neck. "Oh, Cutty!"

Cutty's heart, which had bumped along an astonishing number of million times in fifty-two years, registered a memorable bump against his ribs. The touch of her soft arms and the faint, indescribable perfume which emanates from a dainty woman's hair thrilled him beyond any thrill he had ever known. For Kitty's mother had never put her arms round old Cutty's neck. Of course he understood readily enough: Molly's girl, flesh of her flesh. And she had rushed to him as she would have rushed to her father. He patted her shoulder clumsily, still a little dazzled for all the revelation in the analysis. The sweet intimacy of it! The door of Paradise opened for a moment, and then shut in his face.

"I did not recognize you at all!" she cried, standing off. "I shouldn't have known you on the street. And it is so simple. What a wonderful man you are!"

"For an old codger?" Cutty's heart registered another sizable bump.

Kitty laughed. "Never call yourself old to me again. Are you always doing these things?"

"Well, I keep moving. I suspected something like this might happen. Those two will go to the Tombs to await deportation if they are aliens. Perhaps we can dig something out of them relative to this man Gregor. Anyhow, we'll try."

"Cutty, I saw a man in the court with a pocket lamp before I went to bed. He was hunting for something."

"I didn't find anything but a lot of fresh food someone had thrown out."

"It was you, then?"

"Yes. There was a vague possibility that your protege might have thrown out something valuable during the struggle."

"What?"

"Lord knows! A queer business, Kitty, you've lugged me into--my own! And there is one thing I want you to remember particularly: Life means nothing to the men opposed, neither chivalry nor ethics. Annihilation is their business. They don't want civilization; they want chaos. They have lost the sense of comparisons or they would not seek to thrust Bolshevism down the throats of the rest of the world. They say democracy has failed, and their substitute is murder and loot. Kitty, I want you to leave this roost."

"I shall stay until my lease expires."

"Why? In the face of real danger?"

"Because I intend to, Cutty--unless you kidnap me."

"Have you any good reason?"

"You'll laugh; but something tells me to stay here."

But Cutty did not laugh. "Very well. Tomorrow an assistant janitor will be installed. His name is Antonio Bernini. Every night he will whistle up the tube. Whistle back. If you are going out for the evening notify him where you intend to go and when you expect to be back. A wire from your bed to his cot will be installed. In danger, press the button. That's the best I can do for you, since you decide to stick. I don't believe anything more will happen to-night, but from now on you will be watched. Never come directly to my apartment. Break your journey two or three times with taxis. Always use Elevator Four. The boy is mine; belongs to the service. So our Bolshevik friends won't gather anything about you from him."

As a matter of fact, Cutty had now come to the conviction that it would be well to let Kitty remain here as a lure. He had urged her to leave, and she had refused, so his conscience was tolerably clear. Besides, she would henceforth be guarded with a ceaseless efficiency second only to that which encompasses a President of the United States. Always some man of the service would be watching those who watched her. This was going to develop into a game of small nets, one or two victims at a time. Because these enemies of civilization lacked coherence in action there would be slim chance of rounding them up in bulk. But from now on men would vanish-- one here, a pair there, perhaps on occasion four or five. And those who had known them would know them no more. The policy would be that employed by the British in the submarine campaign--mysterious silence after the evanishment.

"It's all so exciting!" said Kitty. "But that poor old man Gregor! He had a wonderful violin, Cutty; and sometimes I used to hear him play folklore music--sad, haunting melodies."

"We'll know in a little while what's become of him. I doubt there is a foreign organization in the city that hasn't one or more of our men on the inside. A word will be dropped somewhere. I'm rarely active on this side of the Atlantic; and what I'm doing now is practically due to interest. But every active operative in New York, Boston, Philadelphia, and Chicago is on the lookout for a man who, if left free, will stir up a lot of trouble. He has leadership, this Boris Karlov, a former intimate here of Trotzky's. We have reason to believe that he slipped through the net in San Francisco. Probably under a cleverly forged passport. Now please describe the man who came in with the policeman. I haven't had time to make inquiries at the precinct, where they will have a minute description of him."

"He made me think of a gorilla, just as I told you. His face was pretty well banged up. Naturally I did not notice any scar. A dreadfully black beard, shaven."

"Squat, powerful, like a gorilla. Lord, I wish I'd had a glimpse of him! He's one of the few topnotchers I haven't met. He's the spark, the hand on the plunger. The powder is all ready in this land of ours; our job is to keep off the sparks until we can spread the stuff so it will only go puff instead of bang. This man Karlov is bad medicine for democracy. Poor devil!"

"Why do you say that?"

"Because I'm honestly sorry for them. This fellow Karlov has suffered. He is now a species of madman nothing will cure. He and his kind have gained their ends in Russia, but the impetus to kill and burn and loot is still unchecked. Sorry, yes; but we can't have them here. They remind me of nothing so much as those blind deep-sea monsters in one of Kipling's tales, thrown up into air and sunlight by a submarine volcano, slashing and bellowing. But we can't have them here any longer. Keep those revolvers under your pillow. All you have to do is to point. Nobody will know that you can't shoot. And always remember, we're watching over you. Good-night."

"Mouquin's for lunch?"

"Well, I'll be hanged! But it can't be, Kitty. You and I must not be seen in public. If that was Karlov you will be marked, and so will any one who travels with you."

"Good gracious!"

"Fact. But come up to the roost--changing taxis--to-morrow at five and have tea."

Down in the street Cutty bore into the slanting rain, no longer a drizzle. With his hands jammed in his side pockets and his gaze on the sparkling pavement he continued downtown, in a dangerously ruminative frame of mind, dangerous because had he been followed he would not have known it.

Molly Conover's girl! That afternoon it had been Tommy Conover's girl; now she was Molly's. It occurred to him for the first time that he was one of those unfortunate individuals who are always able to open the door to Paradise for others and are themselves forced to remain outside. Hadn't he introduced Conover to Molly, and hadn't they fallen in love on the spot? Too old to be a hero and not old enough to die. He grinned. Some day he would use that line.

Of course it wasn't Kitty who set this peculiar cogitation in motion. It wasn't her arms and the perfume of her hair. The actual thrill had come from a recrudescence of a vanished passion; anyhow, a passion that had been held suspended all these years. Still, it offered a disquieting prospect. He was sensible enough to realize that he would be in for some confusion in trying to disassociate the phantom from the quick.

Most pretty young women were flitter-flutters, unstable, shallow, immature. But this little lady had depth, the sense of the living drama; and, Lord, she was such a beauty! Wanted a man who would laugh when he was happy and when he was hurt. A bull's-eye--bang, like that! For the only breed worth its salt was the kind that laughed when happy and when hurt.

The average young woman, rushing into his arms the way she had, would not have stirred him in the least. And immediately upon the heels of this thought came a taste of the confusion he saw in store for himself. Was it the phantom or Kitty? He jumped to another angle to escape the impasse. Kitty's coming to him in that fashion raised an unpalatable suggestion. He evidently looked fatherly, no matter how he felt. Hang these fifty-two years, to come crowding his doorstep all at once!

He raised his head and laughed. He suddenly remembered now. At nine that night he had been scheduled to deliver a lecture on the Italo-Jugoslav muddle before a distinguished audience in the ballroom of a famous hotel! He would have some fancy apologizing to do in the morning.

He stepped into a doorway, then peered out cautiously. There was not a single pedestrian in sight. No need of hiking any further in this rain; so he hunted for a taxi. To-morrow he would set the wires humming relative to old Stefani Gregor. Boris Karlov, if indeed it were he, would lead the way. Hadn't Stefani and Boris been boyhood friends, and hadn't Stefani betrayed the latter in some political affair? He wasn't sure; but a glance among his 1912 notes would clear up the fog.

But that young chap! Who was he? Cutty set his process of logical deduction moving. Karlov--always supposing that gorilla was Karlov--had come in from the west. So had the young man. Gregor's inclinations had been toward the aristocracy; at least, that had been the impression. A Bolshevik would not seek haven with a man like Gregor, as this young man had. But Two-Hawks bothered him; the name bothered him, because it had no sense either in English or in Russian. And yet he was sure he had heard it somewhere. Perhaps his notes would throw some light on that subject, too.

When he arrived home Miss Frances, the nurse, informed him that the patient was babbling in an outlandish tongue. For a long time Cutty stood by the bedside, translating.

"Olga!... Olga!... And she gave me food, Stefani, this charming American girl. Never must we forget that. I was hungry, and she gave me food.... But I paid for it. You, gone, there was no one else.... And she is poor.... The torches!... I am burning, burning!... Olga!"

"What does he say?" asked the nurse.

"It is Russian. Is it a crisis?" he evaded.

"Not necessarily. Doctor Harrison said he would probably return to consciousness sometime to-morrow. But he must have absolute quiet. No visitors. A bad blow, but not of fatal consequence. I've seen hundreds of cases much worse pull out in a fortnight. You'd better go to bed, sir."

"All right," said Cutty, gratefully. He was tired. The ball did not rebound as it used to; the resilience was petering out. But look alive, there! Big events were toward, and he must not stop to feel of his pulse.

Three o'clock in the morning.

The man in the Gregor bedroom sat down on the bed, the pocket lamp dangling from his hairy fingers. Not a nook or cranny in the apartment had he overlooked. In every cupboard, drawer; in the beds and under; the trunks; behind the radiators and the pictures; the shelves and clothes in the closets. What he sought he had not found.

His vengeance would not be complete without those green stones in his hands. Anna would call from her grave. Pretty little Anna, who had trusted Stefani Gregor, and gone to her doom.

All these thousands of miles, by hook and crook, by forged passports, by sums of money, sleepless nights and hungry days--for this! The last of that branch of the breed out of his reach, and the stones vanished! A queer superstition had taken lodgment in his brain; he recognized it now for the first time. The possession of those stones would be a sign from God to go on. Green stones for bread! Green stones for bread! The drums of jeopardy! In his hands they would be talismanic.

But wait! That pretty girl across the way. Supposing he had intrusted the stones to her? Or hidden them there without her being aware of it?

CHAPTER XII

Kitty Conover ate in the kitchen. First off, this statement is likely to create the false impression that there was an ordinary grain here, a wedge of base hemlock in the citron. Not so. She ate in the kitchen because she could not yet face that vacant chair in the dining room without choking and losing her appetite. She could not look at the chair without visualizing that glorious, whimsical, fascinating mother of hers, who could turn grumpy janitors into comedians and send importunate bill collectors away with nothing but spangles in their heads.

So long as she stayed out of the dining room she could accept her loneliness with sound philosophy. She knew, as all sensible people know, that there were ghosts, that memory had haunted galleries, and that empty chairs were evocations.

Her days were so busily active, there were so many first nights and concerts, that she did not mind such evenings as she had to spend alone in the apartment. Persons were in and out of the office all through the day, and many of them entertaining. For only real persons ever penetrated that well-guarded cubby-hole off the noisy city room. Many of them were old friends of her mother. Of course they were a little pompous, but this was less innate than acquired; and she knew that below they were worth while. She had come to the conclusion that successful actors and actresses were the only people in America who spoke English fluently and correctly.

Yes, she ate in the kitchen; but she would have been a fit subject for the fastidious Fragonard. Kitty was naturally an exquisite. Everything about her was dainty, her body and her mind. The background of pans and dishes, gas range and sink did not absorb Kitty; her presence here in the morning lifted everything out of the rut of commonplace and created an atmosphere that was ornamental. Pink peignoir and turquoise-blue boudoir cap, silk petticoat and stockings and adorable little slippers. No harm to tell the secret! Kitty was educating herself for a husband. She knew that if she acquired the habit of daintiness at breakfast before marriage it would become second nature after marriage. Moreover, she was determined that it should be tremendous news that would cause a newspaper to intervene. She had all the confidence in the world in her mirror.

She got her breakfast this morning, singing. She was happy. She had found a door out of monotony; theatrical drama had given way to the living. She had opened the book of adventure and she was going straight through to finis. That there was an undertow of the sinister escaped her or she ignored it.

In all high-strung Irish souls there is a bit of the old wife, the foreteller; the gift of prescience; and Kitty possessed this in a mild degree. Something held her here, when for a dozen reasons she should have gone elsewhere.

She strained the coffee, humming a tune out of The Mikado, the revival of which she had seen lately:

> My object all sublime
> I shall achieve in time
> To make the punishment fit the crime.
> The punishment fit the crime.
> And make the prisoner pent
> Unwillingly represent
> A source of innocent merriment.
> Of innocent merriment!

And there you were! To make the punishment fit the crime. Wall in the Bolsheviki, the I.W.W.'s, the Red Socialist, the anarchists--and let them try it for ten years. Those left would be glad enough to embrace democracy and sanity. The poor benighted things, to imagine that they were going forward there in Russia! What kind of mentality was it that could conceive a blessing to humanity in the abolition of baths and work? And Cutty felt sorry for them. Well, as for that, so did Kitty Conover; and she would continue feeling sorry for them so long as they remained thousands of miles away. But next door!

"Grapefruit, eggs on toast, and coffee; mademoiselle is served!" she cried, gayly, sitting down and attacking her breakfast with the zest of healthy youth.

Often the eyes are like the lenses of a camera minus the sensitized plate; they see objects without printing them. Thus a dozen times Kitty's glance absently swept the range and the racks on each side of the stovepipe, one rack burdened with an empty pancake jug and the other cluttered with old-fashioned flatirons; but she saw nothing.

She was carefully reviewing the events of the night before. She could not dismiss the impression that Cutty knew Stefani Gregor or had heard of him; and in either case it signified that Gregor was something more than a valet. And decidedly Two-Hawks was not of the Russian peasantry.

By the time she was ready to leave for the office the Irish blood in her was seething and bubbling and dancing. She knew she would do crazy, impulsive things all day. It was easy to analyze this exuberance. She had reached out into the dark and touched danger, and found a new thrill in a humdrum world.

The Great Dramatist had produced a tremendous drama and she had watched curtain after curtain fall from the wrong side of the lights. Now she had been given a speaking part; and she would be down stage for a moment or two--dusting the furniture--while the stars were retouching their make-up. It was not the thought of Cutty, of Gregor, of Johnny Two-Hawks, of hidden treasure; simply she had arrived somewhere in the great drama.

When she reached the office she had a hard time of it to settle down to the day's work.

"Hustle up that Sunday stuff," said Burlingame. Kitty laughed. Just as she had pictured it. She hustled.

"I have it!" she cried, breaking a spell of silence.

"What--St. Vitus?" inquired Burlingame, patiently.

"No; the Morgue!"

"What the dickens--!"

But Kitty was no longer there to answer.

In all newspaper offices there is a department flippantly designated as the Morgue. Obituaries on ice, as it were. A photograph or an item concerning a great man, a celebrated, beauty or some notorious rogue; from the king calibre down to

Gyp-the-Blood brand, all indexed and laid away against the instant need. So, running her finger tip down the K's, Kitty found Karlov. The half tone which she eventually exhumed from the tin box was an excellent likeness of the human gorilla who had entered her rooms with the policeman. She would be able to carry this positive information to Cutty that afternoon.

When she left the office at four she took the Subway to Forty-second Street. She engaged a taxi from the Knickerbocker and discharged it at the north entrance to the Waldorf, which she entered. She walked through to the south entrance and got into another taxi. She left this at Wanamaker's, ducking and dodging through the crowded aisles. She selected this hour because, being a woman, she knew that the press of shoppers would be the greatest during the day. Karlov's man and the secret-service operative detailed by Cutty both made the same mistake--followed Kitty into the dry-goods shop and lost her as completely as if she had popped up in China. At quarter to five she stepped into Elevator Number Four of the building which Cutty called his home, very well pleased with herself.

CHAPTER XIII

To understand Kitty at this moment one must be able to understand the Irish; and nobody does or can or will. Consider her twenty-four years, her corpuscular inheritance, the love of drama and the love of adventure. Imagine possessing sound ideas of life and the ability to apply them, and spiritually always galloping off on some broad highway--more often than not furnished by some engaging scoundrel of a novelist--and you will be able to construct a half tone of Kitty Conover.

That civilization might be actually on its deathbed, that positively half of the world was starving and dying and going mad through the reaction of the German blight touched her in a detached way. She felt sorry, dreadfully sorry, for the poor things; but as she could not help them she dismissed them from her thoughts every morning after she had read the paper, the way most of us do here in these United States. You cannot grapple with the misery of an unknown person several thousand miles away.

That which had taken place during the past twenty-four hours was to her a lark, a blindman's buff for grown-ups. It was not in her to tremble, to shudder, to hesitate, to weigh this and to balance that. Irish curiosity. Perhaps in the original that immortal line read: "The Irish rush in where angels fear to tread," and some proofreader had a particular grudge against the race.

When the elevator reached the seventeenth floor, the passengers surged forth. All except Kitty, who tarried.

"We don't carry to the eighteenth, miss.

"I am Miss Conover," she replied. "I dared not tell you until we were alone."

"I see." The boy nodded, swept her with an appraising glance, and sent the elevator up to the loft.

"You understand? If any one inquires about me, you don't remember."

"Yes, miss. The boss's orders."

"And if any one does inquire you are to report at once."

"That, too."

The boy rolled back the door and Kitty stepped out upon a Laristan runner of rose hues and cobalt blue. She wondered what it cost Cutty to keep up an establishment like this. There were fourteen rooms, seven facing the north and seven facing the west, with glorious vistas of steam-wreathed roofs and brick Matterhorns and the dim horizon touching the sea. Fine rugs and tapestries and furniture gathered from the four ends of the world; but wholly livable and in no sense atmospheric of the museum. Cutty had excellent taste.

She had visited the apartment but twice before, once in her childhood and again when she was eighteen. Cutty had given a dinner in honour of her mother's birthday. She smiled as she recalled the incident. Cutty had placed a box of candles at the side of her mother's plate and told her to stick as many into the cake as she thought best.

"Hello!" said Cutty, emerging from one of the doors. "What the dickens have you been up to? My man has just telephoned me that he lost track of you in Wanamaker's."

Kitty explained, delighted.

"Well, well! If you can lose a man such as I set to watch you, you'll have no trouble shaking the others."

"It was Karlov, Cutty."

"How did you learn?"

"Searched the morgue and found a half tone of him. Positively Karlov. How is the patient?"

"Harrison says he's pulling round amazingly. A tough skull. He'll be up for his meals in no time."

"How do you do it?" she asked with a gesture.

"Do what?"

"Manage a place like this? In a busy office district. It's the most wonderful apartment in New York. Riverside has nothing like it. It must cost like sixty."

"The building is mine, Kitty. That makes it possible. An uncle who knew I hated money and the responsibilities that go with it, died and left it to me."

"Why, Cutty, you must be rich!"

"I'm sorry. What can I do? I can't give it away."

"But you don't have to work!"

"Oh, yes, I do. I'm that kind. I'd die of a broken heart if I had to sit still. It's the game."

"Did mother know?"

"Yes."

With the toe of a snug little bronze boot Kitty drew an outline round a pattern in the rug.

"Love is a funny thing," was her comment.

"It sure is, old-timer. But what put the thought into your head?"

"I was thinking how very much mumsy must have been in love with father."

"But she never knew that I loved her, Kitty."

"What's that got to do with it? If she had wanted money you wouldn't have had the least chance in the world."

"Probably not! But what would you have done in your mother's place?"

"Snapped you up like that!" Kitty flashed back.

"You cheerful little--little--"

"Liar. Say it!" Kitty laughed. "But am I a cheerful little liar? I don't know. It would be an awful temptation. Somebody to wait on you; heaps of flowers when you wanted them; beautiful gowns and thingummies and furs and limousines. I've often wondered what I should do if I found myself with love and youth on one side and money and attraction on the other. I've always been in straitened circumstances. I never spent a dollar in all my days when I didn't think I ought to have held back three or four cents of it. You can't know, Cutty, what it is to be poor and want beautiful things and good times. Of course. I couldn't marry just money. There would have to be some kind of a man to go with it. Someone interesting enough to make me forget sometimes that I'd thrown away a lover for a pocket-book."

"Would you marry me, Kitty?"

"Are you serious?"

"Let's suppose I am."

"No. I couldn't marry you, Cutty I should always be having my mother's ghost as a rival."

"But supposing I fell in love with you?"

"Then I'd always be doubting your constancy. But what queer talk!'"

"Kitty, you're a joy! Lordy, my luck in dropping in to see you yesterday!"

"And a little whippersnapper like me calling a great man like you Cutty!"

"Well, if it embarrasses you, you might switch to papa once in a while."

Kitty's laughter rang down the corridor. "I'll remember that whenever I want to make you mad. Who's here?"

"Nobody but Harrison and the nurse. Both good citizens, and I've taken them into my confidence to a certain extent. You can talk freely before them."

"Am I to see the patient?"

"Harrison says not. About Wednesday your Two-Hawks will be sitting up. I've determined to keep the poor devil here until he can take care of himself. But he is flat broke."

"He said he had money."

"Well, Karlov's men stripped him clean."

"Have you any idea who he is?"

"To be honest, that's one of the reasons why I want to keep him here. He's Russian, for all his Oxford English and his Italian gestures; and from his babble I imagine he's been through seven kinds of hell. Torches and hobnailed boots and the incessant call for a woman named Olga--a young woman about eighteen."

"How did you find that out?"

"From a photograph I found in the lining of his coat. A pretty blonde girl."

"Good heavens!"--recollecting her dream. "Where was it printed?"

"Amateur photography. I'll pick it up on the way to the living room."

It was nothing like the blonde girl of her dream. Still, the girl was charming. Kitty turned over the photograph. There was writing on the back.

"Russian? What does it say?"

"'To Ivan from Olga with all her love.'"

Cutty was conscious of the presence of an indefensible malice in his tones. Why the deuce should he be bitter--glad that the chap had left behind a sweetheart? He knew exactly the basis of Kitty's interest, as utterly detached as that of a reporter going to a fire. On the day the patient could explain himself, Kitty's interest would automatically cease. An old dog in the manger? Malice.

"Cutty, something dreadful has happened to this poor young woman. That's what makes him cry out the name. Caught in that horror, and probably he alone escaped. Is it heartless to be glad I'm an American? Do they let in these Russians?"

"Not since the Trotzky regime. I imagine Two-Hawks slipped through on some British passport. He'll probably tell us all about it when he comes round. But how do you feel after last night's bout?"

"Alive! And I'm going on being alive, forever and ever! Oh, those awful drums! They look like dead eyes in those dim corners. Tumpitum-tump! Tumpitum-tump!" she cried, linking her arm in his. "What a gorgeous view! Just what I'm going to do when my ship comes in--live in a loft. I really believe I could write up here--I mean worth-while things I could enjoy writing and sell."

"It's yours if you want it when I leave."

"And I'd have a fine time explaining to my friends! You old innocent! ... Or are you so innocent?"

"We do live in a cramped world. But I meant it. Don't forget to whistle down to Tony Bernini when you get back home to-night."

"I promise.

"Why the gurgle?"

"Because I'm tremendously excited. All my life I've wanted to do mysterious things. I've been with the audience all the while, and I want to be with the actors."

"You'll give some man a wild dance."

"If I do I'll dance with him. Now lead me to the cookies."

She was the life of the tea table. Her wit, her effervescence, her whimsicalities amused even the prim Miss Frances. When she recounted the exploit of the camouflaged fan, Cutty and Harrison laughed so loudly that the nurse had to put her linger on her lips. They might wake the patient.

"I am really interested in him," went on Kitty. "I won't deny it. I want to see how it's going to turn out. He was very nice after I let him into the kitchen. A perfectly English manner and voice, and Italian gestures when off his guard. I feel so sorry for him. What strangers we races are to each other! Until the war we hardly knew the Canadians. The British didn't know us at all, and the French became acquainted with the British for the first time in history. And the German thought he knew us all and really knew nobody. All the Russians I ever saw were peasants of the cattle type; so that the word Russian conjures up two pictures--the grand duke at Monte Carlo and a race of men who wear long beards and never bathe except when it rains. Think of it! For the first time since God set mankind on earth peoples are becoming acquainted. I never saw a Russian of this type before.".

"A leaf in the whirlpool.--Anyhow, we'll keep him here until he's on his feet. By the way, never answer any telephone call--I mean, go anywhere on a call-- unless you are sure of the speaker."

"I begin to feel important."

"You are important. You have suddenly become a connecting link between this Karlov and the man we wish to protect. I'll confess I wanted you out of that apartment at first; but when I saw that you were bent on remaining, I decided to make use of you."

"You are going to give me a part in the play?"

"Yes. You are to go about your affairs as always, just as if nothing had happened. Only when you wish to come here will you play any game like that of to-day. Then it will be advisable. Switch your route each time. Your real part is to be that of lure. Through you we shall gradually learn who Karlov's associates are. If you don't care to play the role all you have to do is to move."

"The idea! I'm grateful for anything. You men will never understand. You go forth into the world each day--politics, diplomacy, commerce, war--while we women stay at home and knit or darn socks or take care of the baby or make over our clothes and hats or do household work or play the piano or read. Never any adventure. Never any games. Never any clubs. The leaving your house to go to the office is an adventure. A train from here to Philadelphia is an adventure. We women are always craving it. And about all we can squeeze out of life is shopping and hiding the bills after marriage, and going to the movies before marriage with young men our fathers don't like. We can't even stroll the street and admire the handsome gowns of our more fortunate sisters the way you men do. When you see a pretty woman on the street do you ever stop to think that there are ten at home eating their hearts out? Of course you don't. So I'm going through with this, to satisfy suppressed instincts; and I shan't promise to trot along as usual."

"They may attempt to kidnap you, Kitty."

"That doesn't frighten me."

"So I observe. But if they ever should have the luck to kidnap you, tell all you know at once. There's only one way up here--the elevator. I can get out to the fire escape, but none can get in from that direction, as the door is of steel."

"And, of course, you'll take me into your confidence completely?"

"When the time comes. Half the fun in an adventure is the element of the unexpected," said Cutty.

"Where did you first meet Stefani Gregor?"

Captain Harrison laughed. He liked this girl. She was keen and could be depended upon, as witness last night's work. Her real danger lay in being conspicuously pretty, in looking upon this affair as merely a kind of exciting game, when it was tragedy.

"What makes you think I know Stefani Gregor?" asked Cutty, genuinely curious.

"When I pronounced that name you whirled upon me as if I had struck you."

"Very well. When we learn who Two-Hawks is I'll tell you what I know about Gregor. And in the meantime you will be ceaselessly under guard. You are an asset, Kitty, to whichever side holds you. Captain Harrison is going to stay for dinner. Won't you join us?"

"I'm going to a studio potluck with some girls. And it's time I was on the way. I'll let your Tony Bernini know. Home probably at ten."

Cutty went with her to the elevator and when he returned to the tea table he sat down without speaking.

"Why not kidnap her yourself," suggested Harrison, "if you don't want her in this?"

"She would never forgive me."

"If she found it out."

"She's the kind who would. What do you think of her, Miss Frances?"

"I think she is wonderful. Frankly, I should tell her everything--if there is anything more to be told."

When dinner was over, the nurse gone back to the patient and Captain Harrison to his club, Cutty lit his odoriferous pipe and patrolled the windows of his study. Ever since Kitty's departure he had been mulling over in his mind a plan regarding her future--to add a codicil to his will, leaving her five thousand a year, so Molly's girl might always have a dainty frame for her unusual beauty. The pity of it was that convention denied him the pleasure of settling the income upon her at once, while she was young. He might outlive her; you never could tell. Anyhow, he would see to the codicil. An accident might step in.

He got out his chrysoprase. In one corner of the room there was a large port-folio such as artists use for their proofs and sketches; and from this he took a doz-en twelve-by-fourteen-inch photographs of beautiful women, most of them stage beauties of bygone years. The one on top happened to be Patti. The adorable Patti!... Linda, Violetta, Lucia. Lord, what a nightingale she had been! He laughed laid the photograph on the desk, and dipped his hand into a canvas bag filled with polished green stones which would have great commercial value if people knew more about them; for nothing else in the world is quite so beautifully green.

He built tiaras above the lovely head and laid necklaces across the marvellous throat. Suddenly a phenomenon took place. The roguish eyes of the prima donna receded and vanished and slate-blue ones replaced them. The odd part of it was, he could not dissipate the fancied eyes for the replacement of the actual. Patti, with slate-blue eyes! He discarded the photograph and selected another. He began the game anew and was just beginning the attack on the problem uppermost in his mind when the phenomenon occurred again. Kitty's eyes! What infernal nonsense! Kitty had served merely to enliven his tender recollections of her mother. Twenty-four and fifty-two. And yet, hadn't he just read that Maeterlinck, fifty-six, had married Mademoiselle Dahon, many years younger?

In a kind of resentful fury he pushed back his chair and fell to pacing, eddies and loops and spirals of smoke whirling and sweeping behind him. The only light was centred upon the desk, so he might have been some god pacing cloud-riven Olympus in the twilight. By and by he laughed; and the atmosphere--mental--cleared. Maeterlinck, fifty-six, and Cutty, fifty-two, were two different men. Cutty might mix his metaphors occasionally, but he wasn't going to mix his ghosts.

He returned to his singular game. More tiaras and necklaces; and his brain took firm hold of the theme which had in the beginning lured him to the green stones.

Two-Hawks. That name bothered him. He knew he had heard it before, but never in the Russian tongue. It might be that the chap had been spoofing Kitty. Still, he had also called himself Hawksley.

The smoke thickened; there were frequent flares of matches. One by one Cutty discarded the photographs, dropping them on the floor beside his chair, his mind boring this way and that for a solution. He had now come to the point where he ceased to see the photographs or the green stones. The movements of his hands were almost automatic. And in this abstract manner he came to the last photograph. He built a necklace and even ventured an earring.

It was a glorious face--black eyes that followed you; full lipped; every indica-tion of fire and genius. It must be understood that he rarely saw the photographs when he played this game. It wasn't an amusing pastime, a mental relaxation. It was a unique game of solitaire, the photographs and chrysoprase being substituted for cards; and in some inexplicable manner it permitted him to concentrate upon whatever problem filled his thoughts. It was purely accidental that he saw Patti to-night or recalled her art. Coming upon the last photograph without having found a solution of the riddle of Two-Hawks he relaxed the mental pressure; and his sight reestablished its ability to focus.

"Good Lord!" he ejaculated.

He seized the photograph excitedly, scattering the green stones. She! The Ca-labrian, the enchanting colouratura who had vanished from the world at the height of her fame, thirty-odd years gone! Two-Hawks!

Cutty saw himself at twenty, in the pit at La Scala, with music-mad Milan all about him. Two-Hawks! He remembered now. The nickname the young bloods had given her because she had been eternally guarded by her mother and aunt, fierce-beaked Calabrians, who had determined that Rosa should never throw herself away on some beggarly Adonis.

And this chap was her son! Yesterday, rich and powerful, with a name that was open sesame wherever he went; to-day, hunted, penniless, and forlorn. Cutty sank back in his chair, stunned by the revelation. In that room yonder!

4

CHAPTER XIV

For a long time Cutty sat perfectly motionless, his pipe at an upward angle--a fine commentary on the strength of his jaws--and his gaze boring into the shadows beyond his desk. What was uppermost in his thoughts now was the fateful twist of events that had brought the young man to the assured haven of this towering loft.

All based, singularly enough, upon his wanting to see Molly's girl for a few moments; and thus he had established himself in Kitty's thoughts. Instead of turning to the police she had turned to him. Old Cutty, reaching round vaguely for something to stay the current--age; hoping by seeing this living link 'twixt the present and the past to stay the afterglow of youth. As if that could be done! He, who had never paid any attention to gray hairs and wrinkles and time, all at once found himself in a position similar to that of the man who supposes he has an inexhaustible sum at the bank and has just been notified that he has overdrawn.

Cutty knew that life wasn't really coordination and premeditation so much as it was coincident. Trivials. Nothing was absolute and dependable but death; between birth and death a series of accidents and incidents and coincidents which men called life.

He tapped his pipe on the ash tray and stood up. He gathered the chrysoprase and restored the stones to the canvas bag. Then he carefully stacked the photographs and carried them to the portfolio. The green stones he deposited in a safe, from which he took a considerable bundle of small notebooks, returning to the desk with these. Denatured dynamite, these notebooks, full of political secrets, solutions of mysteries that baffle historians. A truly great journalist never writes history as a historian; he is afraid to. Sometimes conjecture is safer than fact. And these little notebooks were the repository of suppressed facts ranging over twenty-odd years.

Gerald Stanley Lee would have recognized them instantly as coming under the head of what he calls Sh!

An hour later Cutty returned the notebooks to their abiding place, his memory refreshed. The poor devil! A dissolute father and uncle, dissolute forbears, corrupt blood weakened by intermarriage, what hope was there? Only one--the rich, fiery blood of the Calabrian mother.

But why had the chap come to America? Why not England or the Riviera, where rank, even if shorn of its prerogatives, is still treated respectfully? But America!

Cutty's head went up. Perhaps that was it--to barter his phantom greatness for money, to dazzle some rich fool of an American girl. In that case Karlov would be welcome. But wait a moment. The chap had come in from the west. In that event there should be an Odyssey of some kind tucked away in the affair.

Cutty resumed his pacing. The moment his imagination caught the essentials he visualized the Odyssey. Across mountains and deserts, rivers and seas, he followed Two-Hawks in fancy, pursued by an implacable hatred, more or less historical, of which the lad was less a cause than an abstract object. And Karlov--Cutty understood Karlov now--always span near, his hate reenergizing his faltering feet.

There was evidently some iron in this Two-Hawks' blood. Fear never would have carried him thus far. Fear would have whispered, "Futility! Futility!" And he would have bent his head to the stroke. So then there was resource and there was courage. And he lay in yonder room, beaten and penniless. The top piece in the grim irony--to have come all these thousands of miles unscathed, to be dropped at the goal. But America? Well, that would be solved later.

"By the Lord Harry!" Cutty stopped and struck his hands together. "The drums!"

From the hour Kitty had pronounced the name Stefani Gregor an idea had taken lodgment, an irrepressible idea, that somewhere in this drama would be the drums of jeopardy. The mark of the thong! Never any doubt of it now. Those magnificent emeralds were here in New York, The mob--the Red Guard--hammering on the doors, what would have been Two-Hawks' most natural first thought? To gather what treasures the hand could be laid to and flee. Here in New York, and in Karlov's hands, ultimately to be cut up for Bolshevik propaganda! The infernal pity of it!

The passion of the gem hunter blazed forth, dimming all other phases of the drama. Here was a real game, a man's game; sport! Cutty rubbed his hands together pleasurably. To recover those green flames before they could be broken up; under the ancient ruling that "Findings is keepings." The stones, of course, meant nothing to Karlov beyond the monetary value; and upon this fact Cutty began developing a plan. He stood ready to buy those stones if he could draw them into the open. Lord, how he wanted them! Murder and loot, always murder and loot!

The thought of those two incomparable emeralds being broken up distressed him profoundly. He must act at once, before the desecration could be consummated. Two-Hawks--Hawksley hereafter, for the sake of convenience--had an equity in the gems; but what of that? In smuggling them in--and how the deuce had he done it?--he had thrown away his legal right to them. Cutty kneaded his conscience into a satisfactory condition of quiescence and went on with his planning. If he succeeded in recovering the stones and his conscience bit a little too deeply for comfort--why, he could pay over to Hawksley twenty per cent. of the price Karlov demanded. He could take it or leave it. In a case like this--to a bachelor without dependents--money was no object. All his life he had wanted a fine emerald to play with, and here was an opportunity to acquire two!

If this plan failed to draw Karlov into the open, then every jeweller and pawn-broker in town would be notified and warned. What with the secret-service operatives and the agents of the Department of Justice on the watch for Karlov--who would recognize his limitations of mobility--it was reasonable to assume that the Bolshevik would be only too glad to dicker secretly for the disposal of the stones. Now to work. Cutty looked at his watch.

Nearly midnight. Rather late, but he knew all the tricks of this particular kind of game. If the advertisement appeared isolated, all the better. The real job would be to hide his identity. He saw a way round this difficulty. He wrote out six advertisements, all worded the same. He figured out the cost and was delighted to find that he carried the necessary currency. Then he got into his engineer's--dungarees, touched up his face and hands to the required griminess, and sallied forth.

Luck attended him until he reached the last morning newspaper on the list. Here he was obliged to proceed to the city room--risky business. A queer advertisement coming into the city room late at night was always pried into, as he knew from experience. Still, he felt that he ought not to miss any chance to reach Karlov.

He explained his business to the sleepy gate boy, who carried the advertisement and the cash to the night city editor's desk. Ordinarily the night city editor would have returned the advertisement with the crisp information that he had no authority to accept advertisements. But the "drums of jeopardy" caught his attention; and he sent a keen glance across the busy room to the rail where Cutty stood, perhaps conspicuously.

"Humph!" He called to one of the reporters. "This looks like a story. I'll run it. Follow that guy in the overalls and see what's in it."

Cutty appreciated the interlude for what it was worth. Someone was going to follow him. When the gate boy returned to notify him that the advertisement had been accepted, Cutty went down to the street.

"Hey, there; just a moment!" hailed the reporter. "I want a word with you about that advertisement."

Cutty came to a standstill. "I paid for it, didn't I?"

"Sure. But what's this about the drums of jeopardy?"

"Two great emeralds I'm hunting for," explained Cutty, recalling the man who stood on London Bridge and peddled sovereigns at two bits each, and no buyer.

"Can it! Can it!" jeered the reporter. "Be a good sport and give us the tip. Strike call among the city engineers?"

"I'm telling you."

"Like Mike you are!"

"All right. It's the word to tie up the surface lines, like Newark, if you want to know. Now, get t' hell out o' here before I hand you one on the jaw!"

The reporter backed away. "Is that on the level?"

"Call up the barns and find out. They'll tell you what's on. And listen, if you follow me, I'll break your head. On your way!"

The reporter dashed for the elevator--and back to the doorway in time to see Cutty legging it for the Subway. As he was a reporter of the first class he managed to catch the same express uptown.

On the way uptown Cutty considered that he had accomplished a shrewd bit of work. Karlov or one of his agents would certainly see that advertisement; and even if Karlov suspected a Federal trap he would find some means of communicating with the issuer of the advertisement.

The thought of Kitty returned. What the dickens would she say--how would she act--when she learned who this Hawksley was? He fervently hoped that she had never read "Thaddeus of Warsaw." There would be all the difference in the world between an elegant refugee Pole and a derelict of the Russian autocracy. Perhaps the best course to pursue would be to say nothing at all to her about the amazing discovery.

Upon leaving Elevator Four Cutty said: "Bob, I've been followed by a sharp reporter. Sheer him off with any tale you please, and go home. Goodnight."

"I'll fix him, sir."

Cutty took a bath, put on his lounging robe, and tiptoed to the threshold of the patient's room. The shaded light revealed the nurse asleep with a book on her knees. The patient's eyes were closed and his breathing was regular. He was coming along. Cutty decided to go to bed.

Meantime, when the elevator touched the ground floor, the operator observed a prospective passenger.

"Last trip, sir. You'll have to take the stairs."

"Where'll I find the engineer who went up with you just now?"

"The man I took up? Gone to bed, I guess."

"What floor?"

"Nothing doing, bo. I'm wise. You're the fourth guy with a subpoena that's been after him. Nix."

"I'm not a lawyer's clerk. I'm a reporter, and I want to ask him a few questions."

"Gee! Has that Jane of his been hauling in the newspapers? Good-night! Toddle along, bo; there's nothing coming from me. Nix."

"Would ten dollars make you talk?" asked the reporter, desperately.

"Ye-ah--about the Kaiser and his wood-sawing. By-by!"

The operator, secretly enjoying the reporter's discomfiture, shut off the lights, slammed the elevator door to the latch, and walked to the revolving doors, to the tune of Garry Owen.

The reporter did not follow him but sat down on the first step of the marble stairs to think, for there was a lot to think about. He sensed clearly enough that all this talk about street-railway strikes and subpoenas was rot. The elevator man and the engineer were in cahoots. There was a story here, but how to get to it was a puzzler. He had one chance in a hundred of landing it--tip the mail clerk in the business office to keep an eye open for the man who called for "Double C" mail.

Eventually, the man who did call for that mail presented a card to the mail clerk. At the bottom of this card was the name of the chief of the United States Secret Service.

"And say to the reporter who has probably asked to watch--hands off! Understand? Absolutely--off!"

When the reporter was informed he blew a kiss into air and sought his city editor for his regular assignment. He understood, with the wisdom of his calling, that one didn't go whale fishing with trout rods.

CHAPTER XV

Early the next morning in a bedroom in a rooming house for aliens in Fifteenth Street, a man sat in a chair scanning the want columns of a newspaper. Occasionally he jotted down something on a slip of paper. This man's job was rather an unusual one. He hunted jobs for other men--jobs in steel mills, great factories, in the textile districts, the street-car lines, the shipping yards and docks, any place where there might be a grain or two of the powder of unrest and discontent. His business was to supply the human matches.

No more parading the streets, no more haranguing from soap boxes. The proper place nowadays was in the yard or shop corners at noontime. A word or two dropped at the right moment; perhaps a printed pamphlet; little wedges wherever there were men who wanted something they neither earned nor deserved. Here and there across the land little flares, one running into the other, like wildfire on the plains, and then--the upheaval. As in Russia, so now in Germany; later, England and France and here. The proletariat was gaining power.

He was no fool, this individual. He knew his clay, the day labourer, with his parrotlike mentality. Though the victim of this peculiar potter absorbs sounds he doesn't often absorb meanings. But he takes these sounds and respouts them and convinces himself that he is some kind of Moses, headed for the promised land. Inflammable stuff. Hence, the strikes which puzzle the average intelligent American citizen. What is it all about? Nobody seems to know.

Once upon a time men went on a strike because they were being cheated and abused. Now they strike on the principle that it is excellent policy always to be demanding something; it keeps capitalism where it belongs--on the ragged edge of things. No matter what they demand they never expect to give an equivalent; and a just cause isn't necessary. Thus the present-day agitator has only one perplexity--

that of eluding the iron hand of the Department of Justice.

Suddenly the man in the chair brought the newspaper close up and stared. He jumped to his feet, ran out and up the next flight of stairs. He stopped before a door and turned the knob a certain number of times. Presently the door opened the barest crack; then it was swung wide enough to admit the visitor.

"Look!" he whispered, indicating Cutty's advertisement.

The occupant of the room snatched the newspaper and carried it to a window.

Will purchase the drums of jeopardy at top price. No questions asked. Address this office.

Double C.

"Very good. I might have missed it. We shall sell the accursed drums to this gentleman."

"Sell them? But--"

"Imbecile! What we must do is to find out who this man is. In the end he may lead us to him."

"But it may be a trap!"

"Leave that to me. You have work of your own to do, and you had best be about it. Do you not see beneath? Who but the man who harbours him would know about the drums? The man in the evening clothes. I was too far away to see his face. Get me all the morning newspapers. If the advertisement is in all of them I will send a letter to each. We lost the young woman yesterday. And nothing has been heard of Vladimir and Stemmler. Bad. I do not like this place. I move to the house to-night. My old friend Stefani may be lonesome. I dare not risk daylight. Some fool may have talked. To work! All of us have much to do to wake up the proletariat in this country of the blind. But the hour will come. Get me the newspapers."

Karlov pushed his visitor from the room and locked and bolted the door. He stepped over to the window again and stared down at the clutter of pushcarts, drays, trucks, and human beings that tried to go forward and got forward only by moving sideways or worming through temporary breaches, seldom directly--the way of humanity. But there was no object lesson in this for Karlov, who was not philosophical in the peculiar sense of one who was demanding a reason for everything and finding allegory and comparison and allusion in the ebb and flow of life. The philosophical is often misapplied to the stoical. Karlov was a stoic, not a philosopher, or he would not have been the victim of his present obsession. The idea of live and let live has never been the propaganda of the anarch. To the anarch the death of some body or the destruction of some thing is the cornerstone to his madhouse.

Nothing would ever cure this man of his obsession--the death of Hawksley and the possession of the emeralds. Moreover, there was the fanatical belief in his poor disordered brain that the accomplishment of these two projects would eventually assist in the liberation of mankind. Abnormally cunning in his methods of approach, he lacked those imaginative scales by which we weigh our projects and which we call logic. A child alone in a house with a box of matches; a dog on one side of Fifth Avenue that sees a dog on the other side, but not the automobiles--inexorable logic--irresistible force--whizzing up and down the middle of that thoroughfare. It is not difficult to prophesy what is going to happen to that child, that dog.

Karlov was at this moment reaching out toward a satisfactory solution relative to the disappearance of the gems. They had not been found on his enemy; they had not been found in the Gregor apartment; the two men assigned to the task of securing them would not have risked certain death by trying to do a little bargaining on their own initiative. In the first instance they had come forth empty-handed. In the second instance--that of intimidating the girl to disclose his whereabouts--neither Vladimir nor Stemmler had returned. Sinister. The man in the dress suit again?

Conceivably, then, the drums were in the possession of this girl; and she was holding them against the day when the fugitive would reclaim them. The advertisement was a snare. Very good. Two could play that game as well as one.

The girl. Was it not always so? That breed! God's curse on them all! A crooked finger, and the women followed, hypnotized. The girl was away from the apartment the major part of the day; so it was in order to search her rooms. A pretty little fool.

But where were they hiding him? Gall and wormwood! That he should slip through Boris Karlov's fingers, after all these tortuous windings across the world! Patience. Sooner or later the girl would lead the way. Still, patience was a galling hobble when he had so little time, when even now they might be hunting him.

Boris Karlov had left New York rather well known.

He expanded under this thought. For the spiritual breath of life to the anarch is flattery, attention. Had the newspapers ignored Trotzky's advent into Russia, had they omitted the daily chronicle of his activities, the Russian problem would not be so large as it is this day. Trotzky would have died of chagrin.

He would answer this advertisement. Trap? He would set one himself. The man who eventually came to negotiate would be made a prisoner and forced to disclose the identity of the man who had interfered with the great projects of Boris Karlov, plenipotentiary extraordinary for the red government of Russia.

Midtown, Cutty tapped his breakfast egg dubiously. Not that he speculated upon the freshness of the egg. What troubled him was that advertisement. Last night, keyed high by his remarkable discovery of the identity of his guest and his cupidity relative to the emeralds, he had laid himself open. If he knew anything at all about the craft, that reporter would be digging in. Fortunately he had resources unsuspected by the reporter. Legitimately he could send a secret-service operative to collect the mail--if Karlov decided to negotiate. Still within his rights, he could use another operative to conduct the negotiations. If in the end Karlov strayed into the net the use of the service for private ends would be justified.

Lord, those green stones! Well, why not? Something in the world worth a hazard. What had he in life but this second grand passion? There shot into his mind obliquely an irrelevant question. Supposing, in the old days, he had proceeded to reach for Molly as he was now reaching for the emeralds--a bit lawlessly? After all these years, to have such a thought strike him! Hadn't he stepped aside meekly for Conover? Hadn't he observed and envied Conover's dazzling assault? Supposing Molly had been wavering, and this method of attack had decided her? Never to have thought of that before! What did a woman want? A love storm, and then an endless after-calm. And it had taken him twenty-odd years to make this discovery.

Fact. He had never been shy of women. He had somehow preferred to play comrade instead of gallant; and all the women had taken advantage of that, used him callously to pair with old maids, faded wives, and homely debutantes.

What impellent was driving him toward these introspections? Kitty, Molly's girl. Each time he saw her or thought of her--the uninvited ghost of her mother. Any other man upon seeing Kitty or thinking about her would have jumped into the future from the spring of a dream. The disparity in years would not have mat-tered. It was all nonsense, of course. But for his dropping into the office and casually picking up the thread of his acquaintance with Kitty, Molly--the memory of her--would have gone on dimming. Actions, tremendous and world-wide, had set his vision toward the future; he had been too busy to waste time in retrospection and introspection. Thus, instead of a gently rising and falling tide, healthily recurrent, a flood of mixed longings that was swirling him into uncertain depths. Those emer-alds had bobbed up just in time. The chase would serve to pull him out of this bog.

He heard a footstep and looked up. The nurse was beckoning to him.

"What is it?"

"He's awake, and there is sanity in his eyes."

"Great! Has he talked?"

"No. The awakening happened just this moment, and I came to you. You never can tell about blows on the skull or brain fever--never any two eases alike."

Cutty threw down his napkin and accompanied the nurse to the bedside. The glance of the patient trailed from Cutty to the nurse and back.

"Don't talk," said Cutty. "Don't ask any questions. Take it easy until later in the day. You are in the hands of persons who wish you well. Eat what the nurse gives you. When the right time comes we'll tell you all about ourselves, You've been robbed and beaten. But the men who did it are under arrest."

"One question," said the patient, weakly.

"Well, just one."

"A girl--who gave me something to eat?"

"Yes. She fed you, and later probably your life."

"Thanks." Hawksley closed his eyes.

Cutty and the nurse watched him interestedly for a few minutes; but as he did not stir again the nurse took up her temperature sheet and Cutty returned to his eggs. Was there a girl? No question about the emeralds, no interest in the day and the hour. Was there a girl? The last person he had seen, Kitty; the first question, after coming into the light: Had he seen her? Then and there Cutty knew that when he died he would carry into the Beyond, of all his earthly possessions--a chuckle. Human beings!

The yarn that reporter had missed by a hair--front page, eight-column head!

But he had missed it, and that was the main thing. The poor devil! Beaten and without a sou marque in his pockets, his trail was likely to be crowded without the assistance of any newspaper publicity. But what a yarn! What a whale of a yarn!

In his fevered flights Hawksley had spoken of having paid Kitty for that meal.

Kitty had said nothing about it. Supposing--

"Telephone, sair," announced the Jap. "Lady."

Molly's girl! Cutty sprinted to the telephone.

"Hello! That you, Kitty?"

"Yes. How is Johnny Two-Hawks?"

"Back to earth."

"When can I see him? I'm just crazy to know what the story is!"

"Say the third or fourth day from this. We'll have him shaved and sitting up then."

"Has he talked?"

"Not permitted. Still determined to stay the run of your lease?" Cutty heard a laugh. "All right. Only I hope you will never have cause to regret this decision."

"Fiddlesticks! All I've got to do in danger is to press a button, and presto! here's Bernini."

"Kitty, did Hawksley pay you for that meal?"

"Good heavens, no! What makes you ask that?"

"In his delirium he spoke of having paid you. I didn't know." Cutty's heart began to rap against his ribs. Supposing, after all, Karlov hadn't the stones? Supposing Hawksley had hidden them somewhere in Kitty's kitchen?

"Anything about Gregor?"

"No. Remember, you're to call me up twice a day and report the news. Don't go out nights if you can avoid it."

"I'll be good," Kitty agreed. "And now I must hie me to the job. Imagine, Cutty!--writing personalities about stage folks and gabfesting with Burlingame and all the while my brain boiling with this affair! The city room will kill me, Cutty, if it ever finds out that I held back such a yarn. But it wouldn't be fair to Johnny Two-Hawks. Cutty, did you know that your wonderful drums of jeopardy are here in New York?"

"What?" barked Cutty.

"Somebody is offering to buy them. There was an advertisement in the paper this morning. Cutty?"

"Yes."

"The first problem in arithmetic is two and two make four. By-by!"

Dizzily Cutty hung up the receiver. He had not reckoned on the possibility of Kitty seeing that damfool advertisement. Two and two made four; and four and four made eight; so on indefinitely. That is to say, Kitty already had a glimmer of the startling truth. The initial misstep on his part had been made upon her pronouncement of the name Stefani Gregor. He hadn't been able to control his surprise. And yesterday, having frankly admitted that he knew Gregor, all that was needed to complete the circle was that advertisement. Cutty tore his hair, literally. The very door he hoped she might overlook he had thrown open to her.

Thaddeus of Warsaw. But it should not be. He would continue to offer a haven to that chap; but no nonsense. None of that sinister and unfortunate blood should meddle with Kitty Conover's happiness. Her self-appointed guardian would attend to that.

He realized that his attitude was rather inexplicable; but there were some adventures which hypnotized women; and one of this sort was now unfolding for Kitty. That she had her share of common sense was negligible in face of the facts that she was imaginative and romantical and adventuresome, and that for the first time she was riding one of the great middle currents in human events. She was Molly's girl; Cutty was going to look out for her.

Mighty odd that this fear for her should have sprung into being that night, quite illogically. Prescience? He could not say. Perhaps it was a borrowed instinct--fatherly; the same instinct that would have stirred her father into action--the protection of that dearest to him.

If he told her who Hawksley really was, that would intrigue her. If he made a mystery of the affair, that, too, would intrigue her. And there you were, 'twixt the devil and the deep blue sea. Hang it, what evil luck had stirred him to tell her about those emeralds? Already she was building a story to satisfy her dramatic fancy. Two and two made four--which signified that she was her father's daughter, that she would not rest until she had explored every corner of this dark room. Wanting to keep her out of it, and then dragging her into it through his cupidity. Devil take those emeralds! Always the same; trouble wherever they were.

The real danger would rise during the convalescence. Kitty would be contriving to drop in frequently; not to see Hawksley especially, but her initial success in playing hide and seek with secret agents, friendly and otherwise, had tickled her fancy. For a while it would be an exciting game; then it might become only a means to an end. Well, it should not be.

Was there a girl! Already Hawksley had recorded her beauty. Very well; the first sign of sentimental nonsense, and out he should go, Karlov or no Karlov. Kitty wasn't going to know any hurt in this affair. That much was decided.

Cutty stormed into his study, growling audibly. He filled a pipe and smoked savagely. Another side, Kitty's entrance into the drama promised to spoil his own fun; he would have to play two games instead of one. A fine muddle!

He came to a stand before one of the windows and saw the glory of the morning flashing from the myriad spires and towers and roofs, and wondered why artists bothered about cows in pastures.

Touching his knees was an antique Florentine bridal chest, with exquisite carving and massive lock. He threw back the lid and disclosed a miscellany never seen by any eye save his own. It was all the garret he had. He dug into it and at length resurrected the photograph of a woman whose face was both roguish and beautiful. He sat on the floor a la Turk and studied the face, his own tender and wistful. No resemblance to Kitty except in the eyes. How often he had gone to her with the question burning his lips, only to carry it away unspoken! He turned over the photograph and read: "To the nicest man I know. With love from Molly." With love. And he had stepped aside for Tommy Conover!

By George! He dropped the photograph into the chest, let down the lid, and rose to his feet. Not a bad idea, that. To intrigue Kitty himself, to smother her with attentions and gallantries, to give her out of his wide experience, and to play the game until this intruder was on his way elsewhere.

He could do it; and he based his assurance upon his experiences and observations. Never a squire of dames, he knew the part. He had played the game occasionally in the capitals of Europe when there had been some information he had particularly desired. Clever, scheming women, too. A clever, passably good-looking elderly man could make himself peculiarly attractive to young women and women in the thirties. Dazzlement for the young; the man who knew all about life, the trivial little courtesies a younger man generally forgot; the moving of chairs, the holding of wraps; the gray hairs which served to invite trust and confidence, which lulled the eternal feminine fear of the male. To the older women, no callow youth but a man of discernment, discretion, wit and fancy and daring, who remembered birthdays husbands forgot, who was always round when wanted.

There was no vanity back of these premises. Cutty was merely reaching about for an expedient to thwart what to his anticipatory mind promised to be an inevitability. Of course the glamour would not last; it never did, but he felt he could sustain it until yonder chap was off and away.

That evening at five-thirty Kitty received a box of beautiful roses, with Cutty's card.

"Oh, the lovely things!" she cried.

She kissed them and set them in a big copper jug, arranged and rearranged them for the simple pleasure it afforded her. What a dear man this Cutty was, to have thought of her in this fashion! Her father's friend, her mother's, and now hers; she had inherited him. This thought caused her to smile, but there were tears in her eyes. A garden some day to play in, this mad city far away, a home of her own; would it ever happen?

The bell rang. She wasn't going to like this caller for taking her away from these roses, the first she had received in a long time--roses she could keep and not toss out the window. For it must not be understood that Kitty was never besieged.

Outside stood a well-dressed gentleman, older than Cutty, with shrewd, inquiring gray eyes and a face with strong salients.

"Pardon me, but I am looking for a man by the name of Stephen Gregory. I was referred by the janitor to you. You are Miss Conover?"

"Yes," answered Kitty. "Will you come in?" She ushered the stranger into the living room and indicated a chair. "Please excuse me for a moment." Kitty went into her bedroom and touched the danger button, which would summon Bernini. She wanted her watchdog to see the visitor. She returned to the living room. "What is it you wish to know?"

"Where I may find this Gregory."

"That nobody seems able to answer. He was carried away from here in an ambulance; but we have been unable to locate the hospital. If you will leave your name--"

"That is not necessary. I am out of bounds, you might say, and I'd rather my name should be left out of the affair, which is rather peculiar."

"In what way?"

"I am only an agent, and am not at liberty to speak. Could you describe Gregory?"

"Then he is a stranger to you?"

"Absolutely."

Kitty described Gregor deliberately and at length. It struck her that the visitor was becoming bored, though he nodded at times. She was glad to hear Bernini's ring. She excused herself to admit the Italian.

"A false alarm," she whispered. "Someone inquiring for Gregor. I thought it might be well for you to see him."

"I'll work the radiator stuff."

"Very well."

Bernini went into the living room and fussed over the steam cock of the radiator.

"Nothing the matter with it, miss. Just stuck."

"Sorry to have troubled you," said the stranger, rising and picking up his hat.

Bernini went down to the basement, obfuscated; for he knew the visitor. He was one of the greatest bankers in New York--that is to say, in America! Asking questions about Stefani Gregor!

CHAPTER XVI

A bout nine o'clock that same night a certain rich man, having established himself comfortably under the reading lamp, a fine book in his hands and a fine after-dinner cigar between his teeth, was exceedingly resentful when his butler knocked, entered, and presented a card.

"My orders were that I was not at home to any one."

"Yes, sir. But he said you would see him because he came to see you regarding a Mr. Gregory."

"What?"

"Yes, sir."

"Damn these newspapers!... Wait, wait!" the banker called, for the butler was starting for the door to carry the anathema to the appointed head. "Bring him in. He's a big bug, and I can't afford to affront him."

"Yes, sir"--with the colourless tone of a perfect servant.

When the visitor entered he stopped just beyond the threshold. He remained there even after the butler closed the door. Blue eye and gray clashed; two masters of fence who had executed the same stroke. The banker laughed and Cutty smiled.

"I suppose," said the banker, "you and I ought to sign an armistice, too."

"Agreed."

"And you've always been rather a puzzle to me. A rich man, a gentleman, and yet sticking to the newspaper game."

"And you're a puzzle to me, too. A rich man, a gentleman, and yet sticking to the banking game."

"What the devil was our row about?"

"Can't quite recall."

"Whatever it was it was the way you went at it."

"A reform was never yet accomplished by purring and pussyfooting," said Cutty.

"Come over and sit down. Now, how the devil did you find out about this Gregory affair?" The banker held out his hand, which Cutty grasped with honest pressure. "If you are here in the capacity of a newspaper man, not a word out of me. Have a cigar?"

"I never smoke anything but pipes that ruin curtains. You should have given your name to Miss Conover."

"I was under promise not to explain my business. But before we proceed, an answer. Newspaper?"

"No. I represent the Department of Justice. And we'll get along easier when I add that I possess rather unlimited powers under that head. How did you happen to stumble into this affair?"

"Through Captain Rathbone, my prospective son-in-law, who is in Coblenz. A cable arrived this morning, instructing me to proceed precisely in the manner I did. Rathbone is an intimate friend of the man I was actually seeking. The apartment of this man Gregory was mentioned to Rathbone in a cable as a possible temporary abiding place. What do you want to know?"

"Whether or not he is undesirable."

"Decidedly, I should say, desirable."

"You make that statement as an American citizen?"

"I do. I make it unreservedly because my future son-in-law is rather a difficult man to make friends with. I am acting merely as Rathbone's agent. On the other hand, I should be a cheerful liar if I told you I wasn't interested. What do you know?"

"Everything," answered Cutty, quietly.

"You know where this young man is?"

"At this moment he is in my apartment, rather seriously battered and absolutely penniless."

"Well, I'll be tinker-dammed! You know who he is, of course?"

"Yes. And I want all your information so that I may guide my future actions accordingly. If he is really undesirable he shall be deported the moment he can stand on his two feet."

The banker pyramided his fingers, rather pleased to learn that he could astonish this interesting beggar. "He has on account at my bank half a million dollars. Originally he had eight hundred thousand. The three hundred thousand, under cable orders from Yokohama, was transferred to our branch in San Francisco. This was withdrawn about two weeks ago. How does that strike you?"

"All in a heap," confessed Cutty. "When was this fund established with you?"

"Shortly before Kerensky's government blew up. The funds were in our London bank. There was, of course, a lot of red tape, excessive charges in exchange, and all that. Anyhow, about eight hundred thousand arrived."

"What brought him to America? Why didn't he go to England? That would have been the safest haven."

"I can explain that. He intends to become an American citizen. Some time ago he became the owner of a fine cattle ranch in Montana."

"Well, I'll be tinker-dammed, too!" exploded Cutty.

"A young man with these ideas in his head ought eventually to become a first-rate citizen. What do you say?"

"I am considerably relieved. His forbears, the blood--"

"His mother was a healthy Italian peasant--a famous singer in her time. His fortune, I take it, was his inheritance from her. She made a fortune singing in the capitals of Europe and speculating from time to time. She sent the boy, at the age of ten, to England. Afraid of the home influence. He remained there, under the name of Hawksley, for something like fourteen years, under the guardianship of this fellow Gregory. Of Gregory I know positively nothing. The young fellow is, to all purposes, methods of living, points of view, an Englishman. Rathbone, who was educated at Oxford, met him there and they shared quarters. But it was only in recent years that he learned the identity of his friend. In 1914 the young fellow returned to Russia. Military obligations. That's all I know. Mighty interesting, though."

"I am much obliged to you. The white elephant becomes a normal drab pachyderm," said Cutty.

"Still something of an elephant on your hands. I see. Bring him here if you wish."

"And sic the Bolshevik at your door."

"That's so. You spoke of his having been beaten and robbed. Bolshevik?"

"Yes. An old line of reasoning first put into effect by Oliver Cromwell. The axe."

"The poor devil!"

"Fact. I'm sorry for him, but I wish he would blow away conveniently."

"Rathbone says he's handsome, gay, but decent, considering. Humanity is being knocked about some. The hour has come for our lawyers to go back to their offices. Politics must step aside for business. We ought to hang up signs in every state capitol in the country: 'Men Wanted--Specialists.' A steel man from Pittsburgh, a mining man from Idaho, a shipowner from Boston, a meat packer from Omaha, a grain man from Chicago. What the devil do lawyers know about these things--the energies that make the wheels of this country go round? By the way, that Miss Conover was a remarkably pretty girl. She seemed to be a bit suspicious of me."

"Good reasons. That chap went to Gregor's--Gregor is his name--and was beaten, robbed, and left for dead. She saved his life."

"Good Lord! Does she know?"

"No. And what's more, I don't want her to. I am practically her guardian."

"Then you ought to get her out of that roost."

"Hang it, I can't get her to leave. I'm not legally her guardian; self-appointed. But she has agreed to leave in May."

"I'm glad you dropped in. Command me in any way you please."

"That's very good of you, considering."

"The war is over. We'd be a fine pair of fools to let an ancient grudge go on. They tell me you've a wonderful apartment on top of that skyscraper of yours."

"Will you come to dinner some night?"

"Any time you say. I should like to bring my daughter."

"She doesn't know?"

"No. Heard of Hawksley; thinks he's English."

"I am certainly agreeable." This would be a distinct advantage to Kitty. "I see you have a good book there. I'll take myself off."

In the Avenue Cutty loaded his pipe. He struck a match on the flagstone and cupped it over the bowl of his pipe, thereby throwing his picturesque countenance into ruddy relief. Opposite emotions filled the hearts of the two men watching him--in one, chagrin; in the other, exultation.

Cutty decided to walk downtown, the night being fine. He set his foot to a long, swinging stride. An elephant on his hands, truly. Poor devil, for a fad! Nobody wanted him, not even those who wished him well. Wanted to become an American citizen. He would have been tolerably safe in England. Here he would never be free of danger. A ranch. The beggar would have a chance out there in the West. The anarchist and the Bolshevik were town cooties. His one chance, actually. The poor devil! Kitty had the right idea. It was a mighty fine thing, these times, to be a citizen under the protection of the American doctrine.

Three hundred thousand! And Karlov had got that along with the drums. The devil's own for luck! The fool would be able to start some fine ructions with all that capital behind him. Episodes in the night.

Kitty dreamed of wonderful rose gardens, endless and changing; but strive as she would she could not find Cutty anywhere, which worried her, even in her dream.

The nurse heard the patient utter a single word several times before he fell asleep.

"What is it?" she asked.

"Fan!" And he smiled.

She hunted for the palm leaf, but with a slight gesture he signified that that was not what he wanted.

Cutty played solitaire with his chrysoprase until the telephone broke in upon his reveries. What he heard over the wire disturbed him greatly.

"You were followed from the Avenue to the apartment."

"How do you know?"

"I am Henderson. You assigned me to watch the apartment in Eightieth through the night. I followed the man who followed you. He saw your face when you lit the pipe. When the banker left Miss Conover he was followed home. That established him in the affair. The follower hung round, and so did I. You appeared. He took a chance shot in the dark. Not sure, but doing a bit of clever guessing."

"You still followed him?"

"Yes."

"Where did he wind up?"

"A house in the warehouse district. Vacant warehouses on each side. Some new nest. I can lead you to it, sir, any time you wish."

"Thanks."

Cutty pushed aside the telephone and returned to his green stones. After all, why worry? It was unfortunate, of course, but the apartment was more inaccessible than the top of the Matterhorn. Still, they might discover what his real business was and interfere seriously with his future work on the other side. A ruin in the warehouse district? A good place to look for Stefani Gregor--if he were still alive.

He was. And in his dark room he cried piteously for water--water--water!

CHAPTER XVII

A March day, sunny and cloudless, with fresh, bracing winds. Green things pushed up from the soil; an eternal something was happening to the tips of the tree branches; an eternal something was happening in young hearts. A robin shook the dust of travel from his wings and bathed publicly in a park basin.

Here and there under the ten thousand roofs of the great city poets were busy with inkpots, trying to say an old thing in a new way. Woe to the pinched soul that did not expand this day, for it was spring. Expansion! Nature--perhaps she was relenting a little, perhaps she saw that humanity was sliding down the scale, withering, and a bit of extra sunshine would serve to check the descension and breed a little optimism.

Cutty's study. The sunlight, thrown westward, turned windows and roofs and towers into incomparable bijoux. The double reflection cast a white light into the room, lifting out the blue and old-rose tints of the Ispahan rug.

Cutty shifted the chrysoprase, irresolutely for him. A dozen problems, and it was mighty hard to decide which to tackle first. Principally there was Kitty. He had not seen her in four days, deeming it advisable for her not to call for the present. The Bolshevik agent who had followed him from the banker's might decide, without the aid of some connecting episode, that he had wasted his time.

It did not matter that Kitty herself was no longer watched and followed from her home to the office, from the office home. Was Karlov afraid or had he some new trick up his sleeve? It was not possible that he had given up Hawksley. He was probably planning an attack from some unexpected angle. To be sure that Karlov would not find reason to associate him with Kitty, Cutty had remained indoors during the daytime and gone forth at night in his dungarees.

Problem Two was quite as formidable. The secret agent who had passed as a negotiator for the drums of jeopardy had disappeared. That had sinister significance. Karlov did not intend to sell the drums; merely wanted precise information regarding the man who had advertised for them. If the secret-service man weakened under torture, Cutty recognized that his own usefulness would be at an end. He would have to step aside and let the great currents sweep on without him. In that event these fifty-two years would pile upon his head, full measure; for the only thing that kept him vigorous was action, interest. Without some great incentive he would shrivel up and blow away--like some exhumed mummy.

Problem Three. How the deuce was he going to fascinate Kitty if he couldn't see her? But there was a bit of silver lining here. If he couldn't see her, what chance had Hawksley? The whole sense and prompting of this problem was to keep Kitty and Hawksley apart. How this was accomplished was of no vital importance. Problem Three, then, hung fire for the present. Funny, how this idea stuck in his head, that Hawksley was a menace to Kitty. One of those fool ideas, probably, but worth trying out.

Problem Four. That night, all on his own, he would make an attempt to enter that old house sandwiched between the two vacant warehouses. Through pressure of authority he had obtained keys to both warehouses. There would be a trap on the roof of that house. Doubtless it would be covered with tin; fairly impregnable if latched below. But he could find out. From the third-floor windows of either warehouse the drop was not more than six feet. If anywhere in town poor old Stefani Gregor would be in one of those rooms. But to storm the house frontally, without being absolutely sure, would be folly. Gregor would be killed. The house was in fact an insane asylum, occupied by super-insane men. Warned, they were capable of blowing the house to kingdom come, themselves with it.

Problem Five was a mere vanishing point. He doubted if he would ever see those emeralds. What an infernal pity!

He built a coronet and leaned back, a wisp of smoke darting up from the bowl of his pipe.

"I say, you know, but that's a ripping game to play!" drawled a tired voice over his shoulder.

Cutty turned his head, to behold Hawksley, shaven, pale, and handsome, wrapped in a bed quilt and swaying slightly.

"What the deuce are you doing out of your room?" growled Cutty, but with the growl of a friendly dog.

Hawksley dropped into a chair weakly. "End of my rope. Got to talk to someone. Go dotty, else. Questions. Skull aches with 'em. Want to know whether this is a foretaste of the life I have a right to live--or the beginning of death. Be a good sport, and let's have it out."

"What is it you wish to know?" asked Cutty, gently. The poor beggar!

"Where I am. Who you are. What happened to me. What is going to happen to me," rather breathlessly. "Don't want any more suspense. Don't want to look over my shoulder any more. Straight ahead. All the cards on the table, please."

Cutty rose and pushed the invalid's chair to a window and drew another up beside it.

"My word, the top of the world! Bally odd roost."

"You will find it safer here than you would on the shores of Kaspuskoi More," replied Cutty, gravely. "The Caspian wouldn't be a healthy place for you now."

With wide eyes Hawksley stared across the shining, wavering roofs. A pause. "What do you know?" he asked, faintly.

"Everything. But wait!" Cutty fetched one of the photographs and laid it upon the young man's knees. "Know who this is--Two-Hawks?"

A strained, tense gesture as Hawksley seized the photograph; then his chin sank slowly to his chest. A moment later Cutty was profoundly astonished to see something sparkle on its way down the bed quilt. Tears!

"I'm sorry!" cried Cutty, troubled and embarrassed. "I'm terribly sorry! I should have had the decency to wait a day or two."

"On the contrary, thank you!" Hawksley flung up his head. "Nothing in all God's muddied world could be more timely--the face of my mother! I am not ashamed of these tears. I am not afraid to die. I am not even afraid to live. But all the things I loved--the familiar earth, the human beings, my dog--gone. I am alone."

"I'm sorry," repeated Cutty, a bit choked up. This was honest misery and it affected him deeply. He felt himself singularly drawn.

"I want to live. Because I am young? No. I want to prove to the shades of those who loved me that I am fit to go on. So my identity is known to you?"--dejectedly.

"Yes. You wish me to forget what I know?"

"Will you?"--eagerly. "Will you forget that I am anything but a naked, friend-less human being?"

"Yes. But your enemies know."

"I rather fancy they will keep the truth to themselves. Let them publish my identity, and a hundred havens would be offered. Your Government would protect me."

"It is doing so now, indirectly. But why do you not want it known?"

"Freedom! Would I have it if known? Could I trust anybody? Would it not be essentially the old life in a new land? I want a new life in a new land. I want to be born again. I want to be what you patently are, an American. That is why I risked life a hundred times in coming all these miles, why I sit in this chair before you, with the room rocking because they battered in my head. I do not offer a human wreck, an illiterate mind, in exchange for citizenship. I bring a tolerably decent manhood. Try me! Always I have admired you people. Always we Russians have. But there is no Russia now that I can ever return to!" Hawksley's head drooped again and his bloodshot eyes closed.

Cutty sensed confusion, indecision; all his deductions were upset in the face of this strange appeal. Russian, born of an Italian mother and speaking Oxford English as if it were his birthright; and wanting citizenship! Wasn't ashamed of his tears; wasn't afraid to die or to live! Cutty searched quickly for a new handhold to his antagonism, but he found only straws. He was honest enough to realize that he had built this antagonism upon a want, a desire; there was no foundation for it. Down-right likeable. A chap who had gone through so much, who was in such a pitiable condition, would not have the wit to manufacture character, camouflage his soul.

"Hang it!" he said, briskly. "You shall have your chance. Talk like that will carry a man anywhere in this country. You shall stay here until you are strong again. Then some night I'll put you on your train for Montana. You want to ask questions. I'll save you the trouble by telling you what I know."

But his narrative contained no mention of the emeralds. Why? A bit conscience-stricken because, if he could, he was going to rob his guest on the basis that findings is keepings? Cutty wasn't ready to analyze the omission. Perhaps he wanted Hawksley himself to inquire about the stones; test him out. If he asked frankly that would signify that he had brought the stones in honestly, paid his obligations to the Customs. Otherwise, smuggling; and in that event conscience wouldn't matter; the emeralds became a game anybody could take a hand in--anybody who considered the United States Customs an infringement upon human rights.

What a devil of a call those stones had for him! Did they mean anything to Hawksley aside from their intrinsic value? But for the nebulous idea, originally, that the emeralds were mixed up somewhere in this adventure, Cutty knew that he would have sent Hawksley to a hospital, left him to his fate, and never known who he was.

All through the narration Hawksley listened motionless, with his eyes closed, possibly to keep the wavering instability of the walls from interfering with his assimilation of this astonishing series of fact.

"Found you insensible on the floor," concluded Cutty, "hoisted you to my shoulders, took you to the street--and here you are!"

Hawksley opened his eyes. "I say, you know, what a devil of an old Sherlock you must be! And you carried me on your shoulders across that fire escape? Ripping! When I stepped back into that room I heard a rushing sound. I knew! But I didn't have the least chance.... You and that bully girl!"

Cutty swore under his breath. He had taken particular pains to avoid mentioning Kitty; and here, first off, the fat was in the fire. He remembered now that he had told Hawksley that Kitty had saved his life. Fortunately, the chap wasn't keen enough with that banged-up head of his to apply reason to the omission.

"Saved my life. Suppose she doesn't want me to know."

Cutty jumped at this. "Doesn't care to be mixed up with the Bolshevik end of it. Besides, she doesn't know who you are."

"The fewer that know the better. But I'll always remember her kindness and that bally pistol with the fan in it. But you? Why did you bother to bring me up here?"

"Couldn't decently leave you where Karlov could get to you again."

"Is Stefani Gregor dead?"

"Don't know; probably not. But we are hunting for him." Cutty had not explained his interest in Gregor. Those plaguey stones again. They were demoralizing him. Loot.

"You spoke of Karlov. Who is he?"

"Why, the man who followed you across half the world."

"There were many. What is he like?"

"A gorilla."

"Ah!" Hawksley became galvanized and extended his fists. "God let me live long enough to put my hands on him! I had the chance the other day--to blot out his face with my boots! But I couldn't do it! I couldn't do it!" He sagged in the chair. "No, no! Just a bit groggy. All right in a moment."

"By the Lord Harry, I'll see you through. Now buck up. Hear that?" cried Cutty, throwing up a window.

"Music."

"Look through that street there. See the glint of bayonets? American soldiers, marching up Fifth Avenue, thousands of them, freemen who broke the vaunted Hindenburg Line. God bless 'em! Americans, every mother's son of 'em; who went away laughing, who returned laughing, who will go back to their jobs laughing. The ability to laugh, that's America. Do you know how to laugh?"

"I used to. I'm jolly weak just now. But I'll grin if you want me to." And Hawksley grinned.

"That's the way. A grin in this country will take you quite as far. All right. In five years you'll be voting. I'll see to that. Now back to bed with you, and no more leaving it until the nurse says so. What you need is rest."

Cutty sent a call to the nurse, who was standing undecidedly in the doorway; and together they put the derelict back to bed. Then Cutty fetched the photograph and set it on top of the dresser, where Hawksley could see it.

"Now, no more gallivanting about."

"I promise, old top. This bed is a little bit of all right. I say!"

"What?"

"How long am I to be here?"

"If you're good, two weeks," interposed the nurse.

"Two weeks? I say, would you mind doing me a trifling favour? I'd like a violin to amuse myself with."

"A fiddle? I don't know a thing about 'em except that they sound good." Cutty pulled at his chin.

"Whatever it costs I'll reimburse you the day I'm up."

"All right. I'll bring you a bundle of them, and you can do your own selecting."

Out in the corridor the nurse said: "I couldn't hold him. But he'll be easier now that he's got the questions off his mind. He will have to be humoured a lot. That's one of the characteristics of head wounds."

"What do you think of him?"

"He seems to be gentle and patient; and I imagine he's hard to resist when he wants anything. Winning, you'd call it. I suppose I mustn't ask who he really is?"

"No. Poor devil. The fewer that know, the better. I'll be home round three."

Once in the street, Cutty was besieged suddenly with the irresistible desire to mingle with the crowd over in the Avenue, to hear the military bands, the shouts, to witness the gamut of emotions which he knew would attend this epochal day. Of course he would view it all from the aloof vantage of the historian, and store away commentaries against future needs.

And what a crowd it was! He was elbowed and pushed, jostled and trod on, carried into the surges, relegated to the eddies; and always the metallic taptap of steel-shod boots on the asphalt, the bayonets throwing back the radiant sunshine in sharp, clear flashes. The keen, joyous faces of those boys. God, to be young like that! To have come through that hell on earth with the ability still to smile! Cutty felt the tears running down his cheeks. Instinctively he knew that this was to be his last thrill of this order. He was fifty-two.

"Quit your crowding there!" barked a voice under his chin.

"Sorry, but it's those behind me," said Cutty, looking down into a florid countenance with a raggedy gray moustache and a pair of blue eyes that were blinking.

"I'm so damned short I can't see anything!"

"Neither can I."

"You could if you wiped your eyes."

"You're crying yourself," declared Cutty.

"Blinking jackass! Got anybody out there?"

"All of 'em."

"I get you, old son of a gun! No flesh and blood, but they're ours all the same. Couple of old fools; huh?"

"Sure pop! What right have two old codgers got here, anyhow? What brought you out?"

"What brought you?"

"Same thing."

"Damn it! If I could only see something!"

Cutty put his hands upon the shoulders of this chance acquaintance and propelled him toward the curb. There were cries of protest, curses, catcalls, but Cutty bored on ahead until he got his man where he could see the tin hats, the bayonets, and the colours; and thus they stood for a full hour. Each time the flag went by the little man yanked off his derby and turned truculently to see that Cutty did the same.

"Say," he said as they finally dropped back, "I'd offer to buy a drink, only it sounds flat."

"And it would taste flat after a mighty wine like this," replied Cutty. "Maybe you've heard of the nectar of the gods. Well, you've just drunk it, my friend."

"I sure have. Those kids out there, smiling after all that hell; and you and me on the sidewalk, blubbering over 'em! What's the answer? We're Americans!"

"You said it. Good-bye."

Cutty pressed on to the flow and went along with it, lighter in the heart than he had been in many a day. These two million who lined Fifth Avenue, who cheered, laughed, wept, went silent, cheered again, what did their presence here signify? That America's day had come; that as a people they were homogeneous at last; that that which laws had failed to bring forth had been accomplished by an ideal.

Bolshevism, socialism--call it what you will--would beat itself into fragments against this Rock of Democracy, which went down to the centre of the world and whose pinnacle touched the stars. Reincarnation; the simple ideals of the forefathers restored. And with this knowledge tingling in his thoughts--and perhaps there was a bit of spring in his heart--Cutty continued on, without destination, chin jutting, eyes shining. He was an American!

He might have continued on indefinitely had he not seen obliquely a window filled with musical instruments.

Hawksley's fiddle! He had all but forgotten. All right. If the poor beggar wanted to scrape a fiddle, scrape it he should. The least he, Cutty, could do would be to accede to any and every whim Hawksley expressed. Wasn't he planning to rob the beggar of the drums, happen they ever turned up? But how the deuce to pick out a fiddle which would have a tune in it? Of all the hypercritical duffers the fiddler was the worst. Beside a fiddler of the first rank the rich old maid with the poodle was a hail fellow well met.

Of course Gregor had taught the chap. That meant he would know instantly; just as his host would instantly observe the difference between green glass and green beryl.

Cutty turned into the shop, infinitely amused. Fiddles! What next? Having constituted a guardianship over Kitty, he was now playing impressario to Hawksley. As if he hadn't enough parts to play! Wouldn't he be risking his life to-night trying to find where Stefani Gregor was? Fiddles! Fiddles and emeralds! What a choice old hypocrite he was!

Fate has a way of telling you all about it--afterward; conceivably, that humanity might continue to reproduce its species. Otherwise humanity would proceed to extinguish itself forthwith. Thus, Cutty was totally unaware upon entering the shop that he was about to tear off its hinges the door he was so carefully bolting and latching and padlocking between Kitty Conover and this duffer who wanted to fiddle his way through convalescence.

Where there is fiddling there is generally dancing. If it be not the feet, then it will be the soul.

CHAPTER XVIII

There are some men who know a little about all things and a great deal about many. Such a man was Cutty. But as he approached the counter behind which stood an expectant clerk he felt for once that he was in a far country. There were fiddles and fiddles, just as there were emeralds and emeralds. Never again would he laugh over the story of the man who thought Botticelli was a manufacturer of spool thread. He attacked the problem, however, like the thoroughbred he was--frankly.

"I want to buy a violin," he began, knowing that in polite musical circles the word fiddle was taboo. "I know absolutely nothing at all about quality or price. Understand, though, while you might be able to fool me, you wouldn't fool the man I'm buying it for. Now what would you suggest?"

The clerk--a salesman familiar with certain urban types, thinly including the Fifth Avenue, which came in for talking-machine records--recognized in this well-dressed, attractive elderly man that which he designated the swell. Hateful word, yes, but having a perfectly legitimate niche, since in the minds of the hoi polloi it nicely describes the differences between the poor gentleman and the gentleman of leisure. To proceed with the digression, to no one is the word more hateful than to the individual to whom it is applied. Cutty would have blushed at the clerk's thought.

"Perhaps I'd better get the proprietor," was the clerk's suggestion.

"Good idea," Cutty agreed. "Take my card along with you." This was a Fifth Avenue shop, and Cutty knew there would be a Who's Who or a Bradstreet somewhere about.

In the interim he inspected the case-lined walls. Trombones. He chuckled. Lucky that Hawksley's talent didn't extend in this direction. True, he himself collected drums, but he did not play them. Something odd about music; human beings had to have it, the very lowest in the scale. A universal magic. He was himself very fond of good music; but these days he fought shy of it; it had the faculty of sweeping him back into the twenties and reincarnating vanished dreams.

After a certain length of time, from the corner of his eye he saw the clerk returning with the proprietor, the latter wearing an amiable smile, which probably connoted a delving into the aforesaid volumes of attainment and worth. Cutty hoped this was so, as it would obviate the necessity of going into details as to who he was and what he had.

"Your name is familiar to me," began the proprietor. "You collect antique drums. My clerk tells me that you wish to purchase a good violin."

"Very good. I have in my apartment rather a distinguished guest who plays the violin for his own amusement. He is ill and cannot select for himself. Now I know a little about music but nothing about violins."

"I suggest that I personally carry half a dozen instruments to your apartment and let your guest try them. How much is he willing to pay?"

"Top price, I should say. Shall I make a deposit?"

"If you don't mind. Merely precautionary. Half a dozen violins will represent quite a sum of money; and taxicabs are unreliable animals. A thousand against accidents. What time shall I call?" The proprietor's curiosity was stirred. Musical celebrities, as he had occasion to know, were always popping up in queer places. Some new star probably, whose violin had been broken and who did not care to appear in public before the hour of his debut.

"Three o'clock," said Cutty.

"Very well, sir. I promise to bring the violins myself."

Cutty wrote out his check for a thousand and departed, the chuckle still going on inside of him. Versatile old codger, wasn't he?

Promptly at three the dealer arrived, his arms and his hands gripping violin cases. Cutty hurried to his assistance, accepted a part of the load, and beckoned to the man to follow him. The cases were placed on the floor, and the dealer opened them, putting the rosin on a single bow.

Hawksley, a fresh bandage on his head, his shoulders propped by pillows, eyed the initial manoeuvres with frank amusement.

"I say, you know, would you mind tuning them for me? I'm not top hole."

The dealer's eyebrows went up. An Englishman? Bewildered, he bent to the trifling labour of tuning the violins. Hawksley rejected the first two instruments after thrumming the strings with his thumb. He struck up a melody on the third but did not finish it.

"My word! If you have a violin there why not let me have it at once?"

The dealer flushed. "Try this, sir. But I do not promise you that I shall sell it."

"Ah!" Hawksley stretched out his hands to receive the instrument.

Of course Cutty had heard of Amati and Stradivari, master and pupil. He knew that all famous violinists possessed instruments of these schools, and that such violins were practically beyond the reach of many. Only through some great artist's death or misfortune did a fine violin return to the marts. But the rejected fiddles had sounded musically enough for him and looked as if they were well up in the society of select fiddles. The fiddle Hawksley now held in his hands was dull, almost black. The maple neck was worn to a shabby gray and the varnish had been sweated off the chin rest.

Hawksley laid his fingers on the strings and drew the bow with a powerful flourishing sweep. The rich, sonorous tones vibrated after the bow had passed. Then followed the tricks by which an artist seeks to discover flaws or wolf notes. A beatific expression settled upon Hawksley face. He nestled the violin comfortably under his chin and began to play softly. Cutty, the nurse, and the dealer became images.

Minors; a bit of a dance; more minors; nothing really begun, nothing really finished--sketches, with a melancholy note running through them all. While that pouring into his ears enchained his body it stirred recollections in Cutty's mind: The fair at Novgorod; the fiddling mountebanks; Russian.

Perhaps the dealer's astonishment was greatest. An Englishman! Who ever heard of an Englishman playing a violin like that?

"I will buy it," said Hawksley, sinking back.

"Sir," began the dealer, "I am horribly embarrassed. I cannot sell that violin because it isn't mine. It is an Amati worth ten thousand dollars."

"I will give you twelve."

"But, sir--"

"Name a price," interrupted Hawksley, rather imperiously. "I want it."

Cutty understood that he was witnessing a flash of the ancient blood. To want anything was to have it.

"I repeat, sir, I cannot sell it. It belongs to a Hungarian who is now in Hungary. I loaned him fifteen hundred and took the Amati as security. Until I learn if he is dead I cannot dispose of the violin. I am sorry. But because you are a real artist, sir, I will loan it to you if you will make a deposit of ten thousand against any possible accident, and that upon demand you will return the instrument to me."

"That's fair enough," interposed Cutty.

"I beg pardon," said Hawksley. "I agree. I want it, but not at the price of any one's dishonesty."

He turned his head toward Cutty, "You're a thoroughbred, sir. This will do more to bring me round than all the doctors in the world."

"But what the deuce is the difference?" Cutty demanded with a gesture toward the rejected violins.

The dealer and Hawksley exchanged smiles. Said the latter: "The other violins are pretty wooden boxes with tolerable tunes in their insides. This has a soul." He put the violin against his cheek again.

Massenet's "Elegie," Moszkowski's "Serenata," a transcription, and then the aria from Lucia. Not compositions professional violinists would have selected. Cutty felt his spine grow cold as this aria poured goldenly toward heaven. He understood. Hawksley was telling him that the shade of his glorious mother was in this room. The boy was right. Some fiddles had souls. An odd depression bore down upon him. Perhaps this surprising music, topping his great emotions of the morning, was a straw too much. There were certain exaltations that could not be sustained.

A whimsical forecast: This chap here, in the dingy parlour of his Montana ranch, playing these indescribable melodies to the stars, his cowmen outside wondering what was the matter with their "inards." Somehow this picture lightened the depression.

"My fingers are stiff," said Hawksley. "My hand is tired. I should like to be alone." He lay back rather inertly.

In the corridor Cutty whispered to the dealer: "What do you think of him?"

"As he says, his touch shows a little stiffness, but the wonderful fire is there. He's an amateur, but a fine one. Practice will bring him to a finish in no time. But I never heard an Englishman play a violin like that before."

"Nor I," Cutty agreed. "When the owner sends for that fiddle let me know. Mr. Hawksley might like to dicker for it. If you know where the owner is you might cable that you have an offer of twelve thousand."

"I'm sorry, but I haven't the least idea where the owner is. However, there is an understanding that if the loan isn't covered in eighteen months the instrument becomes salable for my own protection. There is a year still to run."

Four o'clock found Cutty pacing his study, the room blue with smoke. Of all the queer chaps he had met in his varied career this Two-Hawks topped the lot. The constant internal turmoil that must be going on, the instincts of the blood--artist and autocrat! And in the end, the owner of a cattle ranch, if he had the luck to get there alive! Dizzy old world.

Something else happened at four o'clock. A policeman strolled into Eightieth Street. He was at peace with the world. Spring was in his whistle, in his stride, in the twirl of his baton. Whenever he passed a shop window he made it serve as a mirror. No waistline yet--a comforting thought.

Children swarmed the street and gathered at corners. The older ones played boldly in midstreet, while the toddlers invented games that kept them to the sidewalk and curb. The policeman came stealthily upon one of these latter groups--Italians. At the sight of his brass buttons they fled precipitately. He laughed. Once in a month of moons he was able to get near enough to touch them. Natural. Hadn't he himself hiked in the old days at the sight of a copper? Sure, he had.

A bit of colour on the sidewalk attracted his eye, and he picked up the object. Something those kids had been playing with. A bit of red glass out of a piece of cheap jewellery. Not half bad for a fake. He would put one over on Maggie when he turned in for supper. Certainly this was the age of imitation. You couldn't buy a brass button with any confidence. He put the trinket in his pocket and continued on, soon to forget it.

At six he was off duty. As he was leaving the precinct the desk sergeant called him back.

"Got change for a dollar, an' I'll settle that pinochle debt," offered the sergeant.

"I'll take a look." The policeman emptied his coin pocket.

"What's that yuh got there?"

"Which?"

"The red stone?"

"Oh, that? Picked it up on the sidewalk. Some Italian kids dropped it as they skedaddled."

"Let's have a look."

"Sure." The policeman passed over the stone.

"Gee! That looks like real money. Say, they can do anything with glass these days."

"They sure can."

A man in civilian clothes--a detective from headquarters--went up to the desk. "What you guys got there?"

"A ruby this boob picks up off'n the sidewalk," said the sergeant, winking at the finder, who grinned.

"Let's have a squint at it."

The stone was handed to him. The detective stared at it carefully, holding it on his palm and rocking it gently under the desk light. Crimson darts of flame answered to this treatment. He pushed back his hat.

"Well, you boobs!" he drawled.

"What's the matter?"

"Matter? Why, this is a ruby! A whale of a ruby, an' pigeon blood at that! I didn't work in the' appraiser's office for nothing. But for a broken point--kids probably tried to crack it--it would stack up somewhere between three and four thousand dollars!"

The sergeant and the policemen barked simultaneously: "What?"

"A pigeon blood. Where was it you found it?"

"Holy Moses! On Eightieth."

"Any chance of finding that bunch of kids?"

"Not a chance, not a chance! If I got the hull district here there wouldn't be nothin' doin'. The kids'd be too scared t' remember anything. A pigeon-blood ruby, an' I wasn't gonna pick it up at first!"

"Lock it up, sergeant," ordered the detective. "I'll pass the word to headquarters. Too big for a ring. Probably fallen from a pin. But there'll be a holler in a few hours. Lost or stolen, there'll be some big noise. You two boobs!"

"Well, whadda yuh know about that?" whined the policeman. "An' me thinkin' it was glass!"

But there was no big noise. No one had reported the loss or theft of a pigeon-blood ruby of unusual size and quality.

CHAPTER XIX

Kitty came home at nine that night, dreadfully tired. She had that day been rocked by so many emotions. She had viewed the parade from the windows of a theatrical agency, and she had cheered and cried like everybody else. Her eyes still smarted, and her throat betrayed her every time she recalled what she had seen. Those boys!

Loneliness. She had dined downtown, and on the way home the shadow had stalked beside her. Loneliness. Never before had these rooms seemed so empty, empty. If God had only given her a brother and he had marched in that glorious parade, what fun they two would be having at this moment! Empty rooms; not even a pet.

Loneliness. She had been a silly little fool to stand so aloof, just because she was poor and lived in a faded locality. She mocked herself. Poor but proud, like the shopgirl in the movies. Denied herself companionship because she was ashamed of her genteel poverty. And now she was paying for it. Silly little fool! It wasn't as if she did not know how to make and keep friends. She knew she had attractions. Just a senseless false pride. The best friends in the world, after a series of rebuffs, would drop away. Her mother's friends never called any more, because of her aloofness. She had only a few girl friends, and even these no doubt were beginning to think her uppish.

She did not take off her hat and coat. She wandered through the empty rooms, undecided. If she went to a movie the rooms would be just as lonely when she returned. Companionship. The urge of it was so strong that there was a temptation to call up someone, even someone she had rebuffed. She was in the mood to confess everything and to make an honest attempt to start all over again--to accept friendship and let pride go hang. Impulsively she started for the telephone, when the doorbell rang.

Immediately the sense of loneliness fell away. Another chapter in the great game of hide and seek that had kept her from brooding until to-night? The door-bell carried a new message these days. Nine o'clock. Who could be calling at that hour? She had forgotten to advise Cutty of the fact that someone had gone through the apartment. She could not positively assert the fact. Those articles in her bureau she herself might have disturbed. She might have taken a handkerchief in a hurry, hunted for something under the lingerie impatiently. Still she could not rid herself of the feeling that alien hands had been rifling her belongings. Not Bernini, decid-edly.

Remembering Cutty's advice about opening the door with her foot against it, she peered out. No emissary of Bolshevisim here. A weary little messenger boy with a long box in his arms called her name.

"Miz Conover?"

"Yes."

The boy thrust the box into her hands and clumped to the stairhead. Kitty slammed the door and ran into the living room, tearing open the box as she ran. Roses from Cutty; she knew it. The old darling! Just when she was on the verge of breaking down and crying! She let the box fall to the floor and cuddled the flowers to her heart, her eyes filling. Cutty.

One of those ideas which sometime or another spring into the minds of all pretty women who are poor sprang into hers--an idea such as an honest woman might muse over, only to reject. Sinister and cynical. Kitty was at this moment in rather a desperate frame of mind. Those two inherent characteristics, which she had fought valiantly--love of good times and of pretty clothes--made ingress easy for this sinister and cynical idea. Having gained a foothold it pressed forward bold-ly. Cutty, who had everything--strength, comeliness, wisdom, and money. To live among all those beautiful things, never to be lonely again, to be waited on, fussed over, made much of, taken into the high world. Never more to add up accounts, to stretch five-dollar bills across the chasm of seven days. An old man's darling!

"No, no, no!" she burst out, passionately. She drew a hand across her eyes. As if that gesture could rub out an evil thought! It is all very well to say "Avaunt!" But if the idea will not? "I couldn't, I couldn't! I'd be a liar and a cheat. But he is so nice!

If he did want me!... No, no! Just for comforts! I couldn't! What a miserable wretch I am!"

She caught up the copper jug and still holding the roses to her heart, the tears streaming down her cheeks, rushed out to the kitchen for water. She dropped the green stems into the jug, buried her face in the buds to cool the hot shame on her cheeks, and remembered--what a ridiculous thing the mind was!--that she had three shirt waists to iron. She set the jug on the kitchen table, where it remained for many hours, and walked over to the range, to the flatiron shelf. As she reached for a flatiron her hand stopped in midair.

A fat black wallet! Instantly she knew who had placed it there. That poor Johnny Two-Hawks!

Kitty lifted out the wallet from behind the flatirons. No doubt of it, Johnny Two-Hawks had placed it there when she had gone to the speaking tube to summon the janitor. Not knowing if he would ever call for it! Preferring that she rather than his enemies should have it. And without a word! What a simple yet amazing hiding place; and but for the need of a flatiron the wallet would have stayed there until she moved. Left it there, with the premonition that he was heading into trouble. But what if they had killed him? How would she have explained the wallet's presence in her apartment? Good gracious, what an escape!

Without direct consciousness she raised the flap. She saw the edges of money and documents; but she did not touch anything. There was no need. She knew it belonged to Johnny Two-Hawks. Of course there was an appalling attraction. The wallet was, figuratively, begging to be investigated. But resolutely she closed the flap. Why? Because it was as though Two-Hawks had placed the wallet in her hands, charging her to guard it against the day he reclaimed it. There was no outward proof that the wallet was his. She just knew, that was all.

Still, she examined the outside carefully. In one corner had been originally a monogram or a crest; effectually obliterated by the application of fire.

Who he was and what he was, by a simple turn of the wrist. It was Cutty's affair now, not hers. He had a legal right to examine the contents. He was an agent of the Federal Government. The drums of jeopardy and Stefani Gregor and Johnny Two-Hawks, all interwoven. She had waited in vain for Cutty to mention the emeralds. What signified his silence? She had indirectly apprised him of the fact that she knew the author of that advertisement offering to purchase the drums, no questions asked. Who but Cutty in New York would know about them? The mark of the thong. Johnny Two-Hawks had been carrying the drums, and Karlov's men had torn them from their victim's neck during the battle. Was there any reason why Cutty should not have taken her completely into his confidence? Palaces looted. If Stefani Gregor had lived in a palace, why not his protege? Still, it was possible Cutty was holding back until he could tell her everything.

But what to do with it? If she called him up and made known her discovery, Cutty would rush up as fast as a taxicab could bring him. He had peremptorily ordered her not to come to his apartment for the present. But to sit here and wait, to be alone again after he had gone! It was not to be borne. Orders or no orders, she would carry the wallet to him. He could lecture her as much as he pleased. Tonight, at least, she would lay aside her part as parlour maid in the drama. It would give her something to do, keep her mind off herself. Nothing but excitement would pull her out of this semi-hysterical doldrum.

She hid the wallet in the pocket of her underskirt. Already her blood was beginning to dance. She ran into her bedroom for two veils, a gray automobile puggree and one of those heavy black affairs with butterflies scattered over it, quite as effectual as a mask. She wound the puggree about her hat. When the right moment came she would discard the puggree and drop the black veil. Her coat was of dark blue, lined with steel-gray taffeta. Turned inside out it would fool any man. She wore spats. These she would leave behind when she made the change.

Someone might follow her as far as the Knickerbocker, but beyond there, never. She was sorry, but she dared not warn Bernini. He might object, notify Cutty, and spoil everything.

By the time she reached the street exhilaration suffused her. The melancholia was gone. The sinister and cynical idea had vanished apparently. Apparently. Merely it had found a hiding place and was content to abide there for the present. Such ideas are not without avenues of retreat; they know the hours of attack. Kitty was alive to but one fact: The game of hide and seek was on again. She was going to have some excitement. She was going into the night on an adventure, as children play at bears in the dark. The youth in her still rejected the fact that the woof and warp of this adventure were murder and loot and pain.

En route to the Subway she never looked back. At Forty-second Street she de-trained, walked into the Knickerbocker, entered the ladies dressing room, turned her coat, redraped her hat, checked her gaiters, and sought a taxi. Within two blocks of Cutty's she dismissed the cab and finished the journey on foot.

At the left of the lobby was an all-night apothecary's, with a door going into the lobby. Kitty proceeded to the elevator through this avenue. Number Four was down, and she stepped inside, raising her veil.

"You, miss?"

"Very important. Take me up."

"The boss is out."

"No matter. Take me up.

"You're the doctor!" What a pretty girl she was. No come-on in her eyes, though. "The boss may not get back until morning. He just went out in his engineer's togs. He sure wasn't expecting you.

"Do you know where he went?"

"Never know. But I'll be in this bird cage until he comes back."

"I shall have to wait for him."

"Up she goes!"

As Kitty stepped out into the corridor a wave of confusion assailed her. She hadn't planned against Cutty's absence. There was nothing she could say to the nurse; and if Johnny Two-Hawks was asleep--why, all she could do would be to curl up on a divan and await Cutty's return.

The nurse appeared. "You, Miss Conover?"

"Yes." Kitty realized at once that she must take the nurse into her confidence. "I have made a really important discovery. Did Cutty say when he would return?"

"No. I am not in his confidence to that extent. But I do know that you assumed unnecessary risks in coming here."

Kitty shrugged and produced the wallet. "Is Mr. Hawksley awake?"

"He is."

"It appears that he left this wallet in my kitchen that night. It might buck him up if I gave it to him."

The nurse, eyeing the lovely animated face, conceded that it might. "Come, I've been trying futilely to read him asleep, but he is restless. No excitement, please."

"I'll try not to. Perhaps, after all, you had better give him the wallet."

"On the contrary, that would start a series of questions I could not answer. Come along."

When Kitty saw Hawksley she gave a little gasp of astonishment. Why, he was positively handsome! His dark head, standing out boldly against the bolstering pillows, the fine lines of his face definite, the pallor--he was like a Roman cameo. Who and what could he be, this picturesque foundling?

His glance flashed into hers delightedly. For hours and hours the constant wonder where she was, why no one mentioned her, why they evaded his apparently casual questions. To burst upon his vision in the nadir of his boredom and loneliness like this! She was glorious, this American girl. She made him think of a golden scabbard housing a fine Toledo blade. Hadn't she saved his life? More, hadn't she assumed a responsibility in so doing? Instantly he purposed that she should not be permitted to resign the office of good Samaritan. He motioned toward the nurse's chair; and Kitty sat down, her errand in total eclipse.

"Just when I never felt so lonely! Ripping!"

His quick smile was so engaging that Kitty answered it--kindred spirits, subconsciously recognizing each other. Fire; but neither of them knew that; or that two lonely human beings of opposite sex, in touch, constitute a first-rate combustible.

Quietly the nurse withdrew. There would be a tonic in this meeting for the patient. Her own presence might neutralize the effect. She had not spent all those dreadful months in base hospitals without acquiring a keen insight into the needs of sick men. No harm in letting him have this pretty, self-reliant girl alone to himself for a quarter of an hour. She would then return with some broth.

"How--how are you?" asked Kitty, inanely.

"Top-hole, considering. Quite ready to be killed all over again."

"You mustn't talk like that!" she protested.

"Only to show you I was bucking up. Thank you for doing what you did."

"I had to do it."

"Most women would have run away and left me to my fate."

"Not my kind."

"Rather not! Your kind would risk its neck to help a stray cat. I say, what's that you have in your hand?"

"Good gracious!" Kitty extended the wallet. "It is yours, isn't it?"

"Yes. I wanted you to bring it to me the way you have. If I hadn't come back--out of that--it was to be yours."

"Mine?"--dumfounded. "But----"

"Why not? Gregor gone, there wasn't a soul in the world. I was hungry, and you gave me food. I wanted that to pay you. I'll wager you've never looked into it."

"I had no right to."

"See!" He opened the wallet and spread the contents on the counterpane. "I wasn't so stony as you thought. What? Cash and unregistered bonds. They would have been yours absolutely."

"But I don't--I can't quite," Kitty stammered--"but I couldn't have kept them!"

"Positively yes. You would have shown them to that ripping guardian of yours, and he would have made you see."

"Indeed, yes! He would have been scared to death. You poor man, can't you see? Circumstantial evidence that I had killed you!"

"Good Lord! And you're right, too! So it goes. You can't do anything you want to do. The good Samaritan is never requited; and I wanted to break the rule. Lord, what a bally mix-up I'd have tumbled you in! I forgot that you were you, that you would have gone straight to the authorities. Of course I knew if I pulled through and you found the wallet you would bring it to me."

Kitty no longer had a foot on earth. She floated. Her brain floated, too, because she could not make it think coherently for her. A fortune--for a dish of bacon and eggs! The magnificence, the utter prodigality of such generosity! For a dish of bacon and eggs and a bottle of milk! Had she left home? Hadn't she fallen asleep, the victim of another nightmare? A corner of the atmosphere cleared a little. A desire took form; she wanted the nurse to come back and stabilize things. In a wavering blur she saw the odd young man restore the money and bonds and other documents to the wallet.

"I want you to give this to your guardian when he comes in. I want him to understand. I say, you know, I'm going to love that old thoroughbred! He's fine. Fancy his carrying me on his shoulders and eventually bringing me up here among the clouds! Americans.... Are you all like that? And you!"

Kitty's brain began to make preparations to alight, as it were. Cutty. That gave her a touch of earth. She heard herself say faintly: "And what about me?"

"You were brave and kind. To help an unknown, friendless beggar like that, when you should have turned him over to the police! Makes me feel a bit stuffy. They left me for dead. I wonder--"

"What?"

"If--it wouldn't have been just as well!"

"You mustn't talk like that! You just mustn't! You're with friends, real friends, who want to help you all they can." And then with a little flash of forced humour, because of the recurrent tightening in her throat--"Who could be friendless, with all that money?" Instantly she felt like biting her tongue. He would know nothing of the sad American habit of trying to be funny to keep a wobbly situation on its legs. He would interpret it as heartlessness. "I didn't mean that!" With the Irish impulsiveness which generally weighs acts in retrospection, she reached over and gripped his hand.

"I say, you two!" Hawksley closed his eyes for a second. "Wanting to buck up a chap because you re that sort! All right. I'll stick it out! You two! And I might be the worst scoundrel unhung!"

He drew her hand toward his lips, and Kitty had not the power to resist him. She felt strangely theatrical, a character in a play; for American men, except in playful burlesque, never kissed their women's hands. The moment he released the hand the old wave of hysteria rolled over her. She must fly. The desire to weep, little fool that she was! was breaking through her defences. Loneliness. The two of them all alone but for Cutty. She rose, crushing the wallet in her hand.

Ah, never had she needed that darling mother of hers so much as now. Tears did not seem to afford relief when one shed them into handkerchiefs and pillows. But on that gentle bosom, to let loose this brimming flood, to hear the tender voice consoling!

"Oh, I say, now! Please!" she heard Johnny Two-Hawks cry out.

But she rushed on blindly, knocking against the door jamb and almost upsetting the nurse, who was returning. Somehow she managed to reach the living room, glad it was dark. Alter sundry reaching about she found the divan and flung herself upon it. What would he think? What would the nurse think? That Kitty Conover had suddenly gone stark, raving crazy! And now that she was in the dark, alone, the desire to weep passed over and she lay quietly with her face buried in the pillow. But not for long.

She sat up. Music--violin music! A gay waltz that made her think of flashing water, the laughter of children. Tschaikowsky. Thrilled, she waited for the finale. Silence. Scharwenka's "Polish Dance," with a swing and a fire beyond anything she had ever heard before. Another stretch of silence--a silence full of interrogation points. Then a tender little sketch, quite unfamiliar. But all at once she understood. He was imploring her to return. She smiled in the dark; but she knew she was going to remain right where she was.

"Miss Conover?" It was the voice of the nurse.

"Yes. I'm over here on the divan."

"Anything wrong?"

"Good gracious, no! I'm overtired. A little hysterical, maybe. The parade to-day, with all those wounded boys in automobiles, the music and colour and excitement--have rather done me up. And the way I rushed up here. And not finding Cutty--"

"Anything I can get for you?"

"No, thanks. I'll try to snatch a little sleep before Cutty returns."

"But he may be gone all night!"

"Will it be so very scandalous if I stay here?"

"You poor child! Go ahead and sleep. Don't hesitate to call me if you want anything. I have a mild sedative if you would like it."

"No, thanks. I did not know that Mr. Hawksley played."

"Wonderfully! But does it bother you?"

"It kind of makes me choky."

"I'll tell him."

Kitty, now strangely at peace, snuggled down among the pillows. Some great Polish violinist, who had roused the bitter enmity of the anarchist? But no; he was Russian. Cutty had admitted that. It struck her that Cutty knew a great deal more than Kitty Conover; and so far as she could see there was no apparent reason for this secrecy. She rather believed she had Cutty. Either he should tell her everything or she would run loose, Bolshevik or no Bolshevik.

Sheep. She boosted one over the bars, another and another. Round somewhere in the thirties the bars dissolved. The next thing she knew she was blinking in the light, Cutty, his arms folded, staring down at her sombrely. There was blood on his face and blood on his hands.

CHAPTER XX

Karlov moodily touched the shoulder of the man on the cot. Stefani Gregor puzzled him. He came to this room more often than was wise, driven by a curiosity born of a cynical philosophy to discover what it was that re-enforced this fragile body against threats and thirst and hunger. He knew what he wanted of Gregor--the fiddler on his knees begging for mercy. And always Gregor faced him with that silent calm which reminded him of the sea, aloof, impervious, exasperating. Only once since the day he had been locked in this room had Gregor offered speech. He, Karlov, had roared at him, threatened, baited, but his reward generally had been a twisted wintry smile.

He could not offer physical torture beyond the frequent omissions of food and water; the body would have crumbled. To have planned this for months, and then to be balked by something as visible yet as elusive as quicksilver! Born in the same mudhole, and still Boris Karlov the avenger could not understand Stefani Gregor the fiddler. Perhaps what baffled him was that so valiant a spirit should be housed in so weak a body. It was natural that he, Boris, with the body of a Carpathian bear, should have a soul to match. But that Stefani, with his paper body, should mock him! The damned bourgeoisie!

The quality of this unending calm was understandable: Gregor was always ready to die. What to do with a man to whom death was release? To hold the knout and to see it turn to water in the hand! In lying he had overreached. Gregor, having accepted as fact the reported death of Ivan, had nothing to live for. Having brought Gregor here to torture he had, blind fool, taken away the fiddler's ability to feel. The fog cleared. He himself had given his enemy this mysterious calm. He had taken out Gregor's soul and dissipated it.

No. Not quite dissipated. What held the body together was the iron residue of the soul. Venom and blood clogged Karlov's throat. He could kill only the body, as he had killed the fiddle; he could not reach the mystery within. Ah, but he had wrung Stefani's heart there. There were pieces of the fiddle on the table where Gregor had placed them, doubtless to weep over when he was alone. Why hadn't he thought to break the fiddle a little each day?

"Stefani Gregor, sit up. I have come to talk." This was formula. Karlov did not expect speech from Gregor.

Slowly the thin arms bore up the torso; slowly the legs swung to the floor. But the little gray man's eyes were bright and quick to-night.

"Boris, what is it you want?"

"To talk"--surprised at this unexpected outburst.

"No, no. I mean, what is it all about--these killings, these burnings?"

Karlov was ready at all times to expound the theories that appealed to his dark yet simple mind--humanity overturned as one overturned the sod in the springtime to give it new life.

"To give the proletariat what is his."

"Ha!" said the little man on the cot. "What is his?"

"That which capitalism has taken away from him."

"The proletariat. The lowest in the human scale--and therefore the most helpless. They shall rule, say you. My poor Russia! Beaten and robbed for centuries, and now betrayed by a handful of madmen--with brains atrophied on one side! You are a fool, Boris. Your feet are in strange quicksands and your head among chimeras. You write some words on a piece of paper, and lo! you say they are facts. Without first proving your theories correct you would ram them down the throat of the world. The world rejects you."

"Wait and see, damned bourgeoisie!" thundered Karlov, not alive to the fact that he was being baited.

"Bourgeoisie? Yes, I am of the middle class; the rogue on top and the fool below. I see. The rogue and the fool cannot combine unless the bourgeoisie is obliterated. Go on. I am interested."

"Under the soviet the government shall be everything."

"As it was in Prussia."

Karlov ignored this. "The individual shall never again become rich by exploiting the poor."

Karlov strove to speak calmly. Gregor's willingness to discuss the aims of the proletariat confused him. He suspected some ulterior purpose behind this apparent amiability. He must hold down his fury until this purpose was in the open.

"Well, that is good," Gregor admitted. "But somehow it sounds ancient on my ear. Was there not a revolution in France?"

"Fool, it is the world that is revolting!" Karlov paused. "And no man in the future shall see his sister or his daughter made into a loose woman without redress."

"Your proletariat's sister and daughter. But the daughter of the noble and the daughter of the bourgeoisie--fair game!"

Sometimes there enters a man's head what might be called a sick idea; when the vitality is at low ebb and the future holds nothing. Thus there was a grim and sick idea behind Gregor's gibes. It was in his mind to die. All the things he had loved had been destroyed. So then, to goad this madman into a physical frenzy. Once those gorilla-like hands reached out for him Stefani Gregor's neck would break.

"Be still, fiddler! You know what I mean. There will be no upper class, which is idleness and wastefulness; no middle class, the usurers, the gamblers of necessities, the war makers. One great body of equals shall issue forth. All shall labour."

"For what?"

"The common good."

"Your Lenine offered peace, bread, and work for the overthrow of Kerensky. What you have given--murder and famine and idleness. Can there be common good that is based upon the blood of innocents? Did Ivan ever harm a soul? Have I?"

"You!" Karlov trembled. "You--with your damned green stones! Did you not lure Anna to dishonour with the promise to show her the drums, the sight of which would make all her dreams come true? A child, with a fairy story in her head!"

"You speak of Anna! If you hadn't been spouting your twaddle in taverns you would have had time to instruct Anna against guilelessness and superstition."

"How much did they pay you? Did you fiddle for her to dance?... But I left their faces in the mud!"

A madman, with two obsessions. A pitiable Samson with his arms round the pillars of society to drag it down upon his head because society had defiled his sister! Ah, how many thousands in Russia like him! A great yearning filled Gregor's heart, because he understood; but he suppressed expression of it because the sick idea was stronger.

"Yes, yes! I loved those green stones because it was born in me to love beautiful things. Have you forgotten, Boris, the old days in Moscow, when we were students and I made you weep with my fiddle? There was hope for you then. You had not become a pothouse orator on the rights of the proletariat--the red-combed rooster on the smouldering dungheap! Beauty, no matter in what form, I loved it. Yes, I was mad about those emeralds. I was always stealing in to see them, to hold them to the light, simply because they were beautiful." Gregor's hands flew to his throat, which he bared. "I lured her there! 'Twas I, Boris!... Those beautiful hands of yours, fit for the butcher's block! Kill me! Kill me!"

But Karlov shrank back, covering his eyes. "No! I see now! You wish to die! You shall live!" He rushed toward the far wall, a huge grotesque shadow rising to meet him--his own, thrown upon the wall by the wavering candlelight. He turned shaking, for the temptation had been great.

At once Gregor realized his failure. The tenseness went out of him. He spoke calmly. "Yes, I wanted to die. I no longer possess anything. I lied, Boris; but it is useless to tell you that. I knew nothing of Anna until it was too late. I wanted to die."

Karlov began to pace furiously, the candle flame springing after him each time he passed it.

There was a question in Gregor's mind. It rushed to his lips a dozen times but he dared not voice it. Olga. Since Karlov could not be tempted to murder, it would be futile to ask for an additional burden of mental torture. Perhaps it had not happened--the terrible picture he drew in his mind--since Karlov had not boasted of it.

"Come, Boris. There is blood on your hands. What is one more daub of it?"

Karlov stopped, scowled, and ran his fingers through his hair. Perhaps some ugly memory stirred the roots of it. "You wish to die!"

Gregor bent his head to his hands and Karlov resumed his pacing. After a while Gregor looked up.

"Private vengeance. You begin your rule with private vengeance."

"The vengeance of a people. All the breed. Did France stop at Louis? Do we tear up the roots of the poisonous toadstool that killed someone we loved and leave the other toadstools thriving?"

"To cure the world of all its ills by tearing up the toadstools and the flowers together--do you call that justice? The proletariat shall have everything, and he begins by killing off noble and bourgeoisie and dividing up the loot! Even with his oppression the noble had a right to live. The bourgeoisie must die because of his benefactions to a people. The world for the proletariat, and damnation for the rest!"

"Let each become one of us," cried Karlov, hoarsely. "We give them that right."

"You lie! You have done nothing but assassinate them when they surrendered. But tell me, have not you, Lenine, and Trotzky overlooked something?"

"What?" Karlov was vaguely grateful for this diversion. The lust to kill was still upon him and he was fighting it. He must remember that Gregor wished to die. "What have we overlooked?"

"Human nature. Can you tear it apart and reconstruct it, as you would a clock? What of creative genius in this proletariat millennium of yours?"

"The state will carefully mother that."

Gregor laughed sardonically. "Will there be creative genius under your rule? Will you not suffocate it by taking away the air that energizes it--ambition? You will have all the present marvels of invention to start with, but will you ever go beyond? Have you read history and observed the inexorable? I doubt it. What is progress? A series of almost imperceptible steps."

"Which capitalism has always obstructed," flung back Karlov.

"Which capitalism has always made possible. Curb it, yes; but abolish it, as you have done in unhappy Russia! Why do you starve there? Poor fool, because you have assassinated those forces which created food--that is to say, put it where you could get it. Three quarters of Russia are against you. You read nothing in that? The efficient and the inefficient, they shall lie down together as the lion and the ass, to paraphrase. They shall become equal because you say so. What is, fundamentally, this Bolshevism? The revolt of the inefficient. The mantle of horror that was Germany's you have torn from her shoulders and thrown upon yours. Fools!"

The anarch's huge fists became knotted; wrinkles corrugated his forehead; but he did not stir. Gregor wanted to die.

Gregor pointed with trembling hand toward the brown litter on the table. "To destroy. You shattered a soul there. You tore mine apart when you did it. For what? To better humanity? No; to rend something, to obliterate something that was beautiful. Demolition. Go on. You will tear and rend until exhaustion comes, then some citizen king, some headstrong Napoleon, will step in. The French Revolution taught you nothing. You play 'The Marseillaise' in the Neva Prospekt and miss the significance of that song. Liberty? You choose license. Equality? You deny it in your acts. Fraternity? You slaughter your brothers."

"Be silent!" roared Karlov, wavering.

But Gregor continued with a new-found hope. He saw that his jeers were wearing down the other's control. Perhaps the weak side was the political. Karlov was a fanatic. There might yet be death in those straining fingers.

"To seize by confiscation, without justice, indiscriminately all that the group efficient laboriously constructed. I enter your house, kill your family and steal your silver. Are your acts fundamentally different from mine? Remember, I am speaking from the point of view as three quarters of Russia see it, and all the other civilized nations. There may be something magnificent in that soviet constitution of yours; but you have deluged it in blood and folly. Ostensibly you are dividing up the great estates, but actually you are parcelling them out and charging rent. You will not own anything. The state shall own all the property. What will be the patriotism of the man who has nothing? Why defend something that is only his government's, not his own? You are legalizing women as cows. The sense of motherhood will vanish when a woman may not select her mate. What is the greatest thing in the world? The human need of possession. To own something, however little. The spur of creative genius. Human beings will never be equal except in lawful privileges. The skillful will outpace the unskillful; the thrifty will take from the improvident; genius will overtop mediocrity. And you will change all this with a scrape of your bloody pen!"

Karlov's body began to rock and sway like an angry bear's; but still he held his ground. Gregor wanted to die, to cheat him.

"What of power?" went on his baiter. "Capitalism of might. Lenine and Trotzky; are they--have they been--honest? Has Russia actually voted them into office? They sit in the seats of the mighty by the capitalism of force. For the capitalism of money, which is progress physical and moral, you substitute the capitalism of force, which is terror. You speak of yourselves as internationalists. Bats, that is the judgment day of God--internationalism! For only on the judgment day will nations become a single people."

A short silence. Gregor was beginning to grow weak. Presently he picked up the thread of his diatribe.

"I have lived in England, France, Italy, and here. I am competent to draw comparisons. Where you went to distill poison I went to absorb facts. And I found that here in this great democracy is the true idea. But you will not read the lesson."

Sweat began to drop from Karlov's beetling eyebrows.

"You will fail miserably here. Why? Because the Americans are the greatest of individual property owners. The sense of possession is satisfied. And woe to the fool who suggests they surrender this. Little wooden houses, thousands and thousands of them, with a small plot of ground in the rear where a man in the springtime may dig his hands into the soil and say gratefully to God, 'Mine, mine!' I, too, am a Russ. I thought in the beginning that you would take this country as an example, a government of the people, by the people, for the people. Wrongs? Yes. But day by day these wrongs are being righted. No lesson in this for Trotzky, a beer-hall orator like yourself. Ten million men drafted to carry arms. Did they revolt? Shoulder to shoulder the selected millions marched to the great ships, shoulder to shoulder they pressed toward the Rhine. No lesson in that!

"Capitalism, seeking to save its loans, you rant! Capitalism of blood and money that asked only for simple justice to mankind. The ideal of a great people--a mixture of all bloods, even German! No lessons in these tremendous happenings! And you babble about your damned proletariat who represents the dregs of Russia. What is he? The inefficient, whining that the other man has the luck, so kill him! Russia, the kindly ox, fallen among wolves! You cannot tear down the keystone of civilization--which took seven thousand years to construct--insert it upside down, and expect the arch to stand. You have your chance to prove your theories. Prove them in Petrograd and Moscow, and you will not have to go forth with the torch. And what is this torch but the hidden fear that you may be wrong?... To wreck the world before you are found out! You are idiots, and you have turned Russia into a madhouse! Spawns from the dung-heap!"

"Damn you, Stefani Gregor!" Karlov rushed to the cot, raised his terrible fists, his chest heaving. Gregor waited. "No, no! You wish to die!" The madman swung on his heels and dashed toward the door, sweeping the pieces of the violin to the floor as he passed the table.

Gregor feebly drew himself back upon his cot and laid his face in the pillow.

"Ivan--my violin--all that I knew and loved--gone! And God will not let me die!"

CHAPTER XXI

From a window in one of the vacant warehouses, twenty-odd feet away Cutty, from an oblique angle, had witnessed the peculiar drama without being able to grasp head or tail to it. For two hours he had crouched behind his window, watching the man on the cot and wondering if he would ever turn his face toward the candlelight. Then Karlov had entered. Gregor's ironic calm--with the exception of the time he had bared his throat--and Karlov's tempestuous exit baffled him. To the eye it had the appearance of a victory for Gregor and a defeat for Karlov, but Cutty had long ago ceased to believe his eyes without some corroborative evidence of auricular character.

He had recognized both men. Karlov answered to Kitty's description as an old glove answers to the hand. And no man, once having seen Gregor, could possibly forget his picturesque head. The old chap was alive! This fact made the night's adventure tally one hundred per cent. How to get a cheery word to him, to buck him up with, the promise of help? A hard nut to crack; so many obstacles. Primarily, this was a Federal affair. Yonder hid the werewolf and his pack, and it would be folly to send them scattering just for the sake of advising Gregor that he was being watched over.

Underneath the official obligation there was a personal interest in not risking the game to warn Gregor. Cutty was now positive that the drums of jeopardy were hidden somewhere in this house. To perform three acts, then: Save Gregor, capture Karlov and his pack, and privately confiscate the emeralds. Findings were keepings. No compromise regarding those green stones. It would not particularly hurt his reputation with St. Peter to play the half rogue once in a lifetime. Besides, St. Peter, hadn't he stolen something himself back there in the Biblical days; or got into a scrape or something? The old boy would understand. Cutty grinned in the dark.

Any obsession is a blindfold. A straight course lay open to Cutty, but he chose the labyrinthian because he was obsessed. He wanted those emeralds. Nothing less than the possession of them would, to his thinking, round out a varied and active career. Later, perhaps, he would declare the stones to the customs and pay the duty; perhaps. Thus his subsequent mishaps this night may be laid to the fact that he thought and saw through green spectacles.

The idea that the jewels were hidden near by made it imperative that he should handle this affair exclusively. Coles, the operative he had sent to negotiate with Karlov, was conceivably a prisoner upstairs or down. Coles knew about the drums, and they must not turn up under his eye. Federal property, in that event.

If ever he laid his hands upon the drums he would buy something gorgeous for Kitty. Little thoroughbred!

Time for work. Without doubt Karlov had cellar exits through this warehouse or the other. The job on hand would be first to locate these exits, and then to the trap on the roof. With his pocket lamp blazing a trail he went down to the cellar and carefully inspected the walls that abutted those of the house. Nothing on this side.

He left the warehouse and hugged the street wall for a space. The street was deserted. Instead of passing Karlov's abode he wisely made a detour of the block. He reached the entrance to the second warehouse without sighting even a marauding tom. In the cellar of this warehouse he discovered a newly made door, painted skillfully to represent the limestone of the foundation. Tiptop.

Immediately he outlined the campaign. There should be two drives--one from the front and another from the roof--so that not an anarchist or Bolshevik could escape. The mouth of the Federal sack should be held at this cellar exit. No matter what kind of game he played offside, the raid itself must succeed absolutely. Nothing should swerve him from making these plans as perfect as it was humanly possible. He would be on hand to search Karlov himself. If the drums were not on him he would return and pick the old mansion apart, lath by lath. Gay old ruffian, wasn't he?

Another point worth considering: He would keep his discoveries under cover until the hour to strike came. Some over-zealous subordinate might attempt a coup on his own and spoil everything.

He picked his way to the far end of the cellar, to the doors. Locks gone. He took it for granted that the real-estate agent would not come round with prospective tenants. These doors would take them into the trucking alley, where there were a dozen feasible exits. There was no way out of the house yard, as the brick wall, ten feet high and running from warehouse to warehouse, was blind. Now for the trap on the roof.

He climbed the three flights of stairs crisscrossed and festooned with ancient cobwebs. Occasionally he sneezed in the crook of his elbow, philosophizing over the fact that there was a lot of deadwood property in New York. Americans were eternally on the move.

The window from which he intended dropping to the house roof was obdurate. Only the upper half was movable. With hardly any noise at all he pulled this down, straddled it, balanced himself, secured a good grip on the ledge, and let himself down. The tips of his shoes, rubber-soled, just reached the roof. He landed silently.

The glare of the street lamp at the corner struck the warehouse, and this indirect light was sufficient to work by. He made the trap after a series of extra-cautious steps. The roof was slanting and pebbled, and the least turn of the foot might start a cascade and bell an alarm. A comfort-loving dress-suiter like himself, playing Old Sleuth, when he ought to be home and in bed! It was all of two-thirty. What the deuce would he do when there were no more thrills in life?

He stooped and caught hold of a corner of the trap to test it--and drew back with a silent curse. Glass! He had cut his hand. The beggars had covered the trap with cement and broken glass, sealing it. It would take time to cut round the trap; and even then he wouldn't be sure; they might have nailed it down from the inside. The worst of it was he would have to do the work himself; and in the meantime Karlov would have a fair wind for his propaganda gas, and perhaps the disposal of the drums to some collector who wasn't above bargaining for smuggled emeralds. Odd, though, that Karlov should have made a prisoner of Coles. What lay behind that manoeuvre? Well, this trap must be liberated; no getting round that.

Hang it, he wasn't going to be dishonest exactly; it would be simply a double play, half for Uncle Sam and half for himself. The idea of offering freely his blood and money to Uncle Sam and at the same time putting one over on the old gentleman had a novel appeal.

He stood up and wiped a tickling cobweb from his cheek. As the window from which he had descended came into range he stared, loose-jawed. Then be chuckled, as thoroughbred adventurers generally chuckle when they find themselves at the bottom of the sack, the mouth of which has simultaneously and automatically closed. Wasn't he the brainy old top? Wasn't he Sherlock Holmes plus? Old fool, how the devil was he going to get back through that window?

The drums of jeopardy--even to think of them was unlucky! Not to have planned a retreat; to have climbed down a well and cut the bucket rope! For in effect that was precisely what he had done. Only wings could carry him up to that window. With sardonic humour he felt of his shoulder blades. Not a feather in sight. Then he touched his ears. Ah, here was something definite; they had grown several inches during the past few hours. Monumental ass!

Of course there would be the drain. He could escape; but, dear Lord! with enough noise to wake the dead. And that would write "Finis" to this particular adventure. The quarry and the emeralds would be gone before he could return with help. When everything had gone so smoothly--a jolt like this!

A crowded day, and no mistake, as full of individual acts as a bill at a vaudeville, trained-animal act last. Was it possible that he had gone fiddle hunting that morning, netting an Amati worth ten thousand dollars? Hawksley--no, he couldn't blame Hawksley. Still, if this young Humpty-Dumpty hadn't been pushed off his wall he, Cutty, would not now be marooned upon this roof 'twixt the devil and the deep blue sea. To remain here until sunrise would be impossible; to slide down the drain was equally impossible--that is, if he ever wanted to see Boris Karlov again. The way of the transgressor was hard.

He sat on his heels and let his gaze rove four-square, permitting no object to escape. He saw a clothes pole leaning against the chimney. Evidently the former tenants had hung up their laundry here. There was no clothesline, however. Caught, jolly well, blooming well caught! If ever this got abroad he would be laughed out of the game. He wasn't going to put one over on Uncle Sam after all. There might be some kind of a fire escape on the front of the house. No harm in taking a look; it would serve to pass the time.

There was the usual frontal parapet about three feet in height. Upturned in the shadow lay a gift from the gods-a battered kitchen chair, probably used to reach the clothesline in the happy days when the word "Bolshevism" was known to only a select few dark angels.

Cutty waved a hand cheerfully if vaguely toward his guiding star, picked up the chair, commandeered the clothes pole, and silently manoeuvred to the wall of the warehouse. Standing on the chair he placed the tip of the pole against the top of the upper frame and pushed the frame halfway up. He repeated this act upon the obdurate lower half. He heaved slowly but with all his force. Glory be, the lower half went up far enough to afford ingress! He would eat his breakfast in the apartment as usual. To-morrow night he would establish his line of retreat by fetching a light rope ladder. There was sweat at the roots of his hair, however, when he finally gained the street. He was very tired. He observed mournfully that the vigour which had always recharged itself, no matter how recklessly he had drawn upon it, was beginning to protest. Fifty-two.

Well, his troubles were over for the night. So he believed. Arriving home, dirty and spent, he had to find Kitty asleep on the divan!

CHAPTER XXII

K itty," he said, breaking the tableau, "what are you doing here?"

"You've been hurt! There is blood on you!"

"A trifling cut. But I'm hurt, nevertheless, that you should be so thought-less as to come here against my orders. It doesn't matter that Karlov has given up the idea of having you followed. But for the sake of us all you must be made to understand that we are dealing with high explosives and poison gas. It's not what might happen to me or to Uncle Sam's business. It's you. Any moment they may take it into their heads to get at me and Hawksley through you. That's why we watch over you. You don't want to see Hawksley done in, do you? It's real tragedy, Kitty, and nobody can guess what the end is going to be."

Kitty's lip quivered. "Cutty, if you talk like that to me I shall cry."

"Good Lord, what about?"--bewildered.

"About everything. I've been on the verge of hysterics all day."

"Kitty, you poor child, what's happened?"

"Nothing--everything. Lonesome. When I saw all those mothers and wives and sisters and sweethearts on the curb to-day, watching their boys march by, it hit me hard. I was alone. Nobody. So please don't be cross with me. I'm on the ragged edge. Silly, I know. But we women often go to pieces over nothing, without any logical reason. Ready to face murder and battle and sudden death; and then to blow up, as you men say it, over nothing. I had to move, go somewhere, do something; so I came here. But I came on--what do you call it?--official business. Here!" She offered him the wallet.

"What's this?"

"Belongs to Johnny Two-Hawks. He hid it that night behind my flatirons on the range. Why, Cutty, he's rich!"

"Did he show the contents?"

"Only the money and the bonds. He said if he had died the money and bonds would have been mine.

"Providing Gregor was also dead." Cutty looked into the wallet, but disturbed nothing. "I imagine these funds are actually Gregor's."

"He told me to give the wallet to you. And so I waited. I fell asleep. So please don't scold me."

"I'm a brute! But it's because you've become so much to me that I was angry. You're Tommy and Molly's girl, and I've got to watch out for you until you reach some kind of a port."

"Thank you for the flowers. You'll never know just what they did for me. There was somebody who gave me a thought."

"Kitty, I honestly don't get you. A beauty like you, lonesome!"

"That's it. I am pretty. Why should I deny it? If I'd been homely I shouldn't have been ashamed to invite my friends to my shabby home. I shouldn't have cold shouldered everybody through false pride. But where have you been, and what have you been doing?"

"Official business. But I just missed being a fine jackass. I'll look into the wallet after I've cleaned up. I'm a mess of gore and dust. Is it interesting stuff?" dreading her answer.

"The wallet? I did not look into it. I had no right."

"Ah! Well, I'll be back in two jigs."

He hurried off, relieved to learn that the secret was still beyond Kitty's knowledge. Of course Hawksley wouldn't carry anything in the wallet by which his true identity might be made known. Still, there would be stuff to excite her interest and suspicion. Hawksley had shown her some of that three hundred thousand probably. What a game!

He would say nothing about his own adventures and discoveries. He worked on the theory that the best time to tell about something was after it had become a fact. But no theory is perfect; and in this instance his reticence was going to cost him intolerable agony in the near future.

Within a quarter of an hour he was back in the living room. Kitty was out of sight; probably had curled up on the divan again. He would not disturb her.

Hawksley's wallet! He drew a chair under the reading lamp and explored the wallet. Money and bonds he rather expected, but the customs appraiser's receipt was like a buffet. The emeralds belonged honorably to his guest! All his own plans were knocked galley-west by this discovery.

An odd sense of indignation blazed up in him, as though someone had imposed upon him. The sport was gone, the fun of the thing; it became merely official business. To appropriate a pair of smuggled emeralds was a first-class sporting proposition, with a humorous twist. As it stood now, he would be picking Hawksley's pocket; and he wasn't rogue enough for that. Hang the luck!

Emeralds, rubies, sapphires, pearls, and diamonds! No doubt many of them with histories--in a bag hung to his neck--and all these thousands of miles! Not since the advent of the Gaekwar of Baroda into San Francisco, in 1910, had so many fine stones passed through that port of entry.

But why hadn't Hawksley inquired about them? Stoic indifference? A good loser? How had he got through the customs without a lot of publicity? The Russian consul of the old regime probably; and an appraiser who was a good sport. To have come safely to his destination, and then to have lost out! The magnificent careless generosity of putting the wallet behind Kitty's flatirons, to be hers if he didn't pull through! Why, this fiddling derelict was a man! Stood up and fought Karlov with his bare fists; wasn't ashamed to weep over his mother's photograph; and fiddled like Heifetz. All right. This Johnny Two-Hawks, as Kitty persisted in calling him, was going to reach his Montana ranch. His friend Cutty would take it upon himself to see to that.

It struck him that after all he would have to play the game as he had planned it. Those gems falling into the hands of the Federal agents would surely bring to light Hawksley's identity; and Hawksley should have his chance.

Cutty then came upon the will. Somehow the pathos of it went deep into his heart. The poor devil!--a will that hadn't been witnessed, the handwriting the same as that on the passport. If he had fallen into the hands of the police they would have justifiably locked him up as a murder suspect. Two-Hawks! It was a small world. He returned the contents to the wallet, leaving out the will, however. This he thrust into a drawer.

"Coffee?" said Kitty at his elbow.

"Kitty? I'd forgotten you! I thought I smelt coffee. Just what I wanted, too, only I hadn't brains enough left to think of it. Smells better than anything Kuroki makes.... Tastes better, too. You're going to make some lucky duffer a fine wife."

"Is there anything you can tell me, Cutty?"

"A whole lot, Kitty; only I'm twenty years too old."

"I mean the wallet. Who is he?"

Cutty drained the cup slowly. A good coherent lie, to appease Kitty's curiosity; half a truth, something hard to nail. He set down the empty cup, building. By the time he had filled his pipe and lit it he was ready.

Something bored up through the subconscious, however--a query. Why hadn't he told her the plain truth at the start? Wasn't on account of the drums. He hadn't kept her in the dark because of the drums. He could have trusted her with that part of it--his tentative piracy. That to divulge Hawksley's identity would be a menace to her peace of mind now appeared ridiculous; and yet he had worked forward from this assumption. No answer to the query. Generally he thought clearly enough; but somewhere along this route he had made a muddle of things and couldn't find the spot. The only point clearly defined was that he should wish to keep her out of the affair because there were elements of positive danger. But somewhere inside of him was a question asking for recognition, and it eluded him. Nothing could be solved until this question got out of the fog. Even now he might risk the whole truth; but the lie he had woven appeared too good to waste.

Human frailty. The most accomplished human being is the finished liar. Never to forget a detail, to remember step by step the windings, over a ticklish road. And Cutty, for all his wide newspaper experience, was a poor liar because he had been brought up on facts. Perhaps his lie might have passed had he not been so fagged. The physical labours of the night had dulled his perceptions.

"Ab, but that tastes good!"--as he blew forth a wavering ring of smoke.

"It ought to have at least one merit," replied Kitty, wrinkling her nose. What a fine profile Cutty had! "Now, who and what is he? I'm dying to know."

"An odd story; probably hundreds like it. You see, the Bolsheviki have driven out of the country or killed all the nobles and bourgeoisie. Some of them have escaped--into China, Sweden, India, wherever they could find an open route. To his story there are many loose ends, and Hawksley is not the talking kind. You mustn't repeat what I tell you. Hawksley, with all that money and a forged English passport, would have a good deal of trouble explaining if he ran afoul the police. There is no real proof that the money is his or Gregor's. As a matter of fact, it is Gregor's, and Hawksley was bringing it to him. Hawksley is Gregor's protege."

Kitty nodded. This dovetailed with what Johnny Two-Hawks had told her that night.

"How the two came together originally I don't know. Gregor was in his younger days a great violinist, but unknown to the American public. Early in his career he speculated with his concert earnings and turned a pot of money. He dropped the professional career for that of a country gentleman. He had a handsome estate, and lived sensibly. He sent Hawksley to England to school and spent a good deal of time there with him, teaching him how to play the fiddle, for which it seems Hawksley had a natural bent. He had to Anglicize his name; for Two-Hawks would have made people laugh. To be a gentleman, Kitty, one does not have to be a prince or a grand duke. Gregor was a polished gentleman, and he turned Hawksley into one."

Again Kitty nodded, her eyes sparkling.

"The Russ--the educated Russ--is a queer biscuit. Got to have a finger in some political pie, and political pies in Russia before the war were lese-majesty. The result--Gregor got in wrong with his secret society and the political police and was forced to fly to save his life. But before he fled he had all his convertible funds transferred. Only his estate was confiscated. Hawksley was in London when the war broke out. There was a lot of red tape, naturally, regarding the funds. I shan't bother you with that. Hawksley, hoping to better his protector's future, returned to Russia and joined his regiment and fought until the Czar abdicated. Foretasting the trend of events, he tried to get back to England, but that was impossible. He was permitted to retire to the Gregor estate, where he remained until the uprising of the Bolsheviki. Then he started across the world to join Gregor."

"That was brave."

"It certainly was. I imagine that Hawksley's journey has that of Ulysses laid away on the shelf. Karlov was the head of the society which had voted Gregor's death. So he had agents watching Hawksley. And Karlov himself undertook the chase across Russia, China, and the Pacific."

"I'm glad I gave him something to eat. But Gregor, a valet in a hotel, with all that money!"

"The red tape."

"What a dizzy world we live in, Cutty!"

"Dizzy is the word." Cutty sighed. His yarn had passed a very shrewd censor. "Karlov feels it his duty to kill off all his countryman who do not agree with his theories. He wanted these funds here, but Hawksley was too clever for him. Remember, now, not a word of this to Hawksley. I tell you this in confidence."

"I promise."

"You'll have to spend the night here. It's round four, and the power has been shut off. There's the stairs, but it would be dawn before you reach the street."

"Who cares?"

"I do. I don't believe you're in a good mood to send back to that garlicky warren. I wish to the Lord you'd leave it!"

"It's difficult to find anything desirable within my means. Rents are terrifying. I'll sleep on the divan. A rug or a blanket. I'm a silly fool, I suppose."

"You can have a guest room."

"I'd rather the divan; less scandalous. Cutty, I forgot. He played for me."

"What? He did?"

"I had to run out of the room because some things he said choked me up. Didn't care whether he died or not. He was even lonelier than I. I lay down on the divan, and then I heard music. Funny, but somehow I fancied he was calling me back; and I had to hang on to the divan. Cutty, he is a great violinist."

"Are you fond of music?"

"I am mad about it! I'm always running round to concerts; and I'd walk from Battery to Bronx to hear a good violinist."

Fiddles and Irish hearts. Swiftly came the vision of Hawksley fiddling the heart out of this lonely girl--if he had the chance. And he, Cutty, was going to fascinate her--with what? He rose and took her by the shoulders, bringing her round so that the light was full in her face. Slate-blue eyes.

"Kitty, what would you say if I kissed you?" Inwardly he asked: "Now, what the devil made me say that?"

The sinister and cynical idea leaped from its ambush. "Why, Cutty, I--I don't believe I should mind. It's--it's you!" Vile wretch that she was!

Cutty, noting the lily succeeding the rose, did not kiss her. Fate has a way of reversing the illogical and giving it logical semblance. It was perfectly logical that he should not kiss her; and yet that was exactly what he should have done. The fatherliness of the salute--and he couldn't have made it anything else--would have shamed Kitty's peculiar state of mind out of existence and probably sent back to its eternal sleep that which was strangely reawaking in his lonely heart.

"Forgive me, Kitty. That wasn't exactly nice of me, even if I was trying to be funny."

She tore away from him, flung herself upon the divan, her face in the pillows, and let down the dam.

This wild sobbing--apparently without any reason terrified Cutty. He put both hands into his hair, but he drew them out immediately without retaining any of the thinning gray locks. Done up, both of them; that was the matter. He longed to console her, but knew not what to say or how to act. He had not seen a woman weep like this in so many years that he had forgotten the remedies.

Should he call the nurse? But that would only add to Kitty's embarrassment, and the nurse would naturally misinterpret the situation. He couldn't kneel and put his arms round her; and yet it was a situation that called for arms and endearments. He had sense enough to recognize that. Molly's girl crying like that, and he able to do nothing! It was intolerable. But what was she weeping about?

Covering the divan was a fine piece of Bokhara embroidery. He drew this down over Kitty and tucked her in, turned off the light, and proceeded to his bedroom.

Kitty's sobs died eventually. There was an occasional hiccup. That, too, disappeared. To play--or even think of playing--a game like that! She was despicable. A silly little fool, too, to suppose that so keen a mind as Cutty's would not see through the artifice! What was happening to her that she could let such a thought into her head?

By and by she was able to pick up Cutty's narrative and review it. Not a word about the drums of jeopardy, the mark of the thong round Hawksley's neck. Hadn't she let him know that she knew the author of that advertisement offering to buy the drums, no questions asked? Very well, then; if he would not tell her the truth she would have to find it out herself.

Meanwhile, Cutty sat on the edge of his bed staring blankly at the rug, trying to find a pick-up to the emotions that beset him. One thing issued clearly: He had wanted to kiss the child. He still wanted to kiss her. Why hadn't he? Unanswerable. It was still unanswerable even when the pallor of dawn began slowly to absorb the artificial light of his bed lamp.

CHAPTER XXIII

When Cutty awoke--having had about two hours' sleep--he was instantly conscious that the zest had gone from the adventure. It had resolved itself into official business into which he had projected himself gratuitously; and having assumed the offices of chief factor, he would have to see the affair through, victim of his own greediness. It did not serve to marshal excuses. He had frankly entered the affair in the role of buccaneer; and here he was, high and dry on the reef.

The drums of jeopardy, so far as he was concerned, had been shot into the moon two hundred thousand miles out of reach. He found himself resenting Hawksley's honesty in the matter of the customs.

But immediately this sense of resentment caused him to chuckle. Certainly some ancestor of his had been a Black Bart or a Galloping Dick.

He would put a few straight questions to Hawksley, however. To have lost all those precious stones and not to have inquired about them was a bit foggy, wasn't normal, human. Unless--bang on the plexus came the thought!--the beggar had hidden them himself. He had been exceedingly clever in hiding the wallet. Come to think of it, he hadn't mentioned that, either. Of course he had hidden the stones--either in Gregor's apartment or in Kitty's. Blind as a bat. Now he understood why Karlov had made a prisoner of Coles. The old buzzard had sensed a trap and had countered it. The way of the transgressor was hard. His punishment for entertaining a looter's idea would be work when he wanted to loaf and enjoy himself.

Arriving at Hawksley's door he was confronted by a spectacle not without its humorous touch: The nurse extending a bowl and Hawksley staring at the sky beyond the window, stonily.

"But you must!" insisted Miss Frances.

"Chops or beefsteak!"

"It will give you nausea."

"Permit me to find out. Dash it, I'm hungry!" Hawksley declared. "I'm no fever patient. A smart rap on the head; nothing more than that. Healthy food will draw the blood down from there. Haven't lost anything but a few hours of consciousness, and you treat me as though I'd been jolly well peppered with shrapnel and gassed. Touch that stuff? Rather not! Chops or beefsteak!"

"Let him have it, Miss Frances," advised Cutty from the doorway.

"But it's unusual," replied the nurse as a final protest.

"Give it a try. Is he strong enough to sit up through breakfast?"

"He's really not fit. But if he insists on doing the one he might as well do the other."

"Righto!"--from the patient.

"Will you tell Kuroki to make it a beefsteak breakfast for four? I know how Mr. Hawksley feels. Been through the same bout." Cutty wanted Miss Frances out of the room.

"Very well. Only, I've warned him." Miss Frances left, somewhat miffed.

"Thanks," said Hawksley, smiling. "She thinks I'm a canary."

"Whereas you're an eagle."

"Or a vulture."

Cutty chew up a chair. "Frankly, I believe a good breakfast will put you a peg up."

"A beefsteak!" Hawksley stared ecstatically at the ceiling. "You see, I'm naturally tough. Always went in for rough sports--football, rowing, boxing. Poor old Stefani's idea; and not so bad, either. Of course he was always worrying about my hands; but I always took great care to keep them soft and pliant. Which sounds rummy, considering the pounding I used to give and take. My word, I used to go to bed with my hands done up in ointments like a professional beauty! Of course I'm dizzy yet, and the bally spot is sore; but solid food and some exercise will have me off your hands in no time. I don't fancy being coddled, y'know. I've been trouble enough."

"Don't let that worry you. I'll bring some togs in; flannels and soft shirts. We're about the same height. Anyhow, the difference won't be noticeable in flannels. I've had to tell Miss Conover a bit of fiction. I'll tell you, so if need arises you can back me up."

When Cutty finished his romance Hawksley frowned. "All said and done, if I'm not that splendid old chap's protege, what am I? But for his patience and kindness I'd have run true to the blood. He was with me at the balancing age, when a chap becomes a man or a rotter. He actually gave up a brilliant career because of me. He is a great musician, with that strange faculty of taking souls out of people and untwisting them. I have the gift, too, in a way; but there's always a bit of the devil in me when I play. Natural bent, I fancy. And they've killed him!"

"No," said Cutty, slowly. "But this is for your ear alone: He's alive; and one of these days I'll bring him to you. So buck up."

"Alive! Stefani alive!" whispered Hawksley. He stretched out his hand rather blindly, and Cutty was surprised at the strength of the grip. "Makes me feel choky. I say, are all Americans good Samaritans?"

Cutty put this aside because he did not care to disillusion Hawksley. "I found an appraiser's receipt in your wallet. You carried some fine jewels. Did you hide them or did Karlov get them? It struck me as odd that you haven't inquired about them." The change that came into Hawksley's face alarmed Cutty. The rich olive skin became chalky and the eyes closed. "What is it? Shall I call Miss Frances?"

"No." Hawksley opened his eyes, but looked dully straight ahead. "The stones! I was trying to forget! My God, I was trying to forget!"

"But they were yours?" Cutty was mystified beyond expression.

"Yes, mine, mine, mine!"--panting. "Damn them! Some day I'll tell you. But just now I can't toe the mark. I was trying to forget them! Against my heart, gnawing into my soul like the beetle of the Spanish Inquisition!" Silence. "But they were future bread and butter--for Gregor as well as for myself. They got them, and may they damn Karlov as they have damned me! I had no chance when I returned to Gregor's. They were on me instantly. I put up a fight, but I'd come from a lighted room and was practically blind. Let them go. Most of those stones came out of hell, anyhow. Let them go. There is an unknown grave between those stones and me."

The level despair of the tone appalled Cutty. A crime somewhere? There was still a bottom to this affair he had not plumbed? He rose, deeply agitated.

"I'll fetch those togs for you. Miss Conover will breakfast with us, and the sight of her will give you a brace. I'm sorry. I had to ask you."

"Beefsteak and a pretty girl! That's something. I suppose she was trapped by the lift not running." Hawksley was trying to meet Cutty halfway to cover up the tragedy. "I say, why the deuce do you let her live where she does?"

"Because I'm not legally her guardian. She is the daughter of the man and woman I loved best. All I can do is to watch over her. She lives on her earnings as a newspaper writer. I'd give her half of all I have if I had the least idea she would accept it."

"Fond of her?"

"Fond of her!" repeated Cutty. "Why, of course I'm fond of her!" There was a touch of indignation in his tone.

"Is she fond of you?"

"I suppose so." What was the chap driving at?

"Then marry her," suggested Hawksley with a cynical smile; "make a settlement and give her her freedom. Simple enough. What?"

Cutty stepped back, stunned and terrified. "She would laugh at me!"

"You never can tell," replied Hawksley, maintaining the crooked smile. The devil was blazing in his eyes now. "Try it. It's being done every day; even here in this big America of yours. From the European point of view you have compromised her— or she has compromised herself, by spending the night here. Convention has been disregarded. A ripping good chance, I call it. You tell me she wouldn't accept benefits, and you want to help her. If she's the kind I believe her to be, even if she refuses you she will not be angry. You never can tell what woman will or won't do."

An old and forgotten bit of mental machinery began to set up a ditter-datter in Cutty's brain. Marry Kitty? Make a settlement, and then give her her freedom? Rot! Girls of Kitty's calibre were above such expediencies. He tried to resurrect his interest in the drums of jeopardy, which he might now appropriate without having to shanghai his conscience. The clitter-clatter smothered it; indeed, this new racket upset and demoralized the well-ordered machinery of his thinking apparatus as applied daily. Marry Kitty!

"I'm old enough to be her father."

"What's that to do with it so long as convention is satisfied?"

Cutty was so shaken and confused that he missed the tragic irony of the voice. All the receptive avenues to his brain seemed to have shut down suddenly. He was conscious only of the clitter-clatter. Marry Kitty!

"You can't settle money on her," went on Hawksley, "without scandal. You can't offer her anything without offending her. And you can't let her go to rust without having her bit of good times."

"Utterly impossible," said Cutty, to the idea rather than to his tormentor.

"Oh, of course, if you have an affair--No, God forgive me, I don't mean that! I'm a damned ingrate! But your bringing up those stones and knocking off the top of all the misery piling up in my heart! I was only trying to hurt you, hurt myself, everybody. Please have a little patience with me, for I've come out of hell!" Hawksley turned aside his head.

"Buck up," said Cutty, his blazing wrath dropping to a smoulder. "I'll fetch those togs."

What had the boy done to fill him with such tragic bitterness? Was he Two-Hawks? Cutty dismissed this doubt instantly. He recalled the episode of the boy's conduct when confronted by the photograph of his mother. No human being could be a play actor in such a moment. The boy's emotion had been deep and real. Cutty recognized the fact that he had become as a block in the middle of a Chinese puzzle; only Fate could move him to his appointed place.

But offer marriage to Kitty so that he could provide for her! Mechanically he rummaged his clothes press for the suit he was to take to Hawksley. Well, why not? He could settle five thousand a year on her. His departure for the Balkans--he might be gone a year or more--could be legally construed as desertion. And with pretty clothes and freedom she would soon find some young chap to her liking. But would a girl like Kitty see it from his point of view? The marriage could take place an hour or two before he went aboard his ship. Hang it, Hawksley wasn't so far off. Kitty couldn't possibly be offended if he laid the business squarely on the table. To provide for Molly's girl!

When Kuroki announced that breakfast was ready, Cutty went into the living room for Kitty, whom he had not yet seen. He found her by a window fascinated by the splendour of the panorama as seen in the morning light. Not a vestige of the tears and disorder in which he had left her. What had been behind those tears?

Dainty and refreshing; to the eye as though she had stepped out of a bandbox. Compromised? That was utter rot! Wasn't Miss Frances here? Clitter-clatter, clitter-clatter. But Cutty was not aware that it was no longer in his head but in his heart.

"Breakfast is served, Your Highness," he announced with a grave salaam.

Kitty pirouetted. For some reason she could not explain to herself she wanted to laugh, sing, dance. Perhaps it was because she was only twenty-four. Or it might have had its origin in the tonicky awakening among all these beautiful furnishings.

She assumed a haughty expression--such as the Duchess of Gerolstein assumes when she appoints the private to the office of generalissimo--and with a careless wave of the hand said: "Summon His Highness!"

CHAPTER XXIV

Between Cutty's heart and his throat there was very little space at that moment for the propelment of sound. Kitty Conover had innocently--he understood that almost immediately and recovered his mental balance--Kitty had innocently thrown a bomb at his feet. It did not matter that it was a dud. The result was the same. For a second, then, all the terror, all the astounding suspension of thought and action attending the arrival of a shell on the battlefield were his. As an aftermath he would have liked very much to sit down. Instead, maintaining the mock gravity of his expression, he offered his arm, which Kitty accepted, still the Grand Duchess of Gerolstein. Pompously they marched into the dining room. But as Kitty saw Hawksley she dropped the air confusedly, and hesitated. "Good gracious!" she whispered.

"What's the matter?" Cutty whispered in turn.

"My clothes!"

"What's the matter with 'em?"

"I slept in them!"

If that wasn't like a woman! It did not matter how she might look to an old codger, aetat. fifty-two; he didn't count. But a handsome young chap, now, in white flannels and sport shirt, his head bound picturesquely--

"Don't let that bother you," he said. "Those duds of his are mine."

Still, Cutty was grateful for this little diversion. As he drew back Kitty's chair he was wholly himself again. At once he dictated the trend of the conversation, moved it whither he willed, into strange channels, gave them all a glimpse of his amazing versatility, with vivid shafts of humour to light up corners.

Kuroki, who had travelled far with his master these ten years, sometimes paused in his rounds to nod affirmatively.

Hawksley listened intently, wondering a bit. What was the dear old beggar's idea, throwing such fireworks round at breakfast? He stole a glance at Kitty to see how she was taking it--and caught her stealing a glance at him. Instantly both switched back to Cutty. Shortly the little comedy was repeated because neither could resist the invisible force of some half-conscious inquiry. Third time, they smiled unembarrassedly. Mind you, they were both hanging upon Cutty's words; only their eyes were like little children at church, restless. It was spring.

Without being exactly conscious of what he was doing, Hawksley began to dress Kitty--that is, he visualized her in ball gowns, in sports, in furs. He put her on horses, in opera boxes, in limousines. But in none of these pictures could he hold her; she insisted upon returning to her kitchen to fry bacon and eggs.

Then came a twisted thought, rejected only to return; a surprising thought, so alluring that the sense of shame, of chivalry, could not press it back. Cutty's words began to flow into one ear and out of the other, without sense. There was in his heart--put there by the recollection of the jewels--an indescribable bitterness, a desperate cynicism that urged him to strike out, careless of friend or foe. Who could say what would happen to him when he left here? A flash of spring madness, then to go forth devil-may-care.

She was really beautiful, full of unsuspected fire. To fan it into white flame. The whole affair would depend upon whether she cared for music. If she did he would pluck the soul out of her. She had saved his life. Well, what of that? He had broken yonder man's bread and eaten his salt. Still, what of that? Hadn't he come from a race of scoundrels? The blood--he had smothered and repressed it all his life--to unleash it once, happen what might. If she were really fond of music!

Once again Kitty's glance roved back to Hawksley. This time she encountered a concentration in his unwavering stare. She did not quite like it. Perhaps he was only thinking about something and wasn't actually seeing her. Still, it quieted down the fluttering gayety of her mood. There was a sun spot of her own that became visible whenever her interest in Cutty's monologue lagged. Perhaps Hawksley had his sun spot.

"And so," she heard Cutty say. "Mr. Hawksley is going to become an American citizen. Kitty, what are some of the principles of good citizenship?"

"To be nice to policemen. Not to meddle with politics, because it is vulgar.

To vote perfunctorily. To 'let George do it' when there are reforms to be brought about. To keep your hat on when the flag goes by because otherwise you will attract attention. To find fault without being able to offer remedies. To keep in debt because life here in America would be monotonous without bill collectors."

Cutty interrupted with a laugh. "Kitty, you'll 'scare Hawksley off the map!"

"Let him know the worst at once," retorted Kitty, flashing a smile at the victim.

"Spoofing me--what?" said Hawksley, appealing to his host.

This quality of light irony in a woman was a distinct novelty to Hawksley. She had humour, then? So much the better. An added zest to the game he was planning. He recalled now that she was not of the clinging kind either. A woman with a humorous turn of mind was ten times more elusive than a purely sentimental one. Give him an hour or two with that old Amati--if she really cared for music! She would be coming to the apartment again--some afternoon, when his host was out of the way. Better still, he would call her by telephone; the plea of loneliness. Scoundrel? Of course he was. He was not denying that. He would embark upon this affair without the smug varnish of self-lies. Fire--to play with it!

He ate his portion of beefsteak, potatoes, and toast, and emptied his coffee cup. It was really the first substantial meal he had had in many hours. A feeling of satisfaction began to permeate him. He smiled at Miss Frances, who shook her head dubiously. She could not quite make him out pathologically. Perhaps she had been treating him as shell-shocked when there was nothing at all the matter with his nerves.

Presently Kuroki came in with a yellow envelope, which he laid at the side of Cutty's plate.

"Telegrams!" exploded Cutty. "Hang it, I don't want any telegrams!"

"Open it and have it over with," suggested Kitty.

"If you don't mind."

It was the worst kind of news--a summons to Washington for conference. Which signified that the Government's plans were completed and that shortly he would be on his way to Piraeus.

A fine muddle! Hawksley in no condition to send upon his way; Kitty's affair unsettled; the emeralds still in camera obscura; Karlov at liberty with his infernal schemes, and Stefani Gregor his prisoner. Wild horses, pulling him two ways. A word, and Karlov would come to the end of his rope suddenly. But if he issued that word the whole fabric he had erected so painstakingly would blow away like cardboard. If those emeralds turned up in the possession of any man but himself the ensuing complications would be appalling. For he himself would be forced to tell what he knew about the stones: Hawksley would be thrust conspicuously into the limelight, and sooner or later some wild anarch would kill him. Known, Hawksley would not have one chance in a thousand. Kitty would be dragged into the light and harassed and his own attitude toward her misunderstood. All these things, if he acted upon his oath. Nevertheless, he determined to risk suspension of operations until he returned from Washington. There was one sound plank to cling to. He had first-hand information that anarchistic elements would remain in their noisome cellars until May first. If he were not ordered abroad until after that, no harm would follow his suspension of operations.

"Bad news?" asked Kitty, anxiously.

"Aggravating rather than bad. I am called to Washington. May be gone four or five days. Official business. Leaves things here a bit in the air."

"I'll stay as long as you need me," said Miss Frances.

"I'd rather a man now. You've been a brick. You need rest. I've a chap in mind. He'll make our friend here toe the mark. A physical instructor, ex-pugilist; knows all about broken heads."

"I say, that's ripping!" cried Hawksley. "Give me your man, and I'll be off your hands within a week. The sooner you stop fussing over me the sooner the crack in my head will cease to bother me.

"Kuroki will cook for you and Ryan will put you through the necessary stunts. The roof, when the weather permits, makes a good exercising ground. If you'll excuse me I'll do some telephoning. Kuroki, pack my bag for a five-day trip to Washington. I'll take you down to the office, Kitty."

"I don't fancy I ever will quite understand you," said Hawksley, leaning back in his chair, listlessly. "Honestly, now, you'd be perfectly justified in bundling me off to some hotel. I have funds. Why all this pother about me?"

Cutty smiled. "When I tackle anything I like to carry it through. I want to put you on your train."

"To be reasonably sure that I shan't come back?"

"Precisely"--but without smiling. With a vague yet inclusive nod Cutty hurried off.

"It is because he is such a thorough sportsman. Mr. Hawksley," Kitty explained. "Having accepted certain obligations he cannot abrogate them off hand."

"Did I bother you last night? I mean, did my fiddling?"

"Mercy, no! From the hurdy-gurdy of my childhood, down to Kubelik and his successors, I have been more or less music-mad. You play--wonderfully!" Sudden, inexplicable shyness.

Hawksley smiled. An hour or two with that old Amati.

"I am only an unconventional amateur. You should hear Stefani Gregor when the mood is on. He puts something into your soul that makes you wish to go forth at once to do some fine, unselfish act."

Stefani Gregor! He thought of the clear white soul of the man who had surrendered imperishable fame to stand between him and the curse of his blood; who had for ten years stood between his mother and the dissolute man whom irony had selected for the part of father. Ten years of diplomacy, tact, patience. Stefani Gregor! There was the blood, predatory and untamed; and there was the spirit which the old musician had moulded. He could not harm this girl. Dead or alive, Stefani Gregor would not permit it.

Hawksley rose slowly and without further speech walked to the corridor door. He leaned against the jamb for a moment, then went on to his bedroom.

"I'm afraid that breakfast was too much for him," the nurse ventured. "An odd young man."

"Very," replied Kitty, rather absently. She was trying to analyze that flash of shyness.

Meantime, Cutty sat down before the telephone. He wanted Kitty out of town during his absence. In her present excitable mood he was afraid to trust her. She might surrender to any mad impulse that stirred her fancy. So he called up Burlingame. Kitty's chief, and together they manufactured an assignment that was always a pleasant recollection to Kitty.

Next, Cutty summoned Professor Billy Ryan to the wire, argued and cajoled for ten minutes, and won his point. He was always dealing in futures--banking his favours here and there and drawing checks against them when needed.

Then he tackled his men and issued orders suspending operations temporarily. He was asked what they should do in case Karlov came out into the open. He answered in such an event not to molest him but to watch and take note of those with whom he associated. There were big things in the air, and only he himself had hold of all the threads. He relayed this information to the actual chief of the local service, from whom he had borrowed his men. There was no protest. Green spectacles.

Quarter to nine he and Kitty entered a subway car and found a corner to themselves, while Karlov's agent was content with a strap in the crowded end of the car.

Karlov for once had outthought Cutty. He had withdrawn his watchers, confident that after a day or so his unknown opponent would withdraw his. During the lull Karlov matured his plans, then resumed operations, calculating that he would have some forty-odd hours' leeway.

His agent was clever. He had followed Kitty from Eightieth Street to the Knickerbocker Hotel. There he had lost her. He had loitered on the sidewalk until midnight, and was then convinced that the girl had slipped by. So he had returned to Eightieth Street; but as late as five in the morning she had not returned.

This agent had followed the banker after his visit to Kitty. He had watched the banker's house, seen Cutty arrive and depart. Taking a chance shot in the dark, he had followed Cutty to the office building, learned that Cutty was the owner and lived in the loft. As Kitty had not returned home by five he proceeded to take a second chance shot in the dark, stationing himself across the street from the entrance to the office building, thereby solving the riddle uppermost in Karlov's mind. He had found the man in the dress suit.

"Cutty, I'm sorry I was such a booby last night. But it was the best thing that could have happened. The pentupness of it was simply killing me. I hadn't any one to come to but you--any one who would understand. I don't know of any man who has a better right to kiss me. I know. You were just trying to buck me up."

Clitter-clatter! Clitter-clatter! Cutty stared hard at the cement floor. Marry her, settle a sum on her, and give her her freedom. Molly's girl. Give her a chance to play. He turned.

"Kitty, do you trust me?"

"Of all the foolish questions!" She pressed his arm. "Why shouldn't I trust you?"

"Will you marry me? Wait! Let me make clear to you what I have in mind. I'm all alone. I loved your mother. It breaks my heart that while I have everything in the way of luxuries you have nothing. I can't settle a sum on you--an income. The world wouldn't understand. Your friends would be asking questions among themselves. This telegram from Washington means but one thing: that in a few weeks I shall be on my way to the East. I shall be mighty unhappy if I have to go leaving you in the rut. This is my idea: marry me an hour or so before the ship sails. I will leave you a comfortable income. Lord knows how long I shall be gone. Well, I won't write. After a year you can regain your freedom on the grounds of desertion. Simple as falling off a log. It's the one logical way I can help you. Will you?"

Station after station flashed by. Kitty continued stare through the window across the way, by and by she turned her face toward him, her eyes shining with tears.

"Cutty, there is going to be a nice place in heaven for you some day. I understand. I believe Mother understands, too. Am I selfish? I can't say No to you and I can't say Yes. Yet I should be a liar if I did not say that everything in me leaps toward the idea. It is both hateful and fascinating. Common sense says Yes; and something else in me says No. I like dainty things, dainty surroundings. I want to travel, to see something of the world. I once thought I had creative genius, but I might as well face the fact that I haven't. Only by accident will I ever earn more than I'm earning now. In a few years I'll grow old suddenly. You know what the newspaper game does to women. The rush and hurry of it, the excitements, the ceaseless change. It is a furnace, and women shrivel up in it quicker than men."

"There won't be any nonsense, Kitty. An hour before I go aboard my ship. I'll go back to the job the happiest of men. Molly's girl taken care of! Just before your father died I promised him I'd keep an eye on you. I never forgot, but conditions made it impossible. The apartment will be yours as long as you need it. Kuroki, of course, goes with me. It's merely going by convention on the blind side. To leave you something in my will wouldn't serve at all, I'm a tough old codger and may be marked down for a hale old ninety. All I want is to make you happy and carefree."

"Cutty, I'd like to curl up in some corner and cry, gratefully. I didn't know there were such men. I just don't know what to do. It isn't as if you were asking me to be your wife. And as you say, I can't accept money. There is a pride in me that rejects the whole thing; but it may be the same fool pride that has cut away my friends. I ought to fall on your neck with joy: and here I am trying to look round corners! You are my father's friend, my mother's, mine. Why shouldn't I accept the proposition? You are alone, too. You have a perfect right to do as you please with your money, and I have an equally perfect right to accept your gifts. We are all afraid of the world, aren't we? That's probably at the bottom of my doddering. Cutty, what is love?" she broke off, whimsically.

"Looking into mirrors and hunting for specks," he answered, readily.

"I mean seriously."

"So do I. Before I went round to the stage entrance to take your mother out to supper I used to preen an hour before the mirror. My collar, my cravat, my hair, the nap on my stovepipe, my gloves--terrible things! And what happened? Your dad, dressed in his office clothes, came along like a cyclone, walked all over my toes, and swooped up your mother right from under my nose. Now just look the proposition over from all angles. Think of yourself; let the old world go hang. They'll call it alimony. In a year or so you'll be free; and some chap like Tommy Conover will come along, and bang! You'll know all about love. Here's old Brooklyn Bridge. I'll see you to the elevator. All nonsense that you should have the least hesitance."

Fifteen minutes later he was striding along Park Row. By the swing of his stride any onlooker would have believed that Cutty was in a hurry to arrive somewhere. Instead, one was only walking. Suddenly he stopped in the middle of the sidewalk with the two currents of pedestrians flowing on each side of him, as a man might stop who saw some wonderful cloud effect. But there was nothing ecstatical in his expression; on the contrary, there was a species of bewildered terror. The psychology of all his recent actions had in a flash become vividly clear.

An unbelievable catastrophe had overtaken him. He loved Kitty, loved her with an intense, shielding passion, quite unlike that which he had given her mother. Such a thing could happen! He offered not the least combat; the revelation was too smashing to admit of any doubt. It was not a recrudescence of his love for Molly, stirred into action by the association with Molly's daughter. He wanted Kitty for himself, wanted her with every fibre in his body, fiercely. And never could he tell her--now.

The tragic irony of it all numbed him. Fate hadn't played the game fairly. He was fifty-two, on the far side of the plateau, near sunset. It wasn't a square deal.

Still he stood there on the sidewalk, like a rock in the middle of a turbulent stream, rejecting selfish thoughts. Marry Kitty, and tell her the truth afterward. He knew the blood of her--loyalest of the loyal. He could if he chose play that sort of game--cheat her. He could not withdraw his proposition. If she accepted it he would have to carry it through. Cheat her.

CHAPTER XXV

Kitty hung up her hat and coat. She did not pat her hair or tuck in the loose ends before the mirror--a custom as invariable as sunrise. The coat tree stood at the right of the single window, and out of this window Kitty stared solemnly, at everything and at nothing.

Burlingame eyed her seriously. Cutty had given him a glimmer of the tale-- enough to make known to him that this pretty, sensible girl, though no fault of her own, was in the shadow of some actual if unknown danger. And Cutty wanted her out of town for a few days. Burlingame had intended sending Kitty out of town on an assignment during Easter week. An exchange of telegrams that morning had closed the gap in time.

"Well, you might say 'Good morning.'"

"I beg your pardon, Burly!" In newspaper offices you belong at once or you never belong; and to belong is to have your name sheared to as few syllables as possible. You are formal only to the city editor, the managing editor, and the auditor.

"What's the matter?"

"I've been set in the middle of a fairy story," said Kitty, "and I'm wondering if it's worth the trouble to try to find a way out. A Knight of the Round Table, a prince of chivalry. What would you say if you saw one in spats and a black derby?"

"Why," answered Burlingame, "I suppose I'd consider July first as the best thing that could happen to me."

Kitty laughed; and that was what he wanted.

What had that old rogue been doing now--offering Kitty his eighteen-story office building?

"It's odd, isn't it, that I shouldn't possess a little histrionic ability. You'd think it would be in my blood to act."

"It is, Kitty; only not to mimic. You're an actress, but the Big Dramatist writes your business for you. Now, I've got some fairly good news for you. An assignment."

"Work! What is it?"

"I am going to send you on a visit to the most charming movie queen in the business. She is going to return to Broadway this autumn, and she has a trunkful of plays to read. I have found your judgment ace-high. Mornings you will read with her; afternoons you will visit. She remembers your mother, who was the best comedienne of her day. So she will be quite as interested in you as you are in her. I want you to note her ways, how she amuses herself, eats, exercises. I want you to note the contents of her beautiful home; if she likes dogs or cats or horses. You will take a camera and get half a dozen good pictures, and a page yarn for Easter Sunday. Stay as long as she wants you to."

"But who?"

Burlingame jerked his thumb toward a photograph on the wall.

"Oh! This will be the most scrumptious event in my life. I'm wild about her! But I haven't any clothes!"

Burlingame waved his hands. "I knew I'd hear that yodel. Eve didn't have anything to speak of, but she travelled a lot. Truth is, Kitty, you'd better dress in monotones. She might wake up to the fact that you're a mighty pretty young woman and suddenly become temperamental. She has a husband round the lot somewhere. Make him think his wife is a lucky woman. Here's all the dope--introduction, expenses, and tickets. Train leaves at two-fifty. Run along home and pack. Remember, I want a page yarn. No flapdoodle or mush; straight stuff. She doesn't need any advertising. If you go at it right you two will react upon each other as a tonic."

Kitty realized that this little junket was the very thing she needed--open spaces, long walks in which to think out her problem. She hurried home and spent the morning packing. When this heartrending business was over she summoned Tony Bernini.

"I am going out of town, Mr. Bernini. I may be gone a week."

"All right, Miss Conover." Bernini hid a smile. He knew all about this trip, having been advised by Cutty over the wire.

"Am I being followed any more?"

"Not that we know of. Still, you never can tell. What's your destination?" Kitty told him. "Better not go by train. I can get a fast roadster and run you out in a couple of hours. Right after lunch you go to the boss's garage and wait for me. I'll take care of your grips and camera. I'll follow on your heels."

"Anybody would consider that Karlov was after me instead of Hawksley."

Bernini smiled. "Miss Conover, the moment Karlov puts his hands on you the whole game goes blooey. That's the plain fact. There is death in this game. These madmen expect to blow up the United States on May first. We are easing them along because we want the top men in our net. But if Karlov takes it into his head to get you, and succeeds, he'll have a stranglehold on the whole local service; because we'd have to make great concessions to free you."

"Why wasn't I told this at the start?"

"You were told, indirectly. We did not care to frighten you."

"I'm not frightened," said Kitty.

"Nope. But we wish to the Lord you were, Miss Conover. When you want to come home, wire me and I'll motor out for you."

Another fragment. Karlov's agent sought his chief and found him in the cellar of the old house, sinisterly engaged. The wall bench was littered with paraphernalia well known to certain chemists. Had the New York bomb squad known of the existence of this den, the short hair on their necks would have risen.

"Well?" greeted Karlov, moodily.

"I have found the man in the dress suit."

"He and the Conover girl left that office building together this morning, and I followed them to Park Row. This man uses the loft of the building for his home. No elevator goes up unless you have credentials. Our man is hiding there, Boris."

Karlov dry-washed his hands. "We'll send him one of the samples if we fail in regard to the girl. You say she arrives daily at the newspaper office about nine and leaves between five and six?"

"Every day but Sunday."

"Good news. Two bolts; one or the other will go home."

About the same time in Cutty's apartment rather an amusing comedy took place. Professor Ryan, late physical instructor at one of the aviation camps, stood Hawksley in front of him and ran his hard hands over the young man's body. Miss

Frances stood at one side, her arms folded, her expression skeptical.

"Nothin' the matter with you, Bo, but the crack on the conk."

"Right-o!" agreed Hawksley.

"Lemme see your hands. Humph. Soft. Now stand on that threshold. That's it. Walk t' the' end o' the hall an' back. Step lively."

"But," began Miss Frances in protest. This was cruelty.

"I'm the doctor, miss," interrupted Ryan, crisply. "If he falls down he goes t' bed, an' you stay. If he makes it, he follows my instructions."

When Hawksley returned to the starting line the walls rocked, there were two or three blinding stabs of pain; but he faced this unusual Irishman with never a hint of the torture. A wild longing to be gone from this kindly prison--to get away from the thought of the girl.

"All right," said Ryan. "Now toddle back t' bed."

"Bed?"

"Yep. Goin' t' give you a rub that'll start all your machinery workin'."

Docilely Hawksley obeyed. He wasn't going to let them know, but that bed was going to be tolerably welcome.

"Well!" said Miss Frances. "I don't see how he did it."

"I do," said the ex-pugilist. "I told him to. Either he was a false alarm, or he'd attempt the job even if he fell down. The hull thing is this: Make a guy wanta get well an' he'll get well. If he's got any pride, dig it up. Go after 'em. He hasn't lost any blood. No serious body wound. A crack on the conk. It mighta killed him. It didn't. He didn't wabble an' fall down. So my dope is right. Drop in in a few days an' I'll show yuh."

Miss Frances held out her hand. "You've handled men," she said, with reluctant admiration.

"Oh, boy!--millions of 'em, an' each guy different. Believe me! Make 'em wanta."

Cutty attended his conferences. He learned immediately that he was booked to sail the first week in May. His itinerary began at Piraeus, in Greece, and might end in Vladivostok. But they detained him in Washington overtime because he was a fount of information the departments found it necessary to draw upon constantly. The political and commercial aspects of the polyglot peoples, what they wanted, what they expected, what they needed; racial enmities. The bugaboo of the undesirable alien was no longer bothering official heads in Washington. Stringent immigration laws were in the making. What they wanted to know was an American's point of view, based upon long and intimate associations.

Washington reminded him of nothing so much as a big sheep dog. The hazardous day was over; the wolves had been driven off and the sheep into the fold; and now the valiant guardian was turning round and round and round preparatory to lying down to sleep. For Washington would go to sleep again, naturally.

Often it occurred to him what a remarkable piece of machinery the human brain was. He could dig up all this dry information with the precise accuracy of an economist, all the while his actual thoughts upon Kitty. His nights were nightmares. And all this unhappiness because he had been touched with the lust for loot. Fundamentally, this catastrophe could be laid to the drums of jeopardy.

The alluring possibility of finding those damnable green stones--the unsuspected kink in his moral rectitude--had tumbled him into this pit. Had not Kitty pronounced the name Stefani Gregor--in his mind always linked with the emeralds--he would have summoned an ambulance and had Hawksley carried off, despite Kitty's protests; and perhaps he would have seen her but two or three times before sailing, seen her in conventional and unemotional parts. At any rate, there would have been none of this peculiar intimacy--Kitty coming to him in tears, opening her young heart to him and discovering all its loneliness. If she loved some chap it would not be so hard, the temptation would not be so keen--to cheat her. Marry her, and then tell her. This dogged his thoughts like a murderer's deed, terrible in the watches of the night. Marry her, and then tell her. Cheat her. Break her heart and break his own.

Fifty-two. Never before had he thought old. His splendid health and vigorous mentality were the results of thinking young. But now he heard the avalanche stirring, the whispering slither of the first pebbles. He would grow old swiftly, thunderously. Kitty's youth would shore up the debacle, suspend it indefinitely. Marry her, cheat her, and stay young. Green stones, accursed.

Kitty's days were pleasant enough, but her nights were sieges. One evening someone put Elman's rendition of Schubert's "Ave Maria" on the phonograph. Long after it was over she sat motionless in her chair. Echoes. The Tschaikowsky waltz.

She got up suddenly, excused herself, and went to her room.

Six days, and her problem was still unsolved. Something in her--she could not define it, she could not reach it, it defied analysis--something, then, revolted at the idea of marrying Cutty, divorcing him, and living on his money. There was a touch of horror in the suggestion. It was tearing her to pieces, this hidden repellence. And yet this occult objection was so utterly absurd. If he died and left her a legacy she would accept it gratefully enough. Cutty's plan was only a method of circumventing this indefinite wait.

Comforts, the good things of life, amusements--simply by nodding her head. Why not? It wasn't as if Cutty was asking her to be his wife; he wasn't. Just wanted to dodge convention, and give her freedom and happiness. He was only giving her a mite out of his income. Because he had loved her mother; because, but for an accident of chance, she, Kitty, might have been his daughter. Why, then, this persistent and unaccountable revulsion? Why should she hesitate? The ancient female fear of the trap? That could not be it. For a more honourable, a more lovable man did not walk the earth. Brave, strong, handsome, whimsical--why, Cutty was a catch!

Comfy. Never any of that inherent doubt of man when she was with him. Absolute trust. An evil thought had entered her head; fate had made it honourably possible. And still this mysterious repellence.

Romance? She was not surrendering her right to that. What was a year out of her life if afterward she would be in comfortable circumstances, free to love where she willed? She wasn't cheating herself or Cutty: she was cheating convention, a flimsy thing at best.

Windows. We carry our troubles to our windows; through windows we see the stars. We cannot visualize God, but we can see His stars pinned to the immeasurable spaces. So Kitty sought her window and added her question to the countless millions forlornly wandering about up there, and finding no answer.

But she would return to New York on the morrow. She would not summon Bernini as she had promised. She would go back by train, alone, unhampered.

And in his cellar Boris Karlov spun his web for her.

CHAPTER XXVI

Hawksley heard the lift door close, and he knew that at last he was alone. He flung out his arms, ecstatically. Free! He would see no more of that nagging beggar Ryan until tomorrow. Free to put into execution the idea that had been bubbling all day long in his head, like a fine champagne, firing his blood with reckless whimsicality.

Quietly he stole down the corridor. Through a crack in the kitchen door he saw Kuroki's back, the attitude of which was satisfying. It signified that the Jap was pegging away at his endless studies and that only the banging of the gong would rouse him. The way was as broad and clear as a street at dawn. Not that Kuroki mattered; only so long as he did not know, so much the better.

With careful step Hawksley manoeuvred his retreat so that it brought him to Cutty's bedroom door. The door was unlocked. He entered the room. What a lark! They would hide his own clothes; so much the worse for the old beggar's wardrobe. Street clothes. Presently he found a dark suit, commendable not so much for its style as for the fact that it was the nearest fit he could find. He had to roll up the trouser hems.

Hats. Chuckling like a boy rummaging a jam closet, he rifled the shelves and pulled down a black derby of an unknown vintage. Large; but a runner of folded paper reduced the size. As he pressed the relic firmly down on his head he winced. A stab over his eyes. He waited doubtfully; but there was no recurrence. Fit as a fiddle. Of course he could not stoop without a flash of vertigo; but on his feet he was top-hole. He was gaining every day.

Luck. He might have come out of it with the blank mind of a newborn babe; and here he was, keen to resume his adventures. Luck. They had not stopped to see if he was actually dead. Some passer-by in the hall had probably alarmed them.

That handkerchief had carried him round the brink. Perhaps Fate intended letting him get through--written on his pass an extension of his leave of absence. Or she had some new torture in reserve.

Now for a stout walking stick. He selected a blackthorn, twirled it, saluted, and posed before the mirror. Not so bally rotten. He would pass. Next, he remembered that there were some flowers in the dining room--window boxes with scarlet geraniums. He broke off a sprig and drew it through his buttonhole.

Outside there was a cold, pale April sky, presaging wind and rain. Unimportant. He was going down into the streets for an hour or so. The colour and action of a crowded street; the lure was irresistible. Who would dare touch him in the crowd? These rooms had suddenly become intolerable.

He leaned against the side of the window. Roofs, thousands of them, flat, domed, pinnacled; and somewhere under one of these roofs Stefani Gregor was eating his heart out. It did not matter that this queer old eagle whom everybody called Cutty had promised to bring Stefani home. It might be too late. Stefani was old, highly strung. Who knew what infernal lies Karlov had told him? Stefani could stand up under physical torture; but to tear at his soul, to twist and rend his spirit!

The bubble in the champagne died down--as it always will if one permits it to stand. He felt the old mood seep through the dikes of his gayety. Alone. A familiar face--he would have dropped on his knees and thanked God for the sight of a familiar face. These people, kindly as they were--what were they but strangers? Yesterday he had not known them; to-morrow he would leave them behind forever. All at once the mystery of this bubbling idea was bared: he was going to risk his life in the streets in the vague hope of seeing some face he had known in the days before the world had gone drunk on blood. One familiar face.

Of course he would never forget--at any rate, not the girl whose courage had made possible this hour. Those chaps, scared off temporarily, might have returned. What had become of her? He was always seeing her lovely face in the shadows, now tender, now resolute, now mocking. Doubtless he thought of her constantly because his freedom of action was limited. He hadn't diversion enough. Books and fiddling, these carried him but halfway through the boredom. Where was she? Daily he had called her by telephone; no answer. The Jap shook his head; the slangy boy in the lift shook his.

She was a thoroughbred, even if she had been born of middle-class parentage. He laughed bitterly. Middle class. A homeless, countryless derelict, and he had the impudence to revert to comparisons that no longer existed in this topsy-turvy old world. He was an upstart. The final curtain had dropped between him and his world, and he was still thinking in the ancient make-up. Middle class! He was no better than a troglodyte, set down in a new wilderness.

He heard the curtain rings slither on the pole. Believing the intruder to be Kuroki he turned belligerently. And there she stood--the girl herself! The poise of her reminded him of the Winged Victory in the Louvre. Where there had been a cup of champagne in his veins circumstance now poured a magnum.

"You!" he cried.

"What has happened? Where are you going in those clothes?" demanded Kitty.

"I am running away--for an hour or so."

"But you must not! The risks--after all the trouble we've had to help you!"

"I shall be perfectly safe, for you are going with me. Aren't you my guardian angel? Well, rather! The two of us--people, lights, shop windows! Perfectly splendiferous! Honestly, now, where's the harm?" He approached her rapidly as he spoke, and before the spell of him could be shaken off Kitty found her hands imprisoned in his. "Please! I've been so damnably bored. The two of us in the streets, among the crowds! No one will dare touch us. Can't you see? And then--I say, this is ripping!--we'll have dinner together here. I will play for you on the old Amati. Please!"

The fire of him communicated to the combustibles in Kitty's soul. A wild, reckless irony besieged her. This adventure would be exactly what she needed; it would sweep clear the fog separating one side of her brain from the other. For it was plain enough that part of her brain refused to cooperate with the other. A break in the trend of thought: she might succeed in getting hold of the puzzle if she could drop it absolutely for a little while and then pick it up again.

She had not gone home. She had not notified Bernini. She had checked her luggage in the station parcel room and come directly here. For what? To let the sense of luxury overcome the hidden repugnance of the idea of marrying Cutty, divorcing him, and living on his money. To put herself in the way of visible temptation. What fretted her so, what was wearing her down to the point of fatigue, was the patent imbecility of her reluctance. There would have been some sense of it if Cutty had proposed a real marriage. All she had to do was mumble a few words, sign her name to a document, live out West for a few months, and be in comfortable circumstances all the rest of her life. And she doddered!

She would run the streets with Johnny Two-Hawks, return, and dine with him. Who cared? Proper or improper, whose business was it but Kitty Conover's? Danger? That was the peculiar attraction. She wanted to rush into danger, some tense excitement the strain of which would lift her out of her mood. A recurrent touch of the wild impulsiveness of her childhood. Hadn't she sometimes flown out into thunderstorms, after merited punishment, to punish the mother whom thunder terrorized? And now she was going to rush into unknown danger to punish Fate--like a silly child! Nevertheless, she would go into the streets with Johnny Two-Hawks.

"But are you strong enough to venture on the streets?"

"Rot! Dash it all, I'm no mollycoddle! All nonsense to keep me pinned in like this. Will you go with me--be my guide?"

"Yes!" She shot out the word and crossed the Rubicon before reason could begin to lecture. Besides, wasn't reason treating her shabbily in withholding the key to the riddle? "Johnny Two-Hawks, I will go as far as Harlem if you want me to."

"Johnny Two-Hawks!" He laughed joyously, then kissed her hands. But he had to pay for this bending--a stab that filled his eyes with flying sparks. He must remember, once out of doors, not to stoop quickly. "I say, you're the jolliest girl I ever met! Just the two of us, what?"

"The way you speak English is wonderful!"

"Simple enough to explain. Had an English nurse from the beginning. Spoke English and Italian before I spoke Russian."

He seized the wooden mallet and beat the Burmese gong--a flat piece of brass cut in the shape of a bell. The clear, whirring vibrations filled the room. Long before these spent themselves Kuroki appeared on the threshold. He bobbed.

"Kuroki, Miss Conover is dining here with me to-night. Seven o'clock sharp. The best you have in the larder."

"Yes, sair. You are going out, sair?"

"For a bit of fresh air."

"And I am going with him, Kuroki," said Kitty. Kuroki bobbed again. "Dinner at seven, sair." Another bob, and he returned to the kitchen, smiling. The girl was free to come and go, of course, but the ancient enemy of Nippon would not pass the elevator door. Let him find that out for himself.

When the elevator arrived the boy did not open the door. He noted the derby on Hawksley's head.

"I can take you down, Miss Conover, but I cannot take Mr. Hawksley. When the boss gives me an order I obey it--if I possibly can. On the day the boss tells me you can go strolling, I'll give you the key to the city. Until then, nix! No use arguing, Mr. Hawksley."

"I shan't argue," replied Hawksley, meekly. "I am really a prisoner, then?"

"For your own good, sir. Do you wish to go down, Miss Conover?"

"No."

The boy swung the lever, and the car dropped from sight.

"I'm sorry," said Kitty.

Hawksley smiled and laid a finger on his lips. "I wanted to know," he whispered. "There's another way down from this Matterhorn. Come with me. Off the living room is a storeroom. I found the key in the lock the other day and investigated. I still have the key. Now, then, there's a door that gives to the main loft. At the other end is the stairhead. There is a door at the foot of the first flight down. We can jolly well leave this way, but we shall have to return by the lift. That bally young ruffian can't refuse to carry us up, y' know!"

Kitty laughed. "This is going to be fun!"

"Rather!"

They groped their way through the dim loft--for it was growing dark outside--and made the stairhead. The door to the seventeenth floor opened, and they stepped forth into the lighted hallway.

"Now what?" asked Kitty, bubbling.

"The floor below, and one of the other lifts, what?" Twenty minutes later the two of them, arm in arm, turned into Broadway.

"This, sir," began Kitty with a gesture, "is Broadway--America's backyard in the daytime and Ali Baba's cave at night. The way of the gilded youth; the funnel for papa's money; the chorus lady; the starting point of the high cost of living. We

New Yorkers despise it because we can't afford it."

"The lights!" gasped Hawksley.

"Wreckers' lights. Behold! Yonder is a highly nutritious whisky blinking its bloomin' farewell. Do you chew gum? Even if you don't, in a few minutes I'll give you a cud for thought. Chewing gum was invented by a man with a talkative wife. He missed the physiological point, however, that a body can chew and talk at the same time. Come on!"

They went on uptown, Hawksley highly amused, exhilarated, but frequently puzzled. The pungent irony of her observations conveyed to him that under this gayety was a current of extreme bitterness. "I say, are all American girls like you?"

"Heavens, no! Why?"

"Because I never met one like you before. Rather stilted--on their good behaviour, I fancy."

"And I interest you because I'm not on my good behaviour?" Kitty whipped back.

"Because you are as God made you--without camouflage."

"The poor innocent young man! I'm nothing but camouflage to-night. Why are you risking your life in the street? Why am I sharing that risk? Because we both feel bound and are blindly trying to break through. What do you know about me? Nothing. What do I know about you? Nothing. But what do we care? Come on, come on!"

Tumpitum--tump! tumpitum--tump! drummed the Elevated. Kitty laughed. The tocsin! Always something happened when she heard it.

"Pearls!" she cried, dragging him toward a jeweller's window.

"No!" he said, holding back. "I hate--jewels! How I hate them!" He broke away from her and hurried on.

She had to run after him. Had she hesitated they might have become separated. Hated jewels? No, no! There should be no questions, verbal or mental, this night. She presently forced him to slow down. "Not so fast! We must never become separated," she warned. "Our safety--such as it is--lies in being together."

"I'm an ass. Perhaps my head is ratty without my realizing it. I fancy I'm like a dog that's been kicked; I'm trying to run away from the pain. What's this tomb?"

"The Metropolitan Opera House."

As they were passing a thin, wailing sound came to the ears of both. Seated with his back to the wall was a blind fiddler with a tin cup strapped to a knee. He was out of bounds; he had no right on Broadway; but he possessed a singular advantage over the law. He could not be forced to move on without his guide--if he were honestly blind. Hundreds of people were passing; but the fiddler's "Last Rose of Summer" wasn't worth a cent. His cup was empty.

"The poor thing!" said Kitty.

"Wait!" Hawksley approached the fiddler, exchanged a few words with him, and the blind man surrendered his fiddle.

"Give me your hat!" cried Kitty, delighted.

Carefully Hawksley pried loose his derby and handed it to Kitty. No stab of pain; something to find that out. He turned the instrument, tucked it under his chin and began "Traumerei." Kitty, smiling, extended the hat. Just the sort of interlude to make the adventure memorable. She knew this thoroughfare. Shortly there would be a crowd, and the fiddler's cup would overflow--that is, if the police did not interfere too soon.

As for the owner of the wretched fiddle, he raised his head, his mouth opened. Up there, somewhere, a door to heaven had opened.

True to her expectations a crowd slowly gathered. The beauty of the girl and the dark, handsome face of the musician, his picturesque bare head, were sufficient for these cynical passers-by. They understood. Operatic celebrities, having a little fun on their own. So quarters and dimes and nickels began to patter into Cutty's ancient derby hat. Broadway will always contribute generously toward a novelty of this order. Famous names were tossed about in undertones.

Entered then the enemy of the proletariat. Kitty, being a New Yorker born, had had her weather eye roving. The brass-buttoned minion of the law was always around when a bit of innocent fun was going on. As the policeman reached the inner rim of the audience the last notes of Handel's "Largo" were fading on the ear.

"What's this?" demanded the policeman.

"It's all over, sir," answered Kitty, smiling.

"Can't have this on Broadway, miss. Obstruction." He could not speak gruffly in the face of such beauty--especially with a Broadway crowd at his back.

"It's all over. Just let me put this money in the blind man's cup." Kitty poured her coins into the receptacle. At the same time Hawksley laid the fiddle in the blind man's lap. Then he turned to Kitty and boomed a long Russian phrase at her. Her quick wit caught the intent. "You see, he doesn't understand that this cannot be done in New York. I couldn't explain."

"All right, miss; but don't do it again." The policeman grinned.

"And please don't be harsh with the blind man. Just tell him he mustn't play on Broadway again. Thank you!"

She linked her arm in Hawksley's, and they went on; and the crowd dissolved; only the policeman and the blind man remained, the one contemplating his duty and the other his vision of heaven.

"What a lark!" exclaimed Hawksley.

"Were you asking me for your hat?"

"I was telling the bobby to go to the devil!"

They laughed like children.

"March hares!" he said.

"No. April fools! Good heavens, the time! Twenty minutes to seven. Our dinner!"

"We'll take a taxi.... Dash it!"

"What's wrong?"

"Not a bally copper in my pockets!"

"And I left my handbag on the sideboard! We'll have to walk. If we hurry we can just about make it."

Meantime, there lay in wait for them--this pair of April fools--a taxicab. It stood snugly against the curb opposite the entrance to Cutty's apartment. The door was slightly ajar.

The driver watched the south corner; the three men inside never took their gaze off the north corner.

"But, I say, hasn't this been a jolly lark?"

"If we had known we could have borrowed a dollar from the blind man; he'd never have missed it."

CHAPTER XXVII

Champagne in the glass is a beautiful thing to see. So is water, the morning after. That is the fault with frolic; there is always an inescapable rebound. The most violent love drops into humdrum tolerance. A pessimist is only a poor devil who has anticipated the inevitable; he has his headache at the start. Mental champagnes have their aftermaths even as the juice of the grape.

Hawksley and Kitty, hurrying back, began to taste lees. They began to see things, too--menace in every loiterer, threat in every alley. They had had a glorious lark; somewhere beyond would be the piper with an appalling bill. They exaggerated the dangers, multiplied them; perhaps wisely. There would be no let-down in their vigilance until they reached haven. But this state of mind they covered with smiling masks, banter, bursts of laughter, and flashes of wit.

They were both genuinely frightened, but with unselfish fear. Kitty's fear was not for herself but for Johnny Two-Hawks. If anything happened the blame would rightly be hers. With that head he wasn't strictly accountable for what he did; she was. A firm negative on her part and he would never have left the apartment. And his fear was wholly for this astonishing girl. He had recklessly thrust her into grave danger. Who knew, better than he, the implacable hate of the men who sought to kill him?

Moreover, his strength was leaving him. There was an alarming weakness in his legs, purely physical. He had overdone, and if need rose he would not be able to protect her. Damnable fool! But she had known. That was the odd phase of it. She hadn't come blindly. What mood had urged her to share the danger along with the lark? Somehow, she was always just beyond his reach, this girl. He would never forget that fan popping out of the pistol, the egg burning in the pan.

The apartment was only three blocks away when Kitty decided to drop her mask. "I'd give a good deal to see a policeman. They are never around when you really want them. Johnny Two-Hawks, I'm a little fool! You wouldn't have left the apartment but for me. Will you forgive me?"

"It is I who should ask forgiveness. I say, how much farther is it?"

"Only about two blocks; but they may be long ones. Let's step into this doorway for a moment. I see a taxicab. It looks to be standing opposite the building. Don't like it. Suppose we watch it for a few minutes?"

Hawksley was grateful for the respite; and together they stared at the unwinking red eye of the tail light. But no man approached the cab or left it.

"I believe I've hit upon a plan," said Kitty. "Certainly we have not been followed. In that event they would have had a dozen chances. If someone saw us leave together, naturally they will expect us to return together. We'll walk to the corner of our block, then turn east; but I shall remain just out of sight while you will go round the block. Fifteen minutes should carry you to the south corner. I'll be on watch for you. The moment you turn I'll walk toward you. It will give us a bit of a handicap in case that taxi is a menace. If any one appears, run for it. Where's the cane you had?"

"What a jolly ass I am! I remember now. I left the stick against the wall of the opera house. Blockhead! With a stick, now!... I'm hopeless!"

"Never mind. Let's start. That taxi may be perfectly honest. It's our guilty consciences that are peopling the shadows with goblins. What really bothers us is that we have broken our word to the kindliest man in all this world."

Hawksley wondered if he could walk round the block without falling down. He saw that he was facing a physical collapse, hastened by the knowledge that the safety of the girl depended largely upon himself. What he had accepted at the beginning as strength had been nothing more than exhilaration and nerve energy. There was now nothing but the latter, and only feeble straws at that. Oh, he would manage somehow; he jolly well had to; and there was a bare chance of falling in with a bobby. But run? Honestly, now, how the devil was a chap to run on a pair of spools?

Arriving at the appointed spot they separated. He waved his hand airily and marched off. If he fell it would be out of sight, where the girl could not see him. Clever chap--what? Damned rotter! For himself he did not care. He was weary of this game of hide and seek. But to have lured the girl into it! When he turned the first corner of his journey he paused and leaned against the wall, his eyes shut. When he opened them the sidewalk and the street lamps were normal again.

As soon as he disappeared a new plan came to Kitty. She put it into execution at once, on the basis that yonder taxicab was an enemy machine. She left her retreat and walked boldly down the street, her eyes alert for the least suspicious sign. If she could make the entrance before they suspected the trick, she could obtain help before Johnny Two-Hawks made the south turn. She reached her objective, pushed through the revolving doors, and turned. Dimly she could see the taxi driver; but he appeared to be dozing on the seat.

As a matter of fact, one of the three men in the taxi recognized Kitty, but too late to intercept her. Her manoeuvre had confused him temporarily. And while he and his companions were debating, Kitty had time to summon Cutty's man from Elevator Four.

"Step into the car!" he roughly ordered, after she had given him a gist of her suspicions. He turned off the lights, stepped out, and shut the gates with a furious bang. "And stick to the corner! I'll attend to the other fool."

He rushed into the street, his automatic ready, eyed the taxicab speculatively, wheeled suddenly, and ran south at a dog-trot. He rounded the south corner, but he did not see Hawksley anywhere. The dog-trot became a dead run. As he wheeled round the corner of the parallel street he almost bumped into Hawksley, who had a policeman in tow.

"Officer," said the man with the boy's face, "this is Federal business. Aliens. Come along. There may be trouble. If there should be any shooting don't bother with the atmosphere. Pick out a real target."

"Anarchists?"

"About the size of it."

"Miss Conover?" asked Hawksley.

"Safe. No thanks to you, though. I'd like to knock your block off, if you want to know!"

"Do it! Damned little use to me," declared Hawksley, sagging.

"Here, what's the matter with you?" cried the policeman, throwing his arm round Hawksley.

"They nearly killed him a few days gone. A crack on the bean; but he wasn't satisfied. Help him along. I'll be hiking back."

But the taxicab was gone.

Before Cutty's lieutenant opened the gate to the apartment he spoke to Hawksley. "The boss is doing everything he can to put you through, sir. Miss Conover's wit saved you. For if you hadn't separated they'd have nailed you. I've been running round like a chicken with its head cut off. I forgot that door on the seventeenth floor. I tell you honestly, you've been playing with death. It wasn't fair to Miss Conover."

"It was my fault," volunteered Kitty.

"Mine," protested Hawksley.

"Well, they know where you roost now, for a fact. You've spilled the beans. I'm sorry I lost my temper. The devil fly away with you both!" The boy laughed. "You're game, anyhow. But darn it all, if anything had happened to you the boss would never have forgiven me. He's the whitest old scout God ever put the breath of life into. He's always doing something for somebody. He'd give you the block if you had the gall to ask for it. Play the game fifty-fifty with him and you'll land on both feet. And you, Miss Conover, must not come here again."

"I promise."

"I'll tell you a little secret. It was the boss who sent you out of town. He was afraid you'd do something like this. When you are ready to go home you'll find Tony Bernini downstairs. Sore as a crab, too, I'll bet."

"I'll be glad to go home with him," said Kitty, thoroughly chastened in spirit.

"That's all for to-night."

Kitty and Hawksley stepped out into the corridor, the problem they had sought to shake off reestablished in their thoughts, added too, if anything.

"How do you feel?"

"Top-hole," lied Hawksley. "My word, though, I wobbled a bit going round that block. I almost kissed the hobby. I say, he thought I'd been tilting a few. But it was a lark!"

"Dinner is served," announced Kuroki at their elbows. His expression was coldly bland.

"Dinner!" cried Hawksley, brightening. "What does the American soldier say?"

"Eats!" answered Kitty.

All tension vanished in the double laughter that followed. They approached dinner with something of the spirit that had induced Hawksley to fiddle and Kitty to pass the hat in front of the Metropolitan Opera House. Hawksley's recuperative powers promised well for his future. By the time coffee was served his head had cleared and his legs had resumed their normal functions of support.

"I was so infernally bored!"

"And now?" asked Kitty, recklessly.

"Fancy asking me that!"

"Do you realize that all this is dreadfully improper?"

"Oh, I say, now! Where's the harm? If ever there was a young woman capable of taking care of herself--"

"That isn't it. It's just being here alone with you."

"But you are not alone with me!"

"Kuroki?" Kitty shrugged.

"No. At my side of the table is Stefani Gregor; at yours the man who has be-friended me."

"Thank you for that. I don't know of anything nicer you could say. But the out-side world would see neither of our friends. I did not come here to see you."

"No need of telling me that."

"I had a problem--a very difficult one--to solve; and I believed that I might solve it if I came to these rooms. I had quite forgotten you."

Instantly, upon receiving this blunt explanation, he determined that she should never cease to remember him after this night. His vanity was not touched; it was something far more elusive. It was perhaps a recurrence of that inexplicable desire to hurt. Somehow he sensed the flexible steel behind which lay the soul of this baf-fling girl. He would presently find a chink in the armour with that old Amati.

Blows on the head have few surgical comparisons. That which kills one man only temporarily stuns another. One man loses his identity; another escapes with all his faculties and suffers but trifling inconvenience. In Hawksley's case the blow had probably restricted some current of thought, and that which would have flowed normally now shot out obliquely, perversely. It might be that the natural perverseness of his blood, unchecked by the noble influence of Stefani Gregor and liberated by the blow, governed his thoughts in relation to Kitty. The subjugation of women, the old cynical warfare of sex--the dominant business of his rich and idle forbears, the business that had made Boris Karlov a deadly and implacable enemy--became paramount in his disordered brain.

She had forgotten him! Very well. He would stir the soul of her, play with it, lift it to the stars and dash it down--if she had a soul. Beautiful, natural, alone. He became all Latin under the pressure of this idea.

"I will play for you," he said, quietly.

"Please! And then I'll go home where I belong. I'll be in the living room."

When he returned he found her before a window, staring at the myriad lights.

"Sit here," he said, indicating the divan. "I shall stand and walk about as I play."

Kitty sat down, touching the pillows, reflectively. She thought of the tears she had wept upon them. That sinister and cynical thought! Suddenly she saw light. Her problem would have been none at all if Cutty had said he loved her. There would have been something sublime in making him happy in his twilight. He had loved and lost her mother. To pay him for that! He was right. Those twenty-odd years--his seniority--had mellowed him, filled him with deep and tender understanding. To be with him was restful; the very thought of him now was resting. No matter how much she might love a younger man he would frequently torture her by unconscious egoism; and by the time he had mellowed, the mulled wine would be cold. If only Cutty had said he loved her!

"What shall I play?"

Kitty raised her eyes in frank astonishment. There was a fiercely proud expression on Hawksley's face. It was not the man, it was the artist who was angry.

"Forgive me! I was dreaming a little," she apologized with quick understanding. "I am not quite--myself."

"Neither am I. I will play something to fit your dream. But wait! When I play I am articulate. I can express myself--all emotions. I am what I play--happy, sad, gay, full of the devil. I warn you. I can speak all things. I can laugh at you, weep with you, despise you, love you! All in the touch of these strings. I warn you there is magic in this Amati. Will you risk it?"

Ordinarily--had this florid outburst come from another man--Kitty would have laughed. It had the air of piqued vanity; but she knew that this was not the interpretation. On the streets he had been the most amusing and surprising comrade she had ever known, as merry and whimsical as Cutty--young and handsome--the real man. He had been real that night when he entered through her kitchen window, with the drums of jeopardy about his neck. He had been real that night she had brought him his wallet.

Electric antagonism--the room seemed charged with it. The man had stepped aside for a moment and the great noble had taken his place. It was not because she had been reared in rather a theatrical atmosphere that she transcribed his attitude thus. She knew that he was noble. That she did not know his rank was of no consequence. Cutty's narrative, which she had pretended to believe, had set this man in the middle class. Never in this world. There was only one middle class out of which such a personality might, and often did, emerge--the American middle class. In Europe, never. No peasant blood, no middle-class corpuscle, stirred in this man's veins. The ancient boyar looked down at her.

"Play!" said Kitty. There was a smile on her lips, but there was fiery challenge in her slate-blue eyes. The blood of Irish kings--and what Irishman dares deny it?--surged into her throat.

We wear masks, we inherit generations of masks; and a trivial incident reveals the primordial which lurks in each one of us. Savages--Kitty with her stone hatchet and Hawksley swinging the curved blade of Hunk.

He began one of those tempestuous compositions, brilliant and bewildering, that submerge the most appreciative lay mentality--because he was angry, a double anger that he should be angry over he knew not what--and broke off in the middle of the composition because Kitty sat upright, stonily unimpressed.

Tschaikowsky's "Serenade Melancolique." Kitty, after a few measures, laid aside her stone hatchet, and her body relaxed. Music! She began to absorb it as parched earth absorbs the tardy rain. Then came the waltz which had haunted her. Her face grew tenderly beautiful; and Hawksley, a true artist, saw that he had discovered the fifth string; and he played upon it with all the artistry which was naturally his and which had been given form by the master who had taught him.

For the physical exertions he relied upon nerve energy again. Nature is gener-ous when we are young. No matter how much we draw against the account she always has a little more for us. He forgot that only an hour gone he had been dizzy with pain, forgot everything but the glory of the sounds he was evoking and their visible reaction upon this girl. The devil was not only in his heart, but in his hand.

Never had Kitty heard such music. To be played to in this manner--directly, with embracing tenderness, with undivided fire--would have melted the soul of Gobseck the money lender; and Kitty was warm-blooded, Irish, emotional. The fiddle called poignantly to the Irish in her. She wanted to go roving with this man; with her hand on his shoulder to walk in the thin air of high places. Through it all, however, she felt vaguely troubled; the instinct of the trap. The sinister and cynical idea which had clandestinely taken up quarters in her mind awoke and assailed her from a new angle, that of youth. Something in her cried out: "Stop! Stop!" But her lips were mute, her body enchained.

Suddenly Hawksley laid aside the fiddle and advanced. He reached down and drew her up. Kitty did not resist him; she was numb with enchantment. He held her close for a second, then kissed her--her hair, eyes, mouth--released her and stepped back, a bantering smile on his lips and cold terror in his heart. The devil who had inspired this phase of the drama now deserted his victim, as he generally does in the face of superior forces.

Kitty stood perfectly still for a full minute, stunned. It was that smile--frozen on his lips--that brought her back to intimacy with cold realities. Had he asked her pardon, had he shown the least repentance, she might have forgiven, forgotten. But knowing mankind as she did she could give but one interpretation to that smile--of which he was no longer conscious.

Without anger, in quiet, level tones she said: "I had foolishly thought that we two might be friends. You have made it impossible. You have also abused the kindly hospitality of the man who has protected you from your enemies. A few days ago he did me the honour to ask me to marry him. I am going to. I wish you no evil." She turned and walked from the room.

Even then there was time. But he did not move. It was not until he heard the elevator gate crash that he was physically released from the thraldom of the inner revelation. Love--in the blinding flash of a thunderbolt! He had kissed her not because he was the son of his father, but because he loved her! And now he never could tell her. He must let her go, believing that the man she had saved from death had repaid her with insult. On top of all his misfortunes, his tragedies--love! There was a God, yes, but his name was Irony. Love! He stepped toward the divan, stumbled, and fell against it, his arms spread over the pillows; and in this position he remained.

For a while his thoughts were broken, inconclusive; he was like a man in the dark, groping for a door. Principally, his poor head was trying to solve the riddle of his never-ending misfortunes. Why? What had he done that these calamities should be piled upon his head? He had lived decently; his youth had been normal; he had played fair with men and women. Why make him pay for what his forbears had done? He wasn't fair game.

He! A singular revelation cleared one corner. Kitty had spoken of a problem; and he, by those devil-urged kisses, had solved it for her. She had been doddering, and his own act had thrust her into the arms of that old thoroughbred. That cynical suggestion of his the other morning had been acted upon. God had long ago deserted him, and now the devil himself had taken leave. Hawksley buried his face in the pillow once made wet with Kitty's tears.

The great tragedy in life lies in being too late. Hawksley had learned this once before; it was now being driven home again. Cutty was to find it out on the morrow, for he missed his train that night.

The shuttles of the Weaver in this pattern of life were two green stones called the drums of jeopardy, inanimate objects, but perfect tools in the hands of Destiny. But for these stones Hawksley would not have tarried too long on a certain red night; Cutty would not now be stumbling about the labyrinths into which his looting instincts had thrust him; and Kitty Conover would have jogged along in the humdrum rut, if not happy at least philosophically content with her lot.

CHAPTER XXVIII

Decision is always a mental relief, hesitance a curse. Kitty, having shifted her burdens to the broad shoulders of Cutty, felt as she reached the lobby as if she had left storm and stress behind and entered calm. She would marry Cutty; she had published the fact, burned her bridges.

She had stepped into the car, her heart full of cold fury. Now she began to find excuses for Hawksley's conduct. A sick brain; he was not really accountable for his acts. Her own folly had opened the way. Of course she would never see him again. Why should she? Their lives were as far apart as the Volga and the Hudson.

Bernini met her in the lobby. "I've got a cab for you, Miss Conover," he said as if nothing at all had happened.

"Have you Cutty's address?"

"Yes."

"Then take me at once to a telegraph office. I have a very important message to send him."

"All right, Miss Conover."

"Say: 'Decision made. It is yes.' And sign it just Kitty."

Without being conscious of it her soul was still in the clouds, where it had been driven by the music of the fiddle; thus, what she assumed to be a normal sequence of a train of thought was only a sublime impulse. She would marry Cutty. More, she would be his wife, his true wife. For his tenderness, his generosity, his chivalry, she would pay him in kind. There would be no nonsense; love would not enter into the bargain; but there would be the fragrance of perfect understanding. That he was fifty-two and she was twenty-four no longer mattered. No more loneliness, no more genteel poverty; for such benefits she was ready to pay the score in full. A man she was genuinely fond of, a man she could look up to, always depend upon.

Was there such a thing as perfect love? She had her doubts. She reasoned that love was what a body decided was love, the psychological moment when the physical attraction became irresistible. Who could tell before the fact which was the true and which the false? Lived there a woman, herself excepted, who had not hesitated between two men--a man who had not doddered between two women--for better or for worse? What did the average woman know of the man, the average man know of the woman--until afterward? To stake all upon a guess!

She knew Cutty. Under her own eyes he had passed through certain proving fires. There would be no guessing the manner of man he was. He was fifty-two; that is to say, the grand passion had come and gone. There would be mutual affection and comradeship.

True, she had her dreams; but she could lay them away without any particular regret. She had never been touched by the fire of passion. Let it go. But she did know what perfect comradeship was, and she would grasp it and never loose her hold. Something out of life.

"A narrow squeak, Miss Conover," said Berumi, breaking the long silence.

"A miss is as good as a mile," replied Kitty, not at all grateful for the interruption.

"We've done everything we could to protect you. If you can't see now--why, the jig is up. A chain is as strong as its weakest link. And in a game like this a woman is always the weakest link."

"You're quite a philosopher."

"I have reason to be. I'm married."

"Am I expected to laugh?"

"Miss Conover, you're a wonder. You come through these affairs with a smile, when you ought to have hysterics. I'll bet a doughnut that when you see a mouse you go and get it a piece of cheese."

"Do you want the truth? Well, I'll tell it to you. You have all kept me on the outer edge of this affair, and I've been trying to find out why. I have the reportorial instinct, as they say. I inherited it from my father. You put a strange weapon in my hands, you tell me it is deadly, but you don't tell me which end is deadly. Do you know who this Russian is?"

"Honestly, I don't."

"Does Cutty?"

"I don't know that, either."

"Did you ever hear of a pair of emeralds called the drums of jeopardy?"

"Nope. But I do know if you continue these stunts you'll head the whole game into the ditch."

"You may set your mind at ease. I'm going to marry Cutty. I shall not go to the apartment again until Hawksley, as he is called, is gone."

"Well, well; that's good news! But let me put you wise to one fact, Miss Conover: you have picked some man! I'm not much of a scholar, but knowing him as I do I'm always wondering why they made Faith, Hope, and Charity in female form. But this night's work was bad business. They know where the Russian is now; and if the game lasts long enough they'll reach the chief, find out who he is; and that'll put the kibosh on his usefulness here and abroad. Well, here's home, and no more lecture from me."

"Sorry I've been so much trouble."

"Perhaps we ought to have shown you which end shoots."

"Good-night."

If Kitty had any doubt as to the wisdom of her decision, the cold, gloomy rooms of her apartment dissipated them. She wandered through the rooms, musing, calling back animated scenes. What would the spirit of her mother say? Had she doddered between Conover and Cutty? Perhaps. But she had been one of the happy few who had guessed right. Singular thought: her mother would have been happy with Cutty, too.

Oh, the relief of knowing what the future was going to be! She took off her hat and tossed it upon the table. The good things of life, and a good comrade.

Food. The larder would be empty and there was her breakfast to consider. She passed out into the kitchen, wrote out a list of necessities, and put it on the dumb waiter. Now for the dishes she had so hurriedly left. She rolled up her sleeves, put on the apron, and fell to the task. After such a night--dish-washing! She laughed. It was a funny old world.

Pauses. Perhaps she should have gone to a hotel, away from all familiar objects. Those flatirons intermittently pulled her eyes round. Her fancy played tricks with her whenever her glance touched the window. Faces peering in. In a burst of impatience she dropped the dish towel, hurried to the window, and threw it up. Black emptiness!... Cutty, crossing the platform with Hawksley on his shoulders. She saw that, and it comforted her.

She finished her work and started for bed. But first she entered the guest room and turned on the lights. Olga. She had intended to ask him who Olga was.

A great pity. They might have been friends. The back of her hand went to her lips but did not touch them. She could not rub away those burning kisses--that is, not with the back of her hand. Vividly she saw him fiddling bareheaded in front of the Metropolitan Opera House. It seemed, though, that it had happened years ago. A great pity. The charm of that frolic would abide with her as long as she lived. A brave man, too. Hadn't he left her with a gay wave of the hand, not knowing, for want of strength, if he could make the detour of the block? That took courage. His journey halfway across the world had taken courage. Yet he could so basely disillusion her. It was not the kiss; it was the smile. She had seen that smile before, born of evil. If only he had spoken!

The heavenly magic of that fiddle! It made her sad. Genius, the ability to play with souls, soothe, tantalize, lift up; and then to smile at her like that!

She shut down the curtain upon these cogitations and summoned Cutty, visualized his handsome head, shot with gray, the humour of his smile. She did care for him; no doubt of that. She couldn't have sent that telegram else. Cutty--name of a pipe, as the Frenchmen said! All at once she rocked with laughter. She was going to marry a man whose given name she could not recall! Henry, George, John, William? For the life of her she could not remember.

And with this laughter still bubbling in a softer note she got into bed, twisted about from side to side, from this pillow to that, the tired body seeking perfect relaxation.

A broken melody entered her head. Sleepily she sought one channel of thought after another to escape; still the melody persisted. As her consciousness dodged hither and thither the bars and measures joined.... She sat up, chilled, bewildered. That Tschaikowsky waltz! She could hear it as clearly as if Johnny Two-Hawks and the Amati were in the very room. She grew afraid. Of what? She did not know.

And while she sat there in bed threshing out this fear to find the grain, Cutty was tramping the streets of Washington, her telegram crumpled in his hand. From time to time he would open it and reread it under a street lamp.

To marry her and then to cheat her. It wasn't humanly possible to marry her and then to let her go. He thought of those warm, soft arms round his neck, the absolute trust of that embrace. Molly's girl. No, he could not do it. He would have to back down, tell her he could not put the bargain through, invent some other scheme.

The idea had been repugnant to her. It had taken her a week to fight it out. It was a little beyond his reach, however, why the idea should have been repugnant to her. It entailed nothing beyond a bit of mummery. The repugnance was not due to religious training. The Conover household, as he recalled it, had been rather lax in that respect. Why, then, should Kitty have hesitated?

He thought of Hawksley, and swore. But for Hawksley's suggestion no muddle like this would have occurred. Devil take him and his infernal green stones!

Cutty suddenly remembered his train. He looked at his watch and saw that his lower berth was well on the way to Baltimore. Always and eternally he was missing something.

CHAPTER XXIX

Not unusually, when we burn our bridges, we have in the back of our minds the dim hope that there may be a shallow ford somewhere. Thus, bridges should not be burned impulsively; there may be no ford.

The idea of retreat pushed forward in Kitty's mind the moment she awoke; but she pressed it back in shame. She had given her word, and she would stand by it.

The night had been a series of wild impulses. She had not sent that telegram to Cutty as the result of her deliberations in the country. Impulse; a flash, and the thing was done, her bridges burned. To crush Johnny Two-Hawks, fill his cup with chagrin, she had told him she was going to marry Cutty. That was the milk in the cocoanut. Morning has a way of showing up night-gold for what it is--tinsel. Kitty saw the stage of last night's drama dismantled. If there was a shallow ford, she would never lower her pride to seek it. She had told Two-Hawks, sent that wire to Cutty, broke the news to Bernini.

But did she really want to go back? Not to know her own mind, to swing back and forth like a pendulum! Was it because she feared that, having married Cutty, she might actually fall in love with some other man later? She could still go through the mummery as Cutty had planned; but what about all the sublime generosity of the preceding night?

A queer feeling pervaded her: She was a marionette, a human manikin, and some invisible hand was pulling the wires that made her do all these absurd things. Her own mind no longer controlled her actions. The persistence of that waltz! It had haunted her, broken into her dreams, awakened her out of them. Why should she be afraid? What was there to be afraid of in a recurring melody? She had heard a dozen famed violinists play it. It had never before affected her beyond a flash of emotionalism. Perhaps it was the romantic misfortune of the man, the mystery sur-rounding him, the menace which walled him in.

Breakfast. Human manikins had appetites. So she made her breakfast. Before leaving the kitchen she stopped at the window. The sun filled the court with bril-liant light. The patches of rust on the fire-escape ladder, which was on the Gregor side of the platform, had the semblance of powdered gold.

Half an hour later she was speeding downtown to the office. All through the day she walked, worked, talked as one in the state of trance. There were periods of stupefaction which at length roused Burlingame's curiosity.

"Kitty, what's the matter with you? You look dazed about something."

"How do you clean a pipe?" she countered, irrelevantly.

"Clean a pipe?" he repeated, nearly overbalancing his chair.

"Yes. You see, I may make up my mind to marry a man who smokes a pipe," said Kitty, desperately, eager to steer Burlingame into another channel; "and cer-tainly I ought to know how to clean one."

"Kitty, I'm an old-timer. You can't sidetrack me like this. Something has hap-pened. You say you had a great time in the country, and you come in as pale as the moon, like someone suffering from shell shock. Ever since Cutty came in here that day you've been acting oddly. You may not know it, but Cutty asked me to send you out of town. You've been in some kind of danger. What's the yarn?"

"So big that no newspaper will ever publish it, Burly. If Cutty wants to tell you some day he can. I haven't the right to."

"Did he drag you into it or did you fall into it?"

"I walked into it, as presently I shall walk out of it--all on my own."

"Better keep your eyes open. Cutty's a stormy petrel; when he flies there's rough weather."

"What do you know about him?"

"Probably what he has already told you--that he is a foreign agent of the Gov-ernment. What do you know?"

"Everything but one thing, and that's a problem particularly my own."

"Alien stuff, I suppose. Cutty's strong on that. Well, mind your step. The boys are bringing in queer scraps about something big going to happen May Day--no facts, just rumours. Better shoot for home the shortest route each night and stick round there."

There are certain spiritual exhilarants that nullify caution, warning the presence of danger. The boy with his first pay envelope, the lover who has just been accepted, the debutante on the way to her first ball; the impetus that urges us to rush in where angels fear to tread.

At a quarter after five Kitty left the office for home, unaware that the attribute designated as caution had evaporated from her system. She proceeded toward the Subway mechanically, the result of habit. Casually she noted two taxicabs standing near the Subway entrance. That she noted them at all was due to the fact that Subway entrances were not fortuitous hunting grounds for taxicabs. Only the unusual would have attracted her in her present condition of mind. It takes time and patience to weave a good web--observe any spider--time in finding a suitable place for it; patience in the spinning. All that worried Karlov was the possibility of her not observing him. If he could place his taxicabs where they would attract her, even casually, the main difficulty would be out of the way. The moment she turned her head toward the cabs he would step out into plain view. The girl was susceptible and adventuresome.

Kitty saw a man step out of the foremost taxicab, give some instructions to the chauffeur, and get back into the cab, immediately to be driven off at moderate speed. She recognized the man at once. Never would she forget that squat, gorilla-like body. Karlov! Yonder, in that cab! She ran to the remaining cab; wherein she differed from angels.

"Are you free?"

"Yes, miss."

"See that taxi going across town? Follow it and I will give you ten extra fare."

"You're on, miss."

Karlov peered through the rear window of his cab. If she had in tow a Federal agent the manoeuvre would fail, at a great risk to himself. But he would soon be able to tell whether or not she was being followed.

As a matter of fact, she was not. She had returned to New York a day before she was expected. Her unknown downtown guardian would not turn up for duty until ordered by Cutty to do so. She entered the second cab with no definite plan in her head. Karlov, the man who wanted to kill Johnny Two-Hawks, the man who held

Stefani Gregor a prisoner! For the present these facts were sufficient. "Don't get too near," said Kitty through the speaking tube. "Just keep the cab in sight."

A perfectly logical compensation. She herself had set in motion the machinery of this amazing adventure; it was logically right that she should end it. Poor dear old Cutty--to fancy he could pull the wool over Kitty Conover's eyes! Cutty, the most honest man alive, had set his foot upon an unethical bypath and now found himself among nettles. To keep Johnny Two-Hawks prisoner in that lofty apartment while he hunted for the drums of jeopardy! Hadn't he said he had seen emeralds he would steal with half a chance? Cutty, playing at this sort of game, his conscience biting whichever way he turned! He had been hunting unsuccessfully for the stones that night he had come in with his face and hands bloody. Why hadn't he kissed her?

Johnny Two-Hawks--bourgeois? Utter nonsense! Of course it did not matter now what he was; he had dug a bridgeless chasm with that smile. Sometime to-morrow he and Stefani Gregor would be on their way to Montana; and that would be the last of them both. To-morrow would mark the fork in the road. But life would never again be humdrum for Kitty Conover.

The taxicabs were bumping over cobbles, through empty streets. It was six by now; at that hour this locality, which she recognized as the warehouse district, was always dead. The deserted streets, how ever, set in motion a slight perturbation. Supposing Karlov grew suspicious and turned aside from his objective? Even as this disturbing thought took form Karlov's taxicab stopped. Kitty's stopped also, but without instructions from her. She had intended to drive on and from the rear window observe if Karlov entered that old red-brick house.

"Go on!" she called through the tube.

The chauffeur obeyed, but he stopped again directly behind Karlov's taxicab. He slid off his seat and opened the door. His face was grim.

Tumpitum-tump! Tumpitum-tump! She did not hear the tocsin this time; she felt it on her spine--the drums of fear. If they touched her!

"Come with me, miss. If you are sensible you will not be harmed. If you cut up a racket I'll have to carry you."

"What does this mean?" faltered Kitty.

"That we have finally got you, miss. You can see for yourself that there isn't any help in sight. Better take it sensibly. We don't intend to hurt you. It's somebody else we want. There's a heavy score against you, but we'll overlook it if you act sensibly. You were very clever last night; but the game depends upon the last trick."

"I'll go sensibly," Kitty agreed. They must not touch her!

Karlov did not speak as he opened the door of the house for her. His expression was Buddha-like.

"This way, miss," said the chauffeur, affably.

"You are an American?"

"Whenever it pays."

Presently Kitty found herself in the attic, alone. They hadn't touched her; so much was gained. Poor little fool that she was! It was fairly dark now, but overhead she could see the dim outlines of the scuttle or trap. The attic was empty except for a few pieces of lumber and some soap boxes. She determined to investigate the trap at once, before they came again.

She placed two soap boxes on end and laid a plank across. After testing its stability she mounted. She could reach the trap easily, with plenty of leverage to spare. She was confident that she could draw herself up to the roof. She sought for the hooks and liberated them, then she placed her palms against the trap and heaved. Not even a creak answered her. She pressed upward again and again. The trap was immovable.

Light. She turned, to behold Karlov in the doorway, a candlestick in his hand. "The scuttle is covered with cement, Miss Conover. Nobody can get in or out."

Kitty got down, her knees uncertain. If he touched her! Oh, the fool she had been!

"What are you going to do with me?" she asked through dry lips.

"You are to me a bill of exchange, payable in something more precious to me than gold. I am going to keep you here until you are ransomed. The ransom is the man you have been shielding. If he isn't here by midnight you vanish. Oh, we shan't harm you. Merely you will disappear until my affairs in America are terminated. You are clever and resourceful for so young a woman. You will understand that we are not going to turn aside. You are not a woman to me; you are a valuable pawn. You are something to bargain for."

"I understand," said Kitty, her heart trying to burst through. It seemed impossible that Karlov should not hear the thunder. To placate him, to answer his questions, to keep him from growing angry!

"I thought you would." Karlov set the candle on Kitty's impromptu stepladder. "We saw your interest in the affair, and attacked you on that side. You had seen me once. Being a newspaper writer--the New York kind--you would not rest until you learned who I was. You would not forget me. You were too well guarded uptown. You have been out of the city for a week. We could not find where. You were reported seen entering your office this morning; and here you are. My one fear was that you might not see me. Personally you will have no cause to worry. No hand shall touch you.

"Thank you for that."

"Don't misunderstand. There is no sentiment behind this promise. I imagine your protector will sacrifice much for your sake. Simply it is unnecessary to offer you any violence. Do you know who the man is your protector is shielding?"

Kitty shook her head.

"Has he played the fiddle for you?"

"Yes."

Karlov smiled. "Did you dance?"

"Dance? I don't understand."

"No matter. He can play the fiddle nearly as well as his master. The two of them have gone across the world fiddling the souls of women out of their bodies."

Kitty sat down weakly on the plank. Terror from all points. Karlov's unexcited tones--his lack of dramatic gesture--convinced her that this was deadly business. Terror that for all the promise of immunity they might lay hands on her. Terror for Johnny Two-Hawks, for Cutty.

"Has he injured you?" she asked, to gain time.

"He is an error in chronology. He represents an idea which no longer exists." He spoke English fluently, but with a rumbling accent.

"But to kill him for that!"

"Kill him? My dear young lady, I merely want him to fiddle for me," said Karlov with another smile.

"You tried to kill him," insisted Kitty, the dryness beginning to leave her throat.

"Bungling agents. Do know what became of them--the two who invaded your bedroom?"

"They were taken away the police."

"So I thought. What became of the wallet?"

"I found it hidden on the back of my stove."

"I never thought to look there," said Karlov, musingly. "Who has the drums?"

"The emeralds? You haven't them!" cried Kitty, becoming her mother's daughter, though her heart never beat so thunderously as now. "We thought you had them!"

Karlov stared at her, moodily. "What is that button for, at the side of your bed?"

Kitty comprehended the working of the mind that formulated this question. If she answered truthfully he would accept her statements. "It rings an alarm in the basement."

Karlov nodded. "You are truthful and sensible I haven't the emeralds."

"Perhaps one of your men betrayed you."

"I have thought of that. But if he had betrayed me the drums would have been discovered by the police.... Damn them to hell!" Kitty wondered whether he meant the police or the emeralds.

"Later, food and a blanket will be brought to you. If your ransom does not appear by midnight you will be taken away. If you struggle we may have to handle you roughly. That is as you please."

Karlov went out, locking the door.

Oh, the blind little fool she had been! All those constant warnings, and she had not heeded! Cutty had warned her repeatedly, so had Bernini; and she had deliberately walked into this trap. As if this cold, murderous madman would risk showing himself without some grim and terrible purpose. She had written either Cutty's or Johnny Two-Hawks' death warrant. She covered her eyes. It was horrible.

Perhaps not Cutty, but assuredly Two-hawks. His life for her liberty.

"And he will come!" she whispered. She knew it. How, was not to be analyzed. She just knew that he would come. What if he had smiled like that! The European point of view and her own monumental folly. He would come quietly, without protest, and give himself up.

"God forgive me! What can I do? What can I do?"

She slid to the floor and rocked her body. Her fault! He would come--even as Cutty would have come had he been the man demanded. And Karlov would kill him--because he was an error in chronology! She sensed also that the anarchist would not look upon his act as murder. He would be removing an obstacle from the path of his sick dreams.

Comparisons! She saw how much alike the two were. Cutty was only Johnny Two-Hawks at fifty-two--fearless and whimsical. Had Cutty gone through life without looking at some woman as, last night, Two-Hawks had looked at her? All the rest of her life she would see Two-Hawks' eyes.

Abysmal fool, to pit her wits against such men as Karlov! Because she had been successful to a certain extent, she had overrated her cleverness, with this tragic result... He had fiddled the soul out of her. But death!

She sprang up. It was maddening to sit still, to feel the approach of the tragedy without being able to prevent it. She investigated the windows. No hope in this direction. It was rapidly growing dark outside. What time was it?

The door opened. A man she had not seen before came in with a blanket, a pitcher of water, and some graham crackers. His fingers were stained a brilliant yellow and a peculiar odour emanated from his clothes. He did not speak to her, but set the articles on the floor and departed.

Kitty did not stir. An hour passed; she sat as one in a trance. The tallow dip was sinking. By and by she became conscious of a faint sound, a tapping. Whence it came she could not tell. She moved about cautiously, endeavouring to locate it. When she finally did the blood drummed in her ears. The trap! Someone was trying to get in through the trap!

Cutty! Thus soon! Who else could it be? She hunted for a piece of lumber light enough to raise to the trap. She tapped three times, and waited. Silence. She repeated the signal. This time it was answered. Cutty! In a little while she would be free, and Two-Hawks would not have to pay for her folly with his life. Terror and remorse departed forthwith.

She took the plank to the door and pushed one end under the door knob. Then she piled the other planks against the butt. The moment she heard steps on the stairs she would stand on the planks. It would be difficult to open that door. She sat down on the planks to wait. From time to time she built up the falling tallow. Cutty must have light. The tapping on the trap went on. They were breaking away the cement. Perhaps an hour passed. At least it seemed a very long time.

Steps on the stairs! She stood up, facing the door, the roots of her hair tingling. She heard the key turn in the lock; and then as in a nightmare she felt the planks under her feet stir slightly but with sinister persistence. She presently saw the toe of a boot insert, itself between the door and the jamb. The pressure increased; the space between the door and the jamb widened. Suddenly the boot vanished, the door closed, and the plank fell. Immediately thereafter Karlov stood inside the room, scowling suspiciously.

CHAPTER XXX

Cutty arrived at the apartment in time to share dinner with Hawksley. He had wisely decided to say nothing about the escapade of Hawksley and Kitty Conover, since it had terminated fortunately. Bernini had telegraphed the gist of the adventure. He could readily understand Hawksley's part; but Kitty's wasn't reducible to ordinary terms of expression. The young chap had run wild because his head still wobbled on his shoulders and because his isolation was beginning to scratch his nerves. But for Kitty to run wild with him offered a blank wall to speculation. (As if he could solve the riddle when Kitty herself could not!) So he determined to shut himself up in his study and shuffle the chrysoprase. Something might come of it. Looking backward, he recognized the salient, at no time had he been quite sure of Kitty. She seemed to be a combination of shallows and unfathomable deeps.

From the Pennsylvania Station he had called up the office. Kitty had gone. Bernini informed him that Kitty was dining at a cafe on the way home. Cutty was thorough. He telephoned the restaurant and was advised that Miss Conover had reserved a table. He had forgotten to send down the operative who guarded Kitty at that end. But the distance from the office to the Subway was so insignificant!

"You are looking fit," he said across the table.

"Ought to be off your hands by Monday. But what about Stefani Gregor? I can't stir, leaving him hanging on a peg."

"I am going into the study shortly to decide that. Head bother you?"

"Occasionally."

"Ryan easy to get along with?"

"Rather a good sort. I say, you know, you've seen a good deal of life. Which do you consider the stronger, the inherited traits or environment?"

"Environment. That is the true mould. There is good and bad in all of us. It is brought into prominence by the way we live. An angel cannot touch pitch without becoming defiled. On the other hand, the worst gutter rats in the world saved France. Do you suppose that thought will not always be tugging at and uplifting those who returned from the first Marne?"

"There is hope, then, for me!"

"Hope?"

"Yes. You know that my father, my uncle, and my grandfather were fine scoundrels."

"Under their influence you would have been one, too. But no man could live with Stefani Gregor and not absorb his qualities. Your environment has been Anglo-Saxon, where the first block in the picture is fair play. You have been constantly under the tutelage of a fine and lofty personality, Gregor's. Whatever evil traits you may have inherited, they have become subject to the influences that have surrounded you. Take me, for instance. I was born in a rather puritanical atmosphere. My environments have always been good. Yet there lurks in me the taint of Macaire. Given the wrong environment, I should now have my picture in the Rogues' Gallery."

"You?"

"Yes."

Hawksley played with his fork. "If you had a daughter would you trust me with her?"

"Yes. Any man who can weep unashamed over the portrait of his mother may be trusted. Once you are out there in Montana you'll forget all about your paternal forbears."

Handsome beggar, thought Cutty; but evidently born under the opal. An inexplicable resentment against his guest stirred his heart. He resented his youth, his ease of manner, his fluency in the common tongue. He was theoretically a Britisher; he thought British; approached subjects from a British point of view. A Britisher-- except when he had that fiddle tucked under his chin. Then Cutty admitted he did not know what he was. Devil take him!

There must have been something electrical in Cutty's resentment, for the object of it felt it subtly, and it fired his own. He resented the freedom of action that had always been denied him, resented his host's mental and physical superiority. Did Cutty care for the girl, or was he playing the game as it had been suggested to him? Money and freedom. But then, it was in no sense a barter; she would be giving nothing, and the old beggar would be asking nothing. His suggestion! He laughed.

"What's the joke?" asked Cutty, looking up from his coffee, which he was stirring with unnecessary vigour.

"It isn't a joke. I'm bally well twisted. I laugh now when I think of something tragic. I am sorry about last night. I was mad, I suppose."

"Tell me about it."

Cutty listened intently and smiled occasionally. Mad as hatters, both of them. He and Kitty couldn't have gone on a romp like this, but Kitty and Hawksley could. Thereupon his resentment boiled up again.

"Have you any idea why she took such a risk? Why she came here, knowing me to be absent?"

"She spoke of a problem. I fancy it related to your approaching marriage. She told me."

Cutty laid down his spoon. "I'd like to dump Your Highness into the middle of East River for putting that idea into my head. She has consented to it; and now, damn it, I've got to back out of it!" Cutty rose and flung down his napkin.

"Why?" asked the bewildered Hawksley.

"Because there is in me the making of a first-rate scoundrel, and I never should have known it if you and your affairs hadn't turned up."

Cutty entered his study and slammed the door, leaving Hawksley prey to so many conflicting emotions that his head began to bother him. Back out of it! Why? Why should Kitty have a problem to solve over such a marriage of convenience, and why should the old thoroughbred want to back out?

Kitty would be free, then? A flash of fire, which subsided quickly under the smothering truth. What if she were free? He could not ask her to be his wife. Not because of last night's madness. That no longer troubled him. She was the sort who would understand, if he told her. She had a soul big with understanding. It was that he walked in the shadow of death, and would so long as Karlov was free; and he could not ask any woman to share that.

He pushed back his chair slowly. In the living room he took the Amati from its case and began improvising. What the chrysoprase did for Cutty the fiddle did for this derelict--solved problems.

He reviewed all the phases as he played. That dish of bacon and eggs, the resolute air of her, that popping fan! [Allegretto.] She had found him senseless on the floor. She had had the courage to come to his assistance. [Andante con espressione.] What had been in her mind that night she had taken flight from his bedroom, after having given him the wallet? Something like tears. What about? An American girl, natural, humorous, and fanciful. Somehow he felt assured that it had not been his kisses; she had looked into his eyes and seen the taint. Always there, the beast that old Stefani had chained and subdued. He knew now that this beast would never again lift its head. And he had let her go without a sign. [Dolorosomente.] To have gone through life with a woman who would have understood his nature. The test of her had been last night in the streets. His mood had been hers. [Allegretto con amore.]

"Love," he said, lowering the bow.

"Love," said Cutty, shifting his chrysoprase. There was no fool like an old fool. It did not serve to recall Molly in all her glory, to reach hither and yon for a handhold to pull him out of this morass. Molly had become an invisible ghost. He loved her daughter. Double sunset; the phenomenon of the Indian Ocean was now being enacted upon his own horizon. Double sunset.

But why should Kitty have any problem to solve? Why should she dodder over such a trifle as this prospective official marriage? It was only a joke which would legalize his generosity. She had sent that telegram after leaving this apartment. What had happened here to decide her? Had Hawksley fiddled? There was something the matter with the green stones to-night; they evoked nothing.

He leaned back in his chair, listening, the bowl of his pipe touching the lapel of his coat. Music. Queer, what you could do with a fiddle if you knew how.

After all there was no sense in venting his anger on Hawksley. He was hoist by his own petard. Why not admit the truth? He had had a crack on the head the same night as Hawksley; only, he had been struck by an idea, often more deadly than the butt of a pistol. He would apologize for that roaring exit from the dining room. The poor friendless devil! He bent toward the green stones again. In the living room Hawksley sat in a chair, the fiddle across his knees. He understood now. The old chap was in love with the girl, and was afraid of himself; couldn't risk having her and letting her go.... A curse on the drums of jeopardy! Misfortune followed their wake always. The world would have been different this hour if he--The break in the trend of thought was caused by the entrance of Kuroki, who was followed by a man. This man dropped into a chair without apparently noticing that the room was already tenanted, for he never glanced toward Hawksley. A haggard face, dull of eye. Kuroki bobbed and vanished, but returned shortly, beckoning the stranger to follow him into the study.

"Coles?" cried Cutty delightedly. Here was the man he had sent to negotiate for the emeralds, free. "How did you escape? We've combed the town for you."

"They had me in a room on Fifteenth Street. Once in a while I got something to eat. But I haven't escaped. I'm still a prisoner."

"What do you mean by that?"

"I am here as an emissary. There was nothing for me to do but accept the job."

"Did he have the stones?" asked Cutty, without the least suspicion of what was coming.

"That I don't know. He pretended to have them in order to get me where he wanted me. I've been hungry a good deal because I wouldn't talk. I'm here as a negotiator. A rotten business. I agreed because I've hopes you'll be able to put one over on Karlov. It's the girl."

"Kitty?"

"Karlov has her. The girl wasn't to blame. Any one in the game would have done as she did. Karlov is bugs on politics; but he's shrewd enough at this sort of game. He trapped the girl because he'd studied her enough to learn what she would or would not do. Now they are not going to hurt her. They merely propose exchanging her for the man you've been hiding up here. There's a taxi downstairs. It will carry me back to Fifteenth; then it will return and wait. If the man is not at the appointed place by midnight--he must go in this taxi--the girl will be carried off elsewhere, and you'll never lay eyes on her again. Karlov and his gang are potential assassins; all they want is excuse. Until midnight they will not touch the girl; but after midnight, God knows! What message am I to take back?"

"Do you know where she is?"

Cutty spoke without much outward emotion.

"Not the least idea. Whenever Karlov wanted to quiz me, he appeared late at night from some other part of the town. But he never got much."

"You saw him this evening?"

"Yes. It probably struck him as a fine joke to send me."

"And if you don't go back?"

"The girl will be taken away. I'm honestly afraid of the man. He's too quiet spoken. That kind of a man always goes the limit."

"I see. Wait here."

At Cutty's approach Hawksley looked up apathetically.

"Want me?"

"Perhaps."

"You are pale. Anything serious?"

"Yes. Karlov has got Kitty."

For a minute Hawksley did not stir. Then he got up, put away the Amati, and came back. He was pale, too.

"I understand," he said. "They will exchange her for me. Am I right?"

"Yes. But you are not obliged to do anything like that, you know."

"I am ready."

"You give yourself up?"

"Why not?"

"You're a man!" Cutty burst out.

"I was brought up by one. Honestly, now, could I ever look a white man in the face again if I didn't give myself up? I did begin to believe that I might get through. But Fate was only playing with me. May I use your desk to write a line?"

"Come with me," said Cutty, unsteadily. This was not the result of environment. Quiet courage of this order was race. No questions demanding if there wasn't some way round the inevitable. Cutty's heart glowed; the boy had walked into it, never to leave it. "I'm ready." It took a man to say that when the sequence was death.

"Coles," said Cutty upon reentering the study, "tell Karlov that His Highness will give himself up. He will be there before midnight."

"That's enough for me. But if there's the least sign that you're not playing straight it will be all off. Two men will be watching the taxi and the entrance. If you appear, it's good-night. They told me to warn you."

"I promise not to appear."

Coles smiled enigmatically and reached for his hat. He held his hand out to Hawksley. "You're a white man, sir."

"Thanks," said Hawksley, absently. To have it all over with!

As soon as the captive Federal agent withdrew Hawksley sat down at the desk and wrote.

"Will this hold legally?" he asked, extending the written sheet to Cutty.

Cutty saw that it was a simple will. In it Hawksley gave half of his possessions to Kitty and half to Stefani Gregor. In case the latter was dead the sum total was to go to Kitty.

"I got you into a muddle; this will take you out of it. Karlov will kill me. I don't know how. I am his obsession. He will sleep better with me off his mind. Will this hold legally?"

"Yes. But why Kitty Conover, a stranger?"

"Is a woman who saves your life a stranger?"

"Well, not exactly. This is what we might call zero hour. I gave you a haven here not particularly because I was sorry for you, but because I wanted those emeralds. Once upon a time Gregor showed them to me. Until I examined your wallet I supposed you had smuggled in the stones; and that would have been fair game. But you had paid your way in honestly. Now, what did you do to Kitty Conover last night that decided her to accept that fool proposition? She sent her acceptance after she left you.

"I did not know that. I played for her. She became music-struck, and I took advantage of it--kissed her. Then she told me she was going to marry you."

"And that is why you asked me if I would trust you with a daughter of mine?"

"Yes."

"Conscience. That explains this will."

"No. Why did you accept my suggestion to marry her?"

"To make her comfortable without sidestepping the rules of convention."

"No. Because you love her--the way I do."

Cutty's pipe slipped from his teeth. It did not often do that. He stamped out the embers and laid the pipe on the tray.

"What makes you think I love her?"

"What makes me tell you that I do?"

"Yes, death may be at the end of to-night's work; so I'll admit that I love her. She is like a forest stream, wild at certain turns, but always sweet and clear. I'm an old fool, old enough to be her father. I loved her mother. Can a man love two women with all his heart, one years after the other?"

"It is the avatar; she is the reincarnation of the mother. I understand now. What was a beautiful memory takes living form again. You still love the mother; the daughter has revived that love."

"By the Lord Harry, I believe you've struck it! Walked into the fog and couldn't find the way out. Of course. What an old ass I've been! Simple as daylight. I've simply fallen in love with Molly all over again, thinking it was Kitty. Plain as the nose on my face. And I might have made a fine mess of it if you hadn't waked me up."

All this gentle irony went over Hawksley's head. "When do you wish me to go down to the taxi?"

"Son, I'm beginning to like you. You shall have your chance. In fact, we'll take it together. There'll be a taxi but I'll hire it. I'm quite positive I know where Kitty is. If I'm correct you'll have your chance. If I'm wrong you'll have to pay the score. We'll get her out or we'll stay where she is. In any event, Karlov will pay the price. Wouldn't you prefer to go out--if you must--in a glorious scrap?"

"Fighting?" Hawksley was on his feet instantly. "Do you mean that? I can die with free hands?"

"With a chance of coming out top-hole."

"I say, what a ripping thing hope is--always springing back!"

Cutty nodded. But he knew there was one hope that would never warm his heart again. Molly!... Well, he'd let the young chap believe that. Kitty must never know. Poor little chick, fighting with her soul in the dark and not knowing what the matter was! Such things happened. He had loved Molly on sight. He had loved Kitty on sight. In neither case had he known it until too late to turn about. Mother and daughter; a kind of sacrilege, as if he had betrayed Molly! But what a clear vision acknowledged love lent to the mind! He understood Kitty, who did not understand herself. Well, this night's adventure would decide things.

He smiled. Neither Kitty nor the drums of jeopardy; nothing. The gates of paradise again--for somebody else! Whoever heard of a prompter receiving press notices?

"Let's look alive! We haven't any time to waste. We'll have to change to dungarees--engineer togs. There'll be some tools to carry. We go straight down to the boiler room. We come up the ash exit on the street side. Remember, no suspicious haste. Two engineers off for their evening swig of beer at the corner groggery. Through the side door there, and into my taxi. Obey every order I give. Now run along to Kuroki and say night work for both of us. He'll understand what's wanted. I'll set the machinery in motion for a raid. How do you feel? I want the truth. I don't want to turn to you for help and not get it."

Hawksley laughed. "Don't worry about me. I'll carry on. Don't you understand? To have an end of it, one way or the other! To come free or to die there!"

"And if Kitty is not where I believe her to be?"

"Then I'll return to the taxi outside."

To be young like that! thought Cutty, feeling strangely sad and old. "To come free or to die there!" That was good Anglo-Saxon. He would make a good American citizen--if he were in luck.

At half after nine the two of them knelt on the roof before the cemented trap. Nothing but raging heat disintegrates cement. So the liberation of this trap, considering the time, was a Herculean task, because it had to be accomplished with little or no noise. Cold chisels, fulcrums, prying, heaving, boring. To free the under edge; the top did not matter. Not knowing if Kitty were below--that was the worst part of the job.

The sweat of agony ran down Hawksley's face; but he never faltered. He was going to die to-night, somehow, somewhere, but with free hands, the way Stefani would have him die, the way the girl would have him die. All these thousands of miles--to die in a house he had never seen before, just when life was really worth something!

An hour went by. Then they heard Kitty's signal. Instinctively the two of them knew that the taps came from her. They were absolutely certain when her signal was repeated. She was below, alone.

"Faster!" whispered Cutty.

Hawksley smiled. To say that to a chap when he was digging into his tomb!

When the sides of the trap were free Cutty tapped to Kitty again. There was a long, agonizing wait. Then three taps came from below. Cutty flashed a signal to the warehouse windows. In five minutes the raid would be in full swing--from the roof, from the street, from the cellar.

With their short crowbars braced by stout fulcrums the two men heaved. Noise did not matter now. Presently the trap went over.

"Look out for your hands; there's lots of loose glass. And together when we drop."

"Right-o!" whispered Hawksley, assured that when he dropped through the trap the result would be oblivion. Done in.

CHAPTER XXXI

Karlov, upon forcing his way past Kitty's barricade, stared at her doubtfully. This was a clever girl; she had proved her cleverness frequently. She might have some reason other than fear in keeping him out. So he put a fresh candle in the sconce and began to prowl. He pierced the attic windows with a ranging glance; no one was in the yard or on the Street. The dust on the windows had not been disturbed.

To Kitty the suspense was intolerable. At any moment Cutty might tap a query to her. How to warn him that all was not well? A scream would do it; but in that event when Cutty arrived there would be no Kitty Conover. Something that would sound unusual to Cutty and accidental to Karlov. She hit upon it. She seized a plank from her barricade, raised it to a perpendicular position, then flung it down violently. Would Cutty hear and comprehend that she was warning him? As a matter of fact, Cutty never heard the crash, for at that particular minute he was standing up to get the kinks out of his knees.

Karlov whirled on his heels, ran to Kitty, and snatched her wrist. "Why did you do that?"

Kitty remained mute. "Answer!"--with a cruel twist.

"You hurt!" she gasped. Anything to gain time. She tried to break away.

"Why did you do that?"

"I was going to thrust it through a window to attract attention. It was too heavy."

This explanation was within bounds of reason. It is possible that Karlov--who had merely come up with a fresh candle--would have departed but for a peculiarly grim burst of humour on the part of Fate.

Tap--tap--tap? inquired the unsuspecting man on the roof--exactly to Kitty like some innocent, inquisitive child embarrassing the family before company.

Karlov flung her aside roughly, stepped under the trap, and cupped an ear. He required no explanations from Kitty, who shrank to the wall and remained pinned there by terror. Karlov's intuition was keen. Men on the roof held but one significance. The house was surrounded by Federal agents. For a space he wavered between two desires, the political and the private vengeance.

A call down the stairs, and five minutes afterward there would be nothing on the spot but a jumble of smoking wood and brick. But not to see them die!

His subsequent acts, cold and methodical, fascinated Kitty. He took a step toward her. The scream died in her throat. But he did not go beyond that step. The picture of her terror decided his future actions. He would see them die, here, with the girl looking on. A full measure. Well enough he knew who were digging away the cement of the trap. What gave lodgment to this conviction he did not bother to analyze. The man he had not yet seen, who had balked him, now here, now there, from that first night; and who but the last of that branch of the hated house should be with him? To rend, batter, crush, kill! If he were bound for hell, to go there with the satisfaction of knowing that his private vengeance had been cancelled. The full reckoning for Anna's degradation: Stefani Gregor, broken and dying, and all the others dead!

He would shoot them as they dropped through the trap. Not to kill, but to maim, render helpless; then he would taunt them and grind his heels in their faces. Up there, the two he most hated of all living men!

First he restored Kitty's barricade--to keep assistance from entering before his work was completed. The butt of the first plank he pushed under the door knob. The other planks he laid flat, end to end, with the butt of the last snug against the brick chimney. The door would never give as a whole; it would have to be smashed in by axes. He then set the candle on the floor, backed by an up-ended soapbox. His enemies would drop into a pool of light, while they would not be able to see him at once. The girl would not matter. Her terror would hold her for some time. These manoeuvres completed, he answered the signal, sat down on another box and waited, reminding Kitty of some grotesque Mongolian idol.

Kitty saw the inevitable. Thereupon her terror ceased to bind her. As Cutty flung back the trap she would cry out a warning. Karlov might--and probably would--kill her. Her share in this night's work--her incredible folly--required full payment. Having decided to die with Cutty, all her courage returned. This is the normal result of any sublime resolve. But with the return of her courage she evolved another plan. She measured the distance between herself and Karlov, calculating there would be three strides. As Cutty dropped she would fling herself upon the madman. The act would at least give Cutty something like equal terms. What became of Kitty Conover thereafter was of no importance to the world.

Sounds. She became conscious of noises elsewhere in the house. The floor trembled. There came a creaking and snapping of wood, and she heard the trap fall. Karlov stood up, menacing, terrible. She saw where Cutty would drop, and now understood the cunning of the manoeuvre of placing the candle in front of the soapbox. Cutty would be an absolute mark for Karlov, protected by the shadow. She set herself, as a runner at the tape.

Karlov was not the type criminal, which when cornered, thinks only of personal safety. He was a political fanatic. All who opposed his beliefs must not be permitted to survive. There was a touch of Torquemada of the Inquisition in his cosmos. He could not kill directly; he had to torture first.

He knew by the ascending sounds that there would be no way out of this for him. To the American, Russia was an outlaw. He would be treated as a dangerous alien enemy and locked up. Boris Karlov should never live to eat his heart out behind bars.

Unique angle of thought, he mused. He wanted mud to trample them in, Russian mud. The same mud that had filled the mouth of Anna's destroyer.

He was, then, a formidable antagonist for any two strong men; let alone two one of whom was rather spent, the other dizzy with pain, holding himself together by the last shreds of his will. They dropped through the trap, Cutty in front of the candle, Hawksley a little to one side. The elder man landed squarely, but Hawksley fell backward. He crawled to his feet, swaying drunkenly. For a space he was not sure of the reality of the scene.... Torches and hobnailed boots!

"So!" said Karlov.

The torturer must talk; he must explain the immediate future to double the agony. He could have maimed them both, then trampled them to death, but he had to inform them of the fact. He pointed the automatic at Cutty because he considered this man the more dangerous of the two. He at once saw that the other was a negligible factor. He spoke slowly.

"And the girl shall witness your agonies," he concluded.

Cutty, bereft of invention, could only stare. Death! He had faced it many times, but always with a chance. There was none here, and the absolute knowledge paralyzed him.

Had Cutty been alone Kitty would have rushed at the madman; but the sight of Hawksley robbed her of all mobility. His unexpected appearance was to her the Book of Revelation. The blind alley she had entered and reentered so many times and so futilely crumbled.... Johnny Two-Hawks!

As for Hawksley, he knew he had but little time. The floor was billowing; he saw many candles where he knew there was only one. He was losing his senses. There remained but a single idea--to do the old thoroughbred one favour for the many. Scorning death--perhaps inviting it--he lunged headlong at Karlov's knees.

This reckless challenge to death was so unexpected that Karlov had no time to aim. He fired at chance. The bullet nipped the left shoulder of Hawksley's coat and shattered the laths of the partition between the attic and the servant's quarters. Under the impact of the human catapult Karlov staggered back, desperately striving to maintain his balance. He succeeded because Hawksley's senses left him in the instant he struck Karlov's knees. Still, the episode was a respite for Cutty, who dashed at Karlov before the latter could set himself or raise the smoking automatic.

Kitty then witnessed--dimly--a primordial, titanic conflict which haunted her dreams for many nights to come. They were no longer men, but animals; the tiger giving combat to the gorilla, one striking the quick, terrible blows of the tiger, the other seeking always to come to grips.

The floor answered under the step and rush. Rare athletes, these two; big men who were light on their feet. Kitty could see their faces occasionally and the flash of their bare hands, but of their bodies little or nothing. Nor could she tell how the struggle was going. Indeed until the idea came that they might be trampling Johnny Two-Hawks there was no coherent thought in her head, only broken things.

She ran to the soapbox and kicked it aside. She saw Hawksley on his face, motionless. At least they should not trample his dead body. She caught hold of his arms and dragged him to the wall--to discover that she was sobbing, sobs of rage and despair that tore at her breast horribly and clogged her throat. She was a woman and could not help; she could not help Cutty! She was a woman, and all she could do was to drag aside the lifeless body of the man who had given Cutty his chance!

She knelt, turning Hawksley over on his back. There was a slight gash on one grimy cheek, possibly caused by contact with the latchets of Karlov's boots. She raised the handsome head, pressed it to her bosom, and began to sway her body from side to side. Tumult. The Federal agents were throwing their bodies against the door repeatedly. In the semi-darkness Cutty fought for his life. But Kitty neither heard nor saw. The world had suddenly contracted; there was only this beautiful head in her arms; beyond and about, nothing.

Cutty felt his strength ebbing; soon he would not be able to wrench himself loose from those terrible arms. He knew all the phases of the fighting game. Chivalry and fair play had no part in this contest. Clear light, to observe what his blows were accomplishing; a minute or two of clear light! Half the time his blows glanced. The next time those arms wound about him, that would be the end. He was growing tired, winded; he had not gone into battle fresh. He knew that many of his blows had gone home. Any ordinary man would have dropped; but Karlov came on again and again.

And all the while Karlov was not fighting Cutty; he was endeavouring to remove him. He was an obstacle. What Karlov wanted was that head the girl was holding in her arms; to grind his heel into it. Had Cutty stepped aside Karlov would have rushed for the other man.

"Kitty, the door, the door!" Cutty shouted in despair, taking a terrible kick on the thigh. "The door!"

Kitty did not stir.

A panel in the door crushed in. The sole of a boot appeared and vanished. Then an arm reached in, groping, touched the plank propped under the door knob, wrenched and tugged until it fell. Immediately the attic became filled with men. It was time. Karlov had Cutty in his arms.

This turn in the affair roused Kitty. Presently she saw men in a snarl, heaving and billowing, with a sudden subsidence. The snarl untangled itself; men began to step back and produce pocketlamps. Kitty saw Cutty's face, battered and bloody, appear and disappear in a flash. She saw Karlov's, too, as he was pulled to his feet, his hands manacled. Again she saw Cutty. With shaking hand he was trying to attach the loose end of his collar to the button. The absurdity of it!

"Take him away. But don't be rough with him. He's only a poor devil of a madman," said Cutty.

Karlov turned and calmly spat into Cutty's face. A dozen fists were raised, but Cutty intervened.

"No! Let him be. Just take him away and lock him up. He's a rough road to travel. And hustle a comfortable car for me to go home in. Not a word to the newspapers. This isn't a popular raid."

As soon as the attic was cleared Cutty limped over to Molly Conover's daughter. The poor innocent! The way she was holding that head was an illumination. With a reassuring smile--an effort, for his lips were puffed and burning--he knelt and put his hand on Hawksley's heart.

"Done in, Kitty; that's all."

"He isn't dead?"

"Lord, no! He had nine lives, this chap, and only one of 'em missing to date. But I had no right to let him come. I thought he was fairly fit, but he wasn't. Saved my life, though. Kitty, your Johnny Two-Hawks is a real man; how real I did not know until to-night. He has earned his American citizenship. Fights like he fiddles--on all four strings. All our troubles are at an end; so buck up."

"Alive? He is alive?"

The wild joy in her voice! "Yes, ma'am; and we two can regularly thank him for being alive also. That lunge gave me my chance. He's only stunned. Perhaps he'll need a nurse again. Anyhow, he'll be coming round in a minute or two. I'll wager the first thing he does is to smile. I should."

Suddenly Kitty grew strangely shy. She became conscious of her anomalous position. She had promised to marry Cutty, promised herself that she would be his true wife--and here she was, holding another man's head to her heart as if it were the most precious head in all the world. She could not put that head upon the floor at once; that would be a confession of her embarrassment; and yet she could not continue to hold Hawksley while Cutty eyed her with semi-humorous concern. Cutty was merciful, however. "Let me hold him while you make a pillow out of your coat." After he had laid Hawksley's head on the coat he said: "He'll come about quicker this way. We've had some excitement, haven't we?"

"I don't want any more, Cutty; never any more. I've been a silly, romantic fool!"

"Not silly, only glorious."

"Your poor face!"

"Banged up? Well, honestly, it feels as it looks, Kitty, this chap was going to give himself up in exchange for you. Not a word of protest, not a question. All he said was: 'I am ready.' That's why I'm always going to be on his side."

"He did that--for me?"

"For you. Did it never occur to you that you're the sort folks always want to do things for if you'll let them?"

"God bless you, Cutty!"

"He's always blessing me, Kitty. He blessed me with your mother's friendship, now yours. Kitty, I'm going to jilt you."

"Jilt me?"--her heart leaping.

"Yes, ma'am. We can't go through with that mummery. We aren't built that way. I'll figure it out in some other fashion. But marriage is a sacred contract; and this farce would have left a scar on your honest mind. You'd have to tell some man. Your kind can't go through life without being loved. Would he understand? I wonder. He'll be human or you wouldn't fall in love with him; and always he'll be pondering and bedevilling himself with queer ideas--because he'll be human. Of course there's a loophole--you can sue me for breach of promise."

"Please, Cutty; don't laugh! You're one of those men they call Greathearts. And now I'm going to tell you something. It wasn't going to be a farce. I intended to become your true wife, Cutty, make you as happy as I could."

Cutty patted her hand and got up. Lord, how bruised and sore his old body was!... His true wife! She might have been his if he had not missed that train. But for this hour, hot with life, she might never have discovered that she loved Hawksley. His true wife! Ah, she would have been all of that--Molly's girl!

"Will you mind waiting here until I see where old Stefani Gregor is?"

"No," answered Kitty, dreamily.

Cutty limped to the door. Outside he leaned against the partition. Done in, body and soul. Always opening the gates of paradise for somebody else... His true wife! Slowly he descended the stairs.

Alone, Kitty smoothed back the dank hair from Hawksley's brow, which she kissed. Benediction and good-bye.

CHAPTER XXXII

Because it was assumed that some of Karlov's pack might be at large and unsuspectingly return to the trap, Federal agents would remain on guard all night. They explored the house, hunting for chemicals, documents, letters, and addresses. They found enough high explosive to blow up the district. And they found Stefani Gregor. They were standing by the cot as Cutty came in.

"Yes, sir. Just this minute went out."

"Did he speak?"

"A woman's name."

"Rosa?"

"Yes, sir. Looks to me as if he had been starved to death. Know who he was?"

"Yes. Tell the coroner to be gentle. Once upon a time Stefani Gregor spoke to kings by right of genius."

The thought that he himself might have been the indirect cause of Gregor's death shocked Cutty, who was above all things tender.

He had held back the raid for several days, to serve his own ends. He could have ordered the raid from Washington, and it would have gone through as smoothly as to-night. The drums of jeopardy. Well, that phase of the game was done with. He had held up this raid so that he might be on hand to search Karlov; and until now he had forgotten the drums. Accurst! They were accurst. The death of Stefani Gregor would always be on his conscience.

Cutty stared--not very clearly--at the cameo-like face so beautifully calm. As in life, so it was in death; the calm that had brooked and beaten down the turbulent instincts of the boy, the imperturbable calm of a great soul. Rosa. The sublime unselfishness of the man! He had sacrificed wealth and fame for the love of the boy's mother--unspoken, unrequited love, the quality that passes understanding. And his reward: to die on this cot, in horrid loneliness. Rosa.

All at once Cutty felt himself little, trivial, beside this forlorn bier. What did he know about love? He had never made any sacrifices; he had simply carried in his heart a bittersweet recollection. But here! Twenty-odd years of unremitting devotion to the son of the woman he had loved--Stefani Gregor. Creating environments that would develop the noble qualities in the boy, interposing himself between the boy and the evil pleasures of the uncle, teaching him the beautiful, cleansing his soul of the inherited mud. Reverently Cutty drew the coverlet over the fine old head.

"What's this?" asked one of the operatives. "Looks like the pieces of a broken fiddle."

Out of those dark red bits of wood--some of them bearing the imprints of hob-nails--Cutty constructed the scene. A wave of bitter rage rolled over him. The beast! Karlov had done this thing, with poor old Gregor looking on, too weak to intervene. Not so many years ago these bits of wood, under the master's touch, had entranced the souls of thousands. Cutty recalled a fairy tale he had read when a boy about a prince whose soul had been transformed into a flower which, if plucked or broken, died. Karlov had murdered Stefani Gregor, perhaps not legally but actually nevertheless.

Rehabilitated in soul, Cutty left the room. He had read a compelling lesson in self-sacrifice. He was going to pick up his cross and go on with it, smiling. After all, Kitty was only an interlude; the big thing was the game; and shortly he would be in the thick of great events again. But Kitty should be happy.

His old analytical philosophy resumed its functions. The contempt and jealousy of one race for another; what was God's idea in implanting that in souls? Hawksley was at base Russian. The boy's English education, his adopted outlook upon life, made it possible for Cutty to ignore the racial antagonism of the Anglo-Saxon for all other races. Stefani Gregor at one end of the world and he at the other, blindly working out the destinies of Kitty Conover and Ivan Mikhail Feodorovich and so forth and so on, with the blood of Catharine in his veins! Made a chap dizzy to think of it. Traditions were piling up along with crowns and sceptres in the abyss.

When he returned to the attic he felt himself fortified against any inevitability. Hawksley was sitting up, his back to the wall, staring groggily but with reckless adoration into Kitty's lovely face. Youth will be served. As if, watching these two, there could be any doubt of it! And he had bent part of his energies toward keeping them separated.

"Ha!" he cried, cheerfully. "Back on top again, I see. How's the head?"

"Haven't any; no legs; I'm nothing at all but a bit of my own imagination. How do you feel?"

"Like the aftermath of an Irish wake." Then Cutty's battered face assumed an expression that was meant to typify gravity. "John," he aid, "I've bad news for you."

John. A glow went over the young man's aching body. John. What could that signify except that he had passed into the eternal friendship of this old thorough-bred? John.

"About Stefani?"

"Stefani is dead. He died speaking your mother's name."

Hawksley's head sank; his chin touched his chest. He spoke without looking up. "Something told me I would never see him alive again. Old Stefani! If there is any good in me it will be his handiwork. I say," he added, his eyes now seeking Cutty's, "you called me John. Will you carry on?"

"Keep an eye on you? So long as you may need me."

"I come from a lawless race. Stefani had to fight. Even now I'm afraid some-times. God knows I want to be all he tried to make me."

"You're all right, John. You've reached haven; the storms hereafter will be out-side. Besides, Stefani will always be with you. You'll never pick up that old Amati without feeling Stefani near. Can you stand?"

"Between the two of you, perhaps."

With Kitty on one side and Cutty on the other Hawksley managed the descent tolerably well. Often a foot dragged. How strong she was, this girl! No hysterics, no confusion, after all that racket, with death--or something worse--reaching out toward her; calmly telling him that there was another step, warning him not to bear too heavily on Cutty! Holding him up physically and morally, these two, now all he had in life to care for. Yesterday, unknown to him; this night, bound by hoops of steel. The girl had forgiven him; he knew it by the touch of her arm.... Old Stefani! A sob escaped him. Their arms tightened.

"No; I was thinking of Stefani. Rather hard--to die all alone--because he loved me."

Kitty longed to be alone. There were still many unshed tears--some for Cutty, some for Stefani Gregor, some for Johnny Two-Hawks, and some for herself.

In the limousine Cutty sat in the middle, Kitty on his left and Hawksley on his right, his arms round them both. Presently Hawksley's head touched his shoulder and rested there; a little later Kitty did likewise. His children! Lord, he was going to have a tremendous interest in life, after all! He smiled with kindly irony at the back of the chauffeur. His children, these two; and he knew as he planned their future that they were thinking over and round but not of him, which is the way of youth.

At the apartment Cutty decided to let Hawksley sit in an easy chair in the living room until Captain Harrison arrived. Kuroki was ordered to prepare a supper, which would be served on the tea cart, set at Hawksley's knees. Kitty--because it was impossible for her to remain inactive--set the linen and silver. She was in and out of the room, ill at ease, angry, frightened, bitter, avoiding Hawksley's imploring eyes because she was not sure of her own.

She was sure of one thing, however. All the nonsense was out of her head. Tomorrow she would be returning to the regular job. She would have a page from the Arabian Nights to look upon in the days to come. She understood, though it twisted her heart dreadfully: she was in the eyes of this man a plaything, a pretty woman he had met in passing. If she had saved his life he had in turn saved hers; they were quits. She did not blame him for his point of view. He had come from the top of the world, where women were either ornaments or playthings, while she and hers had always struggled to maintain equilibrium in the middle stratum. Cutty could give him friendship; but she could not because she was a woman, young and pretty.

Love him? Well, she would get over it. It might be only the glamour of the adventure they had shared. Anyhow, she wouldn't die of it. Cutty hadn't. Of course it hurt; she was a silly little fool, and all that. Once he was in Montana he would be sending for his Olga. There wasn't the least doubt in her mind that if ever autocracy returned to power, he'd be casting aside his American citizenship, his chaps and sombrero, for the old regalia. Well--truculently to the world at large--why not?

So she avoided Hawksley's gaze, sensing the sustained persistence of it. But, oh, to be alone, alone, alone!

Cutty washed the patient's hands and face and patched up the cut on the cheek, interlarding his chatter with trench idioms, banter, jokes. Underneath, though, he was chuckling. He was the hero of this tale; he had done all the thrilling stunts, carried limp bodies across fire escapes in the rain, climbed roofs, eluded newspaper reporters, fought with his bare fists, rescued the girl.... All with one foot in the grave! Fifty-two, gray haired--with a prospect of rheumatism on the morrow--and putting it over like a debonair movie idol!

Hawksley met these pleasantries halfway by grousing about being babied when there was nothing the matter with him but his head, his body, and his legs.

Why didn't she look at him? What was the meaning of this persistent avoidance? She must have forgiven last night. She was too much of a thoroughbred to harbour ill feeling over that. Why didn't she look at him?

The telephone called Cutty from the room.

Kitty went into the dining room for an extra pair of salt cellars and delayed her return until she heard Cutty coming back.

"Karlov is dead," he announced. "Started a fight in the taxi, got out, and was making for safety when one of the boys shot him. He hadn't the jewels on him, John. I'm afraid they are gone, unless he hid them somewhere in that--What's the matter, Kitty?"

For Kitty had dropped the salt cellars and pressed her hands against her bosom, her face colourless.

Hawksley, terrified, tried to get up.

"No, no! Nothing is the matter with me but my head.... To think I could forget! Good--heavens!" She prolonged the words drolly. "Wait."

She turned her back to them. When she faced them again she extended a palm upon which lay a leather tobacco pouch, cracked and parched and blistered by the reactions of rain and sun.

"Think of my forgetting them! I found them this morning. Where do you suppose? On a step of the fire-escape ladder."

"Well, I'll be tinker-dammed!" said Cutty.

"I've reasoned it out," went on Kitty, breathlessly, looking at Cutty, "When the anarchist tore them from Mr. Hawksley's neck, he threw them out of the window.

The room was dark; his companion could not see. Later he intended, no doubt, to go into the court and recover them and cheat his master. I was looking out of the window, when I noticed a brilliant flash of purple, then another of green. The pouch was open, the stones about to trickle out. I dared not leave them in the apartment or tell anybody until you came home. So I carried them with me to the office. The drums, Cutty! The drums! Tumpitum-tump! Look!"

She poured the stones upon the white linen tablecloth. A thousand fires!

"The wonderful things!" she gasped. "Oh, the wonderful things! I don't blame you, Cutty. They would tempt an angel. The drums of jeopardy; and that I should find them!"

"Lord!" said Cutty, in an awed whisper. Green stones! The magnificent rubies and sapphires and diamonds vanished; he could see nothing but the exquisite emeralds. He picked up one--still warm with Kitty's pulsing life--and toyed with it. Actually, the drums! And all this time they had been inviting the first comer to appropriate them. Money, love, tragedy, death; history, pageants, lovely women; murder and loot! All these days on the step of the fire-escape ladder! He must have one of them; positively he must. Could he prevail upon Hawksley to sell one? Had he carried them through sentiment?

He turned to broach the suggestion of purchase, but remained mute.

Hawksley's head was sunk upon his chest; his arms hung limply at the sides of his chair.

"He is fainting!" cried Kitty, her love outweighing her resolves. "Cutty!"--desperately, fearing to touch Hawksley herself.

"No! The stones, the stones! Take them away--out of sight! I'm too done in! I can't stand it! I can't--The Red Night! Torches and hobnailed boots!"

CHAPTER XXXIII

Her fingers seemingly all thumbs, her heart swelling with misery and loneliness, wanting to go to him but fearing she would be misunderstood, Kitty scooped up the dazzling stones and poured them hastily into the tobacco pouch, which she thrust into Cutty's hands. What she had heard was not the cry of a disordered brain. There was some clear reason for the horror in Hawksley's tones. What tragedy lay behind these wonderful prisms of colour that the legitimate owner could not look upon them without being stirred in this manner?

"Take them into the study," urged Kitty.

"Wait!" interposed Hawksley. "I give one of the emeralds to you, Cutty. They came out of hell--if you want to risk it! The other is for Miss Conover, with Mister Hawksley's compliments." He was looking at Kitty now, his face drawn, his eyes bloodshot. "Don't be apprehensive. They bring evil only to men. With one in your possession you will be happy ever after, as the saying goes. Oh, they are mine to give; mine by right of inheritance. God knows I paid for them!"

"If I said Mister--" began Kitty, her brain confused, her tongue clumsy.

"You haven't forgiven!" he interrupted. "A thoroughbred like you, to hold last night against me! Mister--after what we two have shared together! Why didn't you leave me there to die?"

Cutty observed that the drama had resolved itself into two characters; he had been relegated to the scenes. He tiptoed toward his study door, and as he slipped inside he knew that Gethsemane was not an orchard but a condition of the mind. He tossed the pouch on his desk, eyed it ironically, and sat down. His, one of them--one of those marvellous emeralds was his! He interlaced his fingers and rested his brow upon them. He was very tired.

Kitty missed him only when she heard the latch snap.

She was alone with Hawksley; and all her terror returned. Not to touch him, not to console him; to stand staring at him like a dumb thing!

"I do forgive--Johnny! But your world and my world--"

"Those stains! The wretches hurt you!"

"What? Where?"--bewildered.

"The blood on your waist!"

Kitty looked down. "That is not my blood, Johnny. It is yours."

"Mine?" Johnny. Something in the way she said it. "Mine?"--trying to solve the riddle.

"Yes. It is where your cheek rested when--I thought you were dead."

The sense of misery, of oppression, of terror, all fell away miraculously, leaving only the flower of glory. She would be his plaything if he wanted her.

Silence.

"Kitty, I came out of a dark world--to find you. I loved you the moment I entered your kitchen that night. But I did not know it. I loved you the night you brought the wallet. Still I did not understand. It was when I heard the lift door and knew you had gone forever that I understood. Loved you with all my heart, with all that poor old Stefani had fashioned out of muck and clay. If you held my head to your heart, if that is my blood there--Do you, can you care a little?"

"I can and do care very much, Johnny."

Her voice to his ears was like the G string of the Amati. "Will you go with me?"

"Anywhere. But you are a prince of some great Russian house, Johnny, and I am nobody."

"What am I, Kitty? Less than nobody--a homeless outcast, with only you and Cutty. An American! Well, when I'm that it will be different; I'll be somebody. God forgive me if I do not give it absolute loyalty, this new country!... Never call me anything but Johnny."

"Johnny." Anywhere, whatever he willed her to be.

"I'm a child, Kitty. I want to grow up--if I can--to be an American, something like that ripping old thoroughbred yonder."

Cutty! Johnny wanted to be something like Cutty. Johnny would have to grow up to be his own true self; for nobody could ever be like Cutty. He was as high and far away from the average man as this apartment was from hers. Would he understand her attitude? Could she say anything until it would be too late for him to interfere? She was this man's woman. She would have her span of happiness, come ill, come good, even if it hurt Cutty, whom she loved in another fashion. But for Johnny dropping through that trap she might never have really known, married Cutty, and been happy. Happy until one or the other died; never gloriously, never furiously, but mildly happy; perhaps understanding each other far better than Johnny and she would understand each other. The average woman's lot. But to give her heart, her mind, her body in a whirlwind of emotions, absolute surrender, to know for once the highest state of exaltation--to love!

All this tender exchange with half a dozen feet between them. Kitty had not stirred from the far side of the tea cart, and he had not opened his arms. She had given herself with magnificent abandon; for the present that satisfied her instincts. As for him, he was not quite sure this miracle might not be a dream, and one false move might cause her to vanish.

"Johnny, who is Olga?" The question was irrepressible. Perhaps it was the last shred of caution binding her. All of him or none of him. There must be no other woman intervening.

Hawksley stiffened in his chair. His hands closed convulsively and his eyes lost their brightness. "Johnny?" Kitty ran round the tea cart. "What is it?" She knelt beside the chair, alarmed, for the horror had returned to his face. "What did they do to you back there?" She clasped one of his hands tensely in hers.

"In my dreams at night!" he said, staring into space. "I could run away from my pursuers, but I could not run away from my dreams! Torches and hobnailed boots!... They trampled on her; and I, up there in the gallery with those damned emeralds in my hands! Ah, if I hadn't gone for them, if I hadn't thought of the extra comforts their sale would bring! There would have been time then, Kitty. I had all the other jewels in the pouch. Horses were ready for us to flee on, loyal servants ready to help us; but I thought of the drums. A few more worldly comforts--with hell forcing in the doors!

"I didn't tell her where I was going. When I came back it was to see her die! They saw me, and yelled. I ran away. I hadn't the courage to go down there and die with her! She thought I was in that hell pit. She went down there to die with me and died horribly, alone! Ah, if I could only shut it out, forget! Olga, my tender young sister, Kitty, the last one of my race I could love. And I ran away like a yellow dog, like a yellow dog! I don't know where her grave is, and I could not seek it if I did! I dared not write Stefani; tell him I had seen Olga go down under Karlov's heels, and then ran away!... Day by day to feel those stones against my heart!"

Nothing is more terrible to a woman than the sight of a brave man weeping. For she knew that he was brave. The sudden recollection of the emeralds; a little more comfort for himself and sister if they were permitted to escape. Not a cowardly instinct, not even a greedy one; a normal desire to fortify them additionally against an unknown future, and he had surrendered to it impulsively, without explaining to Olga where he was going.

"Johnny, Johnny, you mustn't!" She sprang up, seizing his head and wildly kissing him. "You mustn't! God understands, and Olga. Oh, you mustn't sob like that! You are tearing my heart to pieces!"

"I ran away like a yellow dog! I didn't go down there and die with her!"

"You didn't run away to-night when you offered your life for my liberty. Johnny, you mustn't!"

Under her tender ministrations the sobs began to die away and soon resolved into little catching gasps. He was weak and spent from his injuries; otherwise he would not have given way like this, discovered to her what she had not known before, that in every man, however strong and valiant he may be, there is a little child.

"It has been burning me up, Kitty."

"I know, I know! It is because you have a soul full of beautiful things, Johnny. God held you back from dying with Olga because He knew I needed you."

"You will marry me, knowing that I did this thing?"

Marry him! A door to some blinding radiance opened, and she could not see for a little while. Marry him! What a miserable wretch she was to think that he would want her otherwise! Johnny Two-Hawks, fiddling in front of the Metropolitan Opera House, to fill a poor blind man's cup!

"Yes, Johnny. Now, yesterdays never were. For us there is nothing but to-morrows. Out there, in the great country--where souls as well as bodies may stretch themselves--we'll start all over again. You will be the cowman and I'll be the kitchen wench. As in the beginning, so it will always be hereafter, I'll cook your bacon and eggs."

She pulled his chair round and pushed it toward a window, dropped beside it and laid her cheek against his hand.

"Let us look at the stars, Johnny. They know." Kuroki, having arrived with coffee and sandwiches, paused on the threshold, gazed, wheeled right about face, and returned to the kitchen.

By and by Kitty looked up into Hawksley's face. He was asleep. She got up carefully, lightly kissed the top of his head--the old wound--and crossed to Cutty's door. She must tell dear old Cutty of the wonderful happiness that was going to be hers. She opened the study door, but did not enter at once. Asleep on his arms. Why, he hadn't even opened that Ali Baba's bag! Tired out--done in, as Johnny Two-Hawks called it in his English fashion. She waited; but as he did not stir she approached with noiseless step. The light poured full upon his head. How gray he was! A boundless pity surged over her that this tender, valiant knight should have missed what first her mother had known--now she herself--requited love. To have everything in the world without that was to have nothing. She would not wake him; she would let him sleep until Captain Harrison came. Lightly she touched the gray head with her lips and stole from the study.

"Oh, Molly, Molly!" Cutty whispered into his rigid fingers.

And so they were married, in the apartment, at the top of the world, on a May night thick with stars. It was not a wedding; it was a marriage. The world never knew because it was none of the world's business. Who was Kitty Conover? A nobody. Who was John Hawksley? Something to be.

Out of the storm into the calm; which is something of a reversal. Generally in love affairs happiness is found in the approach to the marriage contract; the disillusions come afterward. It was therefore logical that Kitty and her lover should be happy, as they had run the gamut of test and fire beforehand.

The young people were to leave for the West soon after the supper for three. At midnight Cutty's ship would be boring down the bay. Did Kitty regret, even a little, the rice and old shoes, the bridesmaids and cake, so dear to the female of the species? She did not. Did she think occasionally of the splendour of the title that was hers? She did. To her mind Mrs. John Hawksley was incomparably above and beyond anything in that Bible of autocracy--the Almanach de Gotha.

After supper Cutty brought in the old Amati.

"Play," he said, lighting his pipe.

So Hawksley played--played as he never had played before and perhaps as he would never play again. We reach zenith sometimes, but we never stay there. But he was not playing to Cutty. Slate-blue eyes, two books with endless pages, the soul of this wife of his. He had come through. The miracle had been accomplished. Love.

Kitty smiled and smiled, the doors of her soul thrown wide to absorb this magic message. Love.

Cutty smoked on, with his eyes closed. He heard it, too. Love.

"Well," he said, sighing, "I see innovations out there in Montana. The round-up will be different. The Pied Fiddler of Bar-K will stand in the corral and fiddle, and the bossies will come galloping in, two by two--and a few jackrabbits!" He laughed. "John, the Amati is yours conditionally. If after one year it is not reclaimed it becomes yours automatically. My wedding present. Remember, next winter, if God wills, you'll come and visit me."

"As if we could forget!" cried Kitty, embracing Cutty, who accepted the embrace stoically. "I'll be needing clothes, and Johnny will have to have his hair cut. Oh, Cutty, I'm so foolishly happy!"

"Time we started for the choo-choo. Time-tables have no souls. But, Lord, what a racket we've had!"

"Well, rather!"--from Hawksley.

"Bo, listen to me. Out there you must remember that 'bally' and 'ripping' and 'rather' are premeditated insults. Gee-whiz! but I'd like a look-see when you say to your rough-and-readies: 'Bally rotten weather. What?' They'll shoot you up."

More banter; which fooled none of the three, as each understood the other perfectly. The hour of separation was at hand, and they were fortifying their courage.

"Funny old top," was Hawksley's comment as they stood before the train gate. "Three months gone we were strangers."

"And now--" began Cutty.

"With hoops of steel!" interrupted Kitty. "You must write, Cutty, and Johnny and I will be prompt."

"You'll get one from the Azores."

"Train going west!"

"Good luck, children!" Cutty pressed Hawksley's hand and pecked at Kitty's cheek. "Shan't go through with you to the car. Kuroki is waiting. Good-bye!"

The redcaps seized the luggage, and Hawksley and his bride followed them through the gate. Because he was tall Cutty could see them until they reached the bumper. Funny old world, for a fact. Next time they met the wounds would be healed--Hawksley's head and old Cutty's heart. Queer how he felt his fifty-two. He began to recognize one of the truths that had passed by: One did not sense age if one ran with the familiar pack. But for an old-timer to jog along for a few weeks with youth! That was it--the youth of these two had knocked his conceit into a cocked hat.

"Poor dear old Cutty!" said Kitty.

"Old thoroughbred!" said Hawksley.

And there you were, relegated to the bracket where the family kept the kaleidoscope, the sea-shell, and the album. His children, though; from now on he would have that interest in life. The blessed infant--Molly's girl--taking a sunbonnet when she might have worn a tiara! And that boy, stepping down from the pomp of palaces to the dusty ranges of Bar-K. An American citizen. It was more than funny, this old top; it was stark raving mad.

Well, he had one of the drums. It reposed in his wallet. Another queer thing, he could not work up a bit of the old enthusiasm. It was only a green stone. One of the finest examples of the emerald known, and he could not conjure up the panorama of murder and loot behind it. Possibly because he was no longer detached; the stone had entered his own life and touched it with tragedy. For it was tragedy to be fifty-two and to realize it. Thus whenever he took out the emerald he found his imagination walled in. Besides, it was a kind of magic mirror; he saw always his own tentative villainy. He was not quite the honest man he had once been.

But what was happening down the line there? The passengers were making way for someone. Kitty, and racing back to the gate! She did not pause until she stood in front of him, breathless.

"Forget something?" he asked, awkwardly.

"Uh-hm!" Suddenly she threw her arms round his neck and kissed him. "If only the three of us could be always together! Take care of yourself. Johnny and I need you." Then she caught his hand, gave it a pressure, and was off again. Cutty stood there, staring blindly in her direction. Old Stefani Gregor; sacrifice. By and by he became conscious of something warm and hard in his palm. He looked down.

A green stone, green as the turban of a Mecca pilgrim, green as the eye of a black panther in the thicket. He dropped the emerald into a vest pocket and fumbled round for his pipe--always his mental crutch. He lit it and marched out of the station into the night--chuckling sardonically. For the second time the thought occurred to him: Of all his earthly possessions he would carry into the Beyond--a chuckle.

Molly, then Kitty; but the drums of jeopardy were his!

The Codes Of Hammurabi And Moses
W. W. Davies

QTY

The discovery of the Hammurabi Code is one of the greatest achievements of archaeology, and is of paramount interest, not only to the student of the Bible, but also to all those interested in ancient history...

Religion   **ISBN:** *1-59462-338-4*   **Pages:132**
MSRP $12.95

The Theory of Moral Sentiments
Adam Smith

QTY

This work from 1749. contains original theories of conscience amd moral judgment and it is the foundation for systemof morals.

Philosophy   ISBN: *1-59462-777-0*   **Pages:536**
MSRP $19.95

Jessica's First Prayer
Hesba Stretton

QTY

In a screened and secluded corner of one of the many railway-bridges which span the streets of London there could be seen a few years ago, from five o'clock every morning until half past eight, a tidily set-out coffee-stall, consisting of a trestle and board, upon which stood two large tin cans, with a small fire of charcoal burning under each so as to keep the coffee boiling during the early hours of the morning when the work-people were thronging into the city on their way to their daily toil...

Pages:84

Childrens   ISBN: *1-59462-373-2*   *MSRP $9.95*

My Life and Work
Henry Ford

QTY

Henry Ford revolutionized the world with his implementation of mass production for the Model T automobile. Gain valuable business insight into his life and work with his own auto-biography... "We have only started on our development of our country we have not as yet, with all our talk of wonderful progress, done more than scratch the surface. The progress has been wonderful enough but..."

Pages:300

Biographies/   **ISBN:** *1-59462-198-5*   *MSRP $21.95* www.bookjungle.com *email: sales@bookjungle.com fax: 630-214-0564 mail: Book Jungle PO Box 2226 Champaign, IL 61825*

The Art of Cross-Examination
Francis Wellman

I presume it is the experience of every author, after his first book is published upon an important subject, to be almost overwhelmed with a wealth of ideas and illustrations which could readily have been included in his book, and which to his own mind, at least, seem to make a second edition inevitable. Such certainly was the case with me; and when the first edition had reached its sixth impression in five months, I rejoiced to learn that it seemed to my publishers that the book had met with a sufficiently favorable reception to justify a second and considerably enlarged edition. ...

QTY

Reference   **ISBN: *1-59462-647-2***

Pages:412

MSRP $19.95

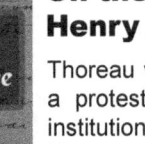

On the Duty of Civil Disobedience
Henry David Thoreau

Thoreau wrote his famous essay, On the Duty of Civil Disobedience, as a protest against an unjust but popular war and the immoral but popular institution of slave-owning. He did more than write—he declined to pay his taxes, and was hauled off to gaol in consequence. Who can say how much this refusal of his hastened the end of the war and of slavery ?

QTY

Law   **ISBN: *1-59462-747-9***

Pages:48

MSRP $7.45

Dream Psychology Psychoanalysis for Beginners
Sigmund Freud

Sigmund Freud, born Sigismund Schlomo Freud (May 6, 1856 - September 23, 1939), was a Jewish-Austrian neurologist and psychiatrist who co-founded the psychoanalytic school of psychology. Freud is best known for his theories of the unconscious mind, especially involving the mechanism of repression; his redefinition of sexual desire as mobile and directed towards a wide variety of objects; and his therapeutic techniques, especially his understanding of transference in the therapeutic relationship and the presumed value of dreams as sources of insight into unconscious desires.

QTY

Psychology   **ISBN: *1-59462-905-6***

Pages:196

MSRP $15.45

The Miracle of Right Thought
Orison Swett Marden

Believe with all of your heart that you will do what you were made to do. When the mind has once formed the habit of holding cheerful, happy, prosperous pictures, it will not be easy to form the opposite habit. It does not matter how improbable or how far away this realization may see, or how dark the prospects may be, if we visualize them as best we can, as vividly as possible, hold tenaciously to them and vigorously struggle to attain them, they will gradually become actualized, realized in the life. But a desire, a longing without endeavor, a yearning abandoned or held indifferently will vanish without realization.

QTY

Self Help   **ISBN: *1-59462-644-8***

Pages:360

MSRP $25.45

QTY

The Rosicrucian Cosmo-Conception Mystic Christianity *by Max Heindel*   ISBN: *1-59462-188-8*   **$38.95**
The Rosicrucian Cosmo-conception is not dogmatic, neither does it appeal to any other authority than the reason of the student. It is: not controversial, but is: sent forth in the, hope that it may help to clear...   New Age/Religion Pages 646

Abandonment To Divine Providence *by Jean-Pierre de Caussade*   ISBN: *1-59462-228-0*   **$25.95**
"The Rev. Jean Pierre de Caussade was one of the most remarkable spiritual writers of the Society of Jesus in France in the 18th Century. His death took place at Toulouse in 1751. His works have gone through many editions and have been republished...   Inspirational/Religion Pages 400

Mental Chemistry *by Charles Haanel*   ISBN: *1-59462-192-6*   **$23.95**
Mental Chemistry allows the change of material conditions by combining and appropriately utilizing the power of the mind. Much like applied chemistry creates something new and unique out of careful combinations of chemicals the mastery of mental chemistry...   New Age Pages 354

The Letters of Robert Browning and Elizabeth Barret Barrett 1845-1846 vol II   ISBN: *1-59462-193-4*   **$35.95**
by Robert Browning and Elizabeth Barrett   Biographies Pages 596

Gleanings In Genesis (volume I) *by Arthur W. Pink*   ISBN: *1-59462-130-6*   **$27.45**
Appropriately has Genesis been termed "the seed plot of the Bible" for in it we have, in germ form, almost all of the great doctrines which are afterwards fully developed in the books of Scripture which follow...   Religion/Inspirational Pages 420

The Master Key *by L. W. de Laurence*   ISBN: *1-59462-001-6*   **$30.95**
In no branch of human knowledge has there been a more lively increase of the spirit of research during the past few years than in the study of Psychology, Concentration and Mental Discipline. The requests for authentic lessons in Thought Control, Mental Discipline and...   New Age/Business Pages 422

The Lesser Key Of Solomon Goetia *by L. W. de Laurence*   ISBN: *1-59462-092-X*   **$9.95**
This translation of the first book of the "Lernegton" which is now for the first time made accessible to students of Talismanic Magic was done, after careful collation and edition, from numerous Ancient Manuscripts in Hebrew, Latin, and French...   New Age/Occult Pages 92

Rubaiyat Of Omar Khayyam *by Edward Fitzgerald*   ISBN:*1-59462-332-5*   **$13.95**
Edward Fitzgerald, whom the world has already learned, in spite of his own efforts to remain within the shadow of anonymity, to look upon as one of the rarest poets of the century, was born at Bredfield, in Suffolk, on the 31st of March, 1809. He was the third son of John Purcell...   Music Pages 172

Ancient Law *by Henry Maine*   ISBN: *1-59462-128-4*   **$29.95**
The chief object of the following pages is to indicate some of the earliest ideas of mankind, as they are reflected in Ancient Law, and to point out the relation of those ideas to modern thought.   Religiom/History Pages 452

Far-Away Stories *by William J. Locke*   ISBN: *1-59462-129-2*   **$19.45**
"Good wine needs no bush, but a collection of mixed vintages does. And this book is just such a collection. Some of the stories I do not want to remain buried for ever in the museum files of dead magazine-numbers an author's not unpardonable vanity..."   Fiction Pages 272

Life of David Crockett *by David Crockett*   ISBN: *1-59462-250-7*   **$27.45**
"Colonel David Crockett was one of the most remarkable men of the times in which he lived. Born in humble life, but gifted with a strong will, an indomitable courage, and unremitting perseverance...   Biographies/New Age Pages 424

Lip-Reading *by Edward Nitchie*   ISBN: *1-59462-206-X*   **$25.95**
Edward B. Nitchie, founder of the New York School for the Hard of Hearing, now the Nitchie School of Lip-Reading, Inc, wrote "LIP-READING Principles and Practice". The development and perfecting of this meritorious work on lip-reading was an undertaking...   How-to Pages 400

A Handbook of Suggestive Therapeutics, Applied Hypnotism, Psychic Science   ISBN: *1-59462-214-0*   **$24.95**
by Henry Munro   Health/New Age/Health/Self-help Pages 376

A Doll's House: and Two Other Plays *by Henrik Ibsen*   ISBN: *1-59462-112-8*   **$19.95**
Henrik Ibsen created this classic when in revolutionary 1848 Rome. Introducing some striking concepts in playwriting for the realist genre, this play has been studied the world over.   Fiction/Classics/Plays 308

The Light of Asia *by sir Edwin Arnold*   ISBN: *1-59462-204-3*   **$13.95**
In this poetic masterpiece, Edwin Arnold describes the life and teachings of Buddha. The man who was to become known as Buddha to the world was born as Prince Gautama of India but he rejected the worldly riches and abandoned the reigns of power when...   Religion/History/Biographies Pages 170

The Complete Works of Guy de Maupassant *by Guy de Maupassant*   ISBN: *1-59462-157-8*   **$16.95**
"For days and days, nights and nights, I had dreamed of that first kiss which was to consecrate our engagement, and I knew not on what spot I should put my lips..."   Fiction/Classics Pages 240

The Art of Cross-Examination *by Francis L. Wellman*   ISBN: *1-59462-309-0*   **$26.95**
Written by a renowned trial lawyer, Wellman imparts his experience and uses case studies to explain how to use psychology to extract desired information through questioning.   How-to/Science/Reference Pages 408

Answered or Unanswered? *by Louisa Vaughan*   ISBN: *1-59462-248-5*   **$10.95**
Miracles of Faith in China   Religion Pages 112

The Edinburgh Lectures on Mental Science (1909) *by Thomas*   ISBN: *1-59462-008-3*   **$11.95**
This book contains the substance of a course of lectures recently given by the writer in the Queen Street Hail, Edinburgh. Its purpose is to indicate the Natural Principles governing the relation between Mental Action and Material Conditions...   New Age/Psychology Pages 148

Ayesha *by H. Rider Haggard*   ISBN: *1-59462-301-5*   **$24.95**
Verily and indeed it is the unexpected that happens! Probably if there was one person upon the earth from whom the Editor of this, and of a certain previous history, did not expect to hear again...   Classics Pages 380

Ayala's Angel *by Anthony Trollope*   ISBN: *1-59462-352-X*   **$29.95**
The two girls were both pretty, but Lucy who was twenty-one who supposed to be simple and comparatively unattractive, whereas Ayala was credited, as her Bombwhat romantic name might show, with poetic charm and a taste for romance. Ayala when her father died was nineteen...   Fiction Pages 484

The American Commonwealth *by James Bryce*   ISBN: *1-59462-286-8*   **$34.45**
An interpretation of American democratic political theory. It examines political mechanics and society from the perspective of Scotsman James Bryce   Politics Pages 572

Stories of the Pilgrims *by Margaret P. Pumphrey*   ISBN: *1-59462-116-0*   **$17.95**
This book explores pilgrims religious oppression in England as well as their escape to Holland and eventual crossing to America on the Mayflower, and their early days in New England...   History Pages 268

QTY

The Fasting Cure by *Sinclair Upton*　　　　　　　　　　ISBN: *1-59462-222-1* **$13.95**
In the Cosmopolitan Magazine for May, 1910, and in the Contemporary Review (London) for April, 1910, I published an article dealing with my experi-ences in fasting. I have written a great many magazine articles, but never one which attracted so much attention...　New Age/Self Help/Health Pages 164

Hebrew Astrology by *Sepharial*　　　　　　　　　　　ISBN: *1-59462-308-2* **$13.45**
In these days of advanced thinking it is a matter of common observation that we have left many of the old landmarks behind and that we are now pressing forward to greater heights and to a wider horizon than that which represented the mind-content of our progenitors...　Astrology Pages 144

Thought Vibration or The Law of Attraction in the Thought World　ISBN: *1-59462-127-6* **$12.95**
by *William Walker Atkinson*　　　　　　　　　　　　　　　　*Psychology/Religion Pages 144*

Optimism by *Helen Keller*　　　　　　　　　　　　　ISBN: *1-59462-108-X* **$15.95**
Helen Keller was blind, deaf, and mute since 19 months old, yet famously learned how to overcome these handicaps, communicate with the world, and spread her lectures promoting optimism. An inspiring read for everyone...　Biographies/Inspirational Pages 84

Sara Crewe by *Frances Burnett*　　　　　　　　　　　ISBN: *1-59462-360-0* **$9.45**
In the first place, Miss Minchin lived in London. Her home was a large, dull, tall one, in a large, dull square, where all the houses were alike, and all the sparrows were alike, and where all the door-knockers made the same heavy sound...　Childrens/Classic Pages 88

The Autobiography of Benjamin Franklin by *Benjamin Franklin*　ISBN: *1-59462-135-7* **$24.95**
The Autobiography of Benjamin Franklin has probably been more extensively read than any other American historical work, and no other book of its kind has had such ups and downs of fortune. Franklin lived for many years in England, where he was agent...　Biographies/History Pages 332

Name	
Email	
Telephone	
Address	
City, State ZIP	

☐ **Credit Card**　　　　　☐ **Check / Money Order**

Credit Card Number	
Expiration Date	
Signature	

Please Mail to:　Book Jungle
PO Box 2226
Champaign, IL 61825
or Fax to:　　630-214-0564

ORDERING INFORMATION

web: *www.bookjungle.com*
email: *sales@bookjungle.com*
fax: *630-214-0564*
mail: *Book Jungle PO Box 2226 Champaign, IL 61825*
or PayPal *to sales@bookjungle.com*

Please contact us for bulk discounts

DIRECT-ORDER TERMS

**20% Discount if You Order
Two or More Books**
Free Domestic Shipping!
Accepted: Master Card, Visa,
Discover, American Express

www.ingramcontent.com/pod-product-compliance
Lightning Source LLC
Chambersburg PA
CBHW080726020726
47503CB00010B/2807